BEING

SIMON

HAINES

Tom Vaughan MacAulay

RedDoor

Published by RedDoor
www.reddoorpublishing.com

ISBN 978-1-910453-35-3

A CIP catalogue record for this book
is available from the British Library

Cover design:
Rawshock Design

Page design and typesetting:
WatchWord Editorial Services
www.watchwordeditorial.co.uk

Printed and bound by Nørhaven, Denmark

BEING SIMON HAINES

PART ONE

1

I FLEW TO HAVANA in memory of earnestness. I was thirty-two years old, professionally accomplished but lacking in wisdom, financially secure but privately adrift, at the point in life when a lawyer recalls Purpose, becomes indignant at the stability afforded by general malaise. It was April 2012 and I had a moment: my eight-month 'Campaign' at the law firm of Fiennes & Plunkett, that family-run, exclusive financing and insolvency boutique of the City of London, was over, and I had to wait for two weeks to see if I would be voted in as a new junior partner; if this blue-eyed boy from Lincoln would become a millionaire. During Campaign, the firm, led by the long legs and mighty silver quiff of Rupert Plunkett, had worked me to a level of nervous exhaustion that required not only a period of recuperation, but also an illusion of escape. Sophie Williams, my now *ex*-girlfriend, had left me only recently. In London spring had been withheld and even the April showers' vitality curbed, so that instead a fine rain, incessant in its listlessness, drifted through cold, hurried streets below a sky of gloom.

'Just disappear for a while, Simon – it'll do you good. God, that sounds banal.'

Dan Serfontein and I had been friends since university – all the way through law school, the training contract and the associate years at Fiennes & Plunkett. Son of a fund manager from Cape Town and his beautiful wife, Dan's towering alpha-male physique held up a boyish, infuriatingly handsome face and a head of thick blond hair. Dan had poise, that special assurance of all of Belgravia's children, but unlike them he had an admirable, manic determination too – despite, or rather because of, the family money. All this Dan Serfontein had – but he did not quite have the mind, the obsessive attention to detail, the neurotic speed of thought, to go all the way at Fiennes & Plunkett. He had left just a couple of weeks before the horror of Campaign had begun, burnt out and unable to go on, and now swam the calmer waters of in-house law.

'No idea how you got through it, mate. You should be proud of yourself, whatever happens – you're far stronger than I am.'

After much pondering, one morning the apotheosis of strength that was Mr Simon Haines decided where to go. Selecting the age category of 28–35s, I booked myself on a group tour of Cuba, through an agency specialising in *bona fide trips for bona fide travellers*. Cuba was, I supposed, a place that I had always wanted to see; and those friends of mine who had made me wince when speaking of 're-connection with your spirit' did perhaps have a point, albeit atrociously expressed. For the idea of a faraway land, of new air, brought about a flicker of an old emotion that lay deeper than consciousness…

I had not been getting much new air. According to Tempo, the firm's electronic timesheet system, I had billed

4

over three thousand hours in the previous twelve months. At one nebulous point, when matters had reached their peak of intensity, I had spent three consecutive days and nights at my desk. Thirty-two, the once attractive face now anaemic and haggard. The once big blue eyes now smaller, the curly brown hair turning grey, beginning to recede; and I was getting through a packet of cigarettes a day in the Fiennes & Plunkett smoking pit. I was still of reasonable, unremarkable height, just below six foot, but at times had the unnerving impression that I was slowly shrinking. Over half a stone in weight had gone since law school, but I had gained at the bottom of my stomach incipient rolls of fat, which seemed unsure of their identity. For years, my only exercise had involved sprinting back and forth to the lifts.

'No running,' Rupert Plunkett had whispered one morning, his distinguished, skeletal figure bending down towards me, minutes before Project Archer had been announced to the market. 'No running in these offices.'

Even before the final test that was Campaign, a sixteen-hour day had been standard for me at Fiennes & Plunkett. Twenty-four-hour days were not rare. Up on the ninth floor of that dome-shaped glass building – the first six floors were populated by an insurance company, and the top three floors belonged to the firm – I spent the end of my twenties and beginning of my thirties as an unappreciative witness of the cycles of nature; of the transience of the days and nights, the seasons, the months, the years. Often, as I made the final tweaks to a loan agreement, I would look up to see the night creeping away, once more defeated by a grey but penetrating light that promised a day of anguish. In the summer, distraught at the abstruse instructions of a man who only ever whispered, I would sometimes gaze out, hands to my temples, just in time to see the sun letting itself down gently into the Thames.

During the early hours, in the refuge of the smoking pit, on occasion my head would rise up to the sky and I would see the moon, at which sight I would panic, and then feel terribly alone.

My relationship with the firm had become akin to a love affair with a narcissist – a beautiful sociopath whom I had courted with desperation, seduced by its lustre and the indifference of its cold heart. Fiennes & Plunkett was far from being one of the big boys of the City – it sat way below the elite Magic Circle firms, below even the Silver Circle and the huge international alliances that came after that. Moreover – and unlike virtually every other serious law firm in the City of London – it had an offering of only two specialisations, with one support department. City law firms generally have corporate departments, finance departments, tax, competition, real estate, intellectual property departments. But at Fiennes & Plunkett...

'At Fiennes & Plunkett we do financing and insolvency,' Rupert Plunkett would whisper proudly, in his Annual Address to the firm – putting particular emphasis on the final two words. He'd whispered this in every Annual Address since the 2008 financial crisis, the time at which a simple fact had transformed into a slogan, a sort of battle cry. 'That is all we do. It's all we will ever do.'

At which point a partner would raise a hand gingerly and Rupert would grimace, then whisper:

'OK. We also have a small real estate department.'

And yet, despite these apparent limitations, Fiennes & Plunkett was the pinnacle of some law graduates' ambition. To the extent that the insolvency sector could be said to have its king in the City, Fiennes & Plunkett was it – and its general financing work was highly regarded too. Unaccountably still a family firm, it had been at the forefront of loans, restructurings and liquidations for four generations of a line of madmen, and was flourishing now under the latest of the line. It was a self-proclaimed 'inventor of market practice', renowned for its commercial approach, and then – let's get to it – there was the money. While its profits as a firm were dwarfed by the US firms and the players in the Magic and Silver Circles, Fiennes & Plunkett had an extremely tight equity structure – there were only thirty partners – so that those who did make it earned considerable sums. Or rather, extraordinary sums – a newly made-up partner, people said, would take home over a million pounds a year. Over a million pounds! For this reason, the intensity of the competition among associates; on this promise, the incomparable demands made of them by the firm; on account of all this the fact that the firm, which had as its mantra the concepts of prudence and clarity, boasted more damaged individuals than any other institution in the City.

'At Fiennes & Plunkett we do financing and insolvency.' Oh, the grave beauty of the whisper!

Infatuated, I had courted it. And the firm had given me its hand: I had been offered a training contract at the age of twenty-two, while still studying languages at Cambridge and knowing nothing about the law. A training contract that included sponsoring me through law school. Signing it, I felt the tingle of glory. I saw constant intellectual stimulation, the biggest restructuring deals, saving famous companies! I saw a million pounds a year, in my early thirties! For a moment I wanted to stop cars in the street… Back in Lincoln, amid the euphoria my parents invited some friends around – the couples who had babysat me as a child – and we had a party in the pleasant and understated sitting room of our small terraced house, which extended through a bright conservatory to a view of a back garden rich with flowers and deliberately imperfect, as if based on a fear of accusations of *petit bourgeois* tidiness.

'Fiennes and bloody Plunkett!' My father – a slight, dishevelled man who practised, in a not overly strenuous manner, as a local psychologist, and whose two distinguishing features would always be a bushy beard and an ability to fall asleep immediately upon sinking into his armchair – was wearing his old green cardigan and older creased corduroys, but his tired face was lit today by a lovely, proud smile. 'I've just read all about them – I can't believe it! Are you sure it's what you want?'

'What? Of course I'm sure!' Oh, the surly conviction…

After law school, there came the two years of training at the firm – years in which the illusions ebbed away but the infatuation intensified, the bond fixed by the glue of a bitter *je ne regrette rien*. They were the years in which we were revealed to one another, naked in the dawn that brings to an end an all-nighter. The firm was indeed an intellectual powerhouse. But it was also an asylum: a home of perfectionists, a sea of insecurity, an uncaring and selfish life partner who demanded dedication twenty-four hours a day. And I, who was I? I was a man who had become addicted, a man who had submitted. A man whose primary emotion was now *terror of getting it wrong*. And for this I was duly rewarded: at the end of the training contract, I was kept on as an 'associate'.

The road ahead, carved through desolate plains, promised soon to straighten out, but I had lost my parents' endorsement on the way: this time I saw only a worried couple, the same old neighbours and a cocky, adolescent cousin who was asking me why I couldn't talk for more than a minute without looking at *that* thing.

'It's the firm's BlackBerry,' I said haughtily. In those days, a junior associate carrying a firm-issued BlackBerry was entitled to be haughty.

'I know what it is, you prick!'

Less than six years of qualified life, I explained to the gathering. The last eight months of it would be Campaign and – if I made it through that – there'd be the possibility of partnership.

'Your dad's right, though,' said Sophie in a soft voice. 'We all just want to see you happy. Not so stressed all the time.'

I was betraying Fiennes & Plunkett. Sophie had been my first girlfriend at school, the first girl I had made love to, and years later we had met again in London, where she now worked as a primary school teacher a couple of miles from the alternative reality of Rupert Plunkett's mother ship. Sophie was very pretty, radiating that transient promise of true beauty that all prettiness brings, and her gentle character concealed a fine intelligence and often sceptical nature that were nevertheless contained within that gentleness. But her most striking feature was her height, standing as she did at just over six feet tall. It was a height that, had she been wired differently, might have brought about a supreme confidence and hauteur, terrifying to men, but for Sophie it was instead a source of faint but perennial embarrassment. Her auburn hair flowed down in tender waves from that height, the fringe stopping above twin seas of dark brown that were the emotional pull of a lovely, captivating face, the charm of which came enhanced by her long, slender figure. Sophie had a teacher's honesty, an ingenuousness that did not allow her to let things go, and she was both alluring and infuriating in her conviction that the business world was an absurd, possibly unnecessary place. She guarded this view, defending it against the violence of reality, and in so doing she had become my hero; and, perversely, a further base for those very ambitions to which she seemed so indifferent.

'You know, I'm not so sure you mean it,' I said. 'Would you *really* be content if I bummed around as – I don't know – an impoverished writer, waiting for you on the sofa when you got back home from work? Would you like that?'

'Simon!' She awoke from the catatonic state which the long lunch had induced in her, and stood up now from the sofa. 'Why wouldn't I like that? Anything would be better than—'

'OK, OK.' My mother's voice was both conciliatory and protective. Like her husband, she was a sensitive soul – but unlike him she had beautiful blue eyes, which flashed under dark curls that belied her age, and an Irish DNA that didn't mind confrontation. 'Enough of that, you two. Come on now, Sophie, I want to show you my rhododendrons.'

And five years went by in seconds, like a confused and unhappy dream, and Sophie and I were arguing every day and of the forty Fiennes & Plunkett associates that had qualified there were only three of us left and then Campaign began. Eight months during which the contenders were required to work on no less than fourteen major transactions – and gain an unconditional endorsement from the client instructing on each. A vortex in which we were spun from deal to deal, from impending catastrophe to financial emergency, our talents and our defects exhibited to all. A major restructuring deal – with its list of documents to be drafted, negotiated, tweaked and renegotiated; its all-night conference calls and its completion agendas; its plaintive requests for approvals, its last-minute obstacles and its chaotic signings – leaves everyone involved broken. The trainees and junior associates are given extra days' holiday to recover. The partners sneak off to their country houses. The directors of the client fly to the Alps or to the beach, having put the noose back in the attic, safe for a rainy day. The lawyer on a Campaign, however, must go on. The lawyer on a Campaign tidies the desk, gets an early night and comes in early the next morning to join the next two major transactions.

Yes, there were only two others left. The first was Angus Peterson – a fair-haired, eerily pale young man with a cruel, wolfish mouth and grey, unblinking eyes that were particularly haunting on what was otherwise a baby face. Angus wore a fixed, very nerdy, very empty smile, the infelicitous façade of bonhomie serving only to underline the ruthlessness of his dream, his coldness. The second of the other two lawyers remaining was the Queen of Keen, Emma Morris – a plump, desperately ambitious girl from Walsall with mousy-brown hair, whose strength derived from both fear and an entire absence of imagination – a closed mind allows for no doubt – and who existed in a state of permanent hysteria, forever flushed, forever promising tears of fury. These two delights, my competitors – and all three of us were to be sent away to recuperate while the partners held the annual vote on whether any new partners should be admitted; and, if so, who they were to be. There was no guarantee that any of us would be admitted: at the tight-knit family firm of Fiennes & Plunkett, often years would pass without any new entries. The only thing for certain was that we had worked three or four times harder than the other lawyers in the building, and that for at least one of us this would have been in vain: there were only two senior partners retiring that year, and the partnership, of course, could never exceed thirty.

'We also have a small real estate department.'

We had not worked harder than *every* lawyer in the building. For there was one man who had worked like a lawyer on a Campaign every working day of his career. That man was Rupert Plunkett – the man who knew how to do nothing else. Each lawyer on a Campaign had a mentor and, to Angus and Emma's dismay, during the partnership meeting Rupert had pulled my name out of the hat. This had its obvious advantage – if he liked me, I reckoned that Rupert, as Executive Chairman, would hold sway when it came to the partners' vote. But he could just as easily blackball me. And he kept following me around as I worked for the different departments and partners, constantly interfering in the deals I was working on.

'I have read the email correspondence, and I believe your deal will sign,' he whispered to me at some point during my final deal of Campaign. 'Where are you headed when this is over?'

'Cuba,' I said.

'Cuba?' The left hand to the quiff, the gaunt face peering down at me, concerned.

'Yes, Rupert. I thought—'

'Cuba?'

Three months earlier, Sophie had walked out of the rented flat in Fulham that we both so adored: it was located on the top floor of a pleasant house on Munster Road, with a skylight in the bedroom and a large roof terrace at the back with a low black railing from which there hung pots of flowers we would buy from a nearby nursery. I had arrived back at 5 a.m. one morning and, as I had entered the living room, I had seen a note on the table.

Can't do this any more. Have gone home to Mum's for the weekend.

The house back in Lincolnshire, up in Hubbard's Hills. Sophie's refuge of fresh green fields and a gurgling river that wound down into the ancient market town of Louth, the capital of the rolling slopes and gentle beauty of the Wolds. That white house high up there alone, that countryside that had bewitched me so long, only to then lose its appeal, quite suddenly, during one long winter's walk. However, by this stage in Campaign nothing evoked emotion, nostalgia, real thoughts. I considered the note for a while, drinking a large glass of whisky, and then passed out on the sofa. Three hours later, I was up.

'The distribution list,' a voice was whispering down the phone. 'Where the hell is it?'

Sophie had erupted a few days before the note. Having not heard from me for over thirty-six hours, and with my secretary not passing on her messages, she had taken the extraordinary step of telephoning Rupert Plunkett, telling him that what he was doing to me was illegal.

'I'm so sorry, Rupert,' I had mumbled, upon my return from the lock-down meeting. 'This is very embarrassing.'

'Par for the course,' he'd whispered. 'It has happened countless – *countless* – times before.'

After her note, I had not seen Sophie again. One evening, while I had been negotiating the final terms of a warranty schedule, she had returned to that flat where we had lived together for over eight years and taken everything she owned – all her myriad classics and schoolbooks from the shelves in the living room, all her low-heeled shoes that spoke so intimately of her insecurity, all her pictures and her computer and the paintings the kids had given her for her birthday, all she owned, all of her – and she had moved in with those dreadful teacher friends of hers, Eleanor Cantle and husband. Eleanor, who was infinitely less intelligent, had trained with Sophie and, to my dismay, was now a geography teacher at a nearby secondary school – as was the husband. I could just imagine Eleanor, the bony frame perched still and tense on the armchair, her eyes gleaming below her short dark hair, her husband dozing on the sofa as she bitches about me with her special subtle venom…

'It's alright, lovely, you can stay as long as you want.'

…failing to reassure, failing to conceal her delight as she talks to the lovely tearful girl whom she's always envied.

But very repressed, poor Eleanor – wincing now, no doubt, when Sophie tells the story directly, and everything Eleanor mumbles in response exuding a sort of horror that something like Fiennes & Plunkett could exist. Munching a chocolate biscuit, beginning timidly to enjoy herself again, but scared by the directness.

'Oh, I'm sure he's just a bit confused, that's all?' she says.

'No, no. He wants the millions.'

Eleanor gets up to make a fresh cup of tea...

Sophie and I had spoken over the phone in the days that followed her leaving the flat, with Sophie saying that she could no longer bear my presence. My agitated voice, my jumping as she came into the room, my inability to concentrate on anything she said, my distant face, my entire absence of interest in her. I kept telling her to be stronger; to be loyal and stay with me. There were only three months to go. There were enormous rewards at the other end.

'For God's sake, don't let Eleanor poison your mind!'

'I'm not!'

Once I became partner, I would be able to manage better my time, delegate the work. Reborn, we would holiday impulsively, extravagantly – oh, how often I daydreamed of this! Snuggled up close in our soft pyjamas, we would clink glasses as the plane's lights dimmed and they flew us away in first class over the night seas... away to hidden romantic hotels, iridescent landscapes, old towns of haunting beauty where we would lose ourselves in the melody of foreign voices, knowing that later we would sleep happy under Egyptian cotton sheets. One day we would buy our own villa, white as white, on the hill clambering up towards the sky from the bay of Portofino. Like king and queen we would stand glowing on its veranda as the sun turned the water milky blue and the pines murmured secrets to the breeze. To dream... to dream! It was a grand theatre that lay waiting – and I was doing this for us both. For the family that we would have together.

'It all makes no sense without you.'

'It's not true!' she cried, shocking me with this new anger that was not of the Sophie I knew. 'You're doing it for yourself! When did you even ask me about my job? And when have you ever talked seriously about marriage, even? You're changing, Simon – you just live in your head now. Even Dan agrees.'

'Dan Serfontein? You're talking to *my* friend about me? What is it with you two?'

'Oh, don't be ridiculous. Listen to what I'm saying.'

'Just three months. Three months!'

'You're repeating yourself – like that mental boss of yours!'

By this stage I *was* – unconsciously, of course – beginning to ape Rupert Plunkett. It was inevitable, I suppose, as my life consisted solely of him. The man who was described as my mentor, and who trained me in the art of anxiety. Great-grandson of Plunkett the founder, grandson of the Plunkett who had screwed Fiennes, son of the Plunkett who had had the foresight to retain the firm's name and the goodwill in it. The son, grandson, great-grandson who fought twenty hours a day to maintain what a legendary City family had bequeathed him. The man who despised those who craved sleep; the man who ate hurriedly, ashamed of his own weakness; the man who had no children and whose white-haired wife, seen out only at the firm's Christmas parties, surely spent her days wandering ghostlike through the rooms of the Pimlico townhouse. A man who earned five million pounds a year, money he had no time to spend, advising some of the largest corporates in Europe – or their creditors – at the beginnings of a new business venture or the final throes of their collapse. The man who, had Sophie addressed to him her words about being ridiculous, would have taken his fountain pen, opened a fresh Fiennes & Plunkett notebook and asked her to clarify.

'You were not at your station,' he noted, the day before Project Bernard was scheduled to complete.

'I was in the canteen, Rupert, getting some breakfast.'

'If you say so.' Rupert's hand pushed down on the quiff, which – insuppressible – shot back up, angrily. 'This promises to be an interesting day for you.'

And Project Bernard did complete, bringing to an end my Campaign. It was at 4 a.m. one grey morning of that April, when I was confronted by this most enormous of thoughts. I had been gazing at the screen of my computer for a thousand years when I was shaken suddenly by an irritating but catchy tune that was blaring out from my mobile phone. As each second passed, the song increased in volume. The suggestion was that there was an emergency, an impending catastrophe: that if I did not wake up properly, act quickly, I and the whole world with me would be engulfed by something so terrible...

I reached over and switched it off. 'So,' I murmured.

An hour earlier, we had received scanned versions of our client's executed counterparts, emailed to us from Luxembourg. There had followed a messy 'virtual exchange', the mess being caused by my trainee, Giles – an Old Harrovian with a mop of reddish-blond hair, infinite enthusiasm and no legal talent whatsoever. The definitive example of a man who would not last beyond his training contract. But now congratulatory emails were flowing in from around the world, and the public relations team from the beleaguered company were preparing the announcement of the rescue deal. Project Bernard had closed. There was nothing else to do. And yes, this was, for me, a somewhat confusing thought.

'Giles! We did get the signed opinion from the Jersey lawyers, didn't we?'

'Yes, I believe so.' Mr Giles Glynne-Ponsonby was displaying to me his strong, plucky jaw.

'Can you check, please? If we didn't, the client will be unprotected. It would be a bloody disaster.'

I watched as he clicked away, opening the attachments to the email. 'Yep, opinion here,' he said. 'Signed. We, um, we checked all these a short time ago, Simon.'

A memory came; I sighed. 'Sorry. Right, you should head off home now. I'll go and tell the common enemy we're done.'

I straightened my tie and stood up from the chair, feeling a vague elation but also vulnerable and redundant, an emptiness exposed by the thought that Fiennes & Plunkett wanted nothing more from me – for now.

'Simon?' Giles had stood up too. 'I'll come with you, if you don't mind. Rupert's asked me to bring him a file.'

'Scared to go alone?'

'Absolutely, indescribably terrified.'

'I understand entirely.'

Four o'clock in the morning. With Giles following behind with a bulky file, I walked down the beige-carpeted corridor to Rupert's office, past a row of identical glass offices, every second or third boasting a lawyer sitting before a bespoke desk lamp. My mind, needing something new to worry about, began to dwell on the point that I was about to leave for Cuba. Was I sure that the trip made sense? Should I really be flying off to what felt like the other side of the world? Didn't I have stuff to sort out? Sophie? I needed to save my relationship, didn't I? But no – no! It had been three months! And she had said that if I phoned her as soon as Campaign was over she would loathe me even more. Maybe she even had another guy by now. Yes, I needed to get away. Go far, far away. Yes, yes, it was fine…

On I walked down the corridor, in the rarefied hush of Fiennes & Plunkett. I walked past strapping, smartly dressed young lawyers who were walking hurriedly to their offices, weighed down by papers; I walked past senior partners with furrowed brows who were looking over the night secretaries' shoulders, quietly tapping their feet as the secretaries typed; I walked past printers spewing out silent rivers of paper. Soon, Giles and I had arrived outside the largest office on the floor. The heart of the firm. The magnificent cage containing the Executive Chairman.

'Here we go,' I said, as I saw Giles's back stiffen. The door of the cage being closed, I knocked a couple of times and then, knowing the rules, opened it just a notch. Seconds later, the whisper came.

'Come in.'

I walked slowly into the room, enchanted as always by the view through the glass walls. A sprawling metropolis, lit up in all its historic glory, could be seen behind the desk of a man who could not have cared less. That silver-haired gentleman – tall and thin, refined and terribly grave – was staring with the intensity of a predator at a sole piece of paper exposed to the glare of his reading lamp. The tie, I noted, was on but loosened. Sweat patches ruined what twenty-four hours earlier had been the crispest of white shirts. The face and neck were red.

'Hi, Rupert.'

To this, there was no response. He was watching that piece of paper; he was waiting for it to move. I looked at Giles and Giles nodded: the red neck was a danger sign. As every person in the building knew, Rupert suffered from a medical issue – a violent rash that flared up when things threatened to become too much. As I stood in my leader's office that morning, the rash was before me. Furious, raw, untreated…

'Well,' I tried again. 'Good news, Rupert: Project Bernard has completed, finally! So I wanted to say goodbye. I'm heading home – I'm off in a few days, to Cuba.'

And then the head shot up suddenly – and I became transfixed by two bloodshot eyes. Eyes that were begging to be allowed to close, but which were held open by that harsh, relentless anxiety. They were the eyes of a captured tiger, a wreck of a tiger, a beast deprived of adequate food and sleep for years, with the consequence that its senses were now acute, its reactions rapid, paranoid.

'Sit down, for Christ's sake.'

I followed the order. The desk now towered above me, reminding me of my position in life. Meanwhile, Giles – having noted that Rupert had not extended the instruction to him – stood still.

'What is that in his hands?' Rupert whispered to me.

'Ah,' intervened Giles. 'I have the file you asked for.'

My leader's eyes narrowed briefly at this. 'And which file might that be?'

'The file sent to us by the corporate lawyers. Containing all the disclosures against the warranties. It's all tabbed—'

Giles was halted by a raised arm.

'That is *not* the file I asked for.'

'Oh. I'm very sorry. I'll sort this straight away.' Following which, a ghastly conundrum: stay in attendance, or go to find the right file? But which *was* the right file? Struggling with all of this, Giles remained standing as Rupert turned his attention back to me.

'Why Cuba?' he whispered.

'Sorry?'

'Why Cuba?'

'Oh, you know, Rupert – I've told you before.' It was difficult, at this time in the morning, to muster a light and friendly tone. 'Everyone wants to go to Cuba; to see it before the regime falls.'

'Before the regime falls?'

'Well, I mean before everything changes there. You know, with Obama charting his "new course" and all that, re-engaging with the Castros, they say it's only a matter of time before the embargo disappears. And Fidel will be gone soon anyway. And then—'

'Obama? You're referring now to President Obama?'

'Well, yes.'

'Christ.' A shake of the head. 'The people survive on rations, you know.'

'Yes, I read about the rations in my guidebook the other day. I couldn't believe it.'

'You couldn't believe it?' Rupert shook his head once more, profoundly disappointed in me. 'But everyone knows that the people survive on rations.'

A brief silence. Then:

'What will you do in Cuba?'

'I'm joining a group tour.' But I was assailed now by doubts. 'We'll have a guide, who'll take us round the island.'

'Good heavens. And the lady?'

'The lady?'

'Yes, the *lady*.' Rupert was scratching his neck furiously. 'Your girlfriend.'

'Ah, Sophie. No, sadly we've broken up. It's quite recent.'

'Yes, fine. Understood. OK.'

He fixed me, appalled by this excessive detail. But then, shaken by some thunderclap of a memory triggered by who knew what, the Lord of Restructurings turned quickly to his computer. I watched him type, hunched and feverish, before he swivelled back around. There followed another period of silence, which, in its heaviness, soon became intolerable.

'Well, Rupert, I'm all in. I haven't slept for over forty-eight hours.'

'Thank you for that – most helpful.' This rare touch of irony hanging in the air, Rupert's nose twisted, like a serpent's head, towards Giles. 'Do you have the file?'

'Not yet,' said Giles, with certainty. 'No, I haven't moved since our earlier conversation.'

The bloodshot eyes now did close. So many conference calls to join; so many emails to compose; so many arcane documents to review; so many billions at stake.

'I need that file,' Rupert whispered.

'Yes. And, just to check, sorry, which precise file would that—'

'The file, man. The file. The damn file.'

Giles, around whom the winds of apocalypse now blew, turned and hurried out, his step that of a City lawyer with much on his mind. Meanwhile:

'Now, you know the rules.'

'The rules?' I asked.

'Yes, the *rules*. The *rules* about emails.'

I saw that Rupert Plunkett – as was often the case when the great man became entangled in prolonged interaction with human beings – was now living a nightmare. He had assumed his particular expression of unspeakable anguish – the tormented face that he was prone to pull when passing on key messages. It was as if he suffered under the weight of ensuring that those messages had been received; that all remained under control.

'You must *not* access your work emails, Simon. Throughout your break. Whether through your BlackBerry or any other way.'

'Ah, yes.'

'As for the partnership appointments – the news that I suspect you'll be rather keen to know – I'll call you on your mobile, as discussed. On the 26th, once the votes have been cast. But you must not access your emails.'

'Yes, Rupert.'

He regarded me carefully. 'Those are the rules, you see.'

'Yes.'

'The rules are there for your benefit. It's most important that you now – relax.'

'I understand.'

'You do? Very good.'

The whisper bore a trace of resignation. My leader knew that he had gone as far as the laws of England would permit in seeking to ensure the safe transmission of the message. He was, perhaps, even quietly confident that I had understood. But I was human – and so there could never be certainty. Bitter at humans, bitter at an abominable world, Rupert Plunkett grimaced, nodded to the door and re-engaged with his piece of paper.

2

FOUR DAYS LATER I found myself on the other side of the Atlantic, being driven at speed through the bumpy streets of Havana. I was on my way to the crumbling Hotel el Rey, the meeting place for the group of travellers, and was reflecting with conflicting emotions that this really was rather far-flung. From my first moment in the country, when I had been pointed at by an airport security guard in faded military uniform, Cuba had elicited in me a vague sense of foreboding. And yet, irreconcilably, there was a sudden, beautiful hope too; a subsiding of doubts as to the rationale, brought about by a thrill at the actuality of this fantasy, the sort of thrill that I had not known for years. Here in the heart of Habana Vieja, here in 2012, I was experiencing the excitement of my year abroad in Naples as a student, the liberating effect of an alien culture. How many years had passed since Naples; how carefree I'd been! Smelling the heavy scent of cigar smoke hanging in the sea air, hearing the beat of the salsa blaring from clapped-out Chevrolets, I was thus lost in thought, and unexpected self-congratulation, when the taxi pulled to a halt and a dwarfish man walked towards us and then spat onto the potholed pavement.

'Jesus,' I murmured. The reconnection, it was clear, was only partial. A susceptibility to panic, germinated in me on my first day at Fiennes & Plunkett, was now a personality trait.

'*Quince pesos*,' grunted the taxi driver.

'*Ah sí, gracias*,' I replied, handing over the coveted tourist currency. And, my first Cuban transaction completed, I nodded at my driver, thanked him again and stepped out, with both wariness and exuberance, into Havana.

On the way out, during the long flight across the Atlantic, I had wondered for hours what my first impressions of Cuba would be: whether I would perceive in the mannerisms and eyes of the people the flickering of a new dream that defied the chains of dictatorship; whether I would be struck instead by a sense of oppression, a resigned belief that things would never really change; or whether, as I stood marvelling at the Capitolio, the anachronistic beauty of a city still suspended in time would make me forget, momentarily, the present. They had all seemed reasonable possibilities, so that it was a bit embarrassing that, as I entered the hotel, my first travel note of substance related to the heat and the humidity. But it was surreally humid. I had never experienced an air like it, and the exoticism fed both of my alternating mental states: it was close to being enjoyable, in the sense that it made me feel far from the familiar cold, far from everything that the familiar cold suggested; but it was fuel also to that sense of looming menace.

I walked across the lobby to a rickety reception desk that was struggling under piles of books and crumpled, yellowed papers, behind which a squat *señora* was either sitting or standing. After I had introduced myself and shown my passport, and she had passed me the keys to my room, I asked the way to the lift. However, from the look on the woman's face, there was no lift.

'*Vale, no pasa nada*,' I said, conciliatory.

'*Eh?*'

Trying not to dwell on her fury, I took my bags and trudged up the creaking stairs, soon to experience another rush of that excitement. There was something incorruptibly romantic about the room, something fine and poetic in the chipped tiles – it was the antithesis of the asepticism of Fiennes & Plunkett. I collapsed onto my bed and lay there for a second, listening to the shouts, screeches of car wheels and deafening salsa from the street.

'I did it,' I murmured. In spite of Rupert Plunkett, in spite of the trauma of Campaign, I still had my youthful spirit – that same open-mindedness, that same curiosity, that same delight in cultural peculiarity that had always been such an important part of me. I had come through Campaign, and I had retained it all! Hadn't I told Sophie that I was still the same person? If she could see me now! As I lay on the bed, I felt a growing pride, which withstood even the ensuing moments of panic as I spotted a hole in the bedroom ceiling.

Possible asbestos, possible asbestos! Need new room, need new room! I reasoned at the speed of a lawyer trained by Rupert Plunkett. But the *señora* at reception looked at me with hostile eyes.

'*No.*'

'Erm.'

'*No.*'

I was thinking that, if this *señora* was in any way representative, then I had been fed lies by my guidebook about the gregarious nature of the Cubans, the light of hope and joviality that strove through shackles. If she was in any

25

way representative, then the truth was that they were, instead, arseholes. I nodded at her and was turning for the stairs when she called to me.

'*Eh!*'

As I lowered my hands, she explained that there was an introductory meeting scheduled for my group in an hour's time.

'*Gracias,*' I said.

Back up in my room, preparing myself for that introductory meeting, I was still proud and determined and hopeful, but edgy now too, increasingly edgy as I discovered that the shower was unusable. It spewed out black oil, so that I had to wash in the sink, or rather to splash water rancorously from the sink onto my bare, overheated body. Once frantic waves had crashed into me, I stood still, dripping, before the mirror, wondering about something of profound importance that I seemed to have forgotten. And then I remembered it – the hole. After much internal debate, much pacing naked around the room, I almost came to the decision that I would have to sleep in the bathroom. Finally, however, stability returned: I told myself to stop it; to go down to meet the team.

The violence of that edginess, which had come alive like an angry rat woken from its slumber by a kick from a boot, had yet failed to defeat positivity: as I walked back down those creaking stairs in a heat and humidity redolent of a tropical jungle, the rat disappeared and I understood the touching little truth that I was desperately looking forward to meeting my group. I hadn't met new people my age for years, outside the firm. Social interaction! Potential new friendships! Maybe even something more – with shock, I realised that I would not at all mind falling in love.

Sophie and I are over. It's been over three months without a word.

Yes, it was true. During that heady descent of the hotel's stairs, I would not at all have minded meeting a beautiful, bona fide traveller. I even imagined her. She was a Parisian girl with a coquettish smile, whose name might turn out to be Hélène and who would sip provocatively from a glass of rum. She was a freelance musician, and her hand would run through her soft, dark hair as we shared a Cohiba on a white-sand beach, looking up at a sky spangled with Castro's stars. As the waves fell in whispers, she would murmur, 'Let's leave the tour – let's go to see our own Cuba, *all* alone.' I would nod, dumb with joy, and her hand would reach out to my cheek. 'How I love your blue eyes. How I love your English voice.'

It was with a sigh that I saw that my group had not yet arrived – a sigh of deflation but also of embarrassment, given the vigour with which I had entered the lobby. I went to perch on a stool in the corner, under an ineffective overhead fan, reminding myself that it was essential that I try to maintain the positive energy. However, I soon began to feel a little restless and uncomfortable. A little anxious. The sense of exoticism had been dimmed by a group of sunburnt English women in their late forties or fifties, who were drinking cocktails and cackling in the middle of the room with an intimacy that suggested lifelong friendship. Their accents suggested somewhere close to, but not in, London. Possibly Reading.

I pondered those English women for a while. And, as I pondered, I experienced once more that unusual sense of foreboding. I looked at my watch. I looked again at my watch. I then began to gaze once more at the English women. One of them had the stiffest, reddest hair I had ever seen. It shot up, straight as an arrow, from her scalp.

Extraordinary, I noted.

Around a quarter of an hour later, someone tapped me on the shoulder and the world, until then held in place only by the finest of cobwebs, imploded. The young Cuban man before me smiled a wild, dangerous smile, while pointing at the women.

'No, no,' I said.

'Welcome, Seemon 'aines! Join the team!'

And then I was sitting at the women's table, listening to the welcome speech.

'OK! Now, you lees'en me! Tonight you all relax, OK? You een the Caribbean now! No more estress! No more appointments! No more eschedules! OK, *amigos*? 'Ere theengs 'appen Cuban time!'

I considered those unlikely words, which had been delivered in a practised, military tone, while regarding a mosquito that hovered ominously under the overhead fan. The mosquito resembled a miniature toy helicopter. A grotesque, shocking thing.

'Come on your own, love?'

And nothing.

'Oi! I said, are you on your own?'

I awoke. 'Sorry! Yes, I'm Simon – nice to meet you all. Sorry – ha! I must look like the little boy lost!'

This reply was met with silence, which was to be expected. My final comment had been a very peculiar, unfortunate one, one of the most peculiar and unfortunate comments I had ever made, and there was in it a suggestion of hysteria.

The silence was broken by the guide.

'Not everyone old, *amigo*! There ees girl comin' too! Not everyone old!'

'Oh, no, I didn't mean that.' I felt myself turning red.

'*Eh?* She ees young, she only eseventeen years!'

Only seventeen? And the women around me, now viewed more closely, must surely be in their fifties. What about the age bracket of 28–35s? What about ... ? A burst of optimism, which disregarded the point that the guide had known my name. As the women returned to their cocktails, I took him aside.

'Listen.' My voice was low, conspiratorial. 'I think maybe we've got mixed up. I'm here for the Yellow Travel tour – the tour for the 28–35s.'

'We are Yellow Travel tour, *amigo*!'

'Please, not so loud. Are you sure this is the only Yellow Travel tour? I paid for the 28–35s, you see. *Veintiocho hasta treinta y cinco.*'

'No age matter for thees tour! Yellow Travel, we not care about age!'

The words were yelled with the fervour and conviction of a brainwashed man. From behind came a hiss.

'There was never an age bracket, was there, Gabs?'

'No. Pablo's right – Yellow Travel don't have age brackets. They've got *suggested* ages, but they're not meant to be exclusive. The whole point of these trips is being open-minded!'

'Yes.' I turned as I spoke. 'Yes, I *completely* agree with that.'

'I'd just leave it, if I were you.'

I left it. The girl arrived shortly thereafter. As I sat in the circle of bona fide travellers, surreptitiously scrutinising the words of my booking confirmation and wondering how I could have gone that evening in the office from an analysis of difficult case law to a comprehensive misreading of a travel company's age policy, we learnt that her name was Victoria. She was a pale, insipid-looking child who was on her first trip outside Europe. Apparently her father had said that it would do her good to explore another culture, and that gaining life experience in this way would hold her in good stead for her interviews at Cambridge. Victoria explained to us that, as a condition of allowing her to go, Daddy had insisted that she keep to the deal that they had made many years earlier: that was to say, that she should still call him twice a day, every day.

'You must be careful using your mobile phone here,' I noted gently. 'I've read that it's very expensive to call abroad from Cuba.'

'Thanks – but my dad pays for the contract, and he wants to hear from me.'

'Fine,' I said. 'Sorry – I'm sure he does.' I had begun to hear a faint humming noise in my head, which I suspected, or hoped, was the result of the long flight. The alternative was that I was having a massive nervous breakdown.

'Don't worry, darling – it don't cost that much to ring abroad. And anyway, you can tell your dad we'll be looking after you.'

The Cuban guide interrupted these initial pleasantries. As I began to muse on the benefits of choosing flight over fight, he was informing us in that ecstatic voice that our first step as bona fide travellers should be to dine in an authentically Cuban state-run restaurant that he knew, and that was only a few metres up the street. Or did we have any other ideas? Taking the question as meant sincerely, and in a monstrous error of judgement, I asked the Cuban guide politely what he thought of *paladares*, the idea of which seemed to me to be rather more appealing. They were privately run and, while some were now becoming more like typical restaurants, the original *paladares*, many of which still existed, were located in family homes. According to my guidebook they offered a better quality of food, giving tourists the chance to sample authentic Cuban home cooking in an intimate, informal atmosphere. The guidebook had come out strongly in favour of the *paladar*, explaining, in a rare example of humour, that by contrast the state-run restaurants in Cuba were of a quality that ranged from the mediocre to the life-threatening. The editors had added that, in most state-run restaurants, you could only eat chicken or pork with rice or beans.

'I'm easy either way, of course, but it might be fun to try a *paladar*.'

'No, man, we go to a restaurant! Real *cubanos*, they go to a restaurant!'

'Thanks, Pablo. We agree. You're the guide, after all!'

'Yes, just to reiterate, I wasn't trying to overrule him.'

'Restaurant sounds good to me, Pablo!'

'Yeah, me too!'

'We should, like, listen to Pablo!'

It was occurring to me that the group of women resembled a small colony of penguins. Disorientated, indignant penguins; penguins far from home and not made for this heat. Of course that vertical red hair did not sit comfortably with the analogy, but there were many factors that did. The large heads, the short necks and even shorter legs, the strangeness of the gaze. They had adopted identical frowns and Victoria, who had moved her chair nearer to the colony, was also forcing an equivocal facial expression that wanted to be a frown. But Victoria didn't look like a penguin.

'*Vamos!*' exclaimed Pablo. 'Eh, my friends – in eSpanish that means: "Let's go!"'

And we waddled out for dinner, to a restaurant that – try as I might – defied rationalisation. For reasons I did not seek to establish, each of the Cuban waiters was dressed as a bullfighter. All of them wore glittering capes, which, in their interplay with the penguins, the shady interior and the concomitant, pervading suggestion of dark farce, elicited vague but traumatic conclusions that I might have become a character in some horrific sequel to *Animal Farm*.

'Chill out,' said Victoria. 'You look so wound up.'

'No, it's just a bit odd in here.'

'It's not odd – it's the authentic Cuba. You need to open up a bit.'

'I'm *not* convinced that these capes represent the authentic Cuba.'

The penguins, unconcerned by the capes and wallowing in a sense of entitlement attributable to their final round of cocktails in the lobby, asked Pablo to please tell them what he recommended, explaining that they did not know the lingo – obviously they didn't; they were English! The guide, sitting at the head of the table, had assumed an expression of general contentment.

'*Amigos*, everytheeng good 'ere. All so great! I not eat in a restaurant for many years!'

This declaration, in its inconsistency with his earlier point that frequenting a restaurant was a typically Cuban thing to do, threatened to throw me into confusion until I realised the truth: Pablo was availing himself of his position as guide to treat himself. Absolutely fair enough, I thought – poor bastard. But he had not really answered the question.

'The translation is on the other side of the menu,' I explained to the table. 'If you just turn—'

'For God's sake, Simon! Apologies, Pablo – please go on.'

The situation, I now knew, was irretrievable: war had broken out between the penguins and me. I fell into troubled contemplation while the guide proceeded to tell the table what I, knowing a bit of the *lingo*, had already read, and which was in any case on the other side of the damn menu: that they would be eating chicken and/or pork with beans and/or rice.

'I can't eat chicken or pork!' cried Victoria.

'Why not, girl?'

'I'm a vegetarian, that's why not!'

'He might not understand that,' I said. 'The Cubans aren't big on—'

'What are you saying?'

'I'm saying that he won't care about chickens the same way you do.'

'But that's just horrible!'

'True, though – unfortunately.' My words were sage; controlled, emotionless.

Presently, a bullfighter arrived. He asked us what we would like to eat. The penguins opted for the *comida criolla de la casa*, which was both chicken and pork with both rice and beans. Victoria followed my suggestion, ordering a plate of rice with beans. Pablo ordered the pork with beans, rice and an extra bowl of beans.

'And you? What would you like, *señor?*'

'I might go for the chicken!' I shouted back – for it was very noisy in the restaurant. 'Would it be possible to have some rice with it?'

'Yes! It is possible!'

'Great stuff! Thank you!'

Many years later, our table was laden with chicken and pork and rice and beans. The penguins' enjoyment of the meat soon put Victoria in difficulty, perhaps leading her fragile and capricious mind to ask itself intrusive questions about the nature and permanence of identity; about the perishability of bonds.

'Chicken's very good, isn't it, Di?' remarked a penguin.

'Sick,' murmured Victoria.

This picture of innocence in the wild spoke no Spanish either, so that in this regard too I stood alone among the travellers. The guide revealed an unflattering side to his character – a form of competitive malice. He tried to catch me out a number of times, often succeeding with great joy.

'Where did you learn Spanish?' asked Victoria.

'Just at school. But I always tried to keep it up – I love romance languages. In fact, I studied languages at uni before going into the law.'

'Really? Which university?'

'Cambridge.'

'Oh! Did I mention that I'm hoping to go?'

Victoria's tone had softened and, as I chewed on my chicken, I saw before she did the curiosity that would soon follow: the evening spent answering her questions about university life and the pros and cons of the various colleges. The premonition soon materialised. I answered question after question, my mind drifting back to London, to the firm, and to a sudden, stark realisation of the consequences of what I had done; of the point that I had reached. Within two weeks, I would be a fêted, stinking-rich young star of City law – or an alumnus of the firm of Fiennes & Plunkett. An alumnus for whom the firm would find a job as an in-house lawyer at one of its creditor clients (i.e. a bank), looking ahead to a more stable life, a competitive salary, decent working hours…

For a fleeting moment I felt a lovely warmth at the prospect of going in-house. In the idea of a job that I might do really well, a job that would give me free evenings and weekends, an amount of money that I would understand. But the potent appeal, I knew, was brought about by a terror of the alternative – the new world I had yet to conceive. The mystery of partnership was fostered to such an extent by the firm that I had dedicated years to a quest for an undeveloped idea. I still did not know what the partners really did. Of course, even though I denied it, I knew in a secret part of me the fallacy of delegation, and that in truth they worked just as hard as any associate – other than an associate on a Campaign. I knew that they bore ultimate responsibility for transactions worth billions of pounds. I knew, or guessed, that they would be involved in business development, pitching for new clients. But it was all abstract, as was the idea of earning a million, two million pounds a year. A million pounds a year at thirty-two? Two million pounds a year at forty? Were these figures true? If so, what would I do with it all? It was a nonsensical amount of money, but money that demanded a commitment of my soul, a comprehensive assumption of an identity. I would be a leading City financing lawyer, for life. Was that who I really was? Was that the guy Sophie had fallen in love with?

But enough! The moment passed, and in its transience I recognised it for what it was: weakness exposed; an instinct to run in the face of the unknown. And, with it given a name, its chaos dissipated, and the same underlying fear that had elicited it now fuelled in its place a proud defiance. I deserved partnership. Yes, it was what I wanted. I would adapt to it just as I had adapted to school, to university, to qualified life. As for Sophie – well, she had let me down. Had three months been so much to ask for? Walking out on me, after so many years! And how did she dare talk to my best friend Dan about me? Although the whole Sophie question, I recognised, was infinitely complicated; a morass of—

'Simon!'

'Hmm?'

'Well?'

'Yes, sorry. Italian and French were my languages.'

'I know! I'm asking which you preferred!'

Indisputably, Victoria had changed sides. Each of the penguins looked on with a mother's jealousy – exacerbated by cheap rum – as I spoke to their former ally and her expression flowered into an unconditional respect that came laced with emotion. When we arrived back at the hotel she giggled at nothing, before asking whether I wanted to hang out in the bar. Once more certain of how things would turn out, I replied that it would probably be an idea to get a good night's sleep, given that we would have to be ready to leave by nine the next morning. Victoria promptly became upset, mumbling something that I did not quite hear but which might have been a statement that I was a freak, and then stormed upstairs with a limp attempt at theatricality.

With her gone, the penguins snoozing hot in their rooms and the Cuban guide having gone home, there arrived a moment of peace, which I decided to spend hanging out in the bar alone, listening to the hotel barmen talking about baseball. As I sat waiting to be served, a couple of women strolled past the glass window of the bar. Looking in for a second, they managed both to glare and to smile in the same expression.

While I reflected, only vaguely, on those proud, hostile smiles, the hotel barmen were telling me that one of the best beers in Cuba was a beer called Bucanero. The exoticism of the name brought about the sense of a lost little fantasy, a recollection of the hopes I had had before meeting the penguins. But it also injected courage, as I reminded myself of the still valid point that I was in Cuba, and supposed to be having fun. I decided to order some local cigarettes – but the smoke was too strong; the tobacco too coarse. I gave the packet to one of the barmen, who took them from my hand without thanking me.

Pleasant, I thought.

My mind was returning to Sophie: the photograph of us in Santorini that she had left on the living room table; her upsetting eagerness to explain that I had got it all wrong and that I needed only to listen to her; whether our break-up had been as one-sided as I had believed. Whether, in fact, I might have been the uncommunicative, self-absorbed partner she had claimed I was. She probably had a point … but how annoying she could be! Putting on the radio at full volume at half past six in the morning, when she knew I had come in only a couple of hours earlier. That raising of her eyebrows whenever I dared mention anything to do with the firm. Coming back tipsy after a dinner with her teacher friends and hiding my BlackBerry in the kitchen. Laughing uncontrollably, and then becoming offended and angry, at my frantic searching. Throwing my cigarettes away, and once locking me out on the roof terrace for a period of time that was too long to be funny, when she had caught me having a sneaky one. That provocative delight she had in reminding me how rewarding her job was; her voice on my birthday when asking whether Rupert had remembered. Her silence during the associate summer parties, and the subsequent unloading of the insecurity on the way home. The contradictory fondness for my tall, handsome, loaded friend Dan. Or perhaps it was something more than fondness – maybe, deep in her subconscious, a small part of Sophie fancied Dan, his manliness and obscene confidence, his physique, his blond hair and green eyes. A physical attraction, an infatuation, seemed the only explanation for their friendship – he represented everything she claimed to despise. Or maybe it was all nonsense, I didn't know – maybe I was just jealous of that physique and charm – but why did she have to look so happy when we met him? So irritating! She really was irritating! And then there was that damned friend of hers, Eleanor Cantle, with her dreadfully boring, dreadfully stupid husband, her plain clothes and plain face and plain conversation, her darting glances at Sophie if I referred to something – anything – outside the comfort zone.

And there was her litany of science documentaries on the television, her silent bitterness when I fell asleep watching them. Her unspoken disgust at London, her unspoken disgust at ambition, the attachment to Louth, the requirement that we go back, nearly every month, to Lincolnshire. At the same time, the bristling at my closeness to my own mother. The envy I perceived at times of my having a father who was present, the insistence on those long weekend walks when she knew I had work to do, the pathological retreat into her books...

I was hurt deeply by her and I adored her and I wanted never to see her again and I missed her so terribly much. I missed the fragility in a smile that pretended to be sure, the constant temptation to stoop that was her loveliest trait, the sincerity with which she would wake me up on a Saturday morning, telling me of all the things we were going to do. I missed the innocence of her conviction, her belief in her job, how she was inspired by her cleverest pupils and had patience for the slowest, and most of all I missed the intimacy of our conversations, how we each knew the other's deepest self. But, after seeing everything of me that there was to see, she had abandoned me – just as she had the first time, when we'd gone to university – and finally in our last conversation she'd told me never to call her again and now I was so alone. A lonely man in Cuba, with the loneliest of plans.

And, there in that bar that night, I could not see any alternative to the plan of increasing my loneliness. I would not manage eleven days traipsing around Cuba with the penguins, and delaying a decision seemed illogical – better alone in Havana than in some remote country village of men rolling cigars. The plan, then, was simple: I would leave the tour before it had started. But its simplicity was so stark, so brutal – like a violently sketched arrow pointing away, but at nothing…

And then – quite suddenly – a voice from behind:

'Hi, mate! Mind if I join you?'

I started – turned quickly and looked up at the man whose Australian voice this was. And I was thinking quickly, too, as I looked. I was daring to wonder: *the sea change?*

It was an optimism that calmed but did not altogether fade out once I had taken in the picture of the man before me. He seemed more or less my age – or rather a bit older than I was: late thirties, perhaps. But the headline point of his appearance was not his age – it was his geekiness. He was very geeky indeed, in his green sleeveless vest, long black shorts and fluorescent trainers. But there was nothing wrong with that: I was a fan of geeks – save for the rare *evil geek*, the type defined by Angus Peterson, my unblinking, baby-faced competitor for partnership. No, harmless geeks I liked, counting many among my acquaintances at the firm – their promise of light eccentricity was charming, engaging, and it was not as if I was entirely non-geeky myself. It was true that this man's appearance was particularly odd, suggesting some strange underlying anger or insecurity: the muscles on his arms and neck appeared to be the result of enormous work in the gym, yet were undermined by the puniest of bone structures. In his attempt to regain self-esteem, he'd managed to create a parody of masculinity. Standing above me at the bar, his arms swelled with proud little bulges – but that was alright. *Don't judge.*

'Of course you can join me,' I said. 'I'm Simon.'

'Nice one, mate. I'm Nathan.' He paused. 'I was watching and thought you could do with some company. You were looking quite reflective for a while there – a bit depressed.'

'Yes,' I said. 'I was thinking of how I've got ten years older without realising it.'

'That *is* sad.'

'Yes – I sort of came out here to meet lots of new people my own age, while forgetting what my own age was. I'd even hoped I might find a new girlfriend. Now I'm about four hours into my trip, and I'd *love* to go home.'

'Shit, mate.'

'I suppose,' I said, warming to my thesis, 'to be honest, I hadn't *forgotten* that I was in my early thirties – I just hadn't thought about what it meant. I'm over a decade late for a gap year.'

'Never too late for a gap year.'

'Hmm? I didn't quite hear her, but I think I might have just been called a freak by a seventeen-year-old. Or maybe it was a creep, in fact. Can you imagine? After *I* told *her* I didn't want a drink with her.'

'Mate – you're making *me* feel depressed.' Nathan smiled. 'And I've just turned forty! Want another cold one?'

'Why not? Bucanero's the beer out here, I understand. It's not too bad.'

'Bucanero sounds excellent.'

'You see, my point is that it would be odd to call a single twenty-two-year-old guy out here a freak or a creep – it wouldn't make sense.'

'Here he comes, mate – the barman.'

'I'll get these,' I said. 'I'm happy to get them.'

'Well, thanks.'

I paid for the beers with a fifty CUC banknote, for I now had no lesser note on me – the Cuban barman, that same grumpy soul to whom I had given the cigarettes, began to curse as he walked away to find me some change. Ignoring him, I continued to talk instead to Nathan, talking about myself, my situation here, and soon found that I rather liked the Australian listener – since a child I had had this tendency to warm to people quickly, sometimes intensely, just so long as it was I who went on talking. But then, with courtesy beginning to demand it, the conversation turned briefly to the listener.

'So, I assume you're a late arrival for the Yellow Travel tour?' I said pleasantly. 'We've all just been for dinner – it was bloody awful, actually.'

'Nah, mate. I'm not here for any group tour. I always travel alone.'

And so, as was equally often the case when it became the turn for the listener to speak, I felt the warmth begin to ebb away and became alternately bored, disappointed, and cross with myself. Cross that, as always, I'd been so impulsive – that I'd built him up in my head, convincing myself that he was fascinating and deep, that he would have a sense of humour similar to mine, all before he had spoken a word. The primary state among these fluctuating states though was boredom: I flitted in and out now as Nathan spoke, my mind drifting – but he wouldn't notice. I had long perfected the look of attentive listening when the mind wandered like this, Sophie the only person in the world who could spot what was happening – she would click her fingers at it.

'Young people don't understand the *dangers* of travel, mate,' Nathan was saying. 'They come out here thinking it's going to be a big party or something. As if the country was a fucking theme park.'

'Yes.'

'Whereas, in truth, Cuba's *fucked*. The economy, the infrastructure, everything! They say it's all going to change – but it won't be overnight, I can tell you.'

'Right – I can imagine that's quite right.'

Nathan's true character, his real weird self, was becoming steadily, depressingly clearer, and suddenly my mind stopped its drifting in order to dwell on a small but curious point upon which it then fixated, developing a little story. For it was quite odd that earlier I'd thought of my competitor at the firm, Angus Peterson – Mr Psycho-Nerd himself. Why had I thought of him? I'd used him as a counterpoint, that was right – I'd drawn a distinction between his type of nerdiness and that other, pleasant type of nerdiness I had for some reason assumed would be Nathan's. But maybe, I thought, as my story spun out, I'd been quite wrong – for there *was* something else about Nathan that evoked Angus, wasn't there? Something I could not quite articulate. Perhaps that hint of coldness underneath?

But it came and went, this intuition, and was probably unfair – he wasn't saying anything cold or sinister, just ranting about the perils of travel, the irresponsibility of 'fake travellers'. My imagination always did run riot when I was overtired – and I was very, very tired now.

'I've been all over the world. I've slept in the desert in Jordan, got buses around Mexico, been to Tibet, India. When you travel alone you learn how to look after yourself. Basic things, you know what I mean?'

'I do.'

As he went on like this, I was sipping my beer, nodding in what I hoped was the manner of a relaxed person who was in agreement with him, while in parallel this new story I'd created transformed slowly into a conversation: an internal discussion about whether Nathan was Good Nerd or Bad Nerd. Reasonable Simon was telling Neurotic Simon to stop it – that the similarity with Angus wasn't there physically and the guy had done nothing to suggest he was bad. But Reasonable Simon tended not to win this sort of debate, for Reasonable Simon didn't have the advantage of *the hunch*: very hard to defeat in an argument, the hunch.

'I'm planning to use Havana as a base,' Nathan said. 'All these idiots charging around the island – foolish, mate! Completely *superficial*. Better to have day trips, using local transport – there's more than enough to do in Havana at night. Get up early, do a full day trip – and then you've still got your base. Now *that* is bona fide.'

'Makes a lot of sense.' Yet it did not – I would have imagined the day trip to be precisely what a man like Nathan disapproved of. How would he manage to see the whole island? Perhaps this was the new avant-garde of authenticity – not to do what others did, even if it meant you missed out on seeing the place you'd come to see. But the bigger point was that I didn't care – I cared so little that it almost pained me to think about it.

'I won't be staying here, though – I can't stand the staff in this hotel. That woman at reception – she's a total bitch, mate. So rude! I'm off tomorrow, not spending another day here.'

'Yes, she's not the kindest, is she? Bit dramatic, though, to leave.'

'It's taken me a long time,' Nathan said, by way of grand *non sequitur*, 'to understand who I am at heart.'

'And who is that?'

'A traveller.'

'That's great, Nathan. It's great that you've found yourself.'

Oh, God, how easy and pleasant and meaningful life might be if people would only let *me* talk to *them* and leave it at that – leave me to imagine them. A short time later my drink was finished and Nathan was broaching the vile idea of my joining him, seeing Cuba his way, on the day trips, instead of going around the island with the Yellow Travel tour. I replied that I needed some time to myself, an answer I was not sure he fully accepted – but he didn't seem too offended. And he also seemed fine with my calling it a night: after a glance at my watch and a comment about the length of the flight, I had let out a reasonably polite little yawn.

'You get yourself to bed, mate. And thanks for the beer – my round next time, if we bump into each other. You never know – we might. Actually, before you go, give me your number – as I say, I'm out of this place first thing tomorrow.'

So, all rather harmless. But then, once I had shaken his hand and walked away towards the stairs, gazing at myself as I approached the large mirror on the bar's wall, it happened: the vindication of Neurotic Simon. I remembered I had forgotten to pick up my change from the fifty-CUC banknote, which the barman had left on a small silver tray on the counter. And it was very strange – a mere second or so after I remembered this, just as I was about to turn, I saw movement in the mirror. I watched Nathan pounce, snatching the notes from the tray and stuffing them into his pocket – it was over in an instant.

I did turn now, experiencing an unfamiliar indignation.

'I've just remembered,' I said, as I walked back towards him, that indignation prevailing over a general awkwardness, newly hot cheeks. 'I left my change, didn't I? There was quite a bit there, I think.'

It was a long silence that ensued – a hard silence that was somehow worse even than the shock of the actual event. For it was not at all natural. Nathan's face was calm and still – shameless.

'Of course!' He laughed, suddenly. 'I'm so *sorry*, mate – I went and stuck the money in my pocket, thinking it was mine!'

'Not a problem,' I said warily. And, as he passed me back the money, I understood finally what it was that had reminded me…

It's his eyes. They're emotionless, just like Angus's eyes.

I spent a restless first night in Havana below the hole in the bedroom ceiling, worrying about how to tell the team that I was leaving the tour, worrying about where I would go, worrying about the hole and worrying about the little sociopath downstairs in the bar. The point that Nathan was off the next morning was cheering to reflect upon, but marred by the thought that he had my mobile phone number. Could he do anything with it? No, no – calm down! Probably I would never see him again – Havana was a big place. It *was* unnerving though to think that I'd just been chatting to a thief. So odd, too. I'd come all the way to Cuba, to meet…

But enough about him! What about me, what was I going to do? As the night outside howled with volatility, inside I was

lying still, too tired even to sleep, too agitated to concentrate on the guidebook that I gripped tightly in my left hand. Perhaps it was best just to stay on at the hotel – with both the thief and the Yellow Travel tour gone in the morning, surely they would have another room, one without a hole in the ceiling? I would stay only for a couple of days, while I explored Havana and made an itinerary for the rest of the island. The comfort offered by this, a solution involving inaction, was fleeting, however, as I turned again to that most English of concerns: how to avoid unpleasantness with the team in the morning. Victoria would take my departure as an affront, and the penguins – secretly delighted, no doubt – would nevertheless make things as difficult as possible for me. They would wake up roasting hot, hungover, pugilistic...
At some point in the early hours, cowardice prevailed. It was very simple: I would send the guide a text message of apology, and then vanish until they were all gone. Things thus not quite satisfactorily resolved, after a final look up at the ceiling I then slept fitfully for a few hours. My dreams returning always to the thief; to Angus Peterson's unblinking eyes.

THE STRATEGY WORKED well: text message sent by 7 a.m., I crept down to the lobby with stealth, found nobody at reception, and then shot out of the hotel with all the conviction in the world. Havana was still quiet at this time of the morning, still dazed by the wildness of the night, and my first lost walk around the city was threatening great disappointment until I found the Universidad de la Habana sitting above a rather grand stone staircase. Apparently it had been founded by Dominican monks, and its alumni included both Fidel and the great liberator, José Martí. I walked around the university several times, coming across peculiar signs to museums that were yet to open, as groups of chattering students began to arrive and the sun continued to rise magnificently, ominously. Soon the heat was creating the beginnings of a sort of rage, and so I sought shelter under a lovely big fan in the university café, a place where, receiving inquisitive looks from all around me, I sat for a full hour, content in my failure, drinking water and the sweetest coffee I had ever tasted.

It was just past nine o'clock when I received a text message from Pablo.

OK. We are sorry.

The timing of my return to the Hotel el Rey nearly led to an excruciating encounter. They should have been gone, but as I turned the street corner I froze before the sight of the Yellow Travel minibus, which was still parked outside the hotel. There followed moments of high anxiety, during which I hid behind a tree at the far end of the street, watching the penguins and a pale adolescent girl climb in, and the minibus then chug away into the distance. Triumphant now, I was about to leave my hiding place when I saw an unimpressive little man rush out of the hotel entrance with an air of great agitation – bum-bag around his waist, military rucksack on his back. *The thief, the thief.* I watched him from behind that tree as he stood still, looking left, then right, then left again. Finally he walked away.

Soon afterwards I was back in the hotel lobby, which was empty except for a receptionist who was different in every conceivable way from her colleague of the previous night – this receptionist smiled, was not a hater, had a perfect Latin face and voluptuous curves that made me wonder whether I hadn't just fallen in love. I stood nervously in front of her, until she reassured me with a second smile.

'You're the guy who left the Yellow Travel tour?'

'Yep, that's me.'

'You're crazy!'

46

The warmth of the personality seemed almost wrong – excessive for such a beautiful young woman. Maybe I had just been unlucky with her colleague, and my guidebook had been right about the Cubans. The only minor annoyance was that she refused to speak in Spanish – but I let it go. The meaningless phrases came and went like memories of a soothing melody that belonged to a distant past; to Naples...

'Yes, you're real crazy. But maybe it is better alone. Cuba is very especial. We have many nice things...'

'I can't wait to see more of the country.'

'And now? Where will you go now?'

'That's what I wanted to talk to you about.' I feigned a cough. 'I wouldn't mind staying here for a couple of nights, but in a different room. You see, mine is lovely...' I paused '...but it has a hole in the ceiling.'

'I'm sorry – there are no rooms in this hotel.'

'None at all?'

'No, no. It is very busy, this period.'

'I see.'

There followed thirty seconds' or so silence, during which the receptionist thought hard, and I thought almost nothing at all, comforted by the knowledge that I had somehow delegated to her the task of rescuing me from danger; guiding me back to a safe road.

'I have a friend, if you want? Good price.'

'Ah, you mean a *casa particular*?'

'Yes!'

I had read about *casas particulares* on the flight out. The background to their existence was hardship and oppression: despite the Cuban regime and the US embargo together subjecting the Cuban people to deprivation, there were only a few ways in which they were even permitted to make extra money. One involved turning their kitchens into *paladares*;

47

another was renting out rooms in their houses. Soon now, surely, this would all be in the past. With the loosening of the restrictions, with the passing of Castro that could not be so long away, there would be a flood of Americans with fat wallets and fat stomachs who would need air-conditioning, big, powerful toilets, internet access – *You got Wi-Fi here, man? You got AC?* The idea led you to wonder whether the Great Change *would* necessarily free the Cubans; whether it might create instead a class of newly rich while the rest became poorer still. But, regardless of the uncertainty of the future, anything seemed better than this present wretchedness.

'His place is great! Near the Malecón, near to Hotel Nacional!'

I had read about the Malecón, too. It was the seafront promenade that spoke of Havana's soul. Faded neocolonial buildings standing before the beating Atlantic; locals sitting in dreamy melancholia on the sea wall, looking out to a freedom denied them so long. The drifting *changüí-son*, that baby of Europe and Africa, played by the double basses of sea-worn men. My guidebook had said that the Malecón was the first 'must see' of Havana.

'Thanks, I might be interested.'

Minutes later, the *amigo* – a white-whiskered man with a shifty smile – was before me. I shook his hand as he told me the unsurprising news that his was the best apartment in the whole of Havana.

'*Graçias. Y el precio?*'

'Sixty *pesos* for night. Like a present. *Eh?*'

'*Rafael!*'

The receptionist and the Cuban fox discussed the matter further, in voices that continued to rise. Presently, he returned.

'Forty *pesos* for night, my friend.'

I looked at the girl – my guidebook had told me to expect to pay around this.

'You must go to see it first.' How lovely she was. 'I'm sure you will like.'

I took a breath, pandering to a desire for melodrama, and to appear to her as courageous and strong. At the same time, behind the façade, the paranoia was contracting with intensity, near to the point of orgasm as it screamed of the range of plausible horror stories. But then – suddenly, out of the airless, humid silence – there was a thrill. So, then: it was to be an escape. A flight into the unfamiliar – into the real Havana. Real, like any competing reality. As real as London, money, as real as getting old. Real like nostalgia … As if illuminated by a flare I saw an ancient Greek alley, hidden deep in the Quartieri Spagnoli in Naples; the profile of an olive-skinned, impossibly beautiful girl whom I had once thought I might have loved. The light came and went, leaving a memory of a warmth that could only be happiness …

3

AROUND NOON, I WAS being driven through Havana in a battered 1950s Cadillac, my driver and potential new landlord slapping me on the shoulder from time to time, as if to remind us both that this was all real. At a certain point in our short journey, he turned to me.

'What you do, *mi amigo*? What is your work?'

'I'm a student,' I said.

'*Eh?*'

'Mature student.'

With the sun now hovering directly above the city, firing down its rays, and the humidity beginning to rise from the streets in scenes that suggested the imminent end of the world, we soon arrived at a dilapidated Rococo apartment block that told of past glamour and luxury. Before us, standing proud on its own little hill, was the regal Hotel Nacional, which I understood to be the finest hotel in Cuba. Beyond it, I had a glimpse of the bluest of seas.

'Beautiful, no?' came the growl.

We entered a high-ceilinged atrium, once surely magnificent but now falling into disrepair. At the far end of it was a lift that threatened to plunge down into the abyss three or four times during its laborious ascent. Once it arrived finally at the top floor, my white-whiskered companion patted me on the back and took out a key, explaining that he lived in an apartment on the floor below with his family. I nodded, thinking that it must be very unusual for a Cuban to own two properties. But an apartment to myself – it sounded rather excellent to me.

'My home is your home,' Rafael announced, as the door swung open.

The apartment was bathed in a golden light that gushed in through windows that stretched up to the ceiling. There was a pretty balcony adorned with flowers, boasting views of what was that morning a limpid, mesmerising Atlantic. A maternal-looking Cuban maid, wearing a starched white apron, was tending to tropical plants that were dotted around the living room, an imposing crucifix overhung the entrance and, as I inspected the spacious bedroom, I made out an infectious yet perturbing beat, which must have been *changüí-son*. The impression was of immediate cultural immersion – with the welcome bonus of material comfort. Of course it was hot but it was hot everywhere in Cuba; and the maid smiled at me with the kindness of all the best grandmothers and I could hear seagulls.

'Rafael,' I said, 'I love it!'

'You want?'

'Yes, I really do!'

Victories, Rupert Plunkett once said, were not to be dwelt upon – the lawyer must move on; must always move on. Rupert tended to be right about things – but that morning, once I had paid the rent and brought my bag up from the landlord's car, I had the cigarette of my life on the balcony. Indeed, if Rupert had been walking down Calle 19, Havana that day, he might have heard me whistling as I looked out at the horizon, imagining how cramped it would be in the Yellow Travel tour minibus. Possibly, I was mere seconds away from breaking out into a jig – but this I would never know. For, turning my gaze back inside, I saw two middle-aged Asian men appear suddenly from a door I had not previously noticed. They caught sight of me at the same time, so that for a moment we simply stared at each other, separated by a glass window.

One of the men acknowledged me with a slight lowering of his head, as the cigarette dropped from my hand. The landlord, I was almost sure, had said that I would be living alone. Even if he hadn't, he certainly hadn't disclosed that I would have flatmates. The two men were now walking towards me as I came in from the balcony. I met them halfway, my hand outstretched. Neither of them took it. Instead we simply stood, each of them bearing a look of curiosity and dread, as if we were re-enacting the roles of our earliest ancestors.

Finally, I introduced myself in Spanish. They spoke no Spanish. I reverted to English but their English was not great either, which, I realised, would make things difficult as I had not come to Cuba equipped with an adequate level of East Asian language skills. The introductions took a long time, but finally I gathered that both of my new flatmates were South Korean, and both, I was pretty sure, went by the name of Kim. They looked hot, which was understandable. The temperature in the apartment was rising.

Go away, Simon, one of the Kims seemed to say, with a courteous smile. I nodded. The humming sound in my head from the night before had cleared up, but the large, ineffectual ceiling fan was giving out a reverberating noise, which, when combined with the increasingly loud beat from the Malecón, was not conducive to an understanding of pidgin English. I looked upwards at the fan, and then at the nearest wall, wondering where the switch was to turn it off. My new flatmates, meanwhile, continued to be still before me, the curiosity in their faces replaced by something that looked to me like expectation. Yet what they were expectant of, I could not know.

'See you shortly, guys,' I said, walking past them to my room, where I then spent some time lying on my bed, dazed by the heat and unhappy at the thought that the shock of the Kims had not only brought to an end my moment of euphoria but also risked upsetting more generally my upward momentum. I needed a nap but the long flight, the brooding until dawn and the general drama of the past twenty-four hours had left me in a strange state of overtiredness, a sort of vague yet insistent alertness… After a while, I decided to go for a stroll. Stepping out into the living room, I bumped into the Cuban maid again. We had a friendly chat, during which she told me the names of the various plants, pointed out some Cuban landmarks from the balcony and gave me a list of the best *paladares*. She ended up telling me that I resembled a famous Englishman, whose name she could not remember. On this high note, I opened the door to the apartment, braved the lift and then went out through the atrium and into the sunshine that I both feared and desired, like a *femme fatale* you know will be your ruin.

Within minutes I was on the Malecón. I walked along the esplanade for a good while, the ocean to my left, a line of grand, washed-out buildings to my right, a voodoo beat in my ears. Swarthy men with crumpled faces were sitting on the famous sea wall, their legs dangling above the waves, their nets cast into the water; the rock pools were alive with children's screeches; a couple of daring young men were bobbing about in the sea. It was all very picturesque and, save for the music and the bite of the sun, even relaxing, so presently I decided to take a break. I perched on the sea wall and, like a contemplative Cuban fisherman, gazed out at the panorama of blue. After a while I sighed, began to remember…

'IT'S MIDNIGHT!' The voice was screaming out from the loud-speaker on my desk. It was a voice not made for screaming – the voice of a quiet young woman who had finally lost control of herself. 'Midnight on our *anniversary*!'

'Yes, and I'm about to come home. I'm not apologising for the tenth time – I don't need this crap now, Sophie.'

'You don't *need* this crap? God, you're selfish – and cold!'

'Thank you for that.' I was so tired that I hardly recognised my own voice, or the unpleasant words that it spat out. 'Anyway, it's not a real anniversary – it's not like we're married or anything.'

'What?' For a second, in her shock, she was calmed – the scream ran out into a tremulous voice. 'You've become a monster. You used to say the day we got back together was the most special day of the year.'

'I don't think you quite understand the pressure I'm under here. We can go out for dinner tomorrow.'

She must have heard the defiance – the anger built again in her words.

'Have you ever asked yourself why we don't have what you call *real* anniversaries? When all the couples around us are getting married, having kids – have you ever asked yourself *why* we're stuck in this limbo, why we haven't even bought a flat yet?'

'I've got to go.'

'Fine! I won't be around tomorrow, as I've already told you – twice. I'm going to the pub quiz, with Eleanor and Jason.'

'Eleanor and hubby? Don't go too wild.'

'You've always been somehow envious of Eleanor, haven't you? It's weird.'

'Envious? I'm not sure what of. I just don't like her – she's negative, and does you no good.'

'You don't like her because she sees through you!'

'Sees through me?'

'Yes! I remember, even at—'

But I never found out what she remembered. With a rapid pressing of a button, the voice had gone. For a man with a silver quiff was squinting at me, a bloodshot eye pressed to the glass wall of my office.

'Sorry, Rupert,' I said, having beckoned him in.

'You were on a conference call?'

'Just a chat with the associate from Tolbert. Dealing with a couple of tweaks to the indemnity letter.'

'Very good. Fine.'

We had spent the last thirty-six hours together, and even in my leader the strain was now threatening to become too much. His face, purple with the rage that drove him, was disfigured by lack of sleep. The quiff was still up, but pointing east. His tie was off and his shirt collar, now missing its top button, was wide open. It was the picture of a man who had pushed himself beyond the perimeter, but who knew only to carry on. Most unsettlingly of all, my leader now had red stains around his lips.

'I wanted to thank you for circulating the comments on the restructuring agreement,' he was whispering. 'The document seems in good shape – at least as concerns the English law aspects. You'll now also circulate the Schedule?'

'I'm about to. I just need to press *send* on the email.'

'OK. Did you see the latest from the boy?'

I was aware that Giles had been called from my room, and

had not returned. I had seen him going down in the lift, his head bowed. But I didn't know why…

'He sent out the commitment letter using our client's actual name. The name of the company.'

'Ah.'

'Not the code name.'

'Yes, I understand.'

'What is the point of a code name, for Christ's sake, if you use the real name? A breach. A breach. I saw it just in time. We have had undertakings from all recipients that they have deleted the email.'

What did this man want from me? Why did I need to hear this? There was nothing left for either of us to do tonight – didn't he realise that these were dangerous levels of sleep-deprivation?

'A breach.'

'Right. We must remember, I suppose, that Giles has had no sleep.'

'We're all tired,' whispered those stained lips. 'The boy is a liability.'

'Well—'

'Incidentally, on these code names…'

And it was at this point that I understood with horror that Rupert didn't want anything from me other than conversation: a pretext to postpone the inevitable. I remembered that my leader was susceptible, particularly at weekends, to a form of panic at the thought that he would be returning to his Pimlico townhouse, where the wife would be wandering from room to room.

'An outrage! Informing us merely of the code name of the new bidder! How am I to perform a conflict check against the name "Alpha"?'

'Yes, it was a little unhelpful of them.'

'We are surrounded by fools on this matter.' But the fury was insincere – these were just stalling tactics.

'Of course, assuming we're not conflicted, there'll be much further work to do,' he noted.

'Yes,' I murmured. 'Yes, that's true.'

'Much further work.'

I watched him as he paced the room, searching for something to say, something to save him from the night outside. It took him a long while but, finally, the mouth opened. I remained still.

'Do you know,' Rupert whispered, 'young Giles ordered me a box of spare ribs for supper.'

And with this he fixed me with a ghastly stare.

'Spare ribs.'

The telephone on my desk rang, saving me from this abyss of howling insanity. As my leader looked on, stunned by his own declaration, I saw my chance.

'It's the guy from Tolbert again,' I said. 'I'd better take this.'

'Yes, you must. Go on, then – take it.'

And now Rupert Plunkett strode out of my room, firm in his quest to find a reason to call someone, a missed email, some drafting in a document – any document – that did not quite work. I waited until he was gone, and then answered the phone.

'I've made the sofabed for you downstairs.' Sophie was crying and I heard in her voice a terrible resignation. 'Please, don't come up when you get back.'

'Look, I'm on my way now!'

'You said that at seven o'clock, remember?'

'Sophie.' And I felt again that old pulling at my heart. 'Just wait for me.'

'No – you'll get delayed. You always get delayed. Please, don't come up tonight.'

And I did get delayed – by Rupert Plunkett, who came rushing back in, left hand pushed down on the quiff in triumph, telling me *not* to send out the Schedule as it contained *errors* – and it was half past two on a Sunday morning when I opened the door to the flat with a blank mind and a bunch of crumpled roses. There was a strange stillness in the living room, I was too tired even to switch off the light by the door, and as I lay on the sofabed a sleepy, defeated voice came drifting down the stairs.

'What's happened to us?'

PERCHED ON THAT SEA WALL in Havana, before the pattern of Atlantic waves tracing back to the horizon, I understood for the first time that those words had represented the end. Sophie and I had not known it, but from then on we had performed tired, conventional roles that were as old as history, the slow and reluctant acceptance that a human attachment, a tacit promise, had turned to dust. Like generations of couples before us, we had tried to run from the day on which we would be compelled to confront this truth, fearful of its enormity. But it had come, and now, perhaps, Sophie was with another guy. A guy who was compatible, serene, a man whose goals were more aligned. While I was in Cuba, waiting for news that would define my future but confused now by memory. Memories of exuberance, of exciting dreams...nostalgia of perhaps the best of me, somewhere lost under the files of Fiennes & Plunkett.

It was time to move. The sun was ferocious, the air heavy, the infinite blue before me dizzying. I lowered myself down from the wall and left the Malecón, turning up one of the narrow streets that led away from the seafront, in search of some water.

What's happened to us?

As I walked up that street – past the barefoot children playing baseball with table legs, the old men huddled below the balconies of crumbling buildings, the line of women chattering as they queued outside a ration shop, next to dogs lying still on the pavement – as I stepped over the streams of water gushing from broken pipes, marched briskly past the hustlers selling cigars, heard the yells and laughter from inside the homes, I began to engage with the entirely self-indulgent question of the morality of what I was doing. Was curiosity really the best of me? I wondered about those Western travellers who would come back inspired by the people of places like this, people whose happiness, they would enthuse, outshone their terrible poverty. It was a comment generated by an appalling egocentricity, a form of studied ignorance, which in its superficiality, its appeal to the most trite of emotions, had a terrible weight. You had to fight it: these people were trapped in their own country. But somehow still there *was*, for me, a vitality to this street that was absent in the London I knew.

My shirt was drenched in sweat by the time that I came across a café. It had a garden of leafy plants bordering its front and there was a plaque nailed to the façade that said that the café had been Ernest Hemingway's favourite drinking hole. For a man who did not yet know that every bar and café in Cuba claims to have been Ernest Hemingway's favourite drinking hole, and that the spectrum of truth is wide, the news was a bonus. I went in, only to nearly bump into a large, gruff man who appeared to be the owner, or in any case the boss, and whose attempt at a welcoming acknowledgement was more of a grimace. Feeling a strange sort of alienation, I asked immediately for a large bottle of sparkling water and then made my way towards a quiet table in the far corner.

The café certainly had an authentic look to it – I was the only tourist. It was the sort of place that a man on a quest to find the untouched Cuba should have been proud to find. And proud I was, although paranoia was back and thriving – in addition to the owner's grimace, there were a number of rowdy Cubans who were shouting at each other at the bar. It was only two o'clock in the afternoon, but they were all plastered.

They could just slit your throat if they took a dislike to you, I thought. *It would be days before the news got back home.*

Sitting alone at my table, I soon understood that it was hotter in the corner of the café than out under the sun. Where was the sparkling water? It was taking an age for them to bring it, but I didn't fancy going up to the bar. Instead I opened my guidebook in an attempt to escape briefly from the immediate reality, and began to leaf through its chapter on 'Cuba in 2012'. There was a detailed piece about Obama's vision, how everything was going to change, but it was the page on China that caught my attention – apparently it had been ploughing money into this country for years and was its second-biggest trading partner. Something Rupert Plunkett would have known; something he would have been appalled to discover that I had not known. It was remarkable how Cuba, this tiny island, regularly found itself involved in global power struggles – there was the Cold War, then there was...

But it's down to its location, Simon. For Christ's sake. That whisper of Rupert's was with me always.

The water arrived, brought to me by the unsmiling owner. After my third or fourth gulp I re-engaged with the guidebook. Soon I realised that my eyes kept returning to a short paragraph at the beginning of the chapter – a paragraph I had skimmed previously on the way out, without really dwelling on it. The words had seemed so irrelevant then, to a man off on a happy tour with a group of happy travellers. But, now that I was a single man in his thirties travelling alone in Cuba, the paragraph was assuming poignancy.

Cuba is now firmly established as a leading sex tourism destination...country can become very irritating for male travellers...harassment from the local pimps...for desperate Cubans, a chance of escape...sex with tourists in return for the promise of help in getting out...polite but firm approach is advised...

I could see Rupert's grave face – *I told you they survived on rations* – and it was strange how, thinking about this more, worrying about this more, the poignancy of what the words meant for *me* – for this was no altruistic unease – unlocked nonetheless an empathy that had been missing as I had crossed the Atlantic in that bubble of giddy selfish anticipation. Or perhaps it was the being here physically when reading the words that brought their sadness to life, gave them meaning. What nonsense, I thought now, that there had been a vitality and warmth to that wretched street. These people lived in poverty, while tourists pranced around their city, crowded into their homes and sat down to be served, gobbled up their food, some taking them up on their offers to sell their bodies. There was no fusion of humanity here! This was not the dream of my past, the dream of Naples! Maybe now, in the present, the only solace to be found was in my own reality, in the cold hard truth that soon I would be back in London, perhaps as a partner, a millionaire.

This truth – that there was no second act for youthful impulsivity – related back to my ruminations of the previous evening. Specifically, the question as to what the hell I was doing here – I'd come on a whim, knowing close to nothing about the

61

country. In Naples, I'd been so young – *that* was the time to be capricious and selfish and ignorant and free. Years brought responsibility – there was something very ugly about an older man being impulsive. Something embarrassing and foolish. And you paid for it, as I was paying for it now. For possibly now I was *suspect*. Possibly everyone I'd met today, everyone around me, thought I was a sex tourist: a man who had no goal but cheap purchased sex, and who had travelled half the world to get it. Perhaps I was being watched, judged, wherever I went. Days ahead of this, too – days and days of being watched. The whole situation brought about by one simple fact: I was too old to be free. I remembered the squat *señora*, the loathing of me that had glared from her eyes. Had she thought…?

You're really fucking mental, Reasonable Simon was saying. Too old to be free? You're thirty-two! And you *are* free – unlike these poor bastards, you insensitive git! And, on that point of your sensitivity, where has all this saintly empathy, this innocence and moral outrage, come from? *No fusion of humanity here?* Are you sure you're not just lonely? Scared because you know you've got a lot of time on your hands now, the chance to really think about your life back in London? Are you sure you're not consciously obsessing about nonsense, a deliberate distraction? You know that nobody thinks you're *suspect*. The Cuban maid treated you like a son earlier. The receptionist this morning was glowingly warm. And look, read on – the guidebook is *telling* you that loads of guys still tour Cuba: this paragraph is intended as a warning for them, not an indictment of them. See? And don't you remember all those men and women, many alone, who were walking the Malecón today? All of those enthusiastic-looking, cheerful tourists, enjoying their little adventure?

—*The thief! The thief's a global sex tourist!*

—You don't know that.

—I shouldn't be here! I'm too old to be here!

—You...

'*Hola,*' came a husky voice – but this was a real voice.

I was a fool. I was too old to be here. And now here she was, the coalescence of thought and reality. She was pouting, really *pouting*, the red top little more than a bra, the smell of liquor penetrating the mist of sweet, cheap perfume that hung over her. She might once have been pretty, with her black hair and high cheekbones, but now she had the bags of heavy drinking under eyes that were haunting in their surrender. Dirty, scuffed boots. And that jolly English couple with backpacks who had come in just minutes ago – with perfect timing, the bastards – I could feel them staring at me. I could feel them *wincing*.

'*Señor,*' the woman said, passing me the food menu. '*Quieres algo?*' She began to list the specials of the day, all the pork and chicken and rice and beans. And for a silly moment, and for so many reasons, I wanted to cry...

'*No, no – gracias,*' I said. '*No tengo hambre.*'

A short time later, having taken no food but another bottle of sparkling water, I was walking back down the street, past the hustlers and onto the Malecón, feeling vague. I stopped before a line of three-wheeled, egg-shaped yellow vehicles that did not allay this vagueness. The humidity was absolutely extraordinary now and I had realised that attempting the full walk back might end with my fainting dramatically before the sea. It was just such a shame that there were no normal taxis hanging around and that I had no numbers on me. For these *cocotaxis* – my guidebook confirmed their designation – were not only surreal, but also, to a man like Neurotic Simon, a little troubling. Inside the three-wheeled eggs were tourists with apprehensive smiles – they elicited images of prisoners of war in antiquity, prisoners captured from exotic lands.

'Where you want to go?' asked one of the drivers.

'Near Hotel Nacional.' I was never going to end up really practising my Spanish in this city.

'Five *pesos*.' He grinned. 'Very quick. Very safe.'

'Hmm.'

'You take?'

'OK,' I said, climbing inside the egg. 'You just need to go down the Malecón. Just drive straight down the seafront.'

But he was turning to go back up into central Havana.

'No, wrong way. That's the wrong way!' I yelled.

'I know way to the Hotel Nacional!'

'I promise you, it's down the Malecón!'

We were soon lost, the egg clattering up and down a thousand broken, identical streets – I had found the only driver in Havana who did *not* in fact know the way to the Hotel Nacional. Finally, though, he escaped the labyrinth he had unnecessarily entered, coming out onto a wide, grey, empty road.

'You know where we are, *amigo*?'

'No.'

He pointed ahead, towards a vast sea of concrete.

'Plaza de la Revolución – in ten minutes, we are home!'

'Marvellous,' I said.

And yet my indifference faded as we approached the enormous square. I became affected by a terrific silence; an eerie desolation. Everywhere in the emptiness there were signs prohibiting entry to something. Here and there in the relentless grey young guards stood to attention, as if protecting from an imaginary crowd of dissenters government buildings that were disquieting in their immenseness. Poking my head out of the egg, I soon found what I was looking for: the vast mural of Che Guevara, rising the full length of a gigantic block of concrete. A replica of Korda's defining photograph, it was the iconic image: Che infinitely resolute, gazing into the future, towards the promise of destiny. Below the frieze was the slogan: *Hasta la Victoria Siempre.* It meant: 'Forever Onwards to Victory'.

'Sorry!' I shouted to the taxi driver. 'Can we stop a minute?'

We came to a stuttering halt. As the oppressive stillness of the square intensified, I stared across at Che, and then at the words, pondering them, appropriating them. I'd had a bad start, I thought, and I was sitting inside an egg – but here I was, at the base of power of one of the most dogged regimes in modern history. The epicentre.

'Two minutes,' mumbled the taxi driver. 'Then we go.'

The setting for the ideation of a failed utopia. The square breathed history, arousing unfamiliar emotions. The pride of Che, the star-shaped tower and the statue of Martí, the harshness of the concrete. Too fresh still to articulate, it was an unfamiliarity you would want to experience together with someone of your own culture; and then discuss afterwards, maybe, over a bottle or two of wine. Experienced alone, it all meant a little less. With a sigh, I took out my mobile phone and began to write.

Hi, Sophie. How are you? I'm in Cuba, in the Plaza de la Revolución in Havana! It's just so unusual. Anyway, I thought of you.

'*Amigo.*'

'God, what am I doing?' I stopped writing and looked out from the egg, only to then start. There was a man now in the square – a man I knew. He had a bum-bag around his waist and was striding towards Che. *The thief, the thief.* I leaned forward to the driver.

'*Vamos.*'

'We can go now?'

'Yes, please. As fast as you can.'

'*Ya.*'

With Nathan still at a distance, the driver started the engine and sped out of the square, letting out an ugly, excited shout as he made it through some traffic lights. Behind him in the egg, I cancelled the draft message to Sophie and rested my head in my hands. And in this position I stayed, as my eyes began to close and the *cocotaxi* rattled on, towards an apartment I shared with two fellow travellers named Kim.

4

IN THE SULTRY, NEBULOUS days that followed, as I pottered in a trancelike state around Havana, I began to lose – in a not unpleasant way – all sense of immediacy, other than when it came to avoiding the thief. In the present, I lived now only to flee Nathan's shadow – we were two ghosts playing a strange game in a strange, haunted city – while my mind wandered back into a complicated past. Time had become amorphous, and one morning I woke up to realise that it was too late to plan a grand tour of the island. There were three nights remaining before my flight back to London, which meant that, since my first excursion into Havana, somehow a week had passed by. The days had been, perhaps, the real Purpose I had sought – a wistful submersion into otherness after years of wild intensity, which had begun even to alleviate fear, that terrible enemy of mine – the worrying about being robbed, being considered a sex tourist, losing my passport had, if not completely disappeared, diminished…replaced by the tentative beginnings of reflection. Finally, after over a decade, I found myself beginning nearly to *think*.

While my memories of those days did not follow a coherent sequence, I knew that, in my pottering, I had seen everything it was worth seeing of Havana. I had visited the Casa Natal de José Martí, the humble birthplace of Cuba's proudest son, without feeling anything at all; I had wandered frustrated and open-mouthed outside the imposing but closed Capitolio Nacional; I had walked around the Museo Nacional de Bellas Artes, for a moment wondering about my BlackBerry tucked away in a pocket of my suitcase, wondering whether when I returned I might have a quick look, before the thought faded away... I had tried out a local *paladar*, where I had been served something like onion soup as a starter, but then chicken with rice and beans as a main. I had enjoyed Cuba libres, mojitos, Bucaneros. One evening, a little drunk, I had bought a Cohiba from a man in the Parque Central. I had become bored in the disappointing Museo de la Revolución; I had ambled around the second-hand book market in the romantic Plaza de Armas, Havana's oldest square, thinking of Sophie... thinking of the day we'd first kissed at sixteen, the day they'd made her cry at school, and thinking of how that day and for another sixteen years she had refused to talk about her dad. I knew only that he was a Welshman who lived alone in Derby, that he too was very tall... and I knew that one day Sophie's mum, Deborah, had held her daughter by the arms and told her that they would be leaving Derby in the summer holidays, once she had finished fifth form, just Sophie and Mum, and going to live with Deborah's parents in their lovely big house near Louth... and that there, from the age of sixteen until university, Sophie had lived, the centre of attention of a newly single mother and two doting grandparents. And this was all I knew, all she had ever said and ever would say; all I would ever know because she'd left me and I needed to move on and here I was in front of a Baroque cathedral, puzzled by its asymmetrical towers, and here I was dining on rice and beans in the opulent setting of the El Patio restaurant, and here I was experiencing a moment of resurgent fear at the sight of the emaciated stray dog that was following me around the Castillo de la Real Fuerza...

So that, to use the terminology of young City professionals, I had 'done Havana'. And, while I had no desire to move elsewhere for the remaining days, and was not keen even on the idea of arduous bus journeys to the other end of the island to see the likes of Santiago de Cuba, I resolved nonetheless that morning to see at least *something* else; something outside the city. My humble ambitions were the result of the calming influence of those days of pottering and also a type of fatalistic lethargy that I had experienced when waking up, but that must have been growing in the subconscious for a while. Today was the 24th. In two days' time, Rupert would call with the news. My passiveness at this prospect seemed perverse, given the immense implications that the news would have. But the apathy was in truth a form of angry denial: the news would come too soon. I needed more time – more thinking time. There were so many years to cover and I might never again have the opportunity to find some truth, to understand...

The Hotel Nacional, I remembered as I rose from the bed, was the place to get information on day trips – it was strange to think that I was about to embrace an idea suggested by the thief. But the recollection of where to go was a happy one, for the Hotel Nacional was also something else: serenity. An icon of luxury at the top of a slope above the Atlantic, boasting that special prestige afforded by history, it was a two-minute walk from the apartment, and I had soon discovered that, for a fee, the attentive staff allowed tourists to use virtually all of the hotel's facilities; and that, if they liked you there, the hotel doubled as an information centre. I had been given maps, booklets, flyers, the telephone numbers and addresses of *paladares*. I had been informed of museum opening times, bus routes, places to see and places to avoid. I had had all of my questions answered patiently, kindly. I had at times continued to ask any question that came to mind, such was the soothing effect of the responses, in harmony with the piano music carrying through the tiled lobby that glistened away under its vast chandeliers, glistened away in the 1930s to which it forever returned. I had begun a number of days in the hotel's grand breakfast room; I had sat in their bar leafing through strange newspapers; I had enjoyed an afternoon's mojito and cigarette while looking down from the princely lawns to the rippling ocean.

In addition, I had from an early stage begun to use the Hotel Nacional's showers in the morning, arriving with a bag containing my toiletries and paying a few *pesos* a day for what I claimed was brief use of the gym. I had found sharing a bathroom with the Kims to be unacceptable. On my second day in the house, my bar of soap had been hacked to pieces. My flatmates displayed great impatience in the morning, knocking on the bathroom door incessantly, with an urgency that suggested the building was on fire. But the definitive reason for my giving up on the apartment's bathroom was my discovery that the Kims shared an equivocal toothbrush, which seemed bloodstained. Each time I had seen it, the instrument had threatened an end to the fragile detachment from the present that carried that promise of reflection, and which was akin almost to peace.

But these were anomalies: living with the South Koreans had generally worked out far better than I had expected. From what I had established, or given up trying to establish, over the course of those hazy days, each Kim was fifty years old. Two years earlier, fate had found them sitting opposite each other in an otherwise empty airport lounge in Dubai and, after a while, one of them had introduced himself – an image I had never quite managed to conjure up. A profound friendship had evolved, a bond that, in its mysterious roots – I had never found out, for example, why either of them had been in Dubai – suggested something like destiny. Kim, I learnt, was an engineer, and Kim was an artist. Apart from that discrepancy – which had no substance, given that it appeared to me that neither of them actually worked, but that both just travelled – the Kims were the same person. A comprehensive, mutual absorption.

The aim of their days in Havana was to photograph the city in its entirety. Every potholed street, every historic square, every eulogy to Castro, every daring protest spray-painted onto the city walls. In the evenings they would share the results of the day's work with me as we sat together on our balcony, drinking cans of Bucanero in the sweltering heat. In turn, I would try to explain to them, try to explain to myself, why I was in Cuba, telling them of how I was waiting to know about a promotion, and after the third or fourth can I would begin to reminisce about Sophie, at which point the Kims would stare at me nervously, unsure of the meaning of the mumbled words. As the vague, tropical hours glided by and the Bucanero flowed, I would sometimes shake myself from the melancholia and in a rush of excitability imitate Rupert Plunkett as he negotiated the closing of a deal, a scene I would help to convey with facial expressions and wild gesticulation. The Kims, by this point turned a dark shade of red by the beer, would laugh hysterically, stand up, and pat me on the back in congratulation. Towards midnight, Kim the artist would stagger off to bed, singing his country's national anthem in a discordant and passionate voice that would wake up the dogs below. A short time later, Kim the engineer, now weeping heavily, would be telling the story of Ji-min, the belle of the village, to whom he had proposed and who had turned him down with a laugh and a disgusted shake of her head – Kim would do me an impression, his fists clenched. And he loved her but she hurt him bad, and he loved her but she hurt him bad; one night, lost in a sea of alcohol, I wept with Kim.

As I walked to the Hotel Nacional that morning, it occurred to me that ideally I would spend the day in a small, undemanding coastal town of faded colours and quiet cafés, a town with beauty or history sufficient to justify the trip, but insufficient to justify staying for too long. This new dream, which some might call shallow, consisting as it did of a simple, uninformed, arbitrary picture, was soon delivered, as shallow dreams often are. The kind staff at the Hotel Nacional confirmed that my guidebook was right: Cojímar, the village where Ernest Hemingway had berthed his fishing boat, was only a short drive away. It was there that he had met Gregorio Fuentes, the inspiration behind the protagonist Santiago in *The Old Man and the Sea*. My guidebook said that it was a nice little place, entirely in line with the dream: *serene, well-kept, residential oasis; break from the frenzy of Havana; pleasant streets; gentle, picturesque bay...*

The hotel staff added some colour that enhanced the appeal. I was told that Gregorio, enjoying in the latter part of his life an improbable fame, had collected *pesos* by recounting tales to tourists in the main restaurant, the Terraza de Cojímar. Apparently, he had died about ten years ago, but his house was still there in the middle of the village. And there was a monument to Hemingway on the seafront, the old genius before the lapping waves.

I needed to hear no more. Spurred on by a sudden impatience, I decided to head immediately to that quaint fishing village, where I too could look at locals in peace. Scooters with yellow eggs by now consigned to the past, I jumped into one of the Hotel Nacional's taxis – and that was when something quite disconcerting occurred.

'Where to?' asked the taxi driver, turning to look at me as I dropped into the passenger seat. He was an ancient, shrivelled soul, as old, surely, as Gregorio Fuentes had ever been. And yet it was not Gregorio's but someone else's face that flashed before me as he spoke; it was someone else's voice, a voice from my past. The driver had light wisps of white hair above a dark, wrinkled forehead, and a fragile, well-meaning, faintly bewildered expression behind his large glasses. Christ – it was Professor Bonini! For a second it really *was* him, my old Italian tutor from university, gazing at me in that charming, distracted manner of his. Asking me:

What's the decision, then, Mr Haines? Come on, hit me with it.

Professor Bonini! When I had known him, the ravages of time were still outshone by his beautiful mind, that indefatigable, humble precision, the overwhelming sense of goodness he exuded. A lovely human being. I had disappointed him in the end – he had offered me the opportunity to stay on at Cambridge as a postgraduate, saying that I had a glittering future in academia – if I wanted it. I'd turned him down. Funny that I should be reminded of him today; that I should think of what he had said to me that evening in the fine quiet of his study, surrounded by piles of dusty books climbing up towards the ceiling. Funny that I should think of his elegant blue calligraphy in the margin of my essay:

A marvellous analysis of the transcript. What a shame that you're giving this all up for City law!

I'd enjoyed that compliment. But I'd felt also some irritation when I'd read it the second time, along with an odd sense of superiority. How silly they were, these academics – didn't they appreciate the *importance* of the corporate world? I was off into reality – I was off to follow my dream!

'*Eh!*'

'Sorry,' I said, shaking myself. 'Cojímar, please.'

'You want to go to Cojímar?'

'You make it sound like an outrageous suggestion,' I said, laughing. But he didn't laugh back. So: 'Yes, please,' I said. 'Cojímar.'

Ten *pesos* later, I was there...

Or rather, ten *pesos* later, I was in the periphery of Cojímar. The driver had stopped at the edge of the village, explaining that he had come the wrong way, and that it would be easier for me to walk into the centre by myself, following a narrow, sandy path that he pointed out to me from inside the taxi. I was relieved to hear that he had got lost, as the route we had taken had not been consistent with my aspirations: we had bumped down stark, desolate streets, through clouds of dust whipped up to a white sky by the taxi's wheels. And now we were at the end of a road, the driver lost in contemplation, gazing through his windscreen at the mound of rubble before us while I asked him if he could come and pick me up once I had taken in the sights. Finally, he stirred. Beyond that mound, he told me in a trembling voice, there had once been a line of small houses and a pretty square where he had played baseball as a boy. I nodded, doubting that it was true. Throughout the journey he had been pointing at things, anything, claiming with a stuttering sincerity a special story. It seemed that in his imagined world the ancient man was seeking a form of validation – as if he was attempting to wash reality clean, erase his poverty, his decades of grey oppression, the pointlessness of it all, by painting cheerful little truths, ascribing meaning to walls, buildings, empty roads.

He said that he would be happy to wait for me, and that we could meet outside the famous restaurant, the Terraza de Cojímar, in an hour's time. I replied firmly, as one must in Cuba, that it would be better for me if he could pick me up in, say, six hours' time – at half past five. If that didn't work, no problem, but I wanted a full afternoon. At this the driver squinted, as if violently confused, and I too then became confused, because again that squint had reminded me...

'Five-thirty, *caballero*? Outside the restaurant?'

'Hmm?'

I've thought about it all night – I couldn't sleep thinking about it. It was so kind of you to go to all the trouble. But, you know what they say: if I don't try I'll never know. Yes, I'll miss it here – oh, the name of the firm? I'm sure you won't have heard of them! Fiennes & Plunkett. They do financing and insolvency. No, to be honest I'm not really sure what that means. No, but, you understand, I'm young. It's an adventure.

'*Caballero!*' The driver waved his hand in my face. 'Five-thirty I come?'

'Yes, five-thirty – outside the restaurant.' I handed over the money and shook his limp hand. '*Gracias.*'

'*Hasta luego,*' he said.

Still discomfited by that squint, by the memories of Professor Bonini, it was nonetheless with a reborn enthusiasm that I began to make my way down that winding, sandy path, the picture of the quaint fishing village, the fine bay, now clear once more in my mind. And yet the path continued to twist, preventing me from seeing into the distance, preventing me from experiencing anything other than the path itself and a rising dust and the next bend ahead, and so all I thought about was how the path would soon straighten out, how the path *must* soon straighten out, how the path was leading me to that quaint fishing village and that fine bay. And the heat was soon overpowering and my throat dry and inflamed by the dust, my back pouring with sweat, and it occurred to me that it was not asking for much; that all I wanted was a quaint fishing village...

Nearly an hour later, hearing myself pant with that peculiar melodrama of a Westerner abroad who, even when alone, has a sense that he is performing to an audience, I came out into a village of silence. A stern face looked out through a window pane as I strode down towards the bay, through the main street of the village – a street that, I conceded, could just about fall within the category of 'well-kept'; but which was not, in my view, pleasant. It was a shrine to torpor, devoid of any vitality, and it seemed to me that it might have been like this forever, boasting as it did a certain cyclical quality. The defeat of progress was manifest in the black dog I saw roaming the street, its rabid, brazen stare.

That dog, I thought, might rule this village.

Bienvenido a Cojímar, said a sign at the bottom of the street. Beyond it was a further path, which, the sign told me, led down to the seafront and the Monument to Hemingway. It said nothing else, giving the impression that this was all a hastily arranged set. I followed the path down, cursing softly, and within minutes I was standing before a view that confirmed the end of the dream.

'My God.'

A Cuban man was lingering in a sinister way on the promenade, in front of a pool of seawater that I understood immediately was a personal thing. It might for some have been inoffensive but for me – in its stillness, in the mud that at points ran down to it and became it, in the profound inconsistency with the image I'd had in my mind – this was

Calamity Bay. I met the man's offers of cigars and women with stony silence as I traipsed up and down that promenade, gaping at the motionless water while applying Deet and trying to form a plan. *Whoa, what was that?* Out of the corner of my eye, I thought that I might have just seen a huge bird swoop down into the sea – I never saw it come out. As I looked across the bay, feeling something akin now to awe, the land and sea became more confused, one's end and the other's beginning more equivocal. On around my fourth lap, I found the Monument to Hemingway, which stood back a little from the seafront. Some squat, thickset men, who from their tools appeared to be builders or plasterers, or in any case men who knew how to use tools, were sitting in a quiet circle around the monument, puffing away on cigarettes.

The Monument to Hemingway in Cojímar. As I looked at it, the strange hurt at the thought of Professor Bonini, which came somehow inextricably linked to the grand disappointment of this village, now merged with a sudden paroxysm of emotion at the break-up with Sophie – emotion that had been repressed for months by Rupert Plunkett, hitherto sublimated to wistfulness – and surged from within me. I saw for a moment a great confusion of images, a stream of memories, and then Sophie appeared out of the mad tapestry with her lovely smile, her magnetic brown eyes, only to change, to grow sad, her expression all betrayed. Then I heard a voice, a whisper down my mobile telephone:

You didn't make it. We like Emma, I'm afraid. However, I would like to talk to you about Uniterra. As you know, they're a key client of ours. If they like you, which I'm sure they will...

It was surely difficult to encounter a monument that spoke more profoundly of disappointment than the Monument to Hemingway in Cojímar. A circle of chipped columns, holding up a strange stone ring, stood with grotesque pride on a plinth that was provocative in its faux grandeur. Inside this circle, high up on a block, was the bust of a resigned and belittled man. A legend mocked. A depiction that spoke somehow of the vulnerability of any man, any man and every man and all men, any man born in any age in any land.

'They got me,' Hemingway was saying quietly. 'And I am all men.'

'*Es el monumento a Hemingway*,' grunted one of the builders or plasterers or handymen or killers, as he struggled to his feet. I nodded and, in dubious scenes, the men then all began to laugh. I turned away from the monument.

'*Es el monumento a Hemingway*.'

'*Lo sé, lo sé*.'

I hurried away back down the promenade, glancing at my watch and understanding now the squint of the taxi driver. A little over an hour had passed. Five more hours in Cojímar to go, and there was only one thing left to see.

'Let's get it over with,' I mumbled.

I headed back up into the village to find the former house of an unremarkable fisherman named Gregorio Fuentes. The day was a blow, and this quiet was not peace, but soon the nothingness was allowing me to disengage slowly... London, Fiennes & Plunkett, Sophie, they were all with me again now, and as I passed the sign welcoming me to Cojímar I began to think in particular of Daniel Serfontein – the Lothario with the green eyes and blond hair who had somehow become my best friend. The man with the self-confidence, or the air of self-confidence, that had once been more intimidating even than his height, his depressingly muscular body.

I thought of handsome Daniel now, as I walked in Cojímar; I thought of a friendship that might have seemed unaccountable and yet had endured, based on the attraction of mutual curiosity – the charm and challenge of the never to be fully known, never to be understood. In my case, initially and for many years the fascination had coexisted with insecurity: a sense of inferiority that had now almost diminished, but which had been acute back in our university days. That intense need to improve myself, reach further…

At university, that unfair combination of height, broad shoulders, strength and boyishness, that lemon-blond hair that would never recede, consigned to the shadows a guy like me – a man whose only physical asset was a pair of nice blue eyes. And Dan's voice – he wasn't public school, and he must have noticed on those first days at Cambridge the class structures imposing themselves – his deep, sure voice, with its tiniest of Essex twangs, it didn't adapt, it didn't change one little bit! And, in its strength, its certainty, it was damning of mine! It underlined the *weirdness* of my voice, which within weeks of university came to inhabit, and forever thereafter inhabited, a no man's land of lost identity, leading friends back in Lincoln to say, 'You've gone all posh! No, really – what's happened to your voice?', while people at Cambridge, then law school, then Fiennes & Plunkett, would continue, intermittently, to ask, 'Where *is* it that you're from, Simon?'

Friendship, of course, should be about support and bonding. It should not be analogous to a boxing match – but in those early days of our knowing each other there was that beautiful uppercut of his physique, the vicious right hook of his success with girls, the repeated jab of the social ease – enough, one might have thought, for Haines to hit the floor. Yet, on the ropes, there was a little flurry from the pretender – the low, painful body shots of academic superiority. These little punches cut deep with Serfontein – they caused bleeding very early on, from our first weeks together at university, though I didn't realise it immediately. He hid it well, feigning indifference towards studying, towards *trying* generally, yet how desperately the man tried – secretly, manically – how desperately he fought to keep up with the rest, throughout his undergraduate years.

Bound up with all this was the further, insidious and complicating point that Dan's family were exhilaratingly rich. But this was not initially a factor in our silent battle, or even a point I dwelt upon or really noticed – as an eighteen-year-old student, I didn't recognise great wealth as being relevant to *anything*. I *had* been prepared for class issues at Cambridge – the public schoolboy prats whom I imagined and feared; stories of initiations, being forced to drink spirits through a condom, girls cleaning with their tongues men covered in whipped cream. I'd been terrified of all that, which was why I had chosen Clare College. Clare is one of the most progressive, open colleges in Cambridge, its students a lovely mix of different backgrounds. It's not devoid of the blazer boys, of course – it's still gigantically intimidating, still full of beautiful posh voices, famous names. But it just didn't, I'd been told, have the yobbishness that was found in certain parts of Oxbridge.

So, all my unease before I arrived at university had been focused on schooling, class or, perhaps more simply, *poshness*. But Dan, although I didn't understand this at first, belonged to a new social class that was threatening to render *posh* people almost charmingly irrelevant – Dan belonged to the super-rich. If the blond hair and green eyes were a gift from his mother – she'd failed as a model, but only on account of laziness, Dan said – the millions, the hundreds of millions, had been made by his father, a man who was somewhat avant-garde in not wanting his son to become *posh*, and who had refused to have him sent to boarding school – hence the accent that was not quite an Essex accent, but was far from Old Etonian. His father had had a somewhat colourful international career, Dan liked to say, laughing fondly. Born into an unremarkable, middle-class family in Cape Town, he had made his way to London via a year in New York and then a decade in West Africa, years that had never been fully accounted for, even to his son. Dan's mother, whom Dan didn't like, now claimed that she had some remote links to Danish nobility, but that story was hilarious to Dan; instead she'd hit gold in a Mayfair club one night when she'd met this dashing businessman, founder of one of the most successful funds in London. Years later I learned that Louis Serfontein had made his fortune by buying up distressed debt in some of the poorest countries on earth...

Anyway, all this money thing was very new and – at first – profoundly uninteresting for the life virgin that was the undergraduate Mr Simon Haines. I had been brought up not to love money, nor to resent money, nor even to actively disregard money, but instead – and most naturally – never to ascribe a value to it that went beyond what was commensurate with our needs. And I hadn't – instead I'd spent a very happy childhood and adolescence wrapped up in my books, in myself, visiting my friends in their family houses almost identical to ours, later falling in love. From my upbringing I had understood that the only index by which human beings should be measured was intelligence, or else some human value.

'John Major's not as bright as Blair,' my dad would mumble through his beard, as his small frame sank into the brown armchair to watch the nine o'clock news, the evening mug of coffee in his hand. 'But the bloke's got integrity. It's painful to watch Blair destroy him like this.'

My parents would talk indulgently about Garry Kasparov and whether he would beat the IBM supercomputer – whether it was possible to calculate the maximum number of chess moves, whether we would all be exterminated the second we created a robot more intelligent than us. We would spend tense evenings locked in games of Trivial Pursuit, enjoy Sunday lunches of eccentric games where we would tell a story together, taking it in turns to add a word, my mother's electric-blue eyes, her soft Irish voice, making me feel warm and loved. I sat up with her till the early hours watching as the Tories fell one by one and handsome, charismatic young Blair declared a new dawn – she seemed so happy to hear my excitement at the simple attraction of hope, the new, though I saw in her face that she had her own private thoughts, which were far away. From a precociously young age, throughout my adolescence, I was educated better at home than I was at school: they taught me maths and sciences and how to love language and literature, insisted on my studying foreign languages, sent me out into the enchanted worlds of a myriad minds. There were those evenings when the three of us would huddle around the kitchen table debating a French text that I needed to read – sometimes they would become so passionate in arguing about this or that line, the historical context, that they would hardly notice as I told them I was off to see my friends for a few drinks. I would come back to find the homework completed and perfect, my dad accepting defeat, my mum uneasily enjoying her victory. A local psychologist and his administrative assistant who had a secret – she was a genius. Just as her simple clothes played down what was a truly beautiful face, so everything she did sought to conceal that special intelligence. A humble couple, they were elated but terrified, just like me, when I was accepted at Cambridge. My dad, scratching his beard, said that I'd inherited the academic vocation from his side of the family, while my mum laughed, telling him to shut up, and then held me close, saying that she hoped it was what I wanted.

Months later, it was time to go…

'Everyone's anxious on the first day of something new – it's normal, Simon. I still remember your first day at school; you were exactly the same. Think of all those new French novelists you're going to read – I'm so excited for you!'

'God, your mum's more stressed than you are – calm down, Abbie! Come on, then, Simon, get into the car – you'll see Sophie again soon. Did you know, both of you, that Clare is the second-oldest college in the whole of Cambridge?'

'Paul! You've told us four times!'

Then we were walking down King's Parade, the grandest street in Cambridge. We'd passed King's College, which was so absurdly *big* that I didn't appreciate its beauty, observing only that it had appropriated the whole blue sky. Then past the lawn and fine white of Senate House...now we were just off Trinity Lane, through the gateposts and after a long, awkward discussion with some college porters we were into Clare's Old Court with its chapel, Master's Lodge and Buttery, enclosed on all four sides as a perfect court must be, light pouring down from above – and it made me feel guilty to imagine that my parents must be feeling as scared as I was. We were crossing the little footbridge over the river, and coming to Memorial Court.

'Right,' said my dad once they'd helped me unpack. 'Look at the bloody time. We need to get going soon, Abbie.'

'You're not staying then for the dinner reception, to meet the Master and the other parents?' I asked – they'd been refusing to answer the question all the way to Cambridge in the car. 'Have you decided?'

'I've been speaking to your dad.' My mum looked down at her feet. 'It's just not our thing, Simon, that's all. You don't mind, do you? If you really want us to—'

'Course he doesn't mind, Abbie – he'll be keen to get rid of us, I'd imagine. Come on, Simon – let your mother take you to Tesco. She's desperate to get you all your treats.'

A couple of hours later I was back with my shopping bags, fumbling with the key to the door of my room in these, my first moments of independence: an insecure eighteen-year-old barely holding back tears of fury at having been forced to say goodbye to Sophie earlier, and now to my parents at the college's iron gates. I had hugged my mum and dad and then just watched them walk away with a sinking, empty apprehension, and loving them, loving them wildly. I was fumbling with my key out of anxiety, a need to get into my room, and in particular to hide from the student representative who was driving me insane in his mission to look after me all day. Already I'd had to attend a confusing number of five-minute meetings – advisory meetings, social meetings, a meeting with the sweet college nurse – and I'd met and received wise words of advice from my two student 'parents'. How weird was that: kids a year or so older than me, being called my 'parents'? I'd met some tutors and directors, real academic eccentrics, the one highlight of this crap day. My mum had bought me all my favourites from Tesco, but just now as I'd walked past the communal kitchen I'd felt too shy to enter with my shopping, so had decided that I would store all my food in my room instead. I had a mini fridge, so in fact I could just live there, if necessary, in my little room, a man in a bunker as the nuclear war of adulthood raged above…

'Hey, mate!' I felt a large hand on my shoulder. And then I turned, looking up to behold Mr Daniel Serfontein. He smiled down at me with a gaze that was nonchalant; he was all tanned, fresh from the gap year in Kenya that he would soon be going on and on about.

'You about to hoard away all this stuff?' He laughed, pointing at my Tesco bags. 'I'm Dan.'

'Nice to meet you – Simon Haines.' I stretched out my hand.

He shook it, with a sort of gentle amusement. 'Well, Mr Haines – we've got lucky here. Have you seen the birds on this corridor yet?'

There was a primitive intimidation, the immediate birth of a complex about Dan's apparent superiority in every possible aspect: his height, his body, his absurd good looks, his obvious extreme confidence. But this came accompanied by relief that at least the bastard didn't sound particularly *posh*. And there was an equally spontaneous attraction to that same confidence, the air of serenity exuded by this man – one of those types of attraction that you half-suspect is not healthy, not in line with your best self. Dan's demeanour contained some sort of promise, and I could never have imagined then that it was empty; that the assurance was the other face of Dan's insecurity, an insecurity deeper even than mine.

'The birds, mate. Have you seen them?'

'No, not yet. Actually – ' and I said this with defiance ' – I'm very girlfriended.'

'Really? Fair enough. Listen, let me give you a hand with these bags.' He bent down.

'Oh, don't worry – no need.'

'Mate, it's fine. These need to go in the kitchen! Come on, I'll introduce you to Ian.'

And so, vaguely against my will, Dan Serfontein was leading me towards the communal kitchen, and I was following obediently. I remember that he opened the big fridge and tossed my mum's Tesco bags inside. And while I was introducing myself to this other confident, tall young man, who was called Ian, I was worrying that Dan might have damaged the strawberries my mum had bought me. I *hated* him now for a moment, this bastard who had insulted the bond symbolised by those strawberries, and I felt angry and then sad again and, oh, what a mess of emotions! Then, with a hand running through his fair hair, Dan said, 'So, what about if we hide from our student parents and go for a little lash? This college is small enough that the students will soon be divided into the swots and the people who want to have fun. We need to get out there, to the Cellars, and stake our social claim!'

I laughed. 'Bit early, isn't it? It's only two o'clock. There're still loads of inductions and stuff.'

'Come on, mate, man up – who needs to spend an afternoon learning about the health and safety policy? Ian, you coming too?'

I hadn't been one of the big drinkers at school in Lincoln. I'd been tipsy a few times, of course – often on those evenings in the pub while my parents debated some theme back in the house. A few times I'd been positively drunk, but I'd never *lashed* during the day – this was a new word for me – I'd never *lashed* all afternoon like I did that first day in Cambridge with Dan and Ian. As the shy students hid away in their rooms just as I had planned to do, and the braver students ventured out to their inductions, Dan, Ian and I marched to the Cellars – Clare's bar is the most atmospheric in Cambridge, located in the crypts beneath the college chapel, all brick arches and pillars and black leather sofas – we marched to the Cellars like lords, and we *lashed it up*. And, like illusions in an underground House of Mirrors, new faces appeared, gliding through the brick arches, pulling up chairs. All of these people were so much more interesting and intense than my friends in Lincoln, and some of them were just so English. Sexy girls with charming names – Tiggy, Arabella, Lottie – beautiful girls with soft fine voices. It seemed that the cool set, even in Clare, was rather *posh*, though not exclusively so. But anyway, I thought, I quite like it, actually!

In those gilded hours in the Cellars I was in a euphoric glow of alcohol – time rolling gently, the auditioning for the cool set begun. The cool set being constructed by words; by our tongues. The tongues constructing it, auditioning for it, were reminding each other, with varying degrees of subtlety, how special and blessed we were; how clever we were. Through words – they're so powerful, words. Soon we would go to sign the Matriculation Book, our names joining those of so many great men and women, so many of life's high-flyers – poet laureates, sopranos and composers, David Attenborough and Andrew Wiles, Archbishops of Canterbury, the Lord Deputy of Ireland, the Duke of Newcastle. And these words, this insistence on the names' achievement *after* Cambridge, the attendant contemplation of the future before the present had begun, I found weird, fascinating, because for me *getting here* had been my achievement – having the chance to learn from the leading minds in the world, to swim deep in foreign literature, the substance of it, the *now*. Perhaps it was I who was strange in never having thought how this place would become a point of departure – maybe one day I would be prime minister too?

'You have the loveliest eyes,' said the girl called Arabella, pulling up close in her chair. She was terribly pretty – pale and red-haired, her own eyes permanently startled, in an endearing, amusing sort of way. Her English was hilariously upper-class, but somehow so natural that it was disarming. She was a little merry, getting a little silly. 'They're the *bluest* eyes. Has anyone ever told you?'

'Well, thank you!' I felt myself beaming at her, like an idiot. And then panic – you love Sophie! You've let her down!

Then we were all back to our college rooms in Memorial Court, freshly cleaned for us by the 'bedders' – another word so old and new – and for a moment we would all gaze through those latticed windows upon the best views England had to offer – the Backs, the lawns falling into the River Cam – and for the first time in our lives we would reflect, with outrageous seriousness, on what we would do to influence society, improve the country, as and when we were given the chance. Next, we would put on our black gowns and cross the stone footbridge to the seventeenth-century Great Hall – inside was all candlelight and grandeur, the glow of History flickering on the stained glass windows. We would stand as the Fellows entered, jump at the gong, sit proud during Latin grace, sip some port, this truth of our futures confirmed as we would listen to the words spoken to us on this, our Matriculation Dinner. Later, we would be back in the Cellars, and the cool set wasn't really full of posh kids – or what Dan had called 'rahs', a very funny new word for me. No, there was a lovely mix – state school kids like me, private school kids like Dan, public school kids. What everyone had in common was *energy* – so many compelling personalities…

…I was drunk now though – we were all a bit drunk…

'Just think,' said Dan, vaguely. *Think what, Dan? Think WHAT?* Many girls listened as he spoke. My gaze wandered, dwelling a moment on the group photographs that hung nearby: earnest-looking rowers on the River Cam during May Bumps – what was May Bumps? The Clare College Choir, their faces straining, last year's Garden Party of strawberries and Pimm's. Strawberries – my mum's strawberries were in the fridge.

'I mean it.' Dan had finished his thought – he'd become a little muddled. 'What are you reading, again?' he asked, turning to me.

'French and Italian.'

'Truth is, it doesn't matter what subject you do.' Dan shrugged. 'Any good degree from here and you're sorted.'

I nodded wisely, aware of a connection between the words and that special, not-quite-right something in Dan that was so interesting, so attractive.

'I've forgotten yours too!' I laughed. 'What did you say your subject was?'

'Hi, there!' Dan stood up suddenly. 'Come and join us – we've got a jug of beer here!' And another girl, this one as blonde as Dan, very sexy but with silly fluttering eyelashes, sat down and owned the sofa with her smile. She was pretending to be ditzy, but it didn't work – the eyelashes were fluttering much too intensely.

'I'm Francesca. Nice to meet you. Hi!'

A short time later, something painful occurred: Dan suddenly became bored with me. Unlike Ian, I was still sitting next to the star of the evening – the other students dancing around us, like moths around the light. It was some joke I had made, a weak joke, and, instead of laughing as I'd expected, he raised his eyebrows to the girl with the silly fluttering eyelashes and coughed in a tired sort of way – and thereby guided the rest of the students towards the conclusion that what I had said was not funny. And tacitly, through those minuscule gestures that we all understand but cannot articulate, he conveyed to the group that they should not think that he and I were in any way a team: we were all friends here and he was Dan and Dan alone; and I was Simon, and Simon alone. I no longer felt well when I understood this – I was embarrassed, suddenly so insecure again, and in this wretched new state I watched him soar ahead, ever higher, as I plummeted, ending up telling pretty Arabella with the red hair how much I was in love with my girlfriend, Sophie Williams. Then I went back to my room, resentful and hurt, but somehow more fascinated still by Dan. It was that childish, somehow superficial anguish that is nevertheless caused by a threat to identity; the wild bitterness that is capable of disappearing in seconds upon a change of heart, an apology.

What a dick. He'd dissolved all my anxieties, led me through the transition, only to make me feel like this, right at the end of my first day away from home. And, oh, God – the strawberries! Please, please tell me he didn't ruin my mum's strawberries! I went into the communal kitchen now and opened the fridge to see what had happened to them, and I felt choked when my worst fears were confirmed – they were all squashed, and the juice had spilt out into the plastic bag.

'Hi, Mum, just checking in!'

Alcohol – sometimes it can make you *so* sad...

'Oh, Simon, how lovely to hear your voice! We weren't expecting to hear from you yet. The mobile phone's working, then?'

I held the heavy black brick to my ear – if not quite a rarity, it was certainly not yet the norm to have one in 1998 – and it was very expensive. We were on the very cusp of the new era; the grand roll-out of a generation's achievement less than a year away.

'And did you like—'

'They were gorgeous!' I said, tears falling from my eyes.

'That's nice.'

An hour or so later, lying in the darkness, I called Sophie.

'I have to tell you – ' I sat up in bed ' – I hate it here!'

'First day's always horrible – it was the same here, in Nottingham. Be strong – remember, nothing will change between us.'

OF COURSE, SIX MONTHS into university *everything* changed – Sophie dumped me, the first of two such occasions in my life. In one sense the hurt it brought was the making of me: I reacted with an aggressive immediacy, began to socialise more at Clare, making new friends, meeting new student girls, eventually going out in a vague way with Arabella, the pretty, wan redhead with the startled eyes. But mainly I threw myself into my studies, discovering the true heart of Cambridge that was twinned with what was perhaps my true heart too – that intensity of academic passion...

Studying like a man enchanted or obsessed and, as a break from the studies that were changing my mind, as a break from the real Cambridge, seeking out from time to time its negative side towards the end of that first year, beginning to drink a little wildly – in that cathartic, very lonely way that was so common among the undergraduates. The Jägerbombs, the super-strength lagers, were somehow tied up with the desire to re-find those golden first hours at Clare, when everything was so thrillingly new, when I was flying with Dan Serfontein. Down in the Cellars, the cool people had been firmly established now; I seemed destined to be forever on the fringes, where I felt perfectly fine, but the sight of Dan at the epicentre would remind me, ever more gently, of how exciting that first day had been. We were friends, of course, and I had long forgiven him for becoming bored with me that first day – for it was impossible not to like Dan Serfontein. He was the source of all fun, the sort of human being capable of changing others' days with ease. He was already captain of the Clare Football First XI, the guy who got all the birds, but what was charming, unique, about him was that he refused to submit to Cambridge – he was the precise same person he had been on day one. I'm not sure it would have worked in certain other colleges, the stuffier ones where there were more blazer boys, more rahs: among the 'cool people' in those colleges Dan's slight accent, his slight lack of class, despite his money, would have been called out, perhaps – or would it – who could tell? Regardless, in Clare he was king...

A complication, though, was that one evening, before the exams at the end of the first year, after Dan had said to us earlier in our little kitchen that he was ill and hungover and that he was taking to his bed with paracetamol, I knocked on his door to ask if he needed anything and the door swung open without my intending it. He was at his desk, head in his hands, staring down at some notes with eyes full of great tears.

'Thought you were bedridden!'

'Ah, yes – was just figuring out which papers to take with me tomorrow.' He turned, wiped his eyes and smiled jovially. 'Filthy bloody cold!'

'Are you OK?'

'Course I'm not OK.' He shook his head at me. 'I just told you, I'm rough as hell!'

I SURPRISED EVEN MYSELF with my performance in those first-year exams: I came fourth in the whole university – not just my college, but in all the colleges combined – in French linguistics, and third in the Dante paper. After a summer in France and Italy I was back for the second year – and now I and a few others lifted off, taking some of the questions beyond the point required to get even a First. This was when lovely old Professor Bonini began to take me aside after supervisions, saying that, while it was outside the scope of the course, if I *was* interested in that specific element of Old Neapolitan syntax, or in the history of Milanese, I might want to read his recent publication, or the publication of his colleague, each of which was available in the university library. It was during the second year too, as we stepped into a new millennium, that I began to hear more, ever more, about Dan's family, how rich he was – the cool people in their own insecurities were exaggerating wildly their knowledge of it – but I still couldn't manage to become interested in the point. In this sense I was no different from my other two main friends at Clare, both of whom, in hindsight, seemed equally oblivious to money in those days. There was the Mancunian Alex Saunders, with his spiky brown hair and his weak, plump face and his predilection for some of the more exotic substances that could be purchased in Cambridge – a Classics student who, at his best, and least stoned, sparkled with vicious irony, brilliant cynicism. A man who, just over a decade later, would be working as a management consultant in the City. How had that happened? Then there was the Chinese guy, Lawrence – what was his surname? He was at least five years younger than everyone else in the year, yet already one of the leading mathematicians in the university by the second year. In the maths exams, apparently you had to answer two questions perfectly to get a First. And so the exam papers included tens of questions for the students to choose from, the idea being that the students would find in the list the couple of questions they had focused on during their revision. The story went that, on the day of the second-year exams, after a heavy drinking session in Cindy's club the night before, Lawrence rushed in a minute or so before it would have been too late, sat down at his designated desk and then answered the first two questions on the list, walking out forty-five minutes later. He still managed a First that year, just as he did every year. Lawrence had a thoughtful, lost face. After the second-year exams some US investment bank invited him down to the City for a three-week internship. And they said that they would pay him:

'Five hundred pounds a week!' he said, frowning with amusement. 'Ridiculous amount of money for crunching numbers – or rather, for watching someone else crunch numbers for a few weeks. It'll be a little embarrassing, to be honest – I might even buy myself a microwave.'

Lawrence, to accept the job offer that the same investment bank made him a year or so later? Lawrence, to wear a sharp suit, to be a banker? Impossible! Who would have bet on that?

We did not know then that one day we would *all* end up in the City, that we were the generation who would necessarily go there – we weren't thinking such things in that second year. To the extent that I was reflecting at all, it was on the subject itself, the way I took to it, how it felt so profoundly right, the most natural thing I had ever experienced. It was that rare, beautiful marriage of a young person and a vocation. But the external consequence of this love affair, my success, while very exciting, felt a little unnatural, creating an intermittent sense of dissociation; and in fact it was crazy what happened – in the exams at the end of that second year, just by working away on the subject I loved, I actually came top this time, number one in the whole university, in three different exam papers. People were now whispering about me in the Cellars, and it was the same, I suppose, as any big achievement in any self-contained world – it had surprising effects, giving you the sense not only that you were no longer quite in control, but also that you were not quite *you*. In May Week I was summoned by Professor Bonini, who told me in a hushed voice that the next day I would be informed that I had won the Cunningham Prize – this was considered a very great honour, he reminded me, bestowed by the faculty on only a couple of dozen or so students since it had been created in the 1950s. I would have to sign a special prizewinners' book, there would be a cheque for two thousand pounds – that bit sounded weird – and I could choose my own book to be embossed with the Cunningham seal. The prize was still sponsored by the descendants of an American financier, the type from the generation who wanted to be associated with Oxbridge faculties instead of sports teams.

'Don't let it go to your head.' Bonini's wrinkled face was gazing down at the River Cam, at some bare-chested students who were causing chaos in the water, three punts having collided. The boats were full of bottles of Pimm's. 'I think these sorts of prizes can be harmful,' he said. 'They distract students from the real stuff, the enjoyment of the subject itself. You must always remember why you've won it – because you have an aptitude for words. It's *this* that you should be proud of.'

People's reactions when I told them the news! It seemed to me that soon the whole of Cambridge, the whole of Lincoln knew. It was the biggest achievement yet on this rollercoaster journey to somewhere, and, while I found myself occasionally looking in on myself with that dissociation thing, there was nevertheless an intense satisfaction, together with a sense that everything seemed to be coming together – that the more I achieved in academia, the closer I seemed to be to that sun from which Dan had stepped. A sun of assurance, of manly self-esteem. There was a deep illogicality in this – it was increasingly clear that Dan was more complex inside, and doing well in linguistics would not necessarily an alpha male make – but I wasn't dwelling on the contradiction as this was just a *feeling,* which didn't need to be explained or analysed. And anyway, during that May Week, as the sun bathed Cambridge in summer, I was drunk on so many things – drunk on literature and words after the mad revision and exams, those recordings of old men in Marseille speaking in dialect, the discovery that Neapolitans referred to lifts as 'trams on the wall', the end of *I promessi sposi*, the rain on my back as Renzo walked through the storm. I was drunk on achievement, on Pimm's in the garden parties of a dozen colleges, on vodka shots in the Cellars, drunk on the sense of stardom exuded by the outrageously extravagant May Balls – champagne receptions, fireworks reaching up into the dark sky to the gasps of locals crowded into punts on the river, ballgowns held high.

One day in May Week, Dan Serfontein knocked on my door.

'Simon, mate – you got a sec?'

I opened, very hungover, as Arabella, who was sort of my girlfriend again now, covered herself with my duvet.

'Congrats on the Cunningham Prize – incredible achievement! Look,' Dan smiled, 'I got an odd invitation last night. Some guy called Freddie from Trinity, an absolute A1 prick, you'll hate him. Anyway, he came over to me, all hilariously formal, and said that, after much deliberation their end, you and I are going to be invited into the Kants.'

'The Kants?'

It turned out that this was an exclusive – the most exclusive – university-wide banned drinking society. All drinking societies were prohibited now in Cambridge, although a lot of the dining, boating and similar societies were just drinking clubs operating under a fake premise. The majority of these were college-based – Clare's were tame and relatively inoffensive – but the real glamour and mystery, we were told – the glamour and mystery I had mocked and scorned and despised for two years – lay in the university-wide societies – particularly the 'illegal' ones. There were the Squirrels, the Bombers, then this relative newbie, formed only five or six years ago…

…the Kants…

…whose mantra, we were told, around a candlelit table in Trinity the next night, was to establish a new league of gentlemen, tomorrow's winners from all fields, who also knew how to take a drink. Accordingly, the initiation would be necessarily brutal.

'Oh, yes, we've had chaps hospitalised,' boasted Freddie, the Kants chairman. His bowl of dark, fuzzy hair loomed large over his very fat, very white face as he played with his Kants tie that was half-hidden under his gown. 'One fellow fucking impaled himself on a railing after nine dirty pints – and I mean *dirty* pints. Taken away in an ambulance with a string of kippers around his neck and trousers full of piss and shit!'

The voice was surreal. Did people *really* speak like this today? Did it come to him naturally? Surely a profound effort was required to sound like this?

'That's another rule of the Kants – no toilet breaks, throughout the day. Excretions are to remain with the initiate.'

'To take a toilet break on initiation is a flagrant offence!' explained the excitable, freckle-faced, tiny man by his side – this was little Benedict, vice chairman of the Kants. He looked up at his superior nervously, obsequiously, until:

'Flagrant!' came the confirmation.

In Freddie's bloated, self-important, horribly pale face was what I hated about my country; what had put me off going to Cambridge; everything that Alex Saunders and I had taken the piss out of, as a form of defence, for two years. But now to the little surprise – now to the weakness of Simon Haines. For I was in a state of wonder, winner of the Cunningham Prize, all these crazy May Balls, the Red Arrows flying overhead as drunken girls dug out magnums of Dom Pérignon from the ice in the punts dotted around the gardens. It was all a bit *Gatsby*, wasn't it? And the initiation wouldn't take long, and it was only a game.

'I'll think about it,' I said proudly.

'Really?' replied Freddie.

Early the next morning Arabella and I were woken by a bunch of fine, strapping young men in blue blazers, beige chinos and Kants ties banging on my door, demanding that I open. Arabella performed her duvet trick, only her face and red hair showing – while I hurried to put on a pair of jeans and a T-shirt...

'Open, sir! Open!'

They sat me down at my desk, held me, and poured a dirty pint down my throat – vodka mixed with cider, Tabasco sauce and bits of a Mars bar that looked like dog turd. And then two shots of something that ripped down into my stomach, burning my insides. And then a small jug of beer which, I saw with terror, had a goldfish in it. But it turned out that this was a joke – it was just a plastic toy. Which might have killed me, actually, if I'd swallowed it...

'Enough,' shouted Arabella from the bed. 'He'll be sick!'

'Offence number one!' yelled Freddie, his sweaty face alive with joy under that absurd jungle of fuzz. 'May this be recorded for later this evening – initiate was found in presence of lady! Flagrant! He is not yet qualified to speak to ladies!'

'Illegitimate encounter with a lady!' they all agreed.

Then they left, and so I had a shower and a bit of sick and was dressed now in the new blazer and the chinos, strangely warm and content, but Arabella was saying that my voice had changed, that it was more like Freddie's, and that it was so freaky. As I strolled down King's Parade with her, people looked at me – some with raised, cynical eyebrows, the same look I would have given, while others seemed sort of resentfully admiring. All knowing the general point – that I'd been initiated into some exclusive club or another! And how was it that I'd despised the idea until I'd become a member, while now, in these brief transitory moments, I had a vague feeling of smugness? It was as if I had climbed up into a new class, the alcohol convincing me of the splendour of it all. Making me ignore what an *utter twat* I must have looked. And making me forget too that, in my case, things like this, spontaneous, capricious decisions that I wasn't really sure about, always went disastrously wrong.

There was no real disaster that day, though – the scandal was to happen a year and a half later, at the Kants dinner that I foolishly attended when I was back in Cambridge after my intervening year abroad in Naples. No, this first time was pretty uneventful – I was just sick again, before I made it to the

Kants initiation lunch, was eventually put to bed by Arabella, and then branded a failure, a disgrace and a 'war criminal' by the Kants leadership. Dan, meanwhile, who with his vast frame could take his drink better than anyone, made it through the fifteen-course 'lunch' relatively unharmed – horse tartare, fourteen shots of grappa, pigs' snouts and beer – although he too was sick, for the first and only time I knew of.

I woke up feeling messy, sullied by the experience, but life was running fast, rich with colour, and within a day or two the whole strange Kants experience was put to the back of my mind. And Dan and I began to bond after that day, really bond this time, perhaps on account of its very strangeness. We began to drink together, often alone, without my even realising it at first – for these were such free, reckless days. Arabella said that she and I shouldn't keep seeing each other once we broke up for the summer. She said my heart wasn't in it, that sometimes I still woke her mumbling Sophie's name – and that was alright, we'd still be the best of friends. She said that we should just enjoy the final days of a May Week we would always remember, not think too much about it. After all, she joked, it was a privilege sleeping with such a star student…

And what was not to savour? The sun was bouncing about the college gardens, I'd won the Cunningham Prize, and after the summer I would be off to magical Naples for the year abroad! And at the end of May Week there would be the final party, too: Dan Serfontein's twenty-first, which was to be held at the family's London residence. He had invited the whole year in Clare, and rumours had been coursing through the college:

'He's got his own cinema, you know.'

'Oh, that's so *nouveau*!'

'It's so *what*? Who are you, the aristocrat?'

'Apparently he's got a swimming pool!'

'Bit narcissistic, inviting the whole year?'

And I found this sort of gossip so unintelligible and boring – was there anything more banal, anything less noteworthy than a home cinema? I didn't get it. But the idea of the party was very exciting – because I would be going to London! To finish off an extraordinary academic year in style.

'You're so sweet,' said Arabella, giggling as I enthused – she'd lived in Chelsea all her life. It was late and we were in the Cellars, on the sofa on which we had first met. Now her face became sad. 'Oh, Simon.'

'What?'

'Nothing, nothing.' She dabbed her eyes. 'It's right what we decided – and you're not in love with me, I know that.'

'Arabella—'

'No, it's alright. Don't say something you don't mean. But, you know, if you ever do want to try with me ... I mean, try properly ... then you'll tell me, won't you?'

'It was you who wanted to split up! And I'm off to Italy soon, for a whole year.'

'I know, I know. It's just that, I was thinking about it yesterday, and I'm not sure I'll meet a person like you again.' She sighed, putting her hand to my cheek. 'I can't quite explain it, how you make me feel – I know you're great at your subject and all that, but at the same time you're somehow so clueless. With this lovely, deep naivety – I suppose that's it. You've got an excitement, Simon – an excitement that's all the excitement I've ever known.'

DAN SERFONTEIN'S twenty-first birthday party was held at a white stucco palace on Walton Square, a square that is the very moment – though I did not yet know it – when Chelsea fades into Belgravia. It was an especially summery late June that year, the wind blowing warm as a carriage of Clare invitees arrived flushed and giddy at King's Cross station. London was bustle and glaring, a vivid cartoon, and my parents laughed happily down the telephone as I noted, with false nonchalance, that I had just popped to the capital for a party…

It was early evening now, the sky surviving, a rich blue, as Lawrence the lost-faced Chinese genius, Mancunian Alex and I sat in a black cab that crossed Parliament Square, raced by the sun-glazed Thames, and then came out, without warning, into a land of white castles, streets of magic. Belgravia gleamed bold, the homes on Walton Square climbing imperiously into the sky.

'Bloody hell,' said Alex. 'Serfontein really *is* the big rich wanker. Look at you, Haines! Look, Lawrence – he's gone into a trance!'

'Simon!'

It wasn't the *money*, of course, at this point – the connection between the picture before me and money had yet to solidify in my mind. Quite the opposite – money was grubby, wasn't it? There was nothing romantic about the sad counting of coins. No, this was about imagination, the mind: one of those rare moments when you experience something *new*, something that takes you beyond your previous understanding of the world. A fresh new otherness that makes that most charming of promises – that you will *never* understand this world fully, that its beauty is unlimited and unknown – affirming the secret hope you've had since you were a child that forever there will be surprises, foreign plains. The grace of Walton Square, enthralling as the best literature I'd read, any painting I'd seen, elicited a strange nostalgia of when I was young. Some film I must have watched about London, some novel I must have read…

Dan's house was the grandest on Walton Square. It stood dead centre, gazing down austerely at the blooming communal gardens, ivy racing up the façade of its five, six floors. Spilling out from the black front door was a queue of men and women of all ages, a colourful mix – finely attired, quaintly absurd old Englishmen; tieless continental Europeans with very white teeth; student rahs, student geeks, chatty girls, aloof girls, timid-looking guys.

'I could have done with a beer or two first,' I said. 'Shall we pop to the pub, come back in a bit?'

'You always want to get pissed when you're stressed or excited!' Lawrence grinned. 'Don't be mental – we're here now!'

'OK, OK.'

We joined the queue undulating towards the black door, like a stream of silk. Soon we had entered Dan's house, floated through a vast hallway into a drawing room where we stood a moment below a mural of a perfect sky – wisps of cloud above soft brown branches, a sky that was an extension of the evening outside so exact that as I gazed upwards I left gravity behind, entering a fantastic space. But the energy of the party, the invisible master of ceremonies, moved you on. We were climbing a marble helical staircase that led into a room of white sofas and white billowing voiles, where a gargantuan bottle of champagne, holding thirty litres, rose up to chest height from its vast golden bucket. Guests stepped through the voiles as if through the air – beyond them was a fine balcony that, looking to the back of the house, offered a glimpse of its jewel: a garden arranged over three levels, the green divided by a limestone terrace made spectacular by an exuberant fountain. It was the apotheosis of summer down there in that garden, I thought – it was the summer of all kings, Roman emperors, Cosimo de' Medici, a summer painted by Cézanne. Here it was, this lovely disturbing fusion was happening again: I was writing about this house in my head, using the material, the appallingly limited material, that I had.

In the far corner of the garden, under the shade of a maple tree, a man sang softly as waiters in white dinner jackets bounced between guests, holding trays of champagne flutes that wavered below the evening sun. We were inside again now, descending the marble staircase, light gushing from the deep sash windows to either side. We stepped out onto the top lawn and made out the music better – the singer was humming 'Somewhere Over the Rainbow', the notes circling and circling in the evening air. Then there was that familiar hand on me.

'Simon, mate – you made it! How do you like my pad?'

'He's overwhelmed,' noted Lawrence, his bland mathematician's accuracy intensified by the rush of his second drink of the evening.

'What's that? Come on, let me show you round.'

Dan really had just stepped from the sun – radiant in his pale blue shirt, his beautiful garden. Around him men milled indecisively, pretty girls lingered with charm. Soon we had lost him and the garden was busy with chinos, dinner jackets, ancient creatures smoking thick cigars, un-English old ladies with extravagant coiffures and the bone structure of baby lambs. Sun-kissed loafers...

'If you analysed it...' Lawrence was saying to Alex. But I couldn't really hear him.

The loafers were the super-rich, popped by from next door on Walton Square; they were that world I had never seen. There were enough of us from Clare not to feel intimidated, though – everyone in that garden was rejoicing, forming private circles, little worlds of pleasure and calm. Towards the end, when people were beginning to leave, after the long, sad kiss goodbye from Arabella, I was lying supine on one of the deckchairs dotted about the garden, champagne glass by my side. As I lay there, thinking very little but somehow about Sophie, I realised that the harsh yet magnetic voice drifting near must have been Dan's father's voice – it was foreign but not really South African, a voice I could not place, and he was talking of how proud he was of his son. I twisted around in the deckchair, and made the man out clearly for the first time. He was tall and handsome like Dan, with that same slightly Nordic aspect that I had always assumed Dan had inherited exclusively from his Danish mother. He was silver-haired, this man from Cape Town, tanned and with some special charm. A wild, captivating, somehow frightening charm. A group of middle-aged men encircled him, hanging on his words – reaching out to endorse them, to catch his mood.

A little drunk on the champagne, I stood up now and ventured nearer, my cigarette giving me company, a pretext to walk alone. Presently I found it difficult to take my eyes from this silver fox – he was alive with a frenzied, youthful energy. To my terror, suddenly he called to me.

'Young man!' The tone was at once beckoning and invasive, while the smile was bewitching – giving off waves and waves of charisma. 'Yes, sir – you. I was wondering if I could ask a favour.'

It was English spoken from some indefinite place, somewhere lost in the oceans of a life of travel. Dan's father laughed now as I hurried up close – his eyes, a snake-charmer's eyes, darting left and right, mischievous and hypnotic.

'My wife's in the house and my son's right over there.' He pointed, and the circle of men laughed obsequiously. 'It's been two years since I had a good honest smoke.'

It took a while for me to register the request. But then: 'Of course,' I said, fumbling for my packet of cigarettes under the glare of the hostile, balding heads.

The snake-charmer seemed touched by my struggle. 'What's your name?' he said. Against the question pressed a wall of impatience from the men around him.

'Sorry, I should have introduced myself. I'm Dan's friend from Clare – Simon Haines. Thank you for inviting me to this – this amazing party.'

'Mr Simon Haines – a pleasure.' Then a pause, and: 'Ah, so *you're* Simon.' And he spoke with deep interest – making me know that for a moment he and I were the only men in the world. 'My Dan, he's told me a great deal about you.'

'Really?' I said.

'Yes, you're the smart one, aren't you?' Mr Serfontein flashed his teeth at me as he shook my hand – he seemed to be constantly restraining himself from smiling. He spoke to the balding heads. 'This boy here's a star. Didn't you get the top mark or something?'

'Well, these were only the second-year exams.'

'The top mark, guys – top mark in Cambridge!'

This was acknowledged with some unhappy nods.

'Well, carry on like that – keep going up and up!' And Mr Serfontein puffed joyously on the cigarette he'd taken from me. 'Decided what to do yet after your studies?'

'No, no. Not yet.'

'There's time.'

We turned now as a feline, slender girl, illuminated by the garden's spotlights, captivating in a mint-green dress, took the microphone that the singer had left and began her own performance. Her quiet voice filled the night, the tender force a thousand times superior to what had come before. She was Gabriella, Dan's new girlfriend, the most talented of Clare's choir, and she was singing 'The Girl From Ipanema', shooting him a smile, gazing winsome into his face. As she sang, I looked around the garden – at the waiters sharing a joke by the fountain, but alert, always alert, to the location of Mr Serfontein beside me; I looked at the remaining students, who were swaying gently to the tune, all drunk but behaving, tamed by the beauty of the garden, the beauty of the voice. As I observed these closing moments of the party more carefully I saw that it was not just the waiters but all of the non-student guests too who were focused upon Louis Serfontein – like miniature spotlights, there were eyes about the garden fixed on the house's master. All waiting for their chance to speak to him, or checking if he was content, but anyway all *thinking* about him. Perhaps it was this that charged the man with the electricity: there was the silly, try-hard organiser with the overly perfect suit, nodding across but getting no response; there were the security guys in the shadows, and the Swiss men who seemed to have come to pitch to him and who were still waiting, maybe they'd given up. Women, lots of women too, peering out from their partners' conversation. My eyes were back on him too now, as I was edged out of the circle slowly, expertly – I'd understood from the conversation that the men around him were a group of bankers. They were going on about his house, his garden, weaving in stories about other clients, stories ever more extravagantly luxurious, making suggestions, giving advice. And he was barely listening – he seemed to be drunk instead on his own private story, a fine story that he was telling himself. Life, I saw, was *good* around this man. And his tanned skin made me think of holidays, and they were talking about holidays, about villas in the Caribbean, and as I was finally removed from the circle one of the bankers mentioned a Brazilian island that had come onto the market. It was called Ilha Preciosa, or something like that – an uninhabited, wild island of cliffs, forest and white sand. Once home to some shipwrecked pirates, maybe, I thought...

Gabriella's voice was passionate as I walked back to my deckchair, as far from England now as it was possible to be. I lay down and was on Ilha Preciosa, the sunlight unremitting,

106

my dad befuddled with joy: they're taking him in a jeep to the Master Lodge where he'll have views of a sparkling sea. My mum's becoming all silly, crying out with excitement in her lovely Irish voice as she puts her feet into the warm water. Sophie and I are on the sand, her eyes open wide with astonishment as we dance to 'The Girl From Ipanema'.

'Simon!' Sophie is laughing. 'How have you done *this*?'

Our own island.

The melodious voice, carrying nostalgia and dreams through the warm night air, hung below the London sky. There were now no more cogent thoughts than if I'd tried a psychedelic pill – you could reason for a hundred years, but my eyes closed as Ilha Preciosa became complete – filled out.

Presently, I was woken:

'Thanks for the cigarette, Simon Haines – you know, I never forget a surname.' Mr Serfontein held his arm out, offering to help me up. 'I understand you're one of the lucky ones staying overnight – your room's in the mews to the back. Now, about that cigarette.' He winked. 'It'll be our little secret, OK?'

'I'm so sorry.' I wiped my eyes – I was the last one in the garden.

'Are you alright? Not out of your head?'

'Oh, no.'

'I'll wish you goodnight, then.' Yet, as he was about to walk away, something occurred to Mr Louis Serfontein. 'Oh, and don't worry – you'll find out what you want to do. If life's taught me one thing, it's this: in the working world – whether it's academia, business or whatever – we all discover our niche in the end.'

Did we? As I entered the mews house behind the garden, I began to wonder what my niche was, then; what my niche couldn't be. Slipping below the sheets that night, I decided that my place in the world must surely be wherever I dared to dream – that my place was Ilha Preciosa, its runway between the cliffs, where you would take off for the sun. An island of validation and self-esteem – where my voice could be *my* voice, settled and clear. A place where either Sophie loved me or else I'd never met her, so I would never know, never care. An island of soft tunes, of maple trees.

5

WE ALL DISCOVER *our niche in the end.* The words flashed
and flashed before me as I leaned against a half-finished brick
wall in the heart of Cojímar, languishing under the Cuban
sun. Maybe this, scouring this deserted town of fire, was my
niche. A further hour had passed, and still I had not found
Gregorio's old house. Indeed I had found nothing, save for
heat, more heat, that same black dog with the brazen stare,
that omnipresent suggestion of labyrinth, of perennial return.
Yet as I languished, reaching suddenly for the bottle of water
and pouring it over my head, unable to control the profound,
animal sigh of relief that this elicited, a native approached.
A man whose father Ernest Hemingway had perhaps once
regarded from his fishing craft. This man looked startled,
wildly agitated, at the sight of me emptying a bottle of water
over my head in the middle of his village, perhaps more still
by that orgasmic moan, and he interrupted me as I tried to
introduce myself. When I explained that I was interested in

Hemingway and that I was desperately keen to find Gregorio's old house, he pointed angrily back down the street, telling me to ask at the Terraza de Cojímar. I had forgotten about the restaurant, having not come across it during my previous roaming. However, on the way back down towards Calamity Bay, I now found what was surely it – it had no sign, but it must be the place, I thought. Partially blocked from view by a moribund tree, it stood quite a distance back from the promenade – far further back than the guidebook suggested – but the windows behind the bar still boasted views of the dismal water. The place was empty except for a line of squat Cuban barmen, who bore a disconcerting resemblance to the men who had laughed at me at the Monument to Hemingway.

I took a seat at the bar.

'*Hola*,' I said. But there was no response – instead they continued to banter among themselves, occasionally banging their fists down on the counter by way of emphasising a point. And so I took out my guidebook, gazed down into it, began to think again…

It was frightening that ten – no, *twelve* – years had gone by since Dan Serfontein's birthday party. How much used to *happen* in those student days, how many experiences, only for everything to stagnate, for there to be a channelling of all development into one sole, all-consuming aspect of life, once I arrived at Fiennes & Plunkett. In those years before the firm there were colours and strands jumping about before they settled into a picture, and like any young person I did not appreciate that these were key building blocks, moments of consequence. Fresh from Dan Serfontein's birthday party, fresh with daydreams of Ilha Preciosa, I was packing for the year abroad – compulsory for all language students – which I would spend in the city that, even before I had visited it, had stolen the heart of that other me, the Simon that Sophie loved.

Naples, Napoli, *Napule*, the city of nostalgia that seduces through the imagination inherent in its words, the promise of theatricality tracing back always to the past, the interplay with its deep violent shades, the warm soft melancholy of the photographs of Posillipo, of the sea at Mergellina, the colours of Piazza del Plebiscito. I did not know then that this year abroad would be *my* year, the time I would look back to always, even perhaps the reason I was here now, in Cojímar. I did not know that I would meet a girl out there in Naples, a girl of dreamlike beauty, yielded up by the city's mad heart. I did not know how brutally it would end, nor how, deflated, sensing that I would never again find that same colour, I would be outside Naples Airport, enjoying the final cigarette of my year abroad, when women began suddenly to scream, men to gesticulate wildly, and I would find myself in a crowd squeezed before the horror playing out on the large television screen in the airport café, the second tower of the World Trade Center collapsing before my eyes.

Then I was back for the final year in Cambridge. The world had turned black, war was brewing and Blair looked older, always more distant, as if a myriad future scenarios were playing out in his mind. And I felt changed, with this conviction that my youth was behind me now, that it was time to decide upon my own future. And then suddenly, as if to alleviate the panic that these grand conclusions elicited, to fill the hole in me, I remembered Walton Square. Dan's garden, the maple tree. They shone clear, a blazing light through the memories of Naples; soon I would become obsessed, deciding that these images were my guide, that they must be my guide. So the dreams of Ilha Preciosa transformed into an impatient anxiety. What was my niche, then? What should I do?

My niche, some part of me knew, was clearly the precise thing that I was doing then, the subject I was excelling at. But the answer didn't satisfy me, didn't curb the agitation, and anyway I wasn't sure that this must be my only niche, that the story must end there. The world was so big, and Ilha Preciosa so vivid! And there was a certain harmony in the manner in which certain events combined to give me the real answer to what I would do: the connection between those events was becoming clearer to me today, as I thought in Cojímar. There was the Cunningham Prize, the resultant promise of heady ascent, the invitation to join the Kants drinking society. There was Dan's twenty-first, the illustration of this higher plain. Then, after the interruption of the year in Naples – that time in Naples was as if something were fighting back, granting that other side of me a chance to pull through, a chance it never took – there came the last key event in the series.

The event was the Kants reunion dinner in Michaelmas term, just before I went home for Christmas in that final year at Clare – a dinner that, as noted, went very wrong. Initially I hadn't even considered attending it – this was due partly to my fear of what they would do to me, given my failed initiation during my second year. But the principal reason I wasn't interested was that the whole idea of the Kants was embarrassing again, shameful even. The perverse little kick it had induced during the end of that second year was, I had realised, a momentary thing, ascribable to its being a new idea, bolstering the sense of limitlessness that had intoxicated that summer. Returning after a year in Naples, the idea of the Kants was painfully childish. Indeed, Clare College generally, the whole university, seemed full of such *young* people, this sensation that I had outgrown the place being underlined by the point that all my friends, everyone except for the language students, had already graduated a year earlier, while we had been abroad.

The reason I did go to the Kants reunion dinner, or at least the only discernible reason, was loneliness. I was lonely and impatient and bored – that strange, anticlimactic fourth year is for language students the *quid pro quo* of the excitement of the year abroad. Now, on those evenings when I needed a release from the intensity of the study, those evenings when I needed to calm my panic about the uncertainty of my future, rather than sitting in the Cellars with the students fresh from sixth form I began to drink alone – not too heavily, of course, but it seemed pointless to force myself through a conversation with teenagers I didn't know when I could finish the day on a quiet high with two or three whiskies at my desk, while writing emails – long, rambling emails to Sophie, to the beautiful girl from Naples, emails I would never send.

So I was alone, studying for up to fifteen hours some days, drinking Jack Daniel's at my desk late at night, and Dan, who was taking another gap year before heading to law school, wanted to come back to Cambridge to see me in December, and suggested we combine it with the Kants dinner. He explained to me what the dinner would actually entail – it wouldn't be just undergraduates, and so I had no reason to be scared about stupid punishments for having failed to get through initiation. No, this would be a more grown-up affair: it was the seventh anniversary dinner, to which the 'Kants alumni' were also invited. Wouldn't it be interesting to meet the *men* who would be coming back here for the occasion? Wasn't I curious to see what these former students were doing now? No doubt the majority would be living in London, big successes down there, and Dan was right, it *would* be fascinating to see how these guys were faring 'out there in the real world'. And this was a very relevant thought, for the empty but insidious words 'out there in the real world' were haunting me now in the depths of the night. What did they mean? What should I do? Professor Bonini had begun to lobby against the proposition that they had any meaning at all, making the occasional caustic, telling remark, frowning below those wisps of white hair, as if he knew the dark places to which my mind might be wandering…

'I have no idea how to translate *outsourcing* into Italian,' he noted to us once in a supervision. 'But then again, what *does* it mean, even in English? What does it really *mean*?' And he smiled, his nostrils flaring a little with indignation…

'This morning, a dear friend of mine from Trapani sent me a link to a newspaper article that made my blood boil,' he told me, as we walked to the lecture hall at Sidgwick Site. 'An interview with the chairmen – the chairmen! – of some of Italy's largest banks. These are intelligent people, and yet the language they used – my God! It was interspersed with English words, words that we Italians don't *need* to borrow – we have a plethora of equivalents, more elegant equivalents. But these men, they were talking *in Italian* about "*partnership*", coming out with observations like "*abbiamo un feeling*". I mean, really! And, worse, it now seems that it's the done thing to misuse Italian words so that they sound as close as possible to English. "*Rilevante*" does not mean "relevant" in Italian. It means something else! It's a false friend!'

'But I thought you would be indifferent to that, excited by it, even,' I argued, fondly – I knew that Bonini, like any academic, loved to argue. 'I mean, as a linguist, a scientist, I thought your job was to judge it all objectively; I thought your fascination was language itself, in its purest sense.'

'You're absolutely right,' he said, shaking his head. 'But this international business world – I just can't stay objective. It's the great enemy of words!'

'I think that's a bit harsh.'

'It's the great enemy of thought!'

Bonini was lobbying, and at times I would decide suddenly, vehemently, that he was right, that applying to stay on here was what I wanted too. But in the evening, with the bottle of Jack Daniel's, I would become assailed by doubts – friends, newspapers, the internet, they were putting a thousand mad ideas into my head, reminding me of the possibility of journalism, politics, human rights, the Bar, founding a start-up – it didn't matter what start-up. Further, there was the point – a slightly disingenuous point, for I couldn't really convince myself that I cared – that the two friends who might have stayed in academia with me had both left the year before. Lawrence was at that investment bank, already beginning to speak a language of different values and ideas, while cynical Alex was now consulting, spending his days *becoming sighted on the issues, listing the deliverables, transitioning the assets* – he would email me his favourite expressions of the week.

My job means nothing, he wrote cheerfully one night. *Zero net, as we say here. And it involves almost nothing too – save for the intense concentration required to ensure that you never actually think. The best way to prevent thinking, I have found, is to say: 'soooooooooo' in a wise, reflective, faintly superior manner whenever asked a question. Incidentally, this also works fine for career development – it is not necessary, from a professional viewpoint, for the 'soooooooooo' to be followed by an answer to the question. All you need to do is to ensure that the 'soooooooooo' lasts for a very, very long time. It cannot last too long. My boss is close to twenty seconds now.*

Anyway, it's kind of extraordinary – the job takes up nineteen hours a day. Yesterday it took up twenty-four hours. Imagine that – twenty-four consecutive hours of saying 'soooooooooo'.

Despite his depressive humour, Alex had still done it, though – he'd abandoned History to focus all his energies on a pursuit that was the diametric opposite in terms of human understanding, cultural substance. Why? Just money, or something else? Did he have his own secrets? Anyway, both he and Laurence had left, Bonini was lobbying for me to stay, and I was changing my mind by the hour, remembering at times that I felt most clean, most free and happy, when I focused on some topic other than myself, or rather some topic other than *my relation to things*. But the effort required to achieve this for any significant period of time was intolerable. I suspected that I wasn't a selfish person, for I'd been told as much since I was a child: I wasn't someone who felt entitled to anything. But, if I wasn't selfish, I was certainly self-obsessed – it was at about this time in my life that I was learning *how* self-obsessed. At night I would try testing it, try breaking free from the self-absorption by forcing myself to imagine something external that made me happy without my being involved: the underdog fighting and winning, the wrongly convicted prisoner as he takes his first step of freedom. I'd soon be straining like a weightlifter to hold the image, to keep *me* out of it, and before I broke there would be a rush of pure serenity…

But then I would appear, even in a small way – a little nod of acknowledgement from the underdog; a whispered 'thank you' from the freed prisoner. And so soon I would be back to fretting about myself, my objectives. What I wanted most was to end this extreme tension created by indecision – an indecision that was threatening my sense of identity.

'For fuck's sake, Simon,' I would whisper. 'Just decide who you are.'

And then there was the Kants dinner, which I didn't tell Professor Bonini about, for fear that he would have looked at me as if I were a stranger, a fraud. The other side of Cambridge, the side that existed in the margins, far from the fine gentle beauty of academia – the other side was not for the Simon Haines he knew.

And maybe I was a fraud – but aren't we all, at times, in our own funny ways? Snow was falling from the December sky as I crossed Old Court in my blazer, white shirt and chinos, my Kants tie in my pocket – no coats were allowed, and the ties had now been identified as connoting membership of a banned drinking society, so could not be put on inside a college. Then I was out and had turned down King's Parade, and, as I walked, I wasn't thinking about Bonini at all – there came stealing over me instead that old Cambridge sensation that this was not real. Trinity, the college boasting Isaac Newton, Lord Byron, over thirty Nobel Prize winners, the wealthiest of all Cambridge colleges, had been chosen as the secret meeting point. I was escorted in by an owl-eyed student called Alastair, and, entering below the statue of Henry VIII, the coats-of-arms, I looked upon the fallen snow stretching out to the clock-tower, a winter court snatched from a fairytale...

Then I was in Trinity's college bar, dropped off dutifully by conspiratorial young Alastair, and there I knew nobody. So I stood alone, drinking a flat pint of beer uneasily. Presently, a group of student girls looked up – the usual sign that my friend had arrived.

'Dan – over here!'

His eyes gleamed as he turned and saw me, strode over. 'You've finished that – let me get us a round,' he said, grinning. 'And then, first on the agenda, I want to hear about this hot bird from Naples!'

'Well, it wasn't dull out there.'

It was pleasant to see Dan again. We were far from best friends in those days, not yet really even close friends, but that chemistry that had begun so suddenly after our experiences of initiation, just before his birthday party, was rekindling within minutes. Soon our anecdotes were spinning out, leading me almost to forget why we were in the bar, at the meeting point for the Kants big night. We'd seen Freddie, the former chairman with the grotesque bush of fuzzy hair and the fleshy white face, and Benedict, the freckled little goblin-acolyte. It was fantastic to think that both of them had graduated now, that these buffoons managed to exist outside Cambridge; possibly, I thought, it was their nastiness that saved them, compensating for the buffoonish aspect, veiled by it. Dan had spotted a few of the others who had made him eat the horse tartare at his initiation, but not so many. It was clear, though, who all the Kants were – men in blazers were sitting together in groups of no more than three, the older Kants alumni in particular apparently rejoicing in the audacity of a banned society's congregating in a college bar. Soon there would be the head count and a secret signal, following which we would leave, in groups of no more than three at a time, and reconvene in the Market Square before heading to a curry house on Jesus Lane – its upstairs room had been booked for the occasion.

'What the hell is the point of all the attendees meeting here first, if they can't speak to each other?' said Dan suddenly. 'We could have just met at the Indian.'

'Presumably that would ruin the intrigue.' I looked at my watch. 'I'll get us another beer.'

'You necked that one in a hurry!'

Then Dan was talking to me about Colombia's women, Ecuador's beaches, and then about the law firm that had offered him a training contract – something of a coup, given that the firm usually offered training contracts only to the leading intellectual lights, the students who obtained or who were on the way to obtaining the First that Dan had not even aimed at. And what an offer it was! They would sponsor him through law school and, provided that he passed the exams, he would go straight in as a trainee solicitor for two years, then an associate, and then – if he excelled – a partner. He was bubbling away.

'My dad's damn proud of me – he's telling anyone who'll listen. Fiennes & Plunkett, it's called. It's not one of the major corporate hitters – there are some *truly* huge ones down there, you know, they're all divided into leagues like football teams: there's the Magic Circle, then the Silver Circle and so on. It's not one of those, but only because it's deliberately small, a family firm, and it's very specialised – it just does financing and insolvency. The work is just as good – actually they say the work is better than the work at the huge firms. And the same goes for the money. And, if you make partner, the money goes crazy.'

'Hmm.'

'People say it's a madhouse! The lawyers are real corporate tigers – they work all night and just keep going the next day! During my interview, a partner told me that recently he'd done a deal where he hadn't left the meeting room for thirty-six hours!'

'Sounds fabulous.'

'Well, it'll be brutal, but it's cutting-edge – they're always in the *FT* for the deals they do. And if I make it as a partner – which, actually, I won't – I'll be on a million quid a year, maybe even more! In my early thirties!'

'Why would you care about that?' I asked absentmindedly. 'A million quid would just be pocket money for you, wouldn't it?'

'What's that? What did you just say, Simon?'

While he'd been enthusing, I'd been surveying the bar. Some small part of my mind had begun to wonder whether we were being looked down upon by the little circles of Kants. I thought I might have caught the odd raised eyebrow, the face that moved away with a trace of disgust upon eye contact. This drinking society was, Dan had confirmed, almost exclusively public school when he'd been initiated, so perhaps he and I were still the only exceptions? It was haunting, this insecurity of mine. I felt out of place and maybe I was – before we'd been invited to join, academic achievement hadn't been a valid credential for admission, but Freddie, good old Freddie, had thought that a new 'type' was needed so as to increase the likelihood that in the future we would have some leading lights to add to the alumni. So people like me were a form of experiment, being watched carefully, maybe – I'd spotted a couple of geeky other trophy invitees too, but even they seemed so *posh*.

Young Dan Serfontein here, the man gazing at me now with a strange expression, had been invited because of his money – his captaincy of the Clare Football First XI, the credential he alleged, being a superfluous, false footnote. Presumably there were a few others like him. But the Kants couldn't all be seriously loaded, so the majority of these guys must have been invited on the basis of some silent, inherent quality; or, more banally, because of whom they'd known at school. Was this why we were getting raised eyebrows? Had I always been right in thinking that Dan, despite his money, wasn't quite *posh* enough for the elite at some of the haughtier colleges? But *were* there really any raised eyebrows? Maybe I was just paranoid – after all, we were not supposed to be acknowledging each other in the bar.

'Simon – I'm talking to you. What did you just say to me?'

A strange voice, to go with the strange face – Dan's, but not quite Dan's.

'Hey – answer me!'

I concentrated now, startled by the venom building in his words. And for a horrible moment as his face completed its transformation I saw in Dan's eyes a new person. A weird person. The face readjusted quickly, the trace of anger crushed out by a smile that strained in its attempt at irony. But still he waited for my answer.

'Oh, come on.' I was wary, but had not yet understood the import of what I had said. 'I was just asking why you'd bother working all day and night if you're richer than any lawyer would ever be anyway? That's all.'

'Simon!' He seemed pained, astonished even. And there was something else – some violence, lurking below the surprise. 'I can't believe you've just said that,' he murmured. 'I thought you didn't give a shit about money.'

'Well, why show off to me that you might make a million a year, then?' I was still half-joking, in an attempt to pull him back to my conception of him.

'I thought you'd just shrug, like you always used to. I thought you didn't… That's what I love, that's what I used to love, about you.' Dan's tone was anxious, as if he was thinking fast.

'Come on. This is a bit mental.'

'Of course, you have no idea what it's *actually* like, coming from a family like mine.' He laughed suddenly, aggressively. 'Knowing that you'll never achieve more than—'

'Happy to try it out for a bit, if you like, just to see. A year or so, on Walton Square. Then we can confirm.'

'You're not funny, Simon. Don't you get it? You're not fucking funny!'

Then I saw the madness, the raw anger bound up with Dan's secrets, his private self. I saw the fists clench, the neck tighten, the eyes go wild – and I thought with a tinge of sadness how I had disturbed him, how there was something not quite right about Dan, something that was perhaps best left alone. Ever since I had seen him in tears at his desk that night years earlier, labouring over his essay, I had understood that there must be another Dan, inconsistent with my friend. But his reaction to my telling him who he was revealed a person as incomprehensible to me as Walton Square itself.

'Alright, alright. Sorry,' I said, but with a bit of a defiance. 'I'm being a dick, I suppose.'

'I'm going to the Gents.'

We made up quickly when he returned – as if we both needed to, in order to save the evening. I told him more about my year abroad, about the Neapolitan girl Mariella, showing him a picture of her that I kept in my wallet...

'Shit! She's like a model or something! Actually, she's *fitter* than most models! Mate! Not even I have pulled a bird like her.'

'Not even *you* – I've missed your narcissism.'

I told him how Mariella had loved me, how she'd thrown the contents of her kitchen at me in a Latin rage. Then I coaxed him gently into telling me more about his law firm, this Fiennes & Plunkett thing, saying in a spirit of conciliation that I was envious that he'd found his path.

'Dan, by the way, do you reckon they're giving us funny looks in this bar? The other Kants?'

'Of course not.' As if summoned by my vulnerability, the handsome, assured young man was back in front of me. 'Why would they be giving us funny looks? We'll be fine, don't worry. As I say, it'll be interesting – a chance to find out what these rahs are up to now.'

'I *love* it when you call them "rahs"! To be honest, though—'

'It'll be fine. We're here now.'

Presently there came the signal from Alastair and the Kants began to leave the bar, one small group at a time, walking proudly out of Trinity to the Market Square, where it was declared – once we had all arrived – that we would now *march like gentlemen* to Tandoori Dream on Jesus Lane. Was the language employed, this obsessive anachronism, actually ironic? A big, splendid, terribly clever joke? Or were they just utter morons? We began to march – or rather, walk – with our

Kants ties on, no coats under the heavy snow, but warmed by the three or four pints, and it was then, on that walk, that it began to fall apart. I had been right, Dan wrong, about the looks, the raised eyebrows. As the Kants crossed the Market Square, more akin to a gang of marauding chimpanzees than soldiers or gentlemen, we heard Freddie refer to me, in a voice too loud to care:

'Hmm? No, I was talking about the little tosser Haines, who never got initiated. I'm not happy, not happy at all at his audacity, showing up like this. All my own fault, this idea of inviting the dweebs. We should reverse the position! Hmm? I said that we should reverse the position, next year.'

Dan told me to ignore it, adding that everyone knew that Freddie was a joke, a guy who would never amount to anything, and that I should be proud that they'd been forced by my achievement, by my capability as a human being, to invite me. And remember, we'd leave early, have some more drinks in a quiet pub to catch up – and don't forget why we're here, to see what some of the non-jokers are up to! God, my friend Dan had charm when he wanted to use it – I stopped obsessing over Freddie's words and, as we passed by the front of Christ's College, Dan and I began to chat to a couple of alumni walking close to us – a man called Harry and a man called Patrick. Both of them were dark-haired, good-looking and extremely smartly dressed, but with that paunch that was something of a common theme among the majority of the Kants. They had graduated six months earlier and now worked together as analysts at some foreign bank or other – and oh, they had stories! They'd just returned from Chicago, business class. But our expectations of what it would be like to talk to this sort of alumnus soon crashed into disappointment. For their stories were empty – they were two children walking lost around a big city, a big world.

Worse, they knew vaguely about Dan's money, they'd heard of his father's fund in Mayfair, and so soon they were trying to charm him, but they were drunk and probably tired and they were getting in knots with the stories they were telling themselves about their own lives. And so, all lost, they began to become provocative. Harry asked Dan suddenly if he was from Essex, as if the question were somehow outrageous, then implied that they'd heard some 'tales' about Dan's dad in the City – Dan shrugged this off, not taking the bait. But the other one, Patrick, who wore a waistcoat under his blazer, couldn't stop grinning at the insinuation, his face a picture of naughty delight, and soon he turned his attention to me, staring at me, most amused, as I spoke in that voice that, despite my best efforts in situations like this, would never be *posh* – a voice that was trying too hard. There was hostility in the air and, as we turned to walk up Jesus Lane, Patrick could contain himself no longer.

'Your dad, mate,' he said to Dan, his eyes laughing hard. 'He's super-well known as the King of Hookers! They say there's not a—'

'Patrick, come on.'

'—not a high-class escort in London he hasn't fucked!'

Not cool. Dan became very quiet and cold, raising his hand to stop me answering back. I didn't know what he was thinking; I didn't know if it was true, if he knew it was true... We followed in a miserable silence as the chimpanzees in blazers charged into the curry house, the owner of the establishment, a short, gentle-looking Indian man, nearly pushed to the ground as he came to greet them.

'Dan,' I said, pulling back, 'let's leave this – let's go to the pub. It was a bad idea.'

But Serfontein was bristling. 'Not a chance,' he said grimly. 'We'll see it through.'

'That's an odd logic. Come on.' I grabbed his arm.

'I'm not backing down,' he said – and there was Weird Face again, suddenly – the face that peeked out for a second, from somewhere dark in Dan. 'It's only two idiots, anyway.'

'It wouldn't be backing down.'

'It would be, in their eyes.'

'Dan.'

'Walk away if you want – I'm going in.'

Where I followed him and where, of course, it soon turned very unpleasant indeed. The upstairs room reserved for the Kants was awash with lager and tequila and Armagnac, alive with excited cries of abuse. And it was the older members, the men Dan had assumed would keep things civil and who would have all these interesting stories to tell, who were behaving the worst by far. Having sat down to some tribal cheers, Dan and I each accepted a beer and then spoke only to each other, a fake conversation. But it was impossible not to hear the things being said around us.

'It was nothing like this on initiation,' Dan whispered quickly, between banal sentences. 'Initiation was harmless compared to this.'

There was so much drink that it was as if the room itself were liquid – as if we were swimming in alcohol. There was alcohol pouring down mouths, soaking the tables and the floor, staining the blazers. And they were saying some really horrific things now about girls, things that were so bad that they held your attention. Fuzzy-haired, obese Freddie – the former *legend* – was on his feet, regaling us with the tale of his experience with Lisa the Whore, a girl who had, in Freddie's day, got through the whole of Trinity's football team, and who had also been *spit-roasted* by Freddie and little Benedict on the goblin's birthday – that was to say, she had had sex with Benedict while giving a sexual favour to his fat-faced hero.

Freddie enjoyed saying *in my day, at Trinity* – he said it many times. The story now, the big one, was of when he came back from his last big Kants night out, and arrived *all messed up* – which I assumed meant drunk – at Lisa's room in Trinity. That night, after he had knocked on her door *all messed up*, she let him in but wasn't up for giving him a blow job. So, given that his cock was already out…

'Hoorah!' the Kants yelled, cutlery flying round the room, a glass smashing.

…given that his cock was already out, Freddie the Legend took the opportunity to use it, and pissed all over her bed – with enormous joy! And Lisa the Whore…

'Hoorah!'

…she chased him around the room in fury while he was squirting, his cock in his hand…

'Freddie plays for England, Freddie plays for England, la la la *la* la, la la la *la* la!' They sang hard, their faces fixed upon each other.

'A flagrant offence, however!' yelled Benedict, who was on his feet too now, quivering with excitement. 'You failed to fuck her!'

'Freddie failed to fuck her, Freddie failed to fuck her, la la la *la* la, la la la *la* la!'

'Stop! Stop and stand, gentlemen. To the Queen!'

'To the Queen!'

I wasn't sure that the Queen would have been flattered to hear the national anthem being sung by the Kants. It was very hot now in the whirlpool and I couldn't contemplate eating, so I was getting through a fair amount of beer. To the extent that I could think at all, I was back to wondering about irony – whether there might be a subtle, English sort of ambivalence here; whether they might be mocking the stereotype at the same time as embracing it. Whether to protest would be to show yourself to be the moron, to have missed the point. These doubts in truth were no more than a desperate hope, but an understandable one...

In any case the question of the extent of the irony didn't matter because, regardless, my body was reacting – I felt not quite pleasant rushes of testosterone, an aggression building in the pit of my stomach: it was the same feeling I'd had once as a teenager when, after we had lost the regional final, our Sunday league football coach, a big, fifty-year-old bully, had continued to scream into the face of our weakest player, who had become so nervous that he hadn't been able to look up. That time, I had sneakily thrown some mud from my boots at the coach's bald head, before cravenly turning away, to the great amusement of the team – it would be my last ever game for the Sunday league club. This time, eight years later in Cambridge, I was staring openly at Freddie, trying to get a reaction, with a kind of certainty that tonight I was going to be that same mix of hero and wimp: that I would say or do something very provocative but then try to run away. Dan, who kept repeating in a barely audible voice that the alumni had come back from London ten times more childish, seemed to know this too and so, as the order came that each Kant was now to down four shots of Armagnac, we changed roles.

'I've had enough, Simon. Come on, let's get out of here.'

'Aw, what are you on about? You're the one who wanted to come. And why cut short a night with these *legends*?' I spoke loudly, grinning at Freddie, who seemed to be wilfully ignoring me.

'Right, I'm serious – we need to go.'

But leaving was not straightforward, for the room had become a Court in Session, and Kant Bailiffs were at the door to prevent anyone who had been sentenced, or anyone else who couldn't take the lash, from escaping. Toilet breaks were permitted, for this was not initiation. But the 'weak, disgraceful souls' who needed to urinate were followed to the Gents by a minder. Oh, this was such fun!

However, one thing that *was* actually funny, as I began to note to Dan in a voice that was very loud now because I was feeling this wild testosterone and I was on my sixth pint, was that these alumni we'd thought would be doing amazing things in the real world, these men who wanted to look like leaders, aristocratic entrepreneurs – they all sounded so mediocre! There was this pathetic dishonesty, the need to mention the name of the friend who was doing outstandingly well, or the bank or the consultancy or the fund or the law firm, the unconscionable hours, the billion-dollar deals – but the story ended there, it being left unclear whether the person even worked for that institution, or even really knew it. It was a delicious thought, that these buffoons had had the shit kicked out of them by London, and that was why, perhaps, they were particularly obnoxious – because back here they felt safe. The chimpanzees had returned to their own Ilha Preciosa.

'Bunch. Of. Fucking. Losers,' I said in Dan's ear.

'Oi, gay boys,' shouted Freddie with exuberance, apparently injected with a sudden courage to look back at me directly. 'Bottom-fuckers – hey you, failed initiate! Let us into your private chat, will you?'

'Bunch. Of. Fucking. Losers.'

'What's he mumbling? What's initiation failure saying?'

But then Freddie became distracted, his attention returning to the task of sentencing a fine specimen of a man, as tall nearly as Dan, whom they called Big Al, and who had been caught eating in his room before the event, allegedly to build up his resistance to the alcohol.

'He stands convicted of a flagrant offence!'

'Flagrant!'

'A severe sentence awaits!'

Ah, the joy on the Kants' faces! But they had to know, surely inside they had to know what they looked like.

'Calm down with the tequila, Simon.'

'I've drunk the same as you have!'

'Yes, but you can't take it, remember.'

'Yeah, yeah. Not like you.'

Yes, the Kants *did* know how laughable they were, didn't they? It was brilliant, because they knew and they were furious about it. And they were angry about something else too and maybe, I thought, they were overdoing the rahness so grotesquely tonight because they had discovered to their dismay that, while still relevant, it was slightly *less* relevant down in the City? That, while they were still given special treatment – while life was infinitely more easy for them than it was for others – nevertheless it was not quite as easy as the Kants had expected it to be? This was perhaps the most prescient of my conclusions as a student. I couldn't know for sure, I had yet to experience how right I was – how, mixed among the old chums, rising above them in the City, there would be people like Angus Peterson from my firm: icy-cold superstars, nerds so devoid of personality that no societal aspect or influence, right or wrong, could ever figure in their identity. This I could only guess at – that tonight the Kants were reclaiming their selfhood, clinging to the relevance of a tribe founded on illusion.

'Bunch. Of. Fucking. Losers.'

'Oi! Shut it there at the back! The Court is in Session!'

'What *is* that little cunt saying?'

'It's Lincoln boy! He's up next. Biggest sentence of all. Only failed initiate in the room!'

'Lincoln boy's a wanker, Lincoln boy's a wanker, la la la *la* la, la la la *la* la!'

A young waitress was let into the room, the Kant Bailiffs standing aside with great theatre. She was dressed smartly in the restaurant's uniform, and she carried a large plate of chocolate éclairs and a bottle of vodka – the former had been ordered surely for their amusement value, their usefulness for those devising punishments. In my agitation I experienced a sudden panic about the waitress being black – I'd sensed undercurrents of jokey racism throughout the evening, heard bits of a repeated story about a male colleague of Patrick's who *really* hated whites; *genuinely hated them*. But nothing terrible happened now: after the waitress had given us a nervously spoken, entirely ignored warning about making too much noise, the door to the room was closed behind her. So she was safe, she had not been racially abused, and the sentencing of Big Al resumed.

'Bailiffs, that door is to remain closed during the accused's punishment!'

The sentencing went on and on, so profoundly lacking in humour, so sickeningly boring. But then the punishments began and soon my aggression was intensifying again, sobering me up, as I looked upon the treatment of the accused, his foolish laughter failing to conceal his discomfort, and thought also of what they were going to do to me next, thought how we were indeed trapped.

'Trousers down, you muppet, get stuck in, you muppet, la la la *la* la, la la la *la* la!' A quarter of an hour or so had passed. Big Al was on punishment number four: he was being ordered to simulate sex with a chocolate éclair. Dan had his arm on my chair – a protective instinct.

'I'll never forgive myself for bringing you here,' he was whispering. 'But you're getting me angry now, Simon. Let's *go – please* – before they start on you. There's no way they can really stop us leaving. I could take out those two Bailiffs

130

at the door easily, if I had to – but it wouldn't even come to that.'

'I can't watch this. I'm going to help him.'

'Big Al's fine – think about yourself! It's going to be a lot worse for you and I'm not standing for it. I'll drag you out if I have to. How did I get this all so fucking wrong?'

Probably I would have agreed with Dan in the end – probably I would have tried to escape. But the decision never needed to be taken – Simon Haines, the failed initiate, did not have to face his sentencing. Because now the event that ended the society was about to occur. Freddie the Legend stood up suddenly, before Dan could react, declared that Big Al had been punished enough, cleared his throat…

'Now, to Lincoln boy,' he said, as I saw Dan's neck muscles tense. 'There is only one man in this room who is not a true member of the society.'

'Foul beast!'

'Enemy of the state!'

'War criminal!'

'Quiet,' said Freddie. 'Quiet, men. Before we proceed to this evening's highlight, the punishment of the failed initiate, may we have another toast? To our society. Please all stand.'

But, with most infelicitous timing for Freddie – who was secretly very angry, remember – just as people began to get to their feet, there was a very loud knock on the closed door. The Bailiffs jumped, unprepared, and then the door was simply pushed open by that young waitress. She looked straight ahead, at nobody, as she said, 'Sorry, gentlemen. It's time to leave now. It's past eleven o'clock.'

There for a few seconds in that room a hostile, intimidating silence, as once more I went cold with fear of what they might say to her, because she was not white like them. Then came Freddie's voice.

'We are toasting our society, young lady,' he said. 'Now, back in your box – clear off. We've booked this room till midnight.'

Dan held me down, as the girl said bravely, 'No, really – it's time to leave.'

'Go and fetch your manager.'

'He's sent me up here. He thought it was best if I ask you first, so that this can be nice. We did warn you – you've been making too much noise.'

A cowardly owner, then – and a brave young girl. She had a sweet, proud face, a gaze that refused to lower. And a strong local accent – it's weird what you remember about big moments. It was the real Cambridgeshire accent, which I'd always liked, found peculiar. She was eighteen or nineteen probably, maybe a year younger, maybe a year older, you couldn't quite tell… The first chocolate éclair crashed hard into her face, the white cream exploding over her dark cheeks, and she jerked back in shock and probably pain – for it had hit her straight between the eyes.

'Éclair blitz, éclair blitz!' Freddie chanted manically, waving his chubby hands to whip up support – his momentary uncertainty at what he had done required reassurance. A validation which he then received – the éclairs began to fly across the room at the girl, who retreated, slipped on her way out and fell backwards onto the floor, to enormous cheers of victory.

'Éclair blitz, éclair blitz!'

Now, it is true, not all of the members of the Kants participated in the horror of those final moments of the society's existence, those moments of sad, filthy rage. Not all of them continued to throw chocolate éclairs, as hard as they could, at a distraught, humiliated teenage girl. Some of the men in the room protested, stood up and began to yell at

Freddie and Benedict and Patrick and the rest of the Presiding Judges, who were having glorious fun launching their missiles. Dan pushed his way out of the insanity and his big frame was in front of the girl now, trying to shield her. He helped her to her feet, took her downstairs, while I...

...while I, true to myself, rather than taking a course of action I would be able to look back upon one day with pride, decided to throw my own chocolate éclair – I decided to throw mine as hard as I could, at Freddie. It missed, and nobody saw it, and so, taken by a sudden delirious conviction, I did something now that was *not* like me at all – I picked up another one, rushed across the room to the Presiding Judges, and then slammed the éclair, with all the strength of my hatred, into Freddie's fat, wide-eyed face. And in the ensuing moments, during that strange silence I had caused, I felt so surreally *not there*, somehow *not me*, the dissociation I had felt at times at the end of my second year reaching an entirely new level, and I watched myself follow up suddenly, unexpectedly, with my right fist, smashing the bastard in the mouth with the first and only real punch I had ever landed anyone. The fuzzy head lurched back, Freddie was staggering and his lip was bloody and his face was covered farcically in cream. I stood still, wildly victorious, before someone hit me hard, winding me, and then I was pushed, and pushed again over a table onto the floor and I looked up to see little Benedict come over and try to stamp on my fingers – he missed. But he kicked me just above my stomach, exactly where I had been winded, and then spat on me, right down into my face, a sensation I would never forget. But then someone threw himself on Benedict and there was a riot now; Freddie was trying to get at me but I was already rolling under the table so his kicks had little impact, and, just as I made it to my feet and saw him preparing to charge, the Indian owner came in, screaming in an effeminate voice that he would call the police, and Dan was back, standing in front of me to protect me from a demonically enraged Freddie and things stopped...

...after that, a blur in memory. The owner probably did not call the police – certainly they never came. Later Dan and I were downstairs, apologising to the girl who, after her silence that was really just shock, was now in hysterics, and the owner was waving us away, telling us to get out as the rest of them had, stuffing the notes Freddie had left from the Kants kitty into my pocket and telling us he didn't want the money. The girl stopped him, began to scream that Dan was the kind one who had helped her, that there were a few kind ones, but the owner told her not to believe it, that we were all scum. And when this insipid man finally found his courage, calling me scum for the second time, looking up into my face – *you're scum, man, you're fucking scum* – I again felt somehow *not me*. I passed the notes to the girl and rushed out of the restaurant, disturbed and frightened, and found myself on King Street, behind Christ's College, where I sat down on the pavement and wept with hatred of myself, my decisions, my weakness. Had Harry really called the girl a silly black bitch as he'd walked out? I wasn't sure if this was true, as my good old imagination was not helped by drink.

I was still sitting in the snow when a Christ's porter came out of the back gate and looked at me in disdain and pity – my blazer was a mess of chocolate and cream, my shirt stained with blood and food and beer, my chinos wet.

'Get yourself to bed. You'll freeze out 'ere. Oi, you! Do I have to call an ambulance?'

I stood up and moved – I wasn't feeling so drunk, just *odd*. I made my way slowly back up through the snow to the Market Square, walking in emptiness. As I turned onto the white majesty of King's Parade, I saw, on the other side of the pavement, another figure walking alone. Dan saw me too and jogged over, nearly slipping.

'Where did you go? Freddie's in serious shit for this. Someone in the society called up Trinity. We'll be alright – the girl said I was her guardian angel.'

'Don't. I don't want to hear it.'

'Look, Simon, we're both a bit pissed. Let's go for a walk.'

'A walk? In this snow? Just get the hell away from me!' Seeing him, being compelled to return to a fierce connection with reality, had woken a rage I did not recognise, could not articulate. I took off my stupid blazer, flung it into the air.

'Well,' he sighed, 'taking that off is really going to warm you up.'

'Shut up! You've done this to me – you've turned me into this *wanker*!'

'What?' Dan sniggered, looking at the blazer lying in the snow. 'Don't be so childish,' he said. 'You know I'm not one of those lot. And nobody's turned you into anything. You're confusing things, as usual. Those guys are morons, terrible human beings. You can hate them for that, but you can't hate people just for being public school – you're so damn chippy, Simon. I used to like your chippiness, but if it's going to turn into—'

'I didn't want any of this! I didn't even want to go tonight!'

'Listen to him crying!' Dan's Weird Face was back. He was nearly ugly, Dan Serfontein himself was nearly unattractive, when Weird Face appeared.

'We've just seen a teenager get assaulted, basically,' he was saying. 'And you're whining about yourself.'

'Dan – you're talking to me about whining?' I felt terribly agitated. 'You, the man who was telling me in the bar how unbearable it is to be so rich? Oh, petal. You poor, spoilt, fucked-up little millionaire. Come here to Mummy. Poor baby.'

We were in front of Myths, a chic bar opposite Trinity, and the snow was falling hard; it was as if a white sky were descending upon us, about to envelop us, veil the world forever. Dan winced, adjusted his position, twisting his frame – and then stood quite still. I waited, goading him silently, looking at him with all the insolence I could muster.

'You chippy, immature little *shit*!' The voice when it came was an animal's cry. Lunging at me, Dan grabbed my shirt, lifted me into the air, held and shook me. 'This jealousy isn't *you*! What's happened to you?'

'Get off me!'

I wriggled in the strong man's grip as he glared into my face. But then I felt the hold loosen, the hatred begin to drain out of him and suddenly, as if he had seen something, he smiled – an amused but empathic smile.

'So *that's* it. You don't know what to do, do you?' Slowly he let me down and then he sighed, wiping the snow from his face. 'I'll tell you what you need to do – you need to grow up, mate.'

'What, like you, Dan?'

'If you're jealous, then you should go out into the world and stake your claim – you should show me how much better than me you are.' The words were ridiculous, the tone was a friend's, or more – a man who felt he had to explain things to me. 'You should show me, show those rahs what you can do.'

'But I'm not jealous, Dan. You don't understand. I don't care about money.'

'Those guys are all losers compared to you.' It was true, he didn't understand a word I was saying, but perhaps he knew that I didn't understand either. 'Half of them haven't got a penny anyway, just a posh voice and a few useful contacts here and there.'

'You're not listening.'

'And none of them are particularly good at anything; none of them are particularly bright. But you are, aren't you? You know you could do anything you wanted – and you're scared shitless about it.'

'Maybe you're right, I haven't grown up yet.' What I was trying to say was that I felt so tired, so indescribably upset. 'Maybe I still want to change things, change how everything works in this stupid country.'

'Nothing's changing, mate.'

'One day things might. I want to fight against what happened this evening, fight those bastards!'

'But the truth is…' Dan sighed again '…you don't really want to fight to protect poor waitresses, do you, Simon? Be honest – you just want to beat Freddie.'

'It's more complicated than that. I can't *stand* bullies, I can't fucking deal with them and—'

'You just want to *win*, Simon. To knock me off my perch, to be able to look down on Freddie one day, all your insecurity gone – and then tell him what a wanker he is. And good for you, I reckon – because you *should* win. You're the cleverest guy I know.'

'What are you *talking* about?'

'Look,' said Dan hurriedly, 'if you want my view, you're made for City law, actually. You should come down to London, with me. The law's just words and hard work, they say – that's all it is. You would utterly dominate it.'

And as he looked at me, two snowmen before each other on King's Parade, there was something earnest inside the voice that held my attention as if by hypnosis.

'And you've admitted you're not going to stay on here.'

'I haven't admitted that! I'm happy here – and Bonini's told me I'm assured the funding. There are loads of bursaries

137

available. Anyway, my options don't begin and end here – I could go into politics, I could—'

'Simon, Simon – you could do a thousand things. But wouldn't it be great if you were brave enough to go down there and really nail it in the City? You could make it as a partner of a top law firm – I won't. A leading mind in international finance, respected the world over. Intellectual, academic even, and you'd be rich, Simon. *Really* rich. And it'd be all your own money. You'd have earned it – not like a spoilt, fucked-up little millionaire, as you would say.'

'I didn't mean that.'

'London's where you need to be,' Dan said, with that disconcerting conviction made somehow stronger by the blithe tone, and it was as if I heard drums, beating away under the whiteness of the world. 'You need to at least try down there, in the City – and after you've tried you'll have a choice. *Then*, if you want, you can engage with this shitty world a little bit, see if you can make a difference. Or leave the world as it is – come back here, treat your mind. But if you try first in the City you'll come back here knowing the truth – that you genuinely prefer academia. That you aren't using it as an excuse, because you're afraid.'

'I'm not afraid of anything.'

'You know, you'd be the perfect lawyer.' Dan's smile had broken through Weird Face, which had faded out – he was Dan again. 'They say that City lawyers are the biggest moaners of all. I can see you now: loaded, still complaining.'

'Why are you so interested in me becoming a lawyer?'

'I'm not. Well, OK, I lie.' He winked. 'I *think* I've already corrupted you a little bit. I'd love to complete what I started.'

'Idiot, I was being serious. So what firm would you suggest, then, all-knowing maestro?' Unashamed, the ignorance, the stirrings under the false banter.

'Well, any of the big firms is a good bet. But come with me, to my firm. In fact, that's just what you'll end up doing.'

'Sure. That's exactly what I'll do. Ha! Which firm is that again, just so I know?'

'I told you a hundred times tonight – Fiennes & Plunkett. A tiny outfit when compared to the top ones. There's a Plunkett who still runs the place. They say he's an absolute nutter. But you could make a fortune there if you made partner. I had to do two vacation schemes, enormous amounts of sucking up, plus my dad knows Plunkett, which helped – and then I just got lucky. Whereas you could just stroll in.'

'Hmm.'

'It'd only be temporary – a brief delay for you before presiding over the restructuring of the social system, ascending to the new post of benign dictator of England.'

'Dickhead – you've made me laugh.'

'Come on.' He put his hand out. 'Tonight was shit. Mates?'

'Mates.'

But I wasn't laughing inside – oh, no. For there is no destiny more certain than that of an insecure young person to whom a goal is identified at a time when all that person wants is a goal. A young person standing under the snow before the Cambridge college he had never believed was real, trying not to think of Freddie and a tearful waitress. Feigning scorn, an entire lack of interest in what his friend is saying, while pretending inside to forget how his soul is wrapped up in words, in a fine hatred of bullies, in a potent, colourful ability to *imagine*. There is no prize more easily obtainable than the prize sought by that young man. As easy as spending on a credit card; as easy as constant flight, avoidance, failure to commit; as easy as a Chablis enjoyed alone on a London summer's evening, when nobody will see you, nobody will know ...

6

'HOLA,' I REPEATED, authoritatively now, to the line of squat barmen in Cojímar, as I leapt out suddenly from the past, like a dolphin from the waves. I'd resurfaced so as to engage, so as to grip a present that was sliding into nonsense. I had been in the Terraza de Cojímar for nearly half an hour, gazing down into my guidebook and retracing a decade's friendship, yet not one of them behind the bar had acknowledged my presence. Instead their banter between themselves continued, which was most improbable – I was the only customer, and tourists could expect to be mobbed, not ignored, in Cuba. I thought worryingly of how not just in this bar but in Cojímar generally nobody had ever spoken to me, nobody except the furious man who had demanded to know what I was doing in his village. Perhaps, I thought, it was because nobody could *see* me. My mind wandered back towards some Latin American literature I'd read at school – *Pedro Páramo*, or, better, that García Márquez novel, *No One Writes to the Colonel*. It felt eerily relevant. *No One Speaks to Simon. No One Can See Simon…*

'*Hola,*' I insisted, straining my face at the little bastards, one of whom now acknowledged me with a shade of reluctance. I was in danger of passing out in this heat if I didn't get some more water – this was a farce! To add to the discomfort, the interior of the Terraza de Cojímar was itself rather troubling. It seemed to be a bar rather than a restaurant, and there was no sign displaying its name, both of which facts might have led me to question whether I was in the right place, had it not been for its consistency with the description given by my guidebook. Consistency in the broadest of senses. For example, the guidebook had remarked merrily that the place had lots of old photos of Ernest Hemingway and Gregorio Fuentes. If ever there were an understatement – the walls of the bar were plastered with photographs of them, and of Castro too, photographs that in their infinite number, their indistinguishability, suggested hysteria. And I saw now that at the far end of the bar, set apart from everything, there was a solitary rocking chair – the chair on which Gregorio had once sat to tell stories? It seemed that, beneath the torpor, there was in this bar, in this village, a silent madness. Why had Hemingway come here? What man would berth his fishing boat at Cojímar? And why the eulogies about the place? Why had everyone told me to come here? Why Cojímar?

'Tell me,' said the barman who could see me.

Why do they all speak in English to me in Cuba? How is it so obvious that I'm English?

'A large bottle of water, please,' I said. 'And also – ' I took another look at my guidebook ' – a Don Gregorio.'

'*Eh?*'

'A Don Gregorio,' I said. 'I thought it was your speciality: dark rum and orange juice.'

'Ah, OK. A Don Gregorio for the man.'

I heard a snigger from the end of the bar. But they shouldn't be sniggering, as it was they who had covered the walls with photographs of Gregorio Fuentes. My guidebook had highlighted the drink as one of the 'things to do' in Cojímar. So what was wrong with ordering a Don Gregorio? Why were they sniggering? Why Cojímar? When, shortly after the bottle of water, a bland rum and orange juice arrived for the outrageous price of eight *pesos*, I refused to admit disappointment, refused to be destroyed by the barman. Instead, commenting that the cocktail looked delicious, I gulped it down in one.

'Another?' he said.

'I might go for a rum and orange juice instead. How much is that?'

'Eight *pesos*. The same.'

'In that case,' I confirmed, 'I will indeed have another Don Gregorio.'

These were precarious moments, as the temptation to find refuge in the security and gentleness lent to the world by the early moments of drunkenness competed with a sense of shame at the prospect of descending into it by midday. But by the third cocktail all my worries were abating. I was beginning to revel in the sensation of performing on a stage, wishing my friends could see me here as I played the role of Englishman lost abroad, and I was telling myself that this was all stupendously funny, that one day I would have Dan and Clemmie, Toby and Arabella, in fits of laughter. This bar was so *shit* that there was something brilliant about it! How polite and serious I had been as I had ordered that sandwich to accompany the third Don Gregorio! They were all so short and ugly and rude … and the day was young and this was all so *funny*. It was in this mood that I remembered Gregorio's house, and the challenge to find it gained a new edge. It would be another let-down, for sure! But I would take a photo of myself outside it, looking ironic and puzzled and infinitely superior! Why Cojímar? Ha!

I got down from my stool. 'I'll be back shortly,' I declared. 'I'm off to see Gregorio's house.' I had to ask three times, but finally the barman drew a map for me on the back of a beer mat.

It was a poor decision. With the alcohol wearing off, leaving irritability and paranoia, for the second time I spent a long period wandering around that village in that extreme heat, in search of the former home of Gregorio Fuentes. The map, and in particular the multiple, contradictory arrows that resembled Rupert Plunkett's manuscript amendments to a contract, became a source of torment, leading me away from the centre of the village, through some admittedly now pretty streets, but then suddenly down, back down to Calamity Bay. There I stopped and turned the beer mat around and around in my hands, wanting to spit at the arrows, staring furiously at the X that marked Gregorio. Finally, I had to accept that I did not understand the map... With a sigh, I let it drop from my hands into a rusty bin on the promenade. Then, standing alone in the sun, suddenly I laughed, thought about heading back to the bar for another Don Gregorio.

...Although first maybe I'd pop inside this desolate souvenir shop looking down onto the muddy water, with its ragged green awning, its dusty windows. Maybe inside, in its sad essential quiet, a Cuban would appear, a man who knew of Gregorio's house. Probably not... The plasterers were shouting again from the Monument to Hemingway and it was all very strange, a City lawyer walking lost and fearful and stressed like this, while waiting to hear the news of whether he was about to become a millionaire. What had Dan said

143

that night? That I could end up rich, seriously rich? Yes, maybe I *would* look around this shop – with a bit of luck it would have a fan, and it would be good to delay the next Don Gregorio because there was so much to ponder with a clear head before it was too late. Years and years of rolling memory. Yes, afterwards, unless the idea of another drink had become irresistible, perhaps I would just keep walking awhile...

YOU COULD MAKE *a fortune there.* I'd been twenty-one, that night under the Cambridge snow, when Dan Serfontein had explained what I would do with my life. Twenty-one: where had eleven years gone? After that conversation, that debacle with the Kants – and somehow I had known it, as I had entered my chilly room in Clare College that night – neither he nor I would ever again be the same person. Dan forfeited some of his coolness that night, lost it to the Weird Face and the clenched fists and the hang-ups about his dad, while I lost or found my path, a schism forming in my soul. Soon I'd achieved my treasured First, been offered a training contract by Fiennes & Plunkett, rejected Professor Bonini... *London's where you need to be...* Down there in the capital, at law school, there were other Dans, men as good-looking, cooler, a couple of international students richer even than him. And despite the fact that he had arrived fresh from a year's break after Cambridge, a year of hedonism spent circumnavigating the earth on the magic carpet of family money, he was soon worn-out, stressed. The school became a torment for him, his struggle no longer capable of concealment now that we all studied the same subject, now that the classes were more 'interactive', people being asked questions on the spot. He had surged ahead for the first week of term, delighting in the formulaic multiple-choice questions, perhaps thinking he had found *his* niche. But then I and many others simply readjusted to the style of thinking, or to the coldness of thought, that was required. And the questions became trickier, more numerous – so we all overtook him, left him flailing.

It was at this time, during our first year of jurisprudence down in London, that Dan and I began to drink harder, and more regularly too – this was hardly remarkable, to be fair: it was impossible to avoid lashing at City Law School. The four pints that had once caused a mild hangover were now the warm-up – the 'microlash', or the 'pre-dinner lash'. The microlash in the Ring of London Bells, the pub opposite the fine school, often merged into megalash in Fulham, apocalash on Upper Street. While our drinking was all wrapped up in the bigger truth that everyone else was doing it, that it was completely normal to do it, Dan and I drank for different reasons in those days, I supposed. He had understood, he must have already understood, that he was chasing an illusion. The goal of making his own millions in the law, rendering his father less relevant, moved farther away the faster he ran, the more he struggled. Perhaps it was that very premature, comprehensive nature of the defeat that led to his refusal to admit it – it would be years and years before he would be compelled to be brave. Whereas I was flying towards Ilha Preciosa, my head brimming with outrageously narcissistic visions – even the vague fantasy of becoming the Executive Chairman of Fiennes & Plunkett came to seem banal, insufficiently extraordinary – I could do *anything*.

So why was I getting pissed all the time? Because everyone else was, because I found the subject dull, the law school students even duller: it was relatively rare to come across a human being in that centre of excellence who had, or rather who admitted to having, anything to say – anything other than the name of the sponsoring law firm, or how wasted we'd all been the previous night. And there should have been so much to say – outside, in the real world, the public was engaged; there was uproar. Blair was taking us into Iraq and millions of protestors, young and old, were marching in Westminster, right past the law school, while inside the school's walls the City's future lawyers prattled on about the electives we'd be taking the next year, how *absurd* it was that the Law Society made us study criminal and probate law, such a waste of time. *Did you see, like, the* state *of Pete last night? Fancy a bit of minilash in a bit? Mate, let's wait till all those people have headed off first. It's, like, really mental out there still with all those protestors!*

But I knew even then that there were other reasons for my drinking, reasons that lay beyond boredom. I missed Sophie still, missed her so much that I felt nauseous when I thought of her, despite my stubborn front, despite ignoring her when she had tried to get back together. And, more disturbing still, ever since the first days of law school there'd been this intermittent, intrusive voice in my head, a voice that I needed to escape from, the voice of the Simon who loved Naples and its colours and words, and who was now repeating neurotically, profoundly unhelpfully, that this law thing was *all wrong*. The voice reminded me when I woke, whispered to me in the night, that I didn't *like* business law, that I was often uncomfortable with its paranoid, sociopathic rules and objectives, its obsessive focus upon ensuring that there were no mistakes, that any advantage be maximised, any opportunity secured, any weakness seized upon. It was true that, in principle – the term 'in principle' was used a lot at law school, only marginally less gratingly than *prima facie* – *in principle*, those rules were equally available for use by the rich and the poor; the strong and the vulnerable. But this didn't seem the true spirit of the course to me – some of these rules seemed so much more useful for a person already in a position of power. We learnt how to ensure that our client, the major bank, would get paid out before the others in the event of the insolvency of the borrower; we learnt how to be ruthless towards the desperate seller of a business, demanding, with haughty self-righteousness, a litany of promises; we learnt how to be even more ruthless to a purchaser, negotiating caveats to those same promises, caveats to the caveats to the caveats to those promises. The whole course, every lesson, every statutory and contractual provision, founded on the extraordinary notion that it was somehow of essential importance to society that the figure that logically *should* prevail *did* prevail. That the rational argument should win. In this way, the freeholders, the couple of aristocrats who owned most of Chelsea, in a thousand years would still have their property; in this way, if you left no will, ultimately all your land would go back to the Monarchy.

'Oh, the boy really does want a revolution!' Dan would enthuse, patting me on the back. 'A closet commie!'

No, no. You don't want a revolution. You just want to slink away, while nobody's looking – to go somewhere far from here. To Naples.

'Very funny!' I stuck two fingers up at him. 'Anyway, it'll be different once we get to the firm. Fiennes & Plunkett's *raison d'être* is basically to rescue companies – I was reading the blurb again the other day. Obviously there'll be some work for the banks too, but the majority of the time we'll be acting for the underdogs.'

'Mate.' Dan had stopped laughing. 'You don't really think – don't tell me you actually think—'

'Think what?'

'Nothing, nothing.'

So I was drinking principally to run from that damn voice, which I began to call 'Mr Naples' in an attempt to destroy it, to delegitimise it through humour. He was malicious, Mr

Naples, intruding when I was at my most tired – he should have just left me alone, I was doing so well! I was on a road to somewhere, and I had never claimed the road itself to be beautiful. And anyway, while it was true that there was no nourishment, I found that if I really tried I could squeeze out some interest from the law school materials – the more you concentrated on the detail of the statutes and the cases, losing yourself in the words, the more the subject became a self-contained intellectual game and you could get close, so close, to forgetting the underlying content. It was just a road, anyway – and once I began at Fiennes & Plunkett it would be all change. Restructuring failing companies, saving them, earning a million pounds a year.

In some parts of the Centro Storico in Naples, the word for a bike is a ting-tang. *A* ting-tang! *And there was a family you knew in Chiaia, they used to call a mirror the* scostumato, *or 'the rude thing' – they had such* fantasia, *as they say over there. Do you remember when you first kissed Mariella, outside L'Arancia? Her lips? Do you remember her insanely beautiful face, the way she spoke, that Italian laced with dialect? Your incredulity that you'd kissed such a beautiful girl? Do you ever think of those mornings when the sun woke you together, entangled on her low bed? That sun in Naples – it was crazy bright, it would skim the Tyrrhenian, tracing a path from the mainland to Capri. Do you remember the morning when the porter delivered you a present from the old woman who lived upstairs on Corso Vittorio Emanuele? She'd made you an enormous cake, soaked in rum, for no reason at all.*

Law school was just a road, and despite my indifference to business I was doing better than so many of the students who actually read the *FT*, the guys who had convinced themselves that they really were interested by the news that a financial institution had sold a subsidiary. Indeed, my ego was blooming – save for when Mr Naples forced himself in – because this stuff was *easy*.

Dan would encourage this sort of thinking when we drank hardest.

'Mate, I despise you – you're pissing these exams! You need to ride the wave! Partnership, mate – a hundred grand a month! Do that for ten years and then, who knows?'

He was still in love with my diminishing innocence, seeming both forlorn and elated to watch it seep out of me, and I felt the same ambivalence at the hint that his old assurance might be abandoning him, slowly. Once when we were in the Ring of London Bells I knocked into a girl who was carrying two large glasses of red wine. The wine was like a sea of blood over my new white shirt – a shirt that in those days I considered precious, extremely expensive. Dan smiled at my turmoil. 'When you're a partner, you'll never wear the same shirt twice. And you certainly won't wear shirts like *that*!'

In this way the first year of City Law School passed. The world outside was aflame: they were searching frantically, unsuccessfully, for weapons of mass destruction in Iraq, the government was at war with the BBC and, just before our results came out, Dr David Kelly was found dead...

'Nuts, isn't it?' Dan said – we were walking through Covent Garden, past the deafening musicians, on the way to an almighty piss-up. 'Don't see where it's all going to end. Now, come on then – out with it.'

'Out with what?'

'You know, dickhead. Your result. You got a Distinction, didn't you?'

'Yep – but loads of other people did too.'

'You git! I hate you!'

A short time later, in the August before the start of the second and final year of law school, there came the big change – the grand reconciliation with Miss Sophie Williams. And so began *Simon and Sophie* Act II. A light had switched back on in my head, maybe Mr Naples had switched it back on, and my love for Sophie – love that had become tied up in humiliation and bitterness – became pure again, so fresh that I forgot even my ego awhile. At times my happiness seemed almost unnatural, reaching such heights that I couldn't express it even to myself; instead I would wander the streets of Fulham, try to write it down in notes to her. I saw less of Dan that year and so was drinking a bit less too, but there was still always the opportunity for a quick microlash with him before heading back home after law school. Or, once arrived at home, sometimes I'd do what City people did: take the sting out of things with a stiff double.

Then came another summer, law school had ended, Sophie had adored the first year at her new school, she was thriving and had found herself, and she and I... *But enough about Sophie for the moment – still not ready to think too much about Sophie. It's too intense, too complicated...* In September of that year I started as a trainee solicitor at Fiennes & Plunkett, and within weeks Mr Naples was getting even louder, and Sophie loved Mr Naples; but Ilha Preciosa was back too, and I became caught up in their war. And as the battle raged I felt myself being pulled away from Sophie, helpless like a man drifting away in space, drifting away from her despite myself, away from the person she wanted me to be.

But it's not 'despite yourself' – it's all within your control, it's your choice, Mr Naples would note, and he would tell me that I was ignoring my heart and so I was doomed, that I might end up mad – but Mr Naples was pretty fucked-up himself, so I wasn't sure about that. I began to work even harder, on a mission to become the best trainee solicitor in the intake, and as a sort of consequence the lashing with Dan soon became more regular again – I would leave the office very late and then party until the early hours with him and the other trainees, sometimes for three, four consecutive nights. Rupert Plunkett had noted to my supervisor that I was a fine young solicitor, and this made me so proud … I was in Rupert's grand office, one of a group of trainees and associates who'd been up all night with him, when the news came that there'd been bombs on the London Tube, on a bus in Tavistock Square. Mobile phones weren't working in London. I spoke to my parents from my office and then tried to call Sophie's mum, but she wasn't answering. My supervisor, a big, kind Geordie, came in panting, saying that he couldn't get in touch with his wife, that one of the trains they were talking about, the one on the Circle line, was the train she always took. That the train was *her* train.

'You don't know that for sure – don't panic, Matt.' What could one say? 'She's probably alright. Just—'

'My wife!'

And it was contagious – I felt hysteria about Sophie, who I knew would have been at the school before the bombs went off, but I needed to hear her voice and it was sickening to think how she would be worrying about me. Some mobile phones were working again, but hers was not. I was telephoning Burnaby Street Primary for the third time when a message came from my secretary that a young lady was waiting for me at reception. Her eyes were swollen, and she was pale.

'Oh, thank God, Simon!' She jumped to her feet, came running into my arms and hugged me hard. 'I had this weird, horrible sense,' she whispered, 'I had almost this *certainty* that you were on one of those trains.'

'I love you.'

'Your switchboard's blocked.'

'I know. Look, we're both OK.'

'No, you don't understand.' She kissed my neck softly. 'It was like I just *knew* that you were on one of those trains – that you'd jumped on, a second before the doors had closed. Oh, all those people. Those poor, poor people.'

Two years ripped by, the training contract was over, Dan and I qualified as associates and now the gloves came off – and between the work and the lashing there wasn't much time for Mr Naples. Slowly he was losing the war, his voice arriving only in the early hours, when my head rested on the pillow and I was so tired that he couldn't speak for long. Mr Naples was also losing because, despite the surreal demands, despite my initial sharp disappointment at the realisation that Fiennes & Plunkett did not have a holy mission to save companies in financial difficulties – an epiphany that Dan found hilarious – there was a part of my job that had become intensely enjoyable. The law was dry, for sure, not rich like literature or linguistics, but at Fiennes & Plunkett the game was so fiercely, absurdly intellectual that there was a physical thrill to be had in solving an apparently unsolvable legal conundrum, ascribing an alternative meaning to a contractual restriction, finding a way through the mass of words to enable the client to do what they wanted to do, drafting a clause packed tight with meaning that satisfied dozens of different stakeholders, for dozens of different reasons. It was a pleasure that was inherently transient, yes, squeezed between one anxiety and another, and there was an extraordinary amount of pain required to get there, but boy was it deep, that pleasure, when it arrived! And as an associate it was seriously cool to be doing well, not something you needed to downplay occasionally like at university, so within the firm's walls I was becoming ever stronger, Dan ever weaker. Although when it came to the now limited time we had outside the firm – our drinking time, effectively – the change in our relationship was less altered. In this context I often recognised our old relationship, my admiring inferiority, his ability to reassure from above.

More years… Now it was 2008, over in America there was a black man full of hope who was going to change the world, and the only secret downtime I had save for the cigarette breaks in the firm's smoking pit and the whiskies on my terrace was my sneaky checking of the BBC website, the *Guardian* website, to follow the excitement out there. In meetings I would Google the latest polls on my BlackBerry; I would think about the stakes for America while Rupert gave me instructions on a term sheet for a loan, acting out my own rebellion, an assumption of a right to care. I felt somehow *involved*, praying that Obama would win, obsessing over whether he would win; it became the only thing that mattered to me. For it was beautiful, I was falling in love with Barack Obama, falling in love with all the abandon of my soul, and nobody knew and nobody could stop me. And then he *did* win, a black guy had finally won, and somehow I felt that I had won too – that he and I had won it together. The next evening seemed an imagined moment, but on an impulse I left the office early, negligently early, with a thousand emails pending. Inside the flat on Munster Road, a space unfamiliar at this time, a slim, tall, pretty girl with beautiful brown eyes was sitting on our beige sofa watching the news, a smile on her face. There was a cheap bottle of champagne open on the table. She looked up, startled, when I came in.

'Simon – you're home early!'

'I couldn't stay late tonight.' My voice felt distant.

'Now, Simon, listen,' Sophie was saying – she seemed nervous. 'Before we start – I really don't want to argue tonight. I'm sorry for anything I said, but can we leave it? It's just that today's special for me – something I believed in happened for once – and so I want to drink this whole bottle of champagne, and be happy. I've been following this election so closely, you know.'

'Obama!'

'What?'

'He bloody won, Sophie! My hero won!'

I ran over to the sofa, laughing wildly, and there Sophie gazed up at me as she took my hand; she looked deep, searchingly, into my eyes. And she was helpless in those moments, begging me silently to forget all the mess of our relationship, to leave it all alone. And so we were on the old sofa, the old Simon and Sophie, drinking her champagne, as we watched Obama's speech again and again and again and again.

'*Change* has come to America,' I said for the twentieth time, as she sobbed with drunken laughter.

'And to think I never even asked you,' she whispered. 'And you never asked me. Honestly, we're such a silly pair.'

A few months before that evening with Sophie, an evening I could never be sure had been quite as I remembered it, Fiennes & Plunkett had had their great stroke of luck – the financial crisis. In the first days of the meltdown we had done no work at all at the firm: our clients, even the creditors, in a sort of stupor, the partners holding austere day-long meetings in their Partners' Meeting Room. On the television, bankers and traders our age were filing out of buildings with cardboard boxes, managing to look pretty cool in the process – among them was a guy who looked just like Lawrence. I'd phoned my old friend, whose arrogant, cold voice did not belong to the distant genius I had known, and he'd clarified that of course it wasn't him. Meanwhile the majority of law firms were freezing immediately all salaries for all young lawyers. In America, terrible things were happening. But at Fiennes & Plunkett...

At Fiennes & Plunkett, one fine day, a month or so before that night with Sophie, Rupert had gone back to first principles.

'At Fiennes & Plunkett, we do financing *and insolvency*,' he had reminded us in his Annual Address, the whisper alive with harsh glory. 'That is all.'

'And, erm, real estate,' his trusted old deputy chairman had added, his face white with tiredness. 'Which is even more relevant now, given the sub-prime mess.'

'Yes, alright. Fine. Yes, we also do real estate.'

The financial crisis had been Rupert Plunkett's *moment* – with a quiet suddenness, his firm, the firm his father had left in his hands, had bolted into life, into levels of work that not even he had ever seen before, would ever see again. Everyone coming to us – the companies, to be saved; the creditors, to claw back anything they could.

'At Fiennes & Plunkett, we do financing and insolvency. That is all.'

And so, already by the time of that night with Sophie, the work had become so dizzying that time no longer made sense – and it continued like this, the years racing by but in slow motion. Trainees were preparing and then sending out piles of termination notices, notices of default, checking frantically whether the financial ratios had been breached, reviewing the terms of the cross-defaults. Associates were taking on obscene amounts of responsibility, negotiating waivers, rescue packages, discussing angrily the terms of the 'waterfall', which dictated who would be paid out first. Every lawyer was insane. Years of this... Dan was on girlfriend number six thousand, the latest in a line of moody, beautiful models he saw only on Friday or Saturday nights, and now we were senior associates and the tipping point had come and gone, that Grand Exodus when lawyers from our intake had deserted, broken by the week. It was *Big Brother* now, the prize millions of pounds. The politics had become acute among those who remained, the group socialising, the team nights out, well over.

But there were no politics between me and Dan, and the beers after work weren't over, not for us – we were back alone in our drinking, where I suppose we were both more comfortable, continuing our secret, insolent party, any time we got a chance. We'd refined the lash to its purest of forms – often we would spend long periods of time not speaking to each other, both on our BlackBerrys, smoking ciggies and drinking our pints outside one place or another. If we were both done at the firm by one o'clock in the morning, we'd find somewhere to drink, even if it was Soho, outside a dodgy bar, surrounded by pushers and pimps. After all, the world was a joke, every day an extended period of hysteria spent in search of those brief intense highs of signing the loan agreement, filing the charge. And over in America they were trying to destroy Obama, preventing him from implementing his dreams, and back at home things were going very badly now with Sophie. The arguments had become far less vehement, far less true, but somehow more exhausting, and some cold, objective *dislike* of me seemed to be growing in her, a faint disgust at how I could go months at a time without a free weekend, without eating properly, without sleeping more than three hours a night. Once she even asked, quite calm, whether I'd faked my excitement about Obama that evening we'd been happy together. I hadn't, but sometimes now, mixed with the shot of anxiety, I would experience a sick delight when Rupert Plunkett arrived in my office with that grave face to ruin my evening, thinking how I would not have to go home to restart some absurdly complex argument with Sophie that had been left pending, an argument I could hardly remember. And of course sometimes Sophie was still up when I returned after the harrowing evening with Rupert and the few drinks of alleviation with Dan, and she would claim that I hadn't worked late at all, that I'd just been boozing all night, at which I'd shake my head, too tired to disagree. She'd go on and on about it as I changed for bed, repeating the same old line:

'Some men are just not made for heavy drinking, Simon.'

But one day this would be over; we'd get through it. I just needed to 'suck it up', as they say in the law, and I would drag us out of this madness with the enormity of my achievement. Emma Morris, Angus Peterson and I were charging ahead and I knew that I was brighter than Emma, and was more or less as bright as Psycho. So I would keep going, work and drink my way through to the conclusion, whatever that might be – this was my contract with the gods.

Some men are just not made for heavy drinking, Simon.

Partly, Sophie was right – I couldn't take my beer the way Dan could, and I knew that my old edginess when drunk was no longer always funny. Occasionally I could be shocking now, outrageously rude, particularly to guys I considered to be overbearing or to have a nasty streak, the secret bullies of trainees, and my jokes had become malicious, thick with a hostility that was out of character. It was Mr Naples meddling again, maybe... I would be woken the next morning by a thunderous anxiety, waves of self-loathing at the vague recollection of what I'd said or done the night before, but then I would see the time, consult the BlackBerry and look in terror at the missed emails. I'd run to the shower, clean my teeth twice, make Sophie her breakfast, which I'd promised myself I would always do, take it up to her and try to look fresh and not hungover when I kissed her sleepy face goodbye. It was lovely, that sleepy face – not yet conscious enough to remember the past, to resurrect the bitterness of yesterday, to remember that she wasn't happy with me. And then I would head to the firm, a leading senior associate at the law firm of Fiennes & Plunkett, the shame of the night before now long gone. Fourteen hours later I'd be fine…

Dan in those days was living a nightmare at the firm worse even than mine – he was by far the weakest of the remaining lawyers in our intake, and he knew it and knew that everyone else knew it too, yet he was just refusing to accept defeat. It was an extraordinary achievement that he was still even there, a testament to his rage at his father's shadow. Things just took him longer, and so he was having to work far more than any of us, hours that were dangerous even for a man of his physical strength, which was why he was also drinking so hard. But still he never became arsey when drunk, remaining always in control. Unlike me – it was frightening sometimes, my new unpredictability with drink: there was a self-destructive element and occasionally Dan had to save me. At a Fiennes & Plunkett Christmas party one year, in the fine reception room reserved usually for client events, looking down onto the lights of the City with champagne and canapés, I just wouldn't let something go. I'd been talking about Italy, as I tended to do when tipsy, as if asking for someone to wind me up, and then others had started talking and one of the firm's oldest partners, Duncan Green – a bespectacled, long-nosed man who also claimed to speak Italian – had been predictably obnoxious about the South. My South! Oh, the fury of Simon Haines!

'Absolutely dreadful. In some areas the rubbish actually *flows* through the streets,' he said to some eager trainee, as the circle of lawyers listened intently. 'Totally corrupt, too. The Bel Paese is like two countries, you see. There's the North: Milan, Turin, Genoa, the engine of the nation. And then, on the other hand, there's Rome, which is already dodgy, and, south of that, Naples and all the rest, it's just wretched, like some godforsaken part of—'

'Ever been to Naples?' I asked pleasantly.

'Did someone speak?' The doyen of credit default swaps turned to me with false humour. I saw a couple of associates looking nervous behind him; a trainee peeling away from the circle.

'Yes, I asked whether you've ever actually been to Naples,' I clarified. 'The city you've just claimed is wretched.'

A senior associate, aiming at partnership. A senior associate with a real chance, who knew full well that lawyers had failed in the past because of the smallest of personal slights, political slips. Yet give a man with a dash of Irish blood some romantic fixation, ply him with a few drinks, stir it all up with a perceived injustice from a snob and what do you get?

But no, it was darker than that, wasn't it? Was it Mr Naples at work?

'I'm not sure I've ever properly made your acquaintance.' Duncan Green had frowned briefly at my impertinence – now he remembered to smile, stretching out an old, wrinkled hand with a fine passive-aggressive animosity. 'It's Haines, isn't it?'

'Yes, Simon Haines,' I said – finding something so intensely comical, hearing the laughter roar inside me. 'So.' I paused. 'Yay or nay? Have you *been* to Naples?'

'Yes, ahm, got it.' A great hush had fallen upon the circle. The wise old partner seemed suddenly excitable – sharpened and enlivened. Then: 'As I say, I've passed through on the way to the islands.'

'Ha!'

'Oh, I'd love to do that!' A tall, strikingly handsome associate with very blond hair had pushed in front of me. 'Which islands? I'd love to see Capri.'

'My wife and I saw all of them – Capri, Procida, Ischia.'

159

'Procida! That's famous for some reason, isn't it?'

'Has. He. Ever. Been. To. Naples?'

The next morning I woke very early, often the case after drinking, and in a state of high anxiety charged to the firm where, after spending the next few hours reliving the conversation, trying to find out more about Green, I discovered to my fleeting delight that the bastard would be retiring in three months' time. Surely he wouldn't pass the story onto the other partners? Would he, Dan? They were vicious, weren't they, the old guard – would he get me for this? Had I blown everything? He was a bit drunk himself, wasn't he? No? He wasn't drinking? Oh, shit! But was he – how angry did he seem? Just cross, or angry? Did I seem drunk? No, I was OK?

Life had turned very ugly, and things felt all out of control, a derailed train. The lack of sleep meant that memories had become mixed up with dreams, and maybe Mr Naples had been right, maybe I would end up seriously insane – sometimes, as we went through the security documentation after an all-nighter, for the briefest of moments I would see Rupert sticking his tongue out at me, his face creased with laughter, or his whisper would become an old witch's voice, and a brass band would begin to play. But the young doctor told me that this was probably just exhaustion, that the human mind was not made to stay up all night and keep going the next day. He added that alcohol certainly didn't help, that it could itself cause psychosis in extreme scenarios. Hardly relevant in my case, I retorted jokingly: I was not exactly an alkie suffering *delirium tremens*. No, he agreed, but you must watch things…

Sophie still lived in the same flat, shared the same bed, but we were not in each other's days. The characters on stage were Dan and Rupert Plunkett and my trainee who changed every six months, and the nice old lady in the canteen who served crappy cappuccinos that burnt your tongue, and the two lawyers who, it was clear, would fight me to the end: red-cheeked Emma with her mousy-brown hair, and the pale man with the unblinking grey eyes. Way back behind us Dan was toiling on, and I was trying to tell him to stop, without offending him. The days and nights really were weird now, *so* weird, and I'd developed these strange new compulsions that would appear only in the early hours, like needing to touch the screen with my right hand if I'd accidentally touched it with my left, or making sure that if I said yes or no I said it a second time to myself, as it was very important that the numbers remained even, you see. And sometimes, when I was really exhausted, it was as if someone had muted all sound – a pure, terrific silence would fall, and eventually I would need to cough or tap my desk to ensure that I hadn't gone deaf. And of course, if I tapped the desk with my right hand, I'd need to tap it again with my left. If I coughed, I would have to cough quietly a second time.

Those fresh bacon sandwiches at dawn, the mad ciggie lash, chaining the ciggies in the smoking pit. Those rare escapes on the day following an all-nighter, the evening running away too fast, neither Dan nor I wanting to go home … *a couple more pints, it's only ten o'clock, we deserve it after what we've just been through* … the rain bitter, no sleep for over thirty-six hours, our hands freezing as we smoke our cigarettes outside the pub in a Dickensian alley of the City, side by side under the semi-shelter of the pub's doorway. And the awfulness of the completed deal dispersing as the two men in their thirties recount it in a fog of catharsis, rewriting it in their minds as they begin to almost babble with tiredness, the deal transforming in memory, becoming hilarious, prestigious and especially *dramatic*. Dan, however, still cooler, more composed.

'That prat Ed Griffiths, at some point during the night he started showing off to us,' he says, shaking his head. 'Such an embarrassment of a partner. His lazy eye was completely out of control, a picture of stress, mate – but he wanted to play Mr Chilled, to show what a cool young partner he is, so he put the phone on mute while we were waiting for the call to begin and began whistling away to himself as he read his notes. Emma was deeply unimpressed, scowling at him, as you'd expect. She's got a kind of honesty about her, hasn't she, Emma Morris?'

'Not sure about that. She's a ball of stress herself, that's all I know!'

'Whereas Angus was just lapping it up, beaming at him! It was like a horror show!'

'Ed Griffiths is a complete *dick*!' I say suddenly – I know I'm shouting, but somehow I can't help it. 'He's the partner I hate most! Do you remember what he did to that tall, weird associate, what was his name? Ed used to come in around eight and leave comments on his desk for him to type up overnight! Overnight, *every* night!'

'Alright, mate, calm down – Jesus! Listen, here's something fucked up for you. Talking about bullies – apparently Mr Evil is leading the juniors off to Infinitum again tonight, to celebrate.'

'Angus? He's going to Infinitum, *again*?'

'Yep. Angus Peterson in a strip club – it's not a great image, is it?'

'I can't, I mean, I just don't get the *point* of a strip club. I've never been in one, you know? Or maybe once, on a stag do. I can't remember.'

'You're not missing much.'

'Fuck, Angus makes me shudder! The blond hair, baby face and the empty eyes!'

'His hair's not real blond. It's kind of colourless. *This*, mate, is blond hair.'

'Fuck off, you love yourself! Ha! Anyway, Angus – do you reckon he's *genuinely* evil?'

'Angus? Oh, definitely. You know he told me he'd mentioned in his self-appraisal with Plunkett that his weakness was that he "didn't delegate enough"? Can you believe it?'

'You've told me that one!'

'He's already made two junior associates leave through his own peculiar form of "delegation". And I reckon it's eight trainees that he's made cry.'

'Those mental eyes! And what's he *doing* in a strip club – he's got a wife!'

'That's a weird enough thought to start with, though – how did Angus Peterson find someone willing to marry him?'

'Fuck knows – they say she's Lithuanian or something. Right – ' I point inside ' – off you go. It's your round.'

'No more drinks now. Home time.'

'Noooo! Peroni lash! One more!'

'OK, one more.'

Two men who knew that they were only just holding on, but who had their friendship, and hoped that this might save them. Then came the day, shortly before Campaign, when, finally, Dan announced he was leaving.

'Can I have a word?' He stood immaculate; sharp and distinguished in the grey light of my office.

'Morning! Why so formal?' I watched as my trainee of the time, judging the mood well, excused herself. The door closed.

'I'm off.' And it seemed to me that Dan Serfontein was fighting to retain his composure – his mouth was pulled tight, his neck all tensed. 'I've landed an in-house role at a hedge fund – Levus.'

'Wow.' I stood up from my desk, feeling waves of relief. 'Well, that's great, Dan. You'll see – things will start to get better the moment you step out of here.'

'Alright – no need to give me the big speech. They didn't want to let me go, by the way.'

'I'm sure they didn't.'

'But it was just too good an offer. Top place, surrounded by bright, commercial people – and guaranteed good hours. My dad says it's one of the best funds going. And, oh, I don't know.'

'Are you OK?' Weird Face had returned suddenly, after years of absence. Dan Serfontein held his hands behind his back now, as if he were a soldier performing a drill.

'I just can't do it any more,' he gasped. 'They've broken me.'

7

BACK IN COJÍMAR the dust rose as I walked, alone with my thoughts. At a certain point I had strayed from the village itself, descending further into Cuban silence. I knew I had exhausted every path, that the search for Gregorio's house was definitively over, that it was time to get back to the Terraza de Cojímar and stay there until the taxi driver came to fish me out of here, take me back to the Kims. And yet, as I passed the tree that told me I was back at base, that it was time for an almighty Don Gregorio, I bumped into an improbably nice old lady whom Castro, or whoever it was who was trying to mess with my head, had presumably planted there, just before the bar. She was a bit like an old grandmother from Naples, all warmth and curiosity, and she asked me her questions in a captivated, laudatory sort of way. She seemed most touched by the story of my abandoned quest to find the house of Gregorio Fuentes, a story I embellished with the strange lie that I was an academic scholar researching Hemingway. Why I did so, I didn't know

– it was, perhaps, an attempt at justification. But it backfired dramatically: to my horror, the old lady purred that she knew where the house was. That, if I cared so much, she would walk me there – it wasn't so far away. Very kind, I said, but not to worry – if she just told me where it was, I would go alone, later. It would be asking far too much of her and I wouldn't—

'*Por aquí.*' She had set off.

No, no – please don't start walking. You don't understand. I've been searching for the house for hours and hours but just now I had taken a decision *to give up on it, a decision that made me feel in* control. *I'm terribly hot and I really would like a drink. I'm English, so I won't be able to say no to you. Just look at my face, though – look at its desperation.*

'*Por aquí.*'

'Coming, coming.'

So we walked. And the old lady began to natter away, talking more to herself, it seemed, than to me. She spoke of her husband, who until recently had worked in a cigar factory in Viñales, the most renowned of the valleys in the sweeping countryside of limestone hillocks that is Pinar del Río – a province I had not visited. The factory workers, she told me, were obliged to roll a certain number of cigars each month. If they failed to meet their monthly target they were not paid at all – while any cigar that they rolled in excess of the target they were allowed to keep.

'*Interesante,*' I offered.

Would I like to meet the husband, to see his cigars? Very kind, but...

She spoke of her children who lived in Havana with their families. And of some cousins who lived in Miami – she was keen to tell me about these cousins, she was very proud of them and this made me sad. But I wasn't really listening. I was thinking instead of the firm, of how Dan had cracked just before

Campaign had begun, of how everyone, all those faces from my intake, had gone except for the three of us. I was thinking of those rivals for partnership Angus Peterson and Emma Morris – Angus's eyes, the vacuous but threatening greeting each morning of 'Hey mate, how's *stuff*?' Of finding Angus in my office, shuffling through papers on my desk, one Sunday afternoon. Of that vicious aggression that woke suddenly in him; of the trainee he'd made work all night, then humiliated in front of the team because of a mistake on the front page of the contract. I remembered how the trainee, with exquisite professionalism, had excused himself from the room...

I was thinking of Miss Tension, stressed-out Emma. She was a complete mess, both in appearance now and psychologically, becoming ever more similar to an angry hamster, able to talk only about her transactions, how this deal was the worst *ever*, mixing always a dash of gallows humour with a deeper message of real panic, or outrage at how Rupert Plunkett and his partners had thrown her in the deep end again. 'I'm telling you, Simon, this time it's true. Real estate just *can't* complete by Saturday morning.' Catastrophizing, repeating the same stories, interrupting you when you tried to change the subject, as if this neuroticism, this constant complaining, was in fact a desperate plea to be heard, an outpouring of unhappiness. I was thinking of what happened during the final stages of that terrible deal, Project Dynamite...

'You'll be liaising with Emma Morris on that new matter of yours,' Rupert had whispered one evening, both hands pressed down on the silver quiff.

'Emma?'

'Yes, that's right, Simon. That's what I said. *Christ*. Emma Morris, Simon. Emma Morris.'

'I know who she is, Rupert. I just thought the rule was, you know, that two lawyers on a Campaign shouldn't work on the same—'

'Let me finish. It's unfortunate, given that you're both on a Campaign.' He fixed me now with a vile, entirely unnecessary stare. 'It's unfortunate, given that you're both on a Campaign,' he repeated.

'Yes, Rupert.'

'But you're both adults, aren't you? And there's no way around it.'

Later that evening, my dear trainee Giles, who at Harrow had been cruelly taught never to give up, always to believe in himself, was sitting proud and confused in the corner of my office, while a young woman with brownish hair and red cheeks interrogated me, Fiennes & Plunkett notebook in her hand.

'Right, Simon – a bit of background please. I need parties' details, timetable, outline of the commercial deal – enough to allow me to do my bit.'

The voice was hostile. Emma worked in the real estate or 'property' department – a department that was thriving, despite Rupert's vague contempt for its work, that anachronistic snobbism of his: the great man was unable to accept fully the notion that a property lawyer was a *true* lawyer, or that real estate in the City was much more difficult than residential conveyancing. You could not resist the conclusion that there might be something lurking below all this; that perhaps Rupert's dark secret was that *he himself was not very good at property law*.

'Of course – I'll fill you in on everything you need.' I sat back in my chair, gazing for a second at the picture of Sophie that stood to the right of my screen – Sophie so light and happy, in a lovely white cotton dress, her eyes gazing back at me. 'On the commercials, I imagine you got the summary but we can go over that again now, if you like.'

'Simon.'

I saw a quivering lip.

'We'll go through the summary,' I confirmed.

'Do you have a list of the leases? And the countries where the properties are located?'

'Erm, dunno. Thought you'd have that, to be honest – I'm not following closely the real estate bits of this.'

'Do you *have* it, Simon?'

I raised my hands – I didn't know if we'd received it and it wouldn't be hard for her to just ask the client. Although a trainee, of course, should be keeping lists of all sorts of things...

'Giles,' I said. 'Do we have a list of all the properties? You know, the leases?'

And Giles looked at me with the brave but vacant expression that I knew so well.

'We'll check,' I said to Emma, who had turned to look at the man in the corner as he put a hand through that reddish-blond mop, his face now one of profound concentration. 'Anyway, here's the deal.'

A couple of nights later, at around 10 p.m. in a meeting room packed with representatives of four different parties and their respective lawyers, some New Yorkers declared finally through the loudspeaker that the fund would drop the requirement for the twenty-million top-up, and that the documents could be signed, the next morning.

'Provided, of course, that the leases are dealt with,' came the clipped voice of a radiant young American with slicked-back hair, who was sitting opposite me in the room. He was daring his first intervention since the real decision-takers, his bosses, had joined the conference call from over in the US.

'Chris, will you shut up?' came the voice of one of those bosses. 'What do we care about the leases? It's an issue for them, not us! It's something for Fiennes & Plunkett to fix.'

'Yes, no need to worry about the remaining legal points,' confirmed Rupert. 'We'll have them fixed in an hour or so. I suggest that signing take place tomorrow morning, in these offices, at 8 a.m.'

'OK. Chris, you stay right there in London and sign. We'll get you a power of attorney.'

'Well, gentlemen, a deal done!' shouted the Welsh finance director of the borrower.

And, as people cheered and Chris nodded sadly, thoroughly undermined, my BlackBerry flashed. An email from Rupert, copying his partner Ed Griffiths, the young partner whose thirty-five years were disputed by that gaunt face, the lazy left eye...

'Simon – why you are still sitting here? Get upstairs. Speak to Emma and get those leases done. Ed – when we're finished down here, you and I need a word.'

'Well, I feel I should offer my congratulations,' Rupert was whispering to the client. 'A good deal struck for all.'

What followed, from half past ten that evening until just after eight the next morning, risked creating lasting psychological damage to all lawyers involved. Save, of course, for Rupert Plunkett, who flourished at such times. But when it was over, and staff dressed in Fiennes & Plunkett livery entered the meeting room carrying silver coffee trays and bottles of Louis Roederer, he whispered to me that he too was now 'feeling a little weary'. The young millionaire Ed Griffiths, that unctuous man with the wandering eye, mentioned to me that I shouldn't worry about the rest of Campaign; that it didn't get worse than the night we'd just had. An extra day's holiday was granted to Giles, a man whose physical stamina had carried him through, despite having soon become – in his inability to file emails, save documents, understand any task which he was set – the focal point of all frustration, a figure of hate for lawyers around the world. As we walked upstairs from that meeting room, Rupert Plunkett mentioned that he did not hold me accountable for what could have been a catastrophe, that the fault had been Ed's for allowing this to be left till the very last minute, as it was Ed who was responsible for co-ordinating the departments, planning the timetable and managing the step plan. He added that I should go home to sleep as soon as I had got hold of Emma and brought her to his room, so that he could thank us both. But Emma, it turned out, had gone missing. As an ordered and discreet search began, my exhausted mind began to remember certain moments that punctuated the fog of the night – scenes that, as I relived them, elicited some horrible fear.

'You negligent *wanker!*' She was screeching. 'I told you, I told you that the leases won't be ready till Saturday!'

But, now that I thought back to it, had she been trying to say something else? Beyond the venomous words, had she been begging me? Perhaps what she'd meant was, *please, Simon. This job is doing me so much harm. Please step in to stop this.*

'Sorry, Emma – but I really can't remember you telling me that.'

'Well, I told *him* to tell you!'

'Who? Giles?'

'Ah,' came a plummy voice from the corner of my office. 'Yes, um, Simon, I may have forgotten to pass that on.'

'Oh, Giles.' My head dropped into my hands. 'I sent you an email from downstairs when I was in the meeting, asking you to check on timing, didn't I? And to let me know if there were any issues.'

'Yes. Sorry. I'd understood something slightly different.'

The properties were located in over twenty-four countries. The overseas firms with which Fiennes & Plunkett customarily worked on international deals did not stretch that far, and so

171

Emma had been liaising with new, local lawyers from Turkey, South Africa, Australia, Portugal, Argentina...

'You've put me in an impossible position!' She was stamping her feet. 'The firm's going to be embarrassed, and I'm the one who's going to get it in the neck!'

'But I didn't know you hadn't—'

'I reckon you've done it on purpose, you twisted little shit!'

'What is happening in here?' came a whisper.

A sharp intake of breath from Emma now, as we both turned to behold a quiff, a purple neck, the blooming of a Man on Fire. For, as noted, it was for these moments of profound anxiety, this anticipation of an insane night ahead, that Rupert Plunkett existed.

'Sorry, Rupert – this is so unfortunate. I think you might have to update the client as to timing – manage expectations. Simon *failed* to pass on the message that we can't do this one to your timescales – it's simply too much work to do over the course of one night.'

'But what could be simpler than a lease?' Rupert was peering down at her, his nose twitching.

'Well, it's the number of leases, Rupert. The law's different in each of the countries. And it'll be impossible to get hold of all the lawyers tonight.'

'What utter nonsense. I shall call the managing partner of each of the firms myself.'

'But it's the amount of documentation, Rupert.' *Please, Rupert – please don't do this to me.*

'What can be simpler than a lease? We have a team of two partners, two lawyers on a Campaign, and a trainee. And they are the only outstanding item. We'll all do it together – you won't have to do it alone.'

'But I'm not sure you financing lawyers are really qualified to help, Rupert. This is quite technical property law.'

'Good God, woman,' whispered Rupert. 'We'll damn well learn, right now, if we need to. We're talking about property law. I'm not asking that we all read *Ulysses*.'

Later on that night, he would steal into my office, the rash gone wild. 'Damn fiddly, these lease things, aren't they? Not intuitive, either. I said they're not intuitive. Now, on yours, how did you…'

'A simple, wretched lease!'

'OK, Rupert – understood. Sorry.' And now a sudden detachment in Emma; a disturbing absence. Seven hours later, as I went down to see her in her office, she bore that same expression.

'We always make it in the end, don't we?' she murmured.

'Oh, yes! Especially when nutcase gets on the phone. He's still so wound up about the lease he was looking at, by the way.'

'He made an absolute hash of it,' she said quietly. 'Obviously I couldn't tell him, so I ended up correcting it on the sly.'

'I know, I know: the five-million-a-year living legend of insolvency law has an Achilles heel! He's not happy – he's questioning the whole intellectual basis of his lease, saying someone needs to write him a long note on it when the dust has settled. Anyway,' I said gently, for Emma really did seem spaced out, 'you alright, though? Happy to finish this off alone if you're knackered.'

'Ah, glory-hunter, are we?' A trace of her old self.

'Don't be silly. You just look tired.'

'You don't look too good yourself. I'll be fine.'

'Fair enough.' I sighed. 'Fair enough, Emma.'

The search was still continuing in the afternoon. The firm had called Emma's personal mobile, spoken to her friends at the firm. Nothing. She lived alone, so the next stage would be to call her family. Rupert Plunkett, sitting with me and Ed

Griffiths in his cage, was looking up intermittently from The Manual and fixing Ed for very long periods, during which Ed would gaze down at the floor, the now deeply exhausted eye rolling around, out of control. There was for me something so destabilising about Rupert's indecisiveness: he was not trained to deal with the unpredictability of human beings. So he was fixating instead on policy; on The Manual.

'Yes, we'll have to call the family soon,' he was whispering, for the thousandth time. 'Four hours have gone. According to The Manual... Simon, can you please let me and Ed have a minute? Just a minute. Just a minute.'

But the rambling was interrupted by a knock on the door. We all jumped, as a pair of flushed cheeks shot into the room, followed closely by the sturdy figure of Giles.

'Ah, there you are, Emma,' whispered Rupert, closing The Manual. 'Very good.'

'Rupert, I'm so sorry if I've caused a fuss, this is absurd. Really *absurd*.' She was glaring at me. 'I'd told people that I had a doctor's appointment that would take up all the morning.'

'Is that so?' Rupert now turned to me too.

'Now hang on,' I said. 'I keep being accused of having been told things that I can't remember ever hearing!'

'Well, I definitely told your trainee.'

'And you keep claiming that too.'

'Well?' Emma looked at Giles. 'Didn't I?'

'Um, yes – *my bad* again, I'm afraid,' said Giles. 'I'd completely forgotten you mentioned it at some point during the night, when I was down in your office. Very briefly, of course.'

'Extraordinary,' whispered Rupert. 'Even for you.'

'It sounds impossible, I know, but I did just forget. I was more or less sleepwalking when she told me. I'm still sleepwalking, in fact.'

'Why didn't you mention it to your secretary, Emma? She said that she saw you just walk out. Any absence should be explained to the secretary. The Manual is clear.'

Emma gave Rupert a nervous smile. 'Well, I'm afraid that I too was sleepwalking by that stage. And we had just signed; there was nothing else to do.'

'But The Manual says – oh, all of you, just go home.' Rupert had had enough. 'Thank you, anyway. Ed and I are extremely grateful.'

With a further accusatory glance in my direction, Emma nodded to Rupert and then marched out of the room. As Rupert turned to his computer, shaking his head at the nonsense of life, Giles and I then also left, and trudged down the corridor to my office, where rival number two, Angus Peterson, was waiting for us.

'Chaps,' he enthused in that icy, empty voice. 'The warriors return to base!'

'Hmm.'

'Oh, doesn't Emma hate you,' he guffawed, and in his laughter there *was* something authentic now – real joy, real pleasure. 'She thinks you've stirred up all the disappearance stuff. Campaign has become personal, ha!'

'As if I'd do that.'

'Yes, but you know…' Angus closed the door to my office and his white face, those cold, reptilian eyes below the insipid fair hair, turned briefly to Giles before coming back to me. 'Let's be honest – women and stressy deals just don't go together. Don't you think?'

'I'm not sure that's right, actually. I—' began Giles. But Angus raised a hand, with that sudden aggression of his, to quieten him. I knew what he was after. He saw that I was beyond myself, liable to say something inane that he knew I didn't believe.

'What a load of bollocks,' I said.

175

It was a while before the little weirdo left. He wanted to know all the details, the names of the parties, the strategy, the margin on the loan. Finally, a look at his BlackBerry ended the interrogation – Angus Peterson darted out to his next deal, leaving a half-finished sentence hanging in the air. With the door closed, I turned to Giles.

'Emma wasn't at the doctor's, was she? You even got into trouble to protect her!'

'Why would you think that?'

'Come on, Giles – you're a useless liar. I won't tell anyone.'

'OK.' Giles's voice had become a murmur. 'Damn it, I thought I'd done a good job. Just between us, then, please.'

'Yes, of course.'

'OK. Well, no, she wasn't at the doctor's. What happened was that Nick, one of the trainees – you probably don't know him – Nick was, um, walking back from Tolbert's offices, taking that shortcut through the little park, Dunham Piece. And he saw her there, sitting on a bench by herself, staring at all the mums pushing their kids on the swings.'

'Well, that's not too bad – she just needed some thinking time.'

'No, Simon – the thing is there was something *wrong* with her. Nick knew it, so he sat down and tried to talk to her. But she was crying, he said, without making a noise. Tears pouring and pouring down from her eyes, but in complete silence – just too strange, and she wouldn't move, wouldn't come round. So Nick emailed me, I came out and after a while she switched back on. And when she did she just made me promise, made me swear I'd never tell.'

'Did she—' But I stopped. Rupert's face had appeared at the glass window. And now the King entered my office, began to walk slowly around the room, the apotheosis of gravitas. Giles sat still and quiet at his computer.

'You've not yet gone home,' Rupert noted, after some time.

'Giles is just about to go. I'm going to circulate the docs by email, for good order, and then I'm done too. I've put the originals in the fireproof cabinet.'

'Yes, fine. Yes, fine.' Such lowly matters were of no interest to a king. But then:

'I should have said, you did very well last night, Simon,' he whispered. 'I was a little short earlier.'

'Thank you, Rupert.'

'Yes. Both you and Emma were excellent.'

'As was Giles here, Rupert, I must say – he deserves huge credit. I've told him his attitude and resilience were absolutely first-class.' Even now though, I couldn't bring myself to suggest any other qualities than these – several times during the night Giles had nearly scuppered the whole deal. And several times he'd put me at risk of being struck off, or worse – I thought of those promises he had begun to make on the conference call he should never have joined. And that list of sensitive commercial information that he kept sending to the wrong Julian.

'Yes, good point. OK. Well done, Giles.' There then appeared a nervous, fleeting smile on my leader's face. I knew what was happening. It was at the end of these sorts of all-nighters, particularly when he decided to carry on through the next day despite *not feeling at his best*, that Rupert knew a brief peace. The obsessions were for the moment under control; he had not let himself down; his father would have been proud of him for the night's work. These were the special golden moments when calm came to Plunkett Ocean, the ripples gentle.

'The leases weren't even your area of expertise, Simon.' He sniffed. 'So you in particular were very impressive.' But then a frown, as the peace became endangered by a thought, a sudden bulge in the water. 'Quite fiddly things, weren't they? Fiddly, fiddly. Irritating even, in their own way.'

'Yes, mine were trickier than I thought – I had to ask Emma a whole range of things.'

'Did you? How odd. I didn't.' Rupert scratched his neck. 'It seems to me that they were badly drafted in the first place – that was the problem at the heart of it. Some damn in-house lawyer going wild with a pen. They were conceptually flawed, in a number of respects. Anyway…' he fixed me '…as I say, you should head off shortly, both of you. It would be counterproductive for you to start on a new transaction today.'

'Agreed.' The idea had not occurred to me. 'I hope you'll do the same.'

'What?' And, look: in an instant, it had happened. He was biting his nails. *Farewell, fine peace. See you again some day.* 'No, I have Mars, Simon – along with various minor matters I need to attend to this afternoon.'

'Mars?'

'Project Mars, of course. Angus Peterson is running it, doing a good job. But we only have today to fix the loan. It needs to go out *today*.'

'Oh. Sorry about that.'

'Hang on, hang on.' The hand was out, resisting a negative energy. 'Please stop interrupting me, Simon. I came in to say, given you're still here, and we've just completed a deal, we might go for a coffee, to celebrate. We've just completed a major deal, Simon.'

'Yes. Well, that'd be great. I'd love a quick coffee.'

'OK.' Rupert exhaled now, thinking. And then: 'You should come too, Giles.'

'Me?'

'Yes, you. Yes, you. We should all go for a coffee. Emma has gone,' he added, bitterly. 'Ed has gone too. It's a pity they rushed off like that.'

'To be fair, I think you told them to go home, Rupert. You told us all to.'

'Erm, just to say, from my side,' Giles's bottom lip trembled under the force of The Stare, 'I wouldn't want to intrude, if you prefer to go just with Simon.'

It was unbearable, witnessing any direct interaction between these two men. Rupert had frozen now, a look of unaccountable horror on his face as Giles continued.

'If you want to talk business, or about anything confidential, you know, that's fine by me – don't feel you have to invite me for the coffee. I'm grateful as it is for the extra day off next week – much appreciated.'

A long silence. Then, once Rupert had recovered from his shock:

'It's a fair point,' he whispered to Giles. 'I don't feel strongly about this. But, if it truly is immaterial to you, then, on balance – ' he paused ' – I would prefer it if you didn't come.'

'Rupert!' I said. 'Giles, of course you should ... ' But Giles's face stopped me – of course, he really didn't want to come. Why would he? Why would anyone?

'Good, good,' Rupert was whispering. 'Mars can wait. Mars can wait. For a *short while*.'

My first and only celebration with Rupert Plunkett of the completion of a Fiennes & Plunkett deal was a modest, deeply odd affair. Rupert took me to the firm's favourite café, a family-run Italian place hidden in a narrow alley behind the Bank of England. The firm's favourite, but not necessarily Rupert's – he whispered to me throughout the walk that he had *misgivings* about the place. As we stepped in, the owner – a very short, impeccably dressed Sicilian known only as Enzo – nearly dropped a tray of coffee cups in his excitement. With a yelp of joy, he rushed towards this tall, important customer with the fine silver quiff.

'*Avvocato Plunkett! Buon pomeriggio, Mistèr! Da quanto tempo! Troppo tempo!*'

'Good afternoon,' the great man replied, courteously. But, when Rupert turned to me, I saw apprehension. 'I have no idea what he's *saying*,' my leader whispered. 'I assume you do.'

'Yes, he's just saying hello, really,' I explained.

'I understood that part.' The red was spreading, slowly, up the neck. 'I was referring to the other part.'

'Well, he was just saying that...' but it was so intimidating, being fixed by The Stare '...that it's been a long time. I imagine you've not been here for a while.'

'It's as if you were *talking* in your damned *sleep*.'

And, on this pleasant note, Rupert turned back to Enzo. 'Two cappuccinos, please,' he whispered, the neck veins testimony to the effort required to force open a little hole in his face that was not quite a smile.

'*Certo!*' sang the ecstatic little man, waving his arms in the air. '*E certo, Mistèr avvocato Plunkett!*'

'Jesus Christ!' With a rapid nod, Rupert darted to the far corner of the café.

The coffee that Enzo served us was, as always, of fine quality. Very expensive, but his was the only coffee in London that reminded me of Southern Italy. My leader and I sipped away in silence, each occasionally glancing at the other but then looking away quickly when eyes met, Rupert sometimes opening his mouth, only to then close it again. After five minutes or so, as was usual, I broke.

'Yes, I must admit – ' I watched poor Rupert jerk back in alarm at this suddenness ' – there's something very satisfying about a successful all-nighter.'

'Yes.' He understood this; he approved of it. 'Yes, that's *right*, Simon.'

But then he frowned as I continued.

'I guess it's the same feeling mountaineers must have. Just pure achievement. Even people who don't get through the training contract, people who have no vocation for the law, even they talk about the thrill.' I had put myself, needlessly, in dangerous territory here. 'I mean, obviously, for people like me, the job *is* a vocation. And for you, too.'

'We'll need to go soon,' Rupert concluded sadly. 'You're not making much sense.' But then, with a little sigh, he astonished me.

'I wouldn't have said that in my case there was any particular calling. I rather enjoyed English at university. It was my family.' He grimaced. 'My grandfather demanded that I join the firm. Good thing I did, as it happens – it was being run very badly by the end of my father's tenure.' A shake of the head. 'So you're telling me that the law is your true vocation? Insolvency law is your true calling?'

'Well...'

'It's alright. Don't answer that. It doesn't matter.'

And the second little sigh came loaded and real, moving me in its directness, its awkward, unqualified honesty. Perhaps I was too sensitive, too tired, but the short deep sigh, together with the admission, seemed an acknowledgement by Rupert Plunkett of a missed chance; a salute to some hope that had never even been fully formed, and which belonged to a time far behind him now.

The moment passed quickly; ended with another bitter frown. Silence resumed. And then a further five, ten minutes had passed.

'This is such a good cappuccino, Rupert. So much better than what they serve up in the coffee chains.'

'What?' He looked up – grave, hostile, terribly concerned that he hadn't understood.

'Enzo's coffee – it's just so good.'

'But he's the *owner*.' He jerked his head towards the counter. 'It's his *business*, Simon.'

'Yes.'

'Everything he has.'

Seconds later, Rupert consulted the BlackBerry. I watched the inevitable: the flinch; the shake of the head. And then came guilt and panic – a hand pressed down onto a quiff. He had been out too long.

'I must move,' he whispered. 'Something has come up.' I nodded, thanked him as he jumped to his feet and then I just watched him: I watched him rush to the door, shake hands with Enzo, bend down to try to hear what he was saying; I watched him become impatient as a group of young men entered, momentarily blocking his escape route. And then, when he had made it out, as I wondered whether I was observing the man I would one day be, I saw him charge away, through the crowd of City workers, down the little alley towards the safety of his institution. Until finally he turned right, and disappeared.

'LA CASA DE GREGORIO,' said the old lady, in elated triumph. We had stopped at the top of a nondescript lane of sand and mud, and she was pointing down it towards a house, and then to a wooden signpost that said nothing at all.

'*La casa!*' I replied, trying to muster suitable emotion as I thanked her again for this. My ears were peeling, my legs and arms and, bizarrely, my right cheek had been savaged by the mosquitoes, and a deep river of sweat poured down every inch of my skin. This point here, this precise place, was the epicentre of the village's fire. At least five degrees hotter even than Calamity Bay. There was in this place no wind; there was pure burning. *La casa, la casa.* I seemed to remember now that, before he had decided upon *Cien años de soledad*,

182

García Márquez had considered *La casa* as a title for his novel – possibly the greatest novel of the twentieth century. A fine title for a book, *La casa* – although *Simón y la casa de Gregorio* had a ring to it, too. After a long, overly zealous embrace in which the old lady kissed me twice on each cheek, her lips grazing the swellings on the right cheek caused by the mosquito attack, she mumbled some words that I did not understand, and then she was gone, hurrying back to the main street. And so I walked alone down the lane, soon to find myself standing directly before the meaning of the day: the X on the beer mat I had long discarded. I stood before it a good while.

'*La casa*,' I murmured finally. '*La casa, la casa.*'

There was nothing to suggest that this was, or that it might plausibly be, the former house of Gregorio Fuentes. No plaque. No indication that anybody had ever visited before. It was just a typical Cuban house, extreme only in its ordinariness. And, like many Cuban houses, it turned out that it was inhabited by a Cuban family – a large family, who became inquisitive as to why I was standing in front of their home. There followed great confusion and the head of the household, a shirtless man, soon began tutting at me, repeating to me that his name was not Gregorio. 'I know that,' I was telling him, 'I *know* that you are not Gregorio.' But, upon hearing the snarl of a dog from inside, noting the rage in the grandmother's eyes, seeing the chubby kid pick up a stone, I ended the game. And so I was trotting in Cojímar – up the lane, down the main street and, finally, back to the restaurant that was really a bar.

They acknowledged me with a cheer as I walked back in – they could all now see me, it appeared. But it was the same barman who spoke to me.

'*Un Don Gregorio, por favor,*' I confirmed.

'Of course, *señor.*'

And now finally the alcohol flowed and it flowed and my cheeks would soon be flushed and my heart would soon palpitate but for a brief period the lights came on again and the world returned to its splendid hilarity and I was handsome. And my voice became intermittently plummy like my trainee Giles's voice as I told them of London, the performance marred only by flashes of impatience. But then the barman asked me what I'd thought of Gregorio's house – and suddenly they all roared and banged down their little fists onto the counter and there was a jolt: out went the lights and up rose waves of hostility and apprehension... They were nasty at the bar and they'd been overcharging me at the bar... and I'd tried hard but nobody wanted to talk to me in this village in a pleasant way, nobody except the old lady and she was probably mad... and look at the barmen laughing at me, my face in the mirror bright red and clownish, with those atrocious mosquito bites... and I didn't understand why Rupert couldn't let me know in advance what he thought of my chances, give me a call with some updates or a reassuring word; I didn't understand how he could be so fucking cold and inhuman. I didn't understand anything now, I hadn't the vaguest idea why I was here in Cuba, but then I remembered that it was more or less because Sophie had walked out on me. And I felt somehow guilty about this, her abandoning me, yet at the same time there was nothing that I wanted to remedy, nothing I felt obliged to put right – instead there was intensified in me a conviction that never in my life had I done anything wrong. I had been rejected – that was all. What was it, then, this sense that I was somehow at fault?

Disorientated now, fragile and scared by the fragility, I contemplated the photographs of Gregorio on the walls. Gregorio with Castro. Gregorio with Hemingway. Gregorio with Hemingway and Castro. Gregorio watching Hemingway shake hands with Castro...

'Another Don Gregorio?'

'One more.'

'OK. *Otro Don Gregorio!*'

'Said one more.'

'Yes, *señor.* I understand!'

And one more became two more and the initial lash rash disappeared, the redness of the cheeks calming despite the alcohol, and I decided that all I needed to think about was that my watch was ticking and that at some wonderful point the taxi driver would arrive. I asked the barman to tell me a story about Gregorio to pass the time – he told me that the protagonist Santiago in *The Old Man and the Sea* had been based on Gregorio.

'Arsehole,' I mumbled.

It had been a terrible move, giving him the opportunity to become a comedian again, and now he was asking me once more whether I had been impressed by Gregorio's house, whether I would like another Don Gregorio, how long I planned to spend in the village. The howling, the banging of the fists. I told him that my taxi was scheduled to pick me up in two hours, to which he replied that there was plenty of time, then, for some more Don Gregorios.

The fists and the howls and the photographs, and through the window the sight of the lonely pimp throwing stones into Calamity Bay. The voice of the barman, bellowing that he had remembered a story about Gregorio: that he had lived in a small, uninteresting house. And then – as his crescendo was reached – he delivered a line.

'The truth is, *señor*, nobody cares about Gregorio.'

'*Jajaja!*' they roared.

'But that makes no sense – your walls are plastered with him.'

'Nobody cares about Gregorio.'

'*Jajaja!*'

'It makes no *sense*.'

But it was a line that in my whimsical state soon came to have a sense, something majestic and profound, a poetic truth that applied to the world in all its loneliness. *Nobody cares about Gregorio*. I was contemplating it later when the barman told me that he had found a friend who would take me back to Havana – I told him that I could not do that to my taxi driver. Instead I repeated the line from time to time, in a quiet voice, as I waited out the final hour, looking down into a glass of half-drunk Don Gregorio. I was still thinking about it when, half an hour after he was scheduled to arrive, bewildered old Professor Bonini from Cambridge entered the bar and cried that he had been waiting for me over at the other side of the bay, at the Terraza de Cojímar, the famous restaurant.

'*Jajaja!*'

'Hey? What is this place? Who the hell are you people?'

Nobody cares about Gregorio. It was on my mind as chaos ensued and this bar of no name erupted into its finest hour and the barmen, doubled up with laughter, gave me a large glass of rum on the house before waving goodbye. Then I was in the taxi, and Bonini barely suppressing his tears was pointing to the places where he'd once played, the places where he'd once played, when the effects of the last drink rushed through me suddenly like the venom of a serpent's bite and my head began to spin ... *nobody cares about Gregorio* ... and the last thing I remember is thinking *fuck it*, taking out my mobile phone and feeling honest, feeling that it was time. Time to write to Sophie, the girl I loved.

PART TWO

8

I WAS WOKEN by the chirping of an agitated bird, which came somehow bound up with the vague sensation that my chest was vibrating. For a brief moment, I knew only this – my mind was still processing the present, preparing itself to develop thoughts, conceptions of the past and the future. Slowly things became a little clearer: I realised that my mobile phone was lying on my bare chest and that in this fact lay the answer to the question of the chirping and the vibrating.

I removed the mobile phone and gulped from the large glass of water by my bedside and it was about then that I remembered why I could hear a man singing – and that he was singing his country's national anthem – and then, also, that I became more acutely aware of how I felt physically, which was not at all well. It was as if my head were in a vice. My mouth, which prior to the gulping had been entirely empty of liquid, was emitting toxic air. A ray of sunshine that strove impudently through a gap in the blinds was burning my left temple, my stomach was all instability, and I needed to be left undisturbed by everyone and everything for a good number of hours … the malaise transformed for a second into a flicker of pure rage – I wanted to swat that mosquito so hard, to get it back for how my exposed left ankle felt. The moment passed and then came anxiety, a sense that I had done something *very* foolish that I would be regretting *very* soon.

Today was the 25th. Tomorrow Rupert would be calling, to tell me if I'd made it.

That *singing*. There was something unbearable about the passion in Kim the artist's voice, the intensity of the joy invading my room as I regarded the screen of the mobile phone with a sudden keenness. For I had received a new message and now came the final step: the completion of the processing of reality.

'Sophie,' I croaked, sitting up in the bed with a start. I had written to her – I was sure of it. But what I had written I did not know: I remembered only the rush of drunken honesty in the taxi back to Havana, the sense of purging of the emotions, and, worse still, the pride that accompanied this – the uncritical, pure satisfaction with myself for being honest. A hungover Englishman's recollection of such a purifying release is no fun thing.

It turned out that Sophie's message was very short:

?

It was very well pitched, a psychological masterpiece in its incitement of fear. The question mark was like a traffic cone by the bedside, saying only, *last night you were very drunk indeed*.

A little groan of panic now as I scrolled upwards to the message that I had sent to Sophie at the height of my madness. And as I read it I had an image of a courtroom; the accused listening in the dock as a recording of his confession is played to the jury. The message read as follows:

> *Nobody cares about Gregorio! I miss you and I was and I LOVE you. Come back to me please, for if not I will xx live with my men friends KIM*

I reflected on that message for some time, letting out little gasps of anxiety. But then I read it again, and then a third time with a strange, sudden calm. Perhaps, I thought, this *was* in some absurd way a healthy release – excruciatingly embarrassing, but necessary after months of a silence that in its impeccable gentlemanliness was entirely unnatural. I wondered now about Sophie's face, wondered whether she had read it a second time; I wondered if she had reflected on all it had to say beneath the words. I wondered where she was, if she was with somebody else. It was so weird: tomorrow Rupert would be calling to tell me if I was a millionaire but I didn't feel ready. Was Sophie with somebody else, somebody new? I rested my head down on the pillow and with a sigh began to think of all those years.

ALL THOSE YEARS...the entirety of my adult life, Sophie Williams had been part of me, permanent inhabitant of my mind, frequenter of dreams. I thought of the morning in September 1996 when she entered my life, sixteen years old like me, the late summer's breeze accompanying her in through the entrance to Longwood's sixth-form common room. The boys' faces turned now, their gazes attaching to this new girl without a name, her long legs, the falling auburn hair, the brown of her eyes. Even then, the first day I saw her, the girl stooped a little, as if knowing that if she held herself up she would be too tall...

The boys' gazes were fixed, while the girls were already looking away – it takes a female no more than a few seconds to assimilate news like this: that the new girl was the prettiest. Sophie sat down on a chair, looked around briefly, then gazed out through the open window onto the sports fields – all alone. A short time later I must have been standing somewhere behind her, for I was struck by the perfect shape of her back, which was held up straight now that she was sitting, the small of her back pressed inwards. Later, as I walked past her on the way to class, I glanced at her, caught her eye.

'Hi,' I half-said, half-mouthed, rushing away as a little smile broke out on her face.

Every time I saw her that day, she was alone. By the afternoon she had a name, the news passed on hurriedly between the boys, but aside from that we knew nothing – she was a girl arrived with no story, a girl stepping fresh from an adolescent dream. She continued to sit alone the next day, the mystery girl, the other girls ostracising her on the silent orders of the group of friends led by Anna Cowley – the girls who had hitherto dominated the boys' attention. The boys meanwhile were cowardly, intimidated by Sophie's solitude, the challenge of being the first to sit down next to her becoming more difficult by the hour. The fierce gaze of the girls prohibited it, and Anna Cowley was watching particularly me. Anna was blonde and faintly pretty too, but horribly spoilt and with a cruel streak – she was endowed with a talent for a peculiarly female form of silent, subtle bullying. I'd made the bad drunken mistake of kissing her once, that summer just passed at a house party full of booze, and after that she had made her feelings clear to me a number of times. She liked me – liked me very much. Her self-esteem would not allow her to accept that it was an unrequited liking.

So I felt Anna watching me while I watched this new girl sitting alone. On the third day we had further information that had leaked from somewhere, and that intensified my belief that I was personally involved already with her, that her arrival was somehow part of *my* story: we were told that she and her mother had only moved to Lincolnshire over the summer, from Derby, that they had left Sophie's father behind, and that now mother and daughter lived with the grandparents up in beautiful Hubbard's Hills, in that white house that I would sometimes gaze up at from afar as my dad drove me to school. Often I had wondered who might live there, daydreaming of the air, the peace high up in the green. That it should now be this girl! That she should have arrived to inhabit the white house of my fantasy! That night was the night she began to appear in dreams – she would be waiting for me at a turn of a country path, her auburn hair blown back...

On the Friday morning, as I was getting out of his old red Renault in the school car park, my dad scratched his beard – and I groaned immediately. For the scratch meant that he had something to say; but I was late, I didn't have time now.

'Just talk to her,' he said.

'Who?'

'This girl, who lives in that white house in the hills. I'm not having another week of this – it's all you talk about.'

'No, it's not!'

'You'll see,' he chuckled. 'As soon as you talk to her, you'll wonder what all the drama was about. I remember the night I saw your mother that Saturday evening in Co-op Hall, in 1968...'

'Dad – I've got to go!'

'Alright – but I'm not talking to you about her tonight when I pick you up unless you've spoken to her. Just be brave and say hello – it'll put hairs on your chest.'

I scurried off, the indignant teenager. But the truth in his words was slowly absorbed into my mind during the morning. In the afternoon, walking into the final class of the day, general studies, I saw Sophie sitting at a desk in the corner

– the desk next to her was vacant. With my blood racing I surprised myself, a strange energy taking possession of me, as if for a moment I were not Simon; as if Simon were not me.

'Hello,' the brave adventurer stuttered as he drew up close. 'Um, can I sit here?' The stares of the other pupils were searing, the air thick with tension, my cheeks raging hot as Sophie's big eyes looked up.

'OK,' she whispered, all nervous. 'What's your name?'

'Go, baby, go!' someone shouted – and there were wolf-whistles now.

'Simon.' I was panting – oddly – as I sat down. 'I'm Simon Haines.' Then, even more oddly, 'Thank you very much.'

'For what?' But she was happy now, I thought, her eyes lowered to her papers, smiling to herself. There was another wolf-whistle, some laughter, but within a minute the voices had moved on, the conversations changed, and in her stillness I saw that Sophie was waiting for me to say something more. But the adventurer had nothing left in the tank for now – there was only the savouring of victory. So I looked away instead, in pride at what I had done and defiance at the rest of the class, but my cheeks were so hot I thought with shame of my appearance, imagining it. And then my eyes met Anna's eyes – theirs were all fury, hurt and anger.

'My name's Sophie,' came a whisper.

I turned. 'Yes, I know. I wanted to sit next to you. To say hello, you know.'

'That's nice.'

I said nothing more to her that day, save for a brief awkward goodbye – but I compensated with the breathless nattering away to a proud father in the car back home that afternoon. Now Sophie waited for me always in my dreams, there at the turn of the path in Hubbard's Hills; the next Tuesday she came into the general studies class after me, and

194

walked boldly towards the desk next to mine, the vacancy of which I had protected obsessively, wild with hope. And for a second I lost my mind, gazing at her with a sort of astonished wonder, a fluttery feeling in my stomach.

'Is it OK if I sit here?' She had taken my staring the wrong way.

'Yes, yes – it's fine. It's great.'

I heard a guffaw from behind me. And then Anna Cowley's voice from the far corner:

'Look at Simon. He's bright red again!'

'Ha!' the laughter rang out. Anna was correct – the bastard cheeks had been disloyal...

'You're all embarrassed,' Sophie whispered.

'No, no – I'm just hot.'

'I don't like that girl.' Her whisper was very low, very sweet – there was no real need to whisper, because the noise had revived around us.

'Don't worry – she's just jealous of you.'

'And I hate this class,' she whispered. 'It's so boring, general studies, isn't it?'

'Oh, yeah,' I said, enthusiastically – for I would have agreed with anything. 'Yeah, it's the one I really hate.'

'Ha – like me. We're the same.'

'Yeah.'

The proposition that we were the same was a little too much, though; the fluttery feeling had gone wild. On an impulse I went for it, seeking to affirm the bond.

'I mean, I *really* hate general studies,' I reiterated. 'It's like ... '

But what to say? How to impress her with the strength of my hatred of general studies?

'Sometimes I want to blow the classroom up!' I said, feverishly – before then falling into a sort of horrified silence, appalled by the nonsense that had spurted from my mouth.

'Weird,' she said. 'Are you a psycho?'

'Oh, yes. Ha! Yes, I've done it before. I've killed dozens of people already.' *Calm down, Simon – what the fuck are you saying?*

'I don't believe you.' Sophie's voice was very faint again, for Mr Dickens had arrived to commence the lesson, and silence had fallen. 'Do you know why I don't believe you?' she continued.

'No. Tell me!'

'Haines!' Mr Dickens cried, as if in anguish. '*Please.* Stop chatting up the ladies, we've started.'

Mortification now – the laughter of the girls in particular was intense, with a nasty undercurrent. Anna wasn't laughing, though – instead she sat still, emitting beams of poison through her fixed stare. One kiss, that was all it had been. I raised my eyebrows at her as if to say: what? Mr Dickens did begin now, at question number one of the endless monotony, and I turned my attention back to the papers on my desk, only to start. Sophie had written on the first page of my exercise book – she'd written down the reason why she didn't think I was a serial bomber.

Because of your eyes. They're too nice for that!

The cheeks – was it possible for cheeks to become hotter?

Your eyes are nicer, I wrote quickly on the next page, turning it so that she could read the words.

You're sweet.

And it was curious that our first real conversation, and all of our real conversations that followed for weeks, should take this form – writing words to each other. Her handwriting was lovely, like a melody – but everything was beautiful about her now. She'd captured all my silly emotions, held them tight in her smile.

How have you found your first weeks, then? I wrote. *Bit difficult, I guess?*

196

The girls are being HORRIBLE, Sophie wrote. *Especially Anna and her gang – blanking me when I try to speak to them.*

Like I said, they're just jealous. You're prettier than all of them!

She blushed a little too when she read this.

I'm not that pretty! x

You ARE!

You're sweet. I've heard you're one of the brainy ones who doesn't have to try so hard – is it true? By the way, Anna fancies you like mad – it's so obvious.

I know, but she's mental! I'm not that brainy – there are just so many morons in our year.

You're one of the cleverest – but not the cleverest. And now I'm here xx

You're clever, are you? Clever AND pretty? That's not fair.

I'm cleverer than you, I reckon.

That's by definition impossible.

We shall see. You do have very nice eyes though. Hers were smiling as she turned the book.

But you reckon you're cleverer, do you – are you a bit of a show-off?

She looked up, startled. 'No,' she mouthed. 'I'm just joking.'

The conversation turned to where she lived, and whether it was true that the white house in the hills, *my* white house, was her home. She seemed very moved by my excitement at her confirmation, and I caught in her face that same thought, the sort of thought that comes to all people of that age – that the coincidence of my daydream and her reality meant that there was a much bigger truth that lay below it. The other rumours were also true: her grandparents owned the house, and she and her mother had arrived only very recently, in August.

So everything's still very new, she wrote. *Completely different from where I was brought up.* She bit her lip. *And my dad didn't come with us. He lives alone now, in our old house in Derby – I don't see him any more.*

Sorry, I wrote, far too young to know what to say, or even to worry about it – I wanted to continue the happy story we were writing; and so, it appeared, did she.

What about you? she wrote quickly. *What's your dad like?*

He's an old man with a big beard! I wrote, to her delight. *A psychologist – analyses crazy people all day.*

I love crazy people. Has he got blue eyes like you?

No – that's my mum. Well, this has been a nice hour writing to you!

It's been my nicest day yet.

My best day too – the best and biggest day I could remember. The end of the class was *not* so good, though. Sophie said goodbye and then rushed out, leaving me sitting in a daze as the class emptied. But the room never emptied completely – behind me Anna Cowley was waiting, alone.

'Well, well,' she said, running a hand through her blonde hair, as I turned in surprise. Now she walked scowling towards my desk. 'He's fallen in love.'

'It's none of your business, Anna – don't be so nasty all the time.'

'She'll end up hurting you – there's something not right about her. I've heard some things.'

'Just stop going *on* about her. You're embarrassing yourself. It's transparent, how jealous you are!'

'What?' And now the face was cold white with anger.

'You heard me.'

'I…' She stopped before the desk, tears gathering in her eyes. 'I *hate* you,' she cried, before turning to storm out of the room. 'You'll pay for this!'

General studies classes were on Tuesdays and Fridays, so that those days had become the centre of meaning in my young universe. It was difficult to speak to Sophie in the sixth-form common room, because that place was all politics and intrigue, the stage of the psychodrama, great weight placed on the location of where you sat, the person to whom you spoke. Sophie had found two friends now from among the girls – the first was a quiet, very timid girl called Isabelle, who had never had many friends. And then, quite suddenly, the day following my disastrous conversation with Anna Cowley, Sophie had Zoe Sutton as a friend too – and this wasn't right, it didn't fit. Zoe was another blonde in Anna Cowley's gang, and had always been one of the bitchiest girls at the school. The friendship was not *real* – I would be kept awake till late at night by my overly busy mind, my imagination painting catastrophes, but returning always to the grim truth that propelled that imagination: Zoe had clearly been sent by Anna to befriend Sophie, *ergo* Zoe wanted to harm Sophie. So that soon, in the early hours, this story that we were writing so fast became enhanced by a new, chivalrous element – the appearance of Simon the Rescuer. It was difficult to be sure which of the emotions was the greater spur to the creation of this character: the real worrying about Sophie or the thrill at the idea of saving her, of how she would look at me when I saved her. With the night over though, in the cold reality of day, things were more complicated and delicate: Sophie was very happy to have Zoe as a friend, and to suggest that Zoe was not her friend was to humiliate Sophie. So how to get the message across without hurting her?

Of course she likes you, I would write in my exercise book. *But she's bad news – she's a close friend of Anna's.*

You're such a worrier! she would write. *Can we talk about something else? It's exhausting!*

No, no – we couldn't talk about anything else. For it was an obsession, you see. Simon the Rescuer.

Just don't tell her any secrets, Sophie – she's not to be trusted.

OK! Jesus!

Meanwhile I had indeed paid for my own insolence to Anna Cowley: there were jokes going around the common room about how much I had been sweating that day in class when she had confronted me; and indeed there was a rumour that I had a problem generally with sweating, that my hands had been pouring with sweat the evening I had kissed Anna. Sophie had either not heard this stuff or, more likely, was too polite to mention it, I thought. Perhaps more likely still, she didn't mention it because she didn't want anything to interrupt the story in the exercise books, the story I was threatening to ruin with the fixation about Zoe. In any case the teasing was never a real threat to it, as it never really stuck or gained substance, allowing me to expend an extraordinary amount of mental energy instead on this Zoe Issue; how to resolve it, how to protect against it. In the brief intervals between such absorptions, I had also a vague comprehension that I needed to take a further step now with regard to Sophie, something more than the occasional continuation of the conversation as we walked out of general studies to the common room – the place where we would bid each other a silent farewell, both go searching for our friends. One afternoon in October, as we were writing away to each other, that next step in the sequence came – its occurrence as simultaneously natural and unnatural as my initial appropriation of a vacant desk weeks earlier. Quite abruptly I asked Sophie for her telephone number, with the immediate written caveat that I was only asking: ... *so that we can help each other out on the homework tonight.*

You need help? she wrote, amused.

Thought you *might need help – but seriously, homework's easier sometimes if you do it with another person.*

Hmm – should I really give my number to a psycho?

Fair point! Why give your number to the Sweat Monster?

Sorry??!

Ah – she hadn't heard the teasing.

Just messing, I wrote. *Just a joke.*

Another very strange joke! It's kind of freaked me out actually!

No, no, I wrote. *It was a joke from that film.*

Which film?

You know, that film – I've forgotten the name now: you're stressing me out, ha ha!

Stressing you out? Sometimes you do seem a bit mental!

She gave me her number though and to my surprise I felt a little frightened when she wrote it down – she'd entrusted me with something intimate, and by doing so had become more vulnerable: the sense of responsibility I felt was acute. Of course in those quaint days obtaining a telephone number was a bigger deal than it would be once mobile phones arrived – in those days it was the number of a whole home, and it took a much greater amount of courage to make that first call, to introduce yourself to the person – who could be anyone – answering the phone. *Anyone could answer.* This truth was heavy for an anxious young man with a rich imagination. That evening I sat on my bed for hours, phone on my lap, playing out the scenarios, thinking of Grandad's surely booming voice: 'You want to speak to my granddaughter, do you?' Or the interrogation from a curious mother: 'So how do you know Sophie? Are you in the same class?'

What my imagination had not extended to was the grandmother answering the telephone and mistaking me for another guy.

'Sophie!' she called. 'It's Leo on the phone again! Le-o!'

Who was Leo? The Zoe Issue, the terrible danger posed by the double agent, was immediately displaced. Who was Leo? I knew that I would be too shy to bring it up directly – and anyhow I hadn't sufficient time to think about it. Yes, better to think about it *after* the call.

Sophie picked the phone up from what I thought must be her bedroom – there was some soppy commercial love song playing in the background, the tune and words of which, I thought, were not so bad after all. The room I soon imagined fiercely – she was looking out of her window onto fields of sloping countryside.

'So,' she said softly. 'You've called about the homework.'

'Yep.'

'You're so funny.'

And indeed this was how every phone call would begin, with Sophie's mum, who soon told me to call her Deborah, playing along, introducing me with the words, 'Sophie! It's Simon, to talk about the homework,' the words spoken in an excited tone of collusion. We came to recount our lives, or bits and pieces of them, over those evening calls – perhaps it was the first time either of us had reflected on anything about our stories. Sophie would tell me about her life up on that hill, depicting in my mind an existence of wonderful stability, a reassuring routine in harmony with time and the weather. And she would enthuse equally about my stories, sighing when I told her of the new pile of books my parents had left on my bed, adding that it was beautiful how we had such different minds – she was studying sciences and maths.

'You love words the way I love numbers,' she said. 'Isn't it lovely?'

Possibly it was – equally, one might have argued that it would have been lovelier still if we had both loved numbers, or both loved words. If I hadn't *hated* numbers. But everything needed to fit into, to enhance the story, so we quickly dispatched things that didn't. Deborah would drive Sophie mad, she said, with her fitness routine: her mother would go jogging at dawn. *So what?* I thought. *She sounds like a nutcase – let's move this along.* Better when Sophie spoke of her grandfather, who would be up at dawn himself – they were all up early there. He would go for long country walks, come in and collapse onto a sofa, soon begin snoring loudly. *My dad snores too – how funny! What? Your mum's favourite restaurant is Kingston's? No way!* We did not yet understand, or did not want to understand, that life is not so varied as for it to be a miracle for two families in the same area to frequent one of the few nearby restaurants; that it would have been infinitely more enriching, and helpful, to talk about all those other things that did not fit immediately into the story. Leo, for example, the mystery caller – although of course in a way he *did* fit into the story. So one evening I was brave – and was stung by the response.

'So who's Leo?' I asked, gripping my pillow. 'Your grandma thought I was a guy called Leo.'

She fell silent. Then: 'Simon, that's a bit nosy.'

'OK, OK – forget I asked.'

'Well, if you must know, he's an ex from my old school.'

The end of the world, back on the other end of the phone. The end of the whole world!

'He still calls me,' Sophie said, 'and he's really nice, but I don't fancy him and I don't really know what to do about it. It was never so serious. Simon?'

'Yes – I'm here,' I confirmed, bravely.

'Listen to your voice! Anyway, what about you and Miss Cowley?'

'I told you – it was only a kiss!'

'Hmm.'

'Now, I heard you did amazingly on that paper...'

Sophie really was intelligent – it was an accepted fact now at Longwood. People said she was whizzing ahead in chemistry in particular. It was very satisfying when I managed through trickery to get her to speak well of herself; suddenly she would realise she was bordering on showing off, and reverse or qualify what she'd said, charmingly.

In this way more weeks passed – the conversations reached eventually a sort of impasse, threatening to soon become formulaic. The challenge of knowing and taking the next step had arisen once more – I heard myself beginning to sound pathetic, pushing the conversation on quickly until it reached the impasse. The range of topics of conversation had reduced as opposed to expanded, which meant that the things that were off limits were heightened in their importance, spoken about silently. There was the mystery of her father – barely even one-dimensional, just a Welshman, living alone now in Derby, very tall like her; there was the Zoe Issue – Sophie had now reached the point of declaring, half-jokingly, that she would hang up if I mentioned it – and then there was the related, sad point that, again tacitly, Sophie had made clear was not to be discussed: she really was being bullied now by Anna and her gang. I knew it hurt her but she would never admit to it... Even a decade later when I would mention the bullying Sophie would look down into her book, telling me not to exaggerate. But they were becoming evil, those girls, to Sophie the pretty girl so infuriatingly good at her schoolwork. I had spoken to Anna three times, and each time had made things worse, intensifying her sense of abandonment, which in turn had triggered a new level of nastiness. They were telling stories about Sophie to the boys to sully the true narrative, and I never mentioned it to her in case she didn't know, but they were vicious, noting how she was abnormally tall, that she was a bitch who only cared about manipulating people and getting attention, that she had Mr Dickens help her with her homework, that Simon chatted her up all the time but she was just playing with him…

And then one day Sophie and I took our first walk together, away from the school and down the secret smokers' lane that, through the wood, led to the main road, where there were cafés and shops and a crappy Italian restaurant that was to us a great extravagance, and I spent my week's lunch money there buying us two pizzas because she had begun to cry so softly, as we'd walked, that I wanted to give her everything I had. It was November, and outside the pizzeria a cold wind whipped up the leaves from the pavement and blew them towards us against the window, while inside, in the warmth of the restaurant, alone at the table in front of us, a man wearing a shabby tweed jacket was sipping his way through a cheap bottle of red wine with an alcoholic's aplomb. Each time a customer opened the door and the wind made a foray into the restaurant, he would mumble at the customer to please close the door. Behind him the two pizzas had hardly been touched and Sophie was looking down at the table and I could see only her cascades of auburn hair, but then she raised her head and leaned over to hold my hand, her brown eyes so big, and I thought of how I loved her, how I had always loved her since the first day I'd seen her. Her hand was soft, and nothing mattered now except my love for Sophie, and nothing had prepared me for this affection. But then she shuddered, jumped to her feet and flew out of the restaurant.

'Nearly real winter now,' the old drunk in the tweed jacket was saying, 'yep, winter's on its way.' But the waiters were staring through the glass window at the girl with the long legs as she ran into the wind and the darkness of an early afternoon that was already night. When I caught up with her at the entrance to the misty wood and reached out to her, held her, the tears began to fall again.

'How could Zoe do that to me?' she cried. 'I should have listened – you were right, you were right.'

'They won't hurt you again.' My voice was loud, competing against the wind.

'Girls always know how to hurt – I can't believe she told Anna. How evil do you need to be?'

'I'll protect you.'

'Oh, Simon.' She looked at me and interrupted her crying with a giggle, which then became real laughter. 'Look at you, standing all straight like that when you say "I'll protect you" – honestly, you're so daft!'

'They—'

'Shhh.'

She lowered her head and pressed her tear-soaked lips against my mouth and as she did I was struck by a fear that I might one day forget this kiss. A heartfelt kiss, electrifying in its emotion, its freshness. Sophie's lips relaxed now and her mouth opened and we kissed more passionately, her salty tears continuing to run down her cheeks and onto my lips; she was stroking the back of my neck, I was pulling her waist towards me and when she opened my coat to slide her hands inside and touched my chest I kissed her harder and we floated away together, far from the horror of earlier that day ...

'Hi, Sophie,' Anna had hissed, and then they were around her, a circle of blonde hair bouncing with excitement, as we all stared, for a second motionless in our surprise.

'Zoe?' Sophie had looked painfully confused, as if looking upon a new person in that circle. Zoe was silent back – proud in her treachery.

'Now, this flirting with Mr Dickens,' said Anna. 'This *obsession* with men.'

'Oh, Anna!' How courageous Sophie was; how nervous she was. 'Not this thing about him doing my homework again. Honestly – ' and she allowed herself to laugh ' – it's not my fault you struggle.'

And in refusing to cower Sophie became beautiful, and the girls understood that and hated her for it, and the hatred intensified as they saw me coming over to break it up.

'Ah, Simon.' Anna shook her head, in bitter amusement. 'Glad you've arrived. I should update you on this one – she's a bit unsure about things. It's complicated because, the thing is, you call her up all the time, but you've never asked her on a date and she's beginning to wonder what your game is; whether you've got the balls. And then there's Leo, you see – what did she tell you about him?'

'Shut up, Anna.'

'She's not quite sure what to do about Leo, or you. He's sweet too, you see.'

'I said shut up.'

'She's probably pretty happy with things as they stand – she *loves* the attention; she's admitted it to Zoe. She does the same with girls, with her friends – it's *all* about attention. Poor thing's lonely, you see – and it must be lonely when your dad doesn't live with you. Her mum walked out on him—'

'Don't you ever!' Sophie's raised voice stopped Anna for a second – but it was a mistake, as in the ensuing seconds it fuelled a glorious, savage satisfaction.

'That's it, isn't it?' murmured Anna. 'That's why you need attention.'

I was still young, did not know much about myself, but *had* already learned that I was not at my best at these sorts of moments – that high drama between members of the opposite sex was not my thing. Sophie, however, surprised us all: in perhaps one of her very best moments, she stepped forward and slapped Anna Cowley in the face, very hard and very cool. 'Don't you ever speak about my family, you stupid little girl.'

'Let's go, Sophie,' I interjected. 'Come on, let's go.'

So said Simon the Rescuer. But I was too slow in moving her away, for seconds later Anna's gang went wild and other girls came to Sophie's aid, with the result that madness broke out in the common room – and I found myself in the awkward position of being stuck in the middle of a bunch of fighting girls. Girls I couldn't hit back, but who were hitting me very hard, scratching at me, so that for months afterwards imitations would be made of my defensive tactics: the arms crossed before the face, the ducking and weaving, the squatting. I had come off worse than Sophie, with two little cuts below my right ear and a swelling on my forehead.

… Now, in the wood, as I held her and the cold rain began to fall on the leaves above us, she was looking at the cuts, stroking the swelling.

'They beat you up quite badly,' she whispered.

'Yes – not allowed to hit back, you see. Was it true though, about Leo?' I was desperate to know – despite all the upset, this was rather important.

'It was a girly chat,' Sophie said. 'And they completely twisted it. What I said was, oh, I don't know – I said I didn't know if you were ever going to ask me. Well, I mean, will you? Will you ask me?'

'Ask you what?'

'Oh, what do you think?'

'Ask you out? Of course!' I pulled back a second. 'If you want it all formal and everything…' I cleared my throat and smiled. 'Sophie Williams, will you go out with me?'

And years later, when we sat in her living room looking out at the harsh London night, she would shake her head in fond laughter, saying that she hadn't meant it that literally –

but that, as it happened, what I had asked was the loveliest thing anyone had ever asked her, and she had remembered it always for its sincerity.

'Will you?'

'Of course I'll go out with you,' she whispered. 'You're lovely.'

SOMEWHERE IN THE words we shared that day, somewhere secret in our kisses, we were telling each other truer things. We're both a bit vulnerable, aren't we? Simon's shy and anxious, sometimes a clown, and Sophie's sad about her father. Sophie's kind, and disappointed with herself for having hurt Simon with her words to Zoe, because she believes him when he keeps telling her now, as they rush back under the rain, how much he cares. Simon's crazy about Sophie and she likes him too – so we'll go forward as a team now, support each other as we go...

And Sophie and I did become a team after that day; and Sophie became always kinder, more affectionate and thoughtful, as if she had limitless reserves of kindness that she'd been afraid to show. Perhaps it was because it takes a lot to convince a kind, sensitive person that the person who fancies her truly wishes her well. She embraced the adventure by my side, always patient, my nervousness as endearing to her as it was transparent. There was trust building between us – and this was essential, because we were approaching something very new.

We were kissing *a lot* now – at lunchtime, in the library, at the end of the day when Sophie was waiting for the school bus and my dad dozed in the Renault. We would spend Saturday evenings at my house, watching films in the sitting room with the door firmly closed, while my parents chatted in the kitchen. There was an element of ritual to those evenings – Deborah would arrive to drop Sophie off, exchange pleasantries with my parents, Sophie would come in, head a little bowed, say hello a little awkwardly, and then we would head to the sitting room. My dad would come in, ask if we were alright, whether we wanted a cup of tea. Then the door would close, the film start, and suddenly there would be a kiss – the thing I had been waiting for all day. Then another and another, and soon, after the kissing became intolerably repetitive, reaching the same sort of impasse as those telephone conversations had, and with me delaying, somehow unable to make the move, Sophie would take the initiative, moving her hands under my shirt and climbing on top of me, straddling me as I sat still, anxious but blissfully happy. She would begin to kiss me again, but frantically now, with us both fully clothed, and in these moments I would be struck by the odd question as to whether this actually constituted a form of sex.

'How's it going with Sophie?' my mates would ask – all of them still without girlfriends. 'Had sex yet?'

'Obviously!' I would tut, arrogantly.

Then one day, as the film played out, unwatched, in the sitting room, Sophie whispered in my ear, 'I think we're ready.'

A week or so earlier, on Sophie's seventeenth birthday, I had finally visited her home. The delay in visiting had been because Sophie had said that we would never have any privacy there – the grandparents would chat to us non-stop, and there were always friends or relatives round. It was lovely to be winding up the hill towards the white house I had thought of so often; and it was funny and somehow bolstering of self-esteem to be the object of such attention there, to suffer the gentle grilling from Deborah, to engage in that serious manly conversation with Grandad. But it would be at my parents' house that *it* was planned to happen – for they would be away an entire weekend in December, and neither they nor Deborah minded Sophie staying over – provided Simon didn't keep going on about it! We planned *it* with growing excitement – for days I had trouble sleeping.

But then the big night arrived – and *it* did not go so well.

'Oh, my God!' I was sitting on the edge of the bed in the low light, my head in my hands – we were in the early hours. 'Oh, my God, you could be pregnant!'

'It's my fault,' Sophie sniffed. 'I should have done something – I should have helped you put it on. Oh, Simon – we're too young for a kid. Stop saying "Oh, my God!", please – you're scaring me.'

'Oh, my God!' I was gazing down at the camel's face on the packet lying on the floor – the camel seemed to be looking back up at me. Below the face were the words *Hump, Grunt, Hump*.

'Where did you get those things, anyway?' Sophie whispered.

'Last ones left in the machine in the pub toilets,' I whispered back, my head down.

'What about the ones we bought in Boots?'

I couldn't bear to look at her as I whispered the truth:

'I used them up – practising. I got too into it and then, by the time you came over, I realised I'd run out and so I had to go to the pub.'

'Camel Condoms, though? And I didn't think condoms were supposed to be black.'

'Me neither. Listen...' I inhaled, trying to control the terror 'I think I put it on the wrong way round!' I looked at her, aghast. 'I was all stressed, and—'

'The thing is...' Sophie was gathering herself. 'I think we're OK, actually, if you think about it calmly. Because...' she paused, as if searching for the words '...I mean, nothing actually *happened*, did it?'

'Not really,' I agreed. 'But there was a hell of a lot of confusion there for a moment – total chaos. And, among one

211

thing and another, there was a second when it was off and – oh, I think it's possible, you know. They say it only takes a second.'

'Right, I'm going to have a test.'

Sophie did have her test soon thereafter – and, somewhat unsurprisingly, given that we had not had sex, she was not pregnant. Meanwhile my days and nights became plagued by camels, the final dance of the insecurities of adolescence – they would pace, grunting, in my dreams, and appear also in my waking hours at the key moment, the very key moment, with the result that things were not working as they should. But then one night, as the snow fell outside and the voices from our neighbours' party drifted through the street of Christmas lights, Sophie, lying on my bed, smiled at me tenderly, and said, 'Don't think – just kiss me.' And so I kissed her, without thinking, without anything entering my mind other than how I loved her, and that the snow was falling outside. 'Don't think,' she repeated, 'there's nothing to think about, except how I love you.' And all the anxieties left me, like clouds dispersing in the sky, while simultaneously I knew that they had never existed, that they had never been real…

'You're not nervous any more,' she whispered. 'See?'

We walked together into 1997, through its bleak winter lit by our togetherness, its bright spring, its cherished summer days. Suddenly it was autumn again, winter again, Christmas again… and we were in 1998. There came the icy morning when I received my offer from Clare, then the spring day on which Sophie – who could have sailed into Oxbridge but who, despite my pleas, had been too unassuming, too embarrassed to apply – received her offer from Nottingham, that spring that with its incipient warmth brought about a happiness intensified by its cruel promise of change. We were soon clawing to hold onto them, those days, our world that excluded everyone else, and the knowledge that we couldn't led to our seeking refuge in nostalgia, reminiscing about the morning when it was still morning, dwelling on memories of the previous night, imagining a coming weekend and, once imagined, guarding it together. We built our own myth, a sunlit tapestry in which we stood against a backdrop of a myriad people who served only to emphasise the comfort, the necessity, of blocking out the rest of the world. Against the menace of the future I defended us with absolutes.

We'll always be together, won't we, Sophie? You'll never leave me?

I'll love you forever, Sophie.

Nothing would make sense without you, Sophie.

We sat together in the library and at assembly and in the common room, Sophie's tormentors long silenced by our unity, and towards the end of the sixth form all but a few of my friends began to drift away as I even stopped smoking with the lads in the wood and drinking in the local pubs and to their disdain and my surprise one day lost my childish cynicism and discovered my love of what I was studying – of French and Spanish and English and Latin, of Ovid and Hardy and Molière, of the Latin American boom and the distant worlds that my whimsical mind conjured up carelessly from excerpts of great literature which were intended to say something else entirely, but all that didn't matter – I still loved those distant worlds. Finally the promise I had shown intermittently throughout school, and on which my conditional offer from Clare was based, was fulfilled, while Sophie excelled in chemistry but also in maths and biology and physics – and general studies too, the subject I never quite mastered. And a gentle rivalry kept us all the more tightly within the safety of our private story.

'Mr Watson said that my Voltaire translation was fantastic again,' I would announce.

'Well, no surprise, Mr Cambridge!'

'Ha! Don't turn that on me when you could have gone too.'

'I didn't want to! The idea of wearing a gown to dinner, surrounded by all those poshos! Ugh! Anyway, it's been a good day for me too.'

'Go on.'

'I got ninety-five per cent in Part A of a past exam paper, in chemistry.'

'Honestly, you're so competitive.'

'I'm *not*!'

And the spring was becoming summer when we were all sent home to study for the exams.

'That's a bull, in that field.'

It was a Saturday morning in late May, and we were walking through the dewy green of Hubbard's Hills – my infatuation with the countryside long over, a residual fondness now co-existing with a new, general fear.

'And the gate's open, too, Sophie.'

'It is *not* a bull – honestly.' Sophie sighed, turning to me. 'I was thinking, you know…' she sighed again '…it *is* a little unfair, this university system. Sending us away, to different parts of the country.'

'Listen, I've told you this before.' I pulled her close, presumptuous in my cowardice. 'I won't go to Clare. I'll wait a year and reapply to Nottingham. I'll come and live with you.'

She laughed. 'You're a silly romantic.'

'I will,' I protested. 'I'll really do it.'

'No, stop it – you're crazy!' She took a breath. 'It'll be fine, nothing will change. We'll just spend the weeks studying and see each other at the weekends. The time will fly – you'll see.'

But her defiant speech had consumed all her certainty, leaving her glum. Above us billowed a sign for Freshers' Week, casting shadows over a garden discovered in a dream.

'Sophie?'

'I'm fine. Nothing will change.'

And that balmy summer, with our results out and our places confirmed, we slipped into a form of light distraction, those words becoming almost sacred between us, repeated like an incantation. They were the last emotion she conveyed to me before my parents drove me to Cambridge – 'Nothing will change,' she whispered – and yet less than six months later, months of increasingly vicious arguments, I was racing to ivy-clad Hugh Stewart Hall in Nottingham, hurrying to have it confirmed to me that the distance of Sophie's voice over the telephone during our last argument now glimmered too on her face. As I sat on the train I was thinking about the last months, trying to rationalise things, to understand how and why everything had gone so wrong. But the more I reflected, the more my position hardened – this was *her* fault, I decided, with the blinkered certainty of an angry teenager. I would moan occasionally, yes, and I would fixate on things, but she *knew* I was a grumbler, and we all have negative sides. And my moaning was only ever because she'd done something dismissive of *us*: I was the one fighting for us here! And surely, if we were adults who loved each other, we should tolerate the traits we didn't like. It was true that I was a bit nagging – but there were things I didn't like about her too. I didn't like this new indifference, for example: how she would blithely decide not to call on an agreed evening. And, as for all this going out partying, it was right that she should do it if she wanted to, and obviously fine by me – even though it wasn't at all like the person I knew – but the point was, could we talk about something else? It was boring! And there was such hypocrisy because, if I *ever* mentioned that I was going out, she would become just the person she'd claimed I was – all jealous and bitter. As for that time I'd mentioned Arabella's name by accident – Sophie had gone ballistic! But at the same time she would forget to call me and ... so many things ... such a mess! Anyway, right: you're here. Don't cry – whatever she says, don't cry.

'Hello, Simon.'

No, it wasn't Sophie – it wasn't the person I knew. What had happened to her? This young woman took my hand in hers, without stopping to look at me. She led me through wood-panelled hallways, across a grassy quad, past what looked like ...

'Ah, you have formal dining here too, after all!'

'You know we do – we talked about it last time.'

'No, we didn't. You're imagining things.'

'We *did*.'

... she led me all the way to her sinuous staircase, and then up those creaking stairs to her room with its single bed and high ceiling and old desk that looked out to a lawn dotted with willow trees. And when she turned to me, illuminated by the daylight gushing in from the bay window, I was horrified to see that I was an intruder in her room.

'You shouldn't have come; I'd said that I'd come to see you.'

'What are you talking about?' I sat down on the bed with a firm expression that was a reaction to the humiliating concern in Sophie's eyes. As if she were trying to break some news gently to a child.

'We're arguing all the time, Simon.' The words were tumbling out awkwardly. 'It's not either of our faults – but it's turned so horrible. It's not going to work. We're both staying in our rooms being unpleasant over the phone when we could be going out and meeting new—'

'New?'

'Well, new friends. What do you think I meant?'

216

'You're making no sense.' I looked at her, trying to conceal my trembling. 'If you want to split up, just have the courage to say it. Because I agree, anyway – that's why I came.'

'Oh, you agree?' A pause. The grey mist of guilt was beginning to lift from Sophie's eyes, uncertainly at first, cautiously now … she was checking for a sign … but my expression was constant and then, yes, the burden had dissipated, for Simon agreed! How lovely, then, that we could both move on, both be happy.

'I just wanted to say it to your face,' I said. 'We deserved that much.'

'Well, this feels weird, doesn't it? After everything we've shared? You're still the most important thing that ever happened to me.' She had begun to cry.

'It's a bit weird – but we'll get used to it.'

'We'll keep in touch though, won't we, Simon? Oh, I don't know – perhaps we can just think of this as a temporary break? Perhaps one day, after we've both found ourselves … I think maybe we both just need to find ourselves, you know … '

'Of course. Listen,' I said, 'I think I'm going to go.'

'Already?'

'It's for the best.'

A hug and a kiss and a second kiss – too emotional, the second kiss – a nod and a turn for the door. A walk back down the wooden stairs to the sound of Sophie sobbing above. A wave from the lawn and then a picture of her leaning out of the window with a sudden doubt.

'Bye, then, Sophie,' I called up to her. Begging her to come running down. Come on, Sophie, come running down the stairs, shout to me to wait. Come on, Sophie, you're throwing everything away.

'Promise me we'll keep in touch!' she cried. 'Part of me will always love you!'

The moping of dumped, broken-hearted young men remains one of the few examples of human emotion that an otherwise psychology-obsessed society still regards with gentle mockery, mixed with a Victorian impatience. The moping is considered by the older generations as sweet, but then silly and over time irksome, a self-indulgence of hormonal little animals who have yet to understand the world. True love, proud women and sorted men say, comes later, and the mark of it is that in its maturity there is peace and an acceptance, without the melodrama, the jealousy and frustrated desire, the unjustified desperation and the brief moments of ecstasy all attributable to unformed character. Such an *ex post facto* analysis of emotion is repeated through generations, in an insane cycle of amnesia so that the world might stay sane: on the other side of the condescension lies the denial, the old fool refusing the memory of a smile; remembering as he denies it his first taste of abandonment...

I arrived back at Clare College in the late evening, wandered to the Cellars, then later around the Market Square, drinking Jack Daniel's from the bottle until reaching a state that I would not remember except for the vomiting up the stairs to my room...and then, the next morning, I woke up and decided not to mope; decided to work. I began to read *properly*, studying late into the crisp Cambridge night, fuelled by Marlboro Lights and endless black coffee, waking in a panic and rushing out of Old Court, Gothic to the north, Classic to the south, the odd Regency touch the only evidence that this was not still the seventeenth century; a court open only to the sky, to the leaden mantle of winter pierced by the rare day of fine blue, to the gossamer clouds blown through the spring...rushing past the chapel and the Great Hall and the Buttery, across the stone footbridge hopping gracefully over the River Cam to Memorial Court, and then out through the iron gates to the Faculty of Modern and Medieval Languages, men brushing away the mountains of fallen leaves in the autumn, bluebells to my left in May, cows grazing in the fields... I became almost unnaturally enamoured with my languages, denying to myself that this was all about Sophie, convincing myself instead that her allure had been replaced now by the pages of Voltaire and Manzoni, the reassurance of her kiss substituted by a professor's compliments, the safety of her holding my hand by the silence of the Forbes Mellon Library. As for the physical desire, well, there was always the outlet of fumbling, perfunctory sex in the early hours with student girls whose departure the next morning would leave an emptiness – an emptiness that I would fill quickly by reminding myself of the preparation needed for that afternoon's supervision. And then, when I realised that I *did* like Arabella, that we should take it slowly but that I was quite fond of her and those funny startled eyes, I ended all contact with Sophie – so that towards the end of the first year I began to believe that I really had got over her and moved on. The long summer break and the concern of bumping into her back at home were dealt with by constant travelling, by wandering through the gentler portraits of southern France and Italy... the cafés of Arles and the lemon groves at Menton, the Gulf of Poets and the Silent Bay of Liguria, the towns in Calabria and Basilicata with Homeric names... Maratea, Scalea, Scilla, Tropea... meeting occasionally a local girl with olive skin and a voice like a song, who the day afterwards would show me around, making me realise with a twinge of sadness that I wasn't really *very* into Arabella... this girl's name was Chloé or Carmine or Lilou or Federica and I was falling quickly in love as we ambled through her town on a sunny afternoon, semi-understanding as the absence of threat led her to unburden herself of a thousand thoughts. Later I would be invited for dinner at her parents' house, maybe, where I would be met by the fascinated stares of extended families and thrive on their laughter as I attempted to pronounce local words, exaggerating my Englishness as we ate our way through bowls of *tagliatelle al ragù, orrechiette* or *soupe au pistou,* plates of *petits farcis, mortadella* or the atrocious *trippa al peperoncino.*

Back for the second year with a growing confidence, soaring in my studies, and the girls came more regularly now: Felicity from Notting Hill, Roberta from Surrey, Mary from Leeds and Lottie from somewhere I never knew, but none of them attracted me the way my lovable redhead Arabella had, and she still liked me too, and kept telling me not to worry, that we were adults and she wouldn't be hurt if it didn't work, we could take it slow again. And so we tried and we did have a lot of fun together that year, but there were always those moments I thought of Sophie instead, when I wished she were Sophie – a moment when walking back drunk up the path from the riverbank, a brief pause before kissing her behind the old yews and chestnuts in the dark of the college gardens, something she said in the Cellars one night. And in late September 2000, Arabella and I now over, after that crazy summer of the Cunningham Prize, the Kants initiation and Dan Serfontein's party, just before I was due to leave for Naples, this delicate stability I had created in relation to Sophie was rocked by a telephone call.

'It's Sophie's mum,' my dad said, regarding me with a quizzical face. 'She asked for your number and – well, I said you were here.'

'What? Oh, Paul, you dozy sod – you could have asked him first!' My mother's blue Irish eyes were particularly brilliant. 'Don't worry, Simon.'

'No, it's OK, I'll take it.'

The cordless phone was lying on the wooden table that had dominated a warm, now distinctly unmodernised kitchen for all of my life. I took it through to the conservatory and sat down on a chair, looking out at the rhododendrons.

'Hello?'

'Oh, there you are. I'm so sorry to ring like this.'

The apology was unconvincing. Single mother of an only daughter, Deborah had joined Sophie in falling in love with her first boyfriend, but the fondness had existed always alongside a sort of protective distrust of me that was natural, something I could understand. It was a fear of my dumping her daughter, perhaps – which was a bit ironic, really…

'Not a problem. Is everything OK?'

'Oh, Sophie's terribly upset.'

I tried to control my pique. 'Sorry to hear that, Deborah. What's happened?'

'It's that *damned* father of hers.' Icy now, the voice. 'The poor girl got it into her head that she wanted to see him. I don't know what she told you about Graham.'

'Nothing. Almost literally nothing. Just that he still lives in Derby, by himself.'

'Well, it doesn't matter now. But yes, Derby. She went there, poor thing, to meet him, and—'

'It went badly?'

She resented that. It must have sounded flippant.

'That's right, Simon, it went badly and she's in quite a state. Anyway, last night she mentioned you and when she did I remembered – oh, I know this sounds silly – but I remembered how you were always able to make her laugh about things. The thing is, Simon, it's so important, it's so lovely, to be able to really laugh together. Well, you know what I mean. I do think it was very extreme of you to decide that you didn't want to keep in touch. I mean, you were only youngsters and—'

'Mum! What are you doing?'

Then silence, followed by some strained, muffled voices. Finally, Deborah again.

'I'm so sorry, I'm told I've got to go.'

The email arrived later that night.

Dear Simon,

First of all, I'm sorry for writing this email as I understood what you said about not staying in touch and I respect that – and have respected it – even though it's not what I would have chosen. I do hope you're well and that things are going swimmingly at uni! I would ask you how the studies are going – there's so much I would like to know – but I don't want you to think you need to reply. I am just writing to say sorry for the bizarre little call from my mum today – can't believe it! Mrs Meddling as always!

I don't actually know why she called you or what she said – I think she might be going dotty! But basically all is well with me. Things are going well at Nottingham – looking forward to my final year although still not decided what I'm going to do afterwards. Of course, you have one more year than me, doing languages – you must be about to depart for some warmer climes; bet you're looking forward to that!

I do often think of you but don't want you to think this is all an attempt to mess you around or anything – not that it would have worked in any case. I wouldn't have planned to tell you like this, but just to be clear I

*am perfectly happy in life and in love, and am seeing
another guy from uni and it's going well. Hope you've
found a lucky girl too.*

Do look after yourself, and I'm so sorry again.

Sophie xx

'After a lifetime devoted to psychology,' said my father that
evening, as he ate his dinner in front of the television and my
mother rolled her eyes to make me smile, 'I can assure you that
all women are nutters.'

I WENT TO NAPLES troubled. It was October and still summer,
the faded beauty of Piazza del Plebiscito bathed in light, hordes
of German tourists queuing for the hydrofoils to Ischia and
Capri, the affluent locals bathing at the quaint Bagni Elena
at Posillipo. There was Piazza Bellini, teeming in the warm,
humid evenings with pretty girls with hard eyes, frenzied
children yelling in a language that was not Italian, young men
without helmets whizzing through the crowds on scooters,
over the rivers of rubbish overflowing from the bins. Elderly
couples ambling past Greek columns, dogs barking savagely
from balconies, clouds of cannabis hanging in the night
air above the street named either Via Toledo or Via Roma,
depending on whom you asked. The music pumping in the hip
district of Chiaia, blaring out from minuscule bars crammed
with pirates' faces, summer still, summer still in Naples…

Yet I spent the majority of October thinking of Sophie.
Brooding in the flat I shared with four other students on the
Corso Vittorio Emanuele, the busy, snaking road that cuts
through the middle of the climbing city, below residential
Vomero and above the chaos of the Quartieri Spagnoli, the

grid of tightly packed alleys that is the heart of Naples and that forms part of the vastest historical city centre in Europe, where the city's less wealthy inhabitants live surrounded by some of our continent's most precious cultural heritage. Brooding as I made my way each morning to the language school, down the flights of ancient steps before a panorama of Tyrrhenian sea stretching out to Capri, and later turned left up the tree-lined Via Chiaia. In its luxury and hint of despair, its gleaming shop windows below neglected apartments, the armed guards outside the banks, the women with Louis Vuitton handbags posing at the beginning of implausibly narrow, ancient Greek alleys that led up, high up into the pulsating insanity of the Quartieri, this was Paris's Avenue Montaigne and the heart of the third world, a *bella figura* struggling to contain the force of the abandonment, the infectious instability, the reckless *vivere 'a jurnata* – living for the day, solely for the day – that surged around it.

I was brooding, though, my senses dimmed, my fascination limited. Deborah had dedicated her life to Sophie and understood her every emotion, and it was inconceivable that she would have invented her story. Sophie still cared, perhaps? Or was she just being nostalgic, capricious, in a moment of weakness? That seemed to be the truth, and her declaration that she was seeing someone had brought about a new sense of humiliation. Finally, in November, I started going out. I joined them, the Erasmus students, the students from Spain and Germany and France and America, in their wild, heedless nights in Piazza Bellini and Piazza del Gesù, the bars of Chiaia and the clubs of Pozzuoli, and one night, as I was smoking a cigarette behind the dance floor of L'Arancia, Naples's oldest club, I met a local girl. She stood before me, slender yet curvaceous, dark-haired and olive-skinned, at once hostile and enchanting in her extraordinary beauty – that raw, harsh beauty that is born in the Quartieri. Her insolence as she looked brazenly into my eyes captured the whole of my attention, eliciting a sudden, deep excitement.

'*Bonasera*,' she said coolly. '*Mariella*.'

From that moment, I convinced myself that I'd consigned Sophie once more to the past. Mariella and I kissed that night, outside the club on Via Toledo, her enormous lips opening softly, with thrilling reassurance, and soon a romance became a liberation, and then an infatuation, as I thought of nothing but Mariella, of her body and those lips and the touch of her skin. For the only time in my undergraduate life the studies began to suffer, and then studying stopped entirely, the dissertation lying half-started on the desk in my room as I was led into the heart of the Quartieri Spagnoli, into the danger and joy of living by the day...I would wake up towards midday in Mariella's studio flat on Vico Conte di Mola, foggy from the partying of the night before, and would lie still, listening, as the housewives hurled news from their balconies with an intensity that could easily be confused for rage: '*'a gatta, 'a gatta! Aggio vist' 'a gatta...èh! Ma ll'aggio vista pur'ie!*' Something about a stray cat that had been jumping from balcony to balcony...the children below were booting footballs before a shrine to Diego Maradona, the church bells ringing hysterically...there was an argument now, surely a fight...no, it was just a conversation...a man was cackling...a deafening bang, what was that? A car's exhaust? Someone bawling that he didn't sell something...no, that he couldn't do something...'*sciuè sciuè! mo' mo'!*'...it was at once tribal and redolent of epic poetry, this dialect, and the volume did not belong to the world I knew. Dozens of people shouting at the same time. I still couldn't understand the meaning of most of the words or the meaning of the tones...the scooters were roaring past below, there was the

225

beeping of a car's horn…confusion now, a form of chanting at the driver that he needed to turn round…and then a bang again, a crash! What had…but then the clapping of hands! Applause! '*Hê visto? Hê visto? Michele! Miche'!!!*'…the neighbour's dog waking up with a bark…and then the cat, the cat was back…'*'a gatta, 'a gatta!*'…a little girl and her mother engaged in a screaming match…a door slamming and a baby crying and the boys cheering as they scored a goal…

Ahead was a day free of endeavour, a walk to Piazza Dante, a cappuccino at Gambrinus, lunch at Da Nennella, maybe. The restlessness that had dominated the last two years would raise its head briefly around now and I would let the anxieties dissolve slowly, feel victorious in my rebellion. Mariella was lying naked, her arms flung out, her head to the side, her olive body radiant…she would open her eyes as I gazed…she was already awake…she was leaning over and kissing my neck, running her hand up and down my chest in slow, confident circles. I was trying to kiss her too, her elusive mouth breaking into a mischievous smile, making its way down from my neck now, her hands reaching under the thin white sheet and she'd darted below it, doing things Sophie had never done; and she was raising herself up from below the sheets, pressing her warm, soft body down onto mine, burying her head again in my neck and beginning to rock…and then she was moaning…and she would still be embracing me later as we lay on the bed in silence, thoughtful now, both of us…

'*Cazzo!*' she shouted one morning, jumping to her feet as her mobile phone rang.

'Mariella?'

'My *mammà e papà*, they arrive! Fast, fast, *muovete, muovete!*'

Mariella's living alone in her studio flat at the age of twenty-two was fairly exceptional – most Neapolitans appeared to me to live with their parents until the age of around forty, at which point the only change would involve the description of the arrangement: suddenly, the elderly parents would be said to be living with them. But Mariella's appearance of independence was deceptive. She stayed at the studio flat only during the working week – which, according to the official account, she spent training as an apprentice at her friend's beauty centre that was really a tanning salon and where she put in about three hours a day – and each Saturday she would return for the weekend to the nearby town of Nola, where her parents lived. I imagined them as a huge, kindly mother and a terrifying, squat father. The studio flat had been procured by the father through a series of deals and favours that was more complex than a step plan for any of Rupert Plunkett's transactions, and occasionally *Papà* came with his wife to Naples to check on his innocent, beloved daughter, a girl who made the sign of the cross before every church in Nola.

'Go, go! They come!'

It was December, almost time to go home to England for Christmas, the days in Naples fluctuating between brief resurgences of summer, dramatic storms, and an insipid cold at which the locals trembled with fear. I had been in the city nearly three months and had yet to articulate the duality of Campania and its culture that was impressing itself on me. The mirage of freedom in poverty that the mirage of wealth elicited by the shops on Via Chiaia sought to conceal; the immediate, effervescent warmth of the locals that was not quite false but that was nonetheless misleading; the initial, exaggerated spontaneity and openness, that lack of inhibition, followed by occasional glimpses, sudden suggestions that this culture might in fact be more closed than any I had ever experienced. The living by the day interplaying with flashes of cold calculation, an interplay that was – or that appeared to a proud Englishman to be – the diametric opposite of an Englishman's own duality of conservatism and ingenuousness. But nowhere was the dichotomy more apparent than in the position of young, single Neapolitan women, in their sentimental affairs, their sexuality. It seemed that the choice for them was 'good girl or prostitute', that there was a threat of immediate expulsion hanging over the head of a woman who dared to test the frontiers, but the situation was more complicated than that, barely held together by intricately woven fabric. Mariella accentuated her sexuality, with her heavily made-up face and lips and the flirtatious delay before she moved away her eyes, and when we went out to the bars of the Quartieri she was tight jeans and bare midriff. She had all the sexual experience of an English girl her age and more, and insisted, as I did too, on protection; and yet on Saturday mornings as she prepared to go back to Nola the jeans were no longer tight, the top was sober, the face suddenly naïve and virginal – and the face would transform back for a second while she laughed mockingly about the latest plaintive text messages from the man at the grocer's store on Via Nicotera, who would growl as she walked past, and to whom for some reason she had given her number. It was occurring to me gradually that the culture risked skewing the self-awareness of women, particularly beautiful young women. There seemed to be so much duplicity and denial, society dictating that a good Neapolitan girl could either be single or *fidanzata* – the fact that the term *fidanzata* did not necessarily mean engaged, but merely 'taken', added to the suggestion that things were trapped in an unenlightened past. Maybe I had it wrong, maybe I was exaggerating, but what I did know for sure, straight from Mariella, was that a relationship such as we had would be unacceptable to a traditional family like hers, and if discovered would result in shame for her and who knew what for me. Yes, there was a repression about all this that flabbergasted me...

But hang on! This wasn't the time for pretentious observations! These weren't the days! No, these were the happy days! We were young, unfamiliar and new and we rejoiced in our otherness, and I liked myself just like that, as fascinating to Mariella as she was to me. Now for a second Mariella forgot her own fear and began to moan with laughter at my English form of terror, my fumbling attempts to put on my shirt as quickly as I could; life was still a game, there was a delicious smell of baked pasta from the street below and I felt so comfortable in this role of uncomfortable Englishman and – shit! – her phone rang again. '*Cia' mammà, mo' t'arape.*' They were coming up the stairs, I was on the balcony and the old women on theirs were watching with fascination. I was only about six, maybe ten feet up – and Mariella was begging me now to go for it – '*Fa ampresso vuttete, vuttete...pe' piacere...ja'!*' – and maybe I would break my leg but oh, sod it – and there I was! There I was flying through the Campanian air, adrift for a second in the midst of the chaos, flying through Naples... landing on a bin bag and peering up to see Mariella closing the doors to the balcony and the gaping mouths of the women standing still on theirs. '*Mamma d''o Carmine! Hê visto, Anna hê visto?! E che r'è?*' And I was staggering away, past the bins and the scooters, and was now a character on that street, cognisant that the day was mine. Then I was out onto the safety of Via Toledo, and later by the library looking out to sea, all giddy...

And Christmas back in Lincoln came and went, with vague but confusing thoughts about Sophie, thoughts that came intertwined with, and perhaps accentuated, my desire, my desperation for Mariella. The days were punctuated by a thrill at the arrival of a message from Signorina Esposito, panic when she didn't reply, a thrill again when she did. There was a morning of real joy, an intense nostalgia, when a big parcel arrived from NAPOLI – inside were beautifully crafted miniature terracotta figurines from the master artisans of San Gregorio Armeno, the depiction of a scene on my street, Corso Vittorio Emanuele – a young Latin woman kissing a pale young man with blue eyes. *Ti amo*, Mariella wrote. *Auguri, vita mia*. The recollection of my dissertation, still lying there on the desk in that flat – it was to be a translation and analysis of a chapter of Calvino, but had so far amounted to a cursory review – the recollection of it I pushed to the back of my mind, resentful at its having dared to intrude on the beauty of my happiness, the colour of my freedom.

And then it was February and then it was April, then May – and it was summer again in Naples. And the exquisite insouciance had remained, crowned now by the Southern Italian sun but otherwise unchanged by the passing of the seasons. Still coffee at Gambrinus, still a walk down Via Toledo, lunch above the waves at Reginella, evenings drinking in decadent squares. I was still on a high, still incredulous that Mariella would want to be with me, still inattentive to the subtle warnings and promises that escape those who are engaged in the present, unable or unprepared to consider the development of this story that would require consideration if it were to last, running from analysis, consolidation or practicalities... because, without having admitted it to myself, all I was really living was a dream. In early June, Mariella told me that it was time to meet her parents; time to be introduced as a *fidanzato*. As the news sank in, I experienced that oddest of feelings that is elicited by the materialising of what you have proclaimed without conviction to be a grand ambition: a sense that something awful and unnatural must have occurred to bring it about.

'Simon,' purred Mariella, stroking my head as I looked up at her ceiling. 'You think my English is good now for London?'

The following Saturday we boarded together an ancient regional train for Cancello, where we then changed for Nola, the hot, sunny day chilled by guilt and the promise of drama ahead. Our story for the parents was now clear and practised: we had met at the language school where I taught, and where Mariella had come to pick up a friend; we had subsequently only seen each other at parties, or nights out in the presence of her friends; I didn't know where her flat was. My emotions though were tied up in a separate, unshared plan that I was reluctant to recognise – a plan that slowly was taking form and that involved escape. And I wondered why I wanted to escape and was ashamed at myself for my inconsistency, unable to decide whether it was something that was wrong with me, some fear of commitment, or whether my distaste at Mariella's new forcefulness was legitimate. She was very clear now about what was going to happen. She would wait until I finished my degree and then, in about a year's time, she would move to London: there was no mention of marriage but I feared this was because she deemed it so obvious that to express it would have been vulgar. We would live in London together and she might take a year or so out, to just relax and explore the city. Maybe she would join a band – she'd always wanted to be a singer! She wasn't interested in studying, in art or books or anything like that, in bettering herself – she just wanted to join a band! After all, she said, she and I were more or less the same age but she had had to work all her life, while I had been having fun at school and then an elite university! It was new, this bitterness – the acute, problematical bitterness of a victor, a person who has found a way out and only upon finding it understands the rancour that has been thundering inside. And, during the previous week, traits of hers that I had once found either attractive or at least excusable in their exoticism I had come to find concerning, unpleasant when viewed as traits of a person who would be concretely part of my own life. The previous night we had eaten at Da Michele, the famous pizzeria, and had been presented with a bill that was all wrong – they had missed off our second round of drinks, and my own third drink – and as I had raised my hand to point this out she had pulled my arm back down and asked me if I was stupid. I had yielded, but then been furious at myself for yielding. And, on the way back from the pizzeria, Riccardo, the man from the grocer's on Via Nicotera, had called her and to make me laugh she had put him on loudspeaker so that I could hear his desperate voice begging to take her out. This she had done before, back in December, and then Riccardo had represented to me merely a stereotype, the ridiculous Southern Italian playing Romeo, absurd to the point of hilarity as he told her that he had loved her before he had even met her, that she was his life, that he had bought her a Tiffany ring that Mariella had told me would probably be stolen or fake. But now as I listened to him I looked at her laughing eyes and found her cold, a touch cruel – and why had she given him her number?

'You should just tell him that you are with me,' I said, still feigning lightness, as we got back to her flat.

'What? I never tell things to Riccardo!'

But I suspected that I was using the Riccardo story as a pretext, in an attempt to flee from an uncomfortable confession. Mariella held my hand firm and proud that morning in the cramped carriage of the little train as it chugged towards Nola, through the madness of the landscape, the fertile, rich plains stretching out below a wondrous Vesuvius violated by the black fires in the distance, fires that years later would become notorious, revealed to be burning

232

with toxic waste brought from the North, from abroad, from a myriad parts of Europe, and dumped on this, once the most serene, delightful of lands. The dioxin in the air, the waste seeping from the illegal landfills to harm the land that had captivated Goethe and Stendhal and Dickens and Lawrence, inspired a thousand poems, the land that Pliny the Elder had called nature's favourite; the dumping and burning that would threaten agriculture, reputation, livelihoods, economy, the health of the people; the land that would one day become known as the *terra dei fuochi*.

As we approached Nola, Mariella patted me on the shoulder like a best friend, and I had never hated myself as I hated myself then, having confessed finally and silently that what I disliked about Mariella was that she was a taker: someone who grasped at what she could, a streetwise fighter prepared to use her beauty to improve her condition. It was vile and disgraceful to dislike her for this – these traits should have given rise to admiration or affectionate pity, or at least understanding, but instead I found them so unbecoming. And there was a grotesque hypocrisy in the fact that I had come to Naples arrogant and uninvited, and had sucked up all it had to offer, enjoyed it to the full, had been more of a taker than she ever had… Naples had seduced me as Mariella had seduced me, or so I liked to say, as if I were that passive observer, the truth being that I had taken it as I had taken her, clawed greedily at all it, and she, had to offer, while not having the courage to admit that I remained in truth uninvolved, that I was captivated but not committed, and that, therefore, it was I who was the taker…

'Simon.' A nervous Mariella stood up from her seat. 'We're here.'

That lunch with Mariella's family, my being presented to them as her boyfriend, was many different things for the many different people involved in it. A throng of people, in fact, as the extended family, more numerous than any extended family I had previously met in France or Italy, came to the family home to meet the *inglese* – or, more accurately, to stare at the *inglese*. For them I hoped – once I had regained my ability to think rationally – that it was an afternoon they would come to remember fondly; that, in being the first Englishman they had met, I had somehow added richness to their lives. For the mother – short, but very pretty and not at all obese as I had imagined her – and for the father, who instead was squatter than my imagination had allowed (he was an apotheosis, in fact: shorter, fiercer, louder than any father I had met, from Provence to Sicily) – for them, it was an afternoon of great import, as an initial hostility and apprehension turned to curiosity, then to affection, and then to a touch of confusion and surprise. For Mariella, it was, I reminded myself with rising nausea, perhaps the loveliest day of her life, the day it all came together. For me it was for the most part an afternoon spent with those two nemeses of mine, guilt and fear... Too much food, too much food, sudden panic, a misunderstanding, sudden panic, a misunderstanding...

'*Saimo*'!' The father had taken the place they all did: at the head of a long table laden with all the food in the world – spaghetti with clams, deep-fried eel, enormous mozzarellas, plates of prosciutto. And he was shouting at me as any good Southerner would, but with a certain added passion. '*Magna!*'

'My dad, he's telling you to have more.' Mariella was laughing.

'Yes, I understood. I'm just not sure I have any more space.'

'*'A trippa, 'a trippa!*'

The steaming bowl passed slowly down the table, from loving aunt to potbellied child, from swarthy uncle dressed in a starched white shirt to a cousin with a black leather jacket he refused to take off, to another potbellied little lad with a Napoli football shirt on that bore the name of Maradona. And then on to a sweet little girl called Imma, whose tenth birthday it was, to a fierce uncle, to a ... Everyone, now, sticking a chin out at me ...

'Now listen, Mariella.' My voice was sure. 'I'm afraid I can't eat tripe. It's the only thing that I simply cannot eat.'

'Is my *mamma*'s speciality.' The eyes open wide with family honour.

'*Magna, magnat' 'a trippa! E' bbona 'a trippa, magna, magna!*'

The head of the household was bellowing at me in a tone that in any part of the world outside Campania, in any region of any country of any continent, would be identifiable as a tone of fury: the tone of a man about to strike you, throw you out of his house, leap on you and beat you wildly to death ... but we were in Naples, so there was a chance all was still fine. Inhumanly squashed down in size, this man, like a dense lump of muscle, his elbows reaching up slightly to the table, his head of short, black hair inches above the bowl.

'He wants you to try it,' said Mariella.

'Yes, I got that.'

The tripe swirled around my mouth as I remembered not to chew – for chewing, I had learnt, would release its overpowering taste of intestine, its suggestion of raw cow. I weighed up the risks of attempting to swallow it whole, deciding against this lest I choke, so that it just continued to swirl and I just continued to nod down the table to the father, who pursed his lips as Mariella began to tell them more about me. About how I studied at Cambridge, the same university at which so many famous men had studied, Charles Darwin ...

'*Kembrig?*' cried the mother. '*Darveen? Maronna!*'

... that after graduating I would likely move to London – *Londra*! That I adored Italy and that my Italian was excellent, as they could see, but I was especially fond of Naples and the Neapolitans – a couple of cousins nodded at me, in respect – and that I was studying Modern and Medieval Languages. But the father raised his hand now, asking what 'modern and medieval languages' meant, what I was studying them for, while rubbing his hands together questioningly. I did not know the meaning of this gesture, but Mariella did – she explained to her father that in England it worked differently, and that you could get a well-paid job after studying languages or humanities. The father looked down at the table, shaking his head, incredulous – and, as he did, up came my napkin and with a feigned little cough out came the tripe, smooth as anything, and the napkin, full of tripe, was back in my pocket. I had made it. But then the father had stood up and was walking down the table towards me and the grandmother by my side, who a short time earlier had fallen in love with the ardour of her hundred years, and who continued to mouth to me with great sentiment the word *santo*.

'What's your dad doing, please, Mariella?'

He was stroking my face. The stubby fingers cracked and harsh against my skin.

'*Tene 'a faccia pulita*,' he announced. And Mariella's happiness blossomed.

'He says you have a clean face,' she whispered, reaching for my hand under the table. 'It is a big compliment in Naples.'

'I see – how nice.' *Got to get out, got to get out, pocket's full of tripe, pocket's full of tripe*. And Mariella's affection was sincere and confirmed.

'It is true.' Her voice flowed to me through the noise of the family. 'Your face is so clean.'

The final course. Baba swimming in rum, mini-sized *sfogliatelle*, the fruit salad, a mandatory further round of cakes, a slice of watermelon, coffee, the shot of limoncello.

And suddenly the lights went out and in came the birthday cake with ten candles and little Imma was now the centre of the world, sitting upright and blowing out the candles amid the compliments, the hugs from uncles and the kisses from a thousand aunts. Then the lights were back on and Imma was ordered by her own father, Mariella's uncle, to do something that I could not quite make out.

'*Sona!*' he repeated.

'She's a genius, this little girl,' whispered Mariella. 'They say she will be a star! She plays the piano so beautiful.'

'Oh, I see – he wants her to play the piano. I hadn't...'

'Ah, wait – yes! You also play!'

'No,' I said quietly. 'Do not tell them that, please. I can't play that well at all. I was just trying to show off to you. I was *lying* to you.'

But it was too late – she wasn't listening to what I was saying. As I turned in terror to look at the battered old piano in the corner of the room, Mariella had already told them that I was a master. That I too...

'*Sona!*' roared the father with all the vicious passion in the world.

All I was able to play was the theme tune to *Titanic*, Celine Dion's 'The Heart Must Go On'. I didn't even play that song very well, having been taught it one afternoon in my first year at university by a strange boy in our corridor who was convinced that beautiful student girls were necessarily superficial, their emotions triggered by the banal, and that a tune such as this would make her yours. I doubted if I even remembered the notes.

'*Sona!*'

'OK, OK. Christ.' I was getting to my feet when I was saved by the uncle. It was Imma's birthday. She was the hope of the family. She should go first.

'*Sona!*' they growled at Imma.

The little girl walked across to the old piano and, as her adoring relatives held their breath, to my unspeakable dismay she began to play 'The Heart Must Go On'. She played it with a precision and depth that went beyond it, a talent that seemed to me to hold a golden promise, the magic of a rhythm known only to those who have been born with the secret... and then this angel upon whose shoulders a family's dreams rested had finished her performance, the aunts were gasping and a heavy, solitary tear was running down the left cheek of Mariella's father's cruel face. They broke out into applause, before he turned to me.

'*Sona!*'

I stood up obediently from my plastic chair and with a very odd serenity walked across the small room whose windows gave views of an empty, sun-baked old square in the heart of Nola, the eyes of the Espositos upon me. It was the contrived calm of a man who has given up on a current situation, and who has told himself to trust in time – a man who has told himself that, in a year, he might even be happy. A peace that is inherently fragile, liable to turn back to nightmare in a flash. I sat down at the piano with a sigh.

'Mariella,' I said, my head bowed. 'Please tell them that I'll play the same tune as Imma has just played. For fun.'

'*Che cosa?* No, Simon, that is really strange! Please, play another.'

'I know no other.'

When it ended a month or so later, the night when Mariella threw our framed photographs down at me from her balcony while I stood on Vico Conte di Mola, calling me a clown, a liar, a man of shit... the night I walked away towards Via Toledo only to turn and see her rush out onto the street, gather all the photographs from the dirt, hysterical in her sadness... when it was all over and I had returned to my flat on Corso Vittorio

Emanuele, to the prospect of two months of solid work to save my degree, I had the conviction that, of everything Mariella had given me, there were two things that I would keep always. The first was the intimacy of the mischief in her eyes once I had finished battering out my own, shocking version of 'The Heart Must Go On' that day in Nola, and had looked up to the silence of a packed room. They were cheeky, those eyes, comprehending in their cheekiness, and, as the situation deteriorated and the father yelled *'Sonane n'ata! Sonane n'ata, sona, sona!'* and I repeated that I had no other song, for a second their intimacy untied the knots of my messy soul. For I knew that she had seen who I really was and whom I didn't like – a man who, rather than a charming buffoon, was a real buffoon, and I wanted suddenly to scream.

And the second thing I would keep was what she said to me before I caught the train back to Naples that afternoon, from the godforsaken train station of Nola, as we stood under the sun with Vesuvius towering in the distance.

'Did you like the girl I was today?' she murmured.

'Mariella, of course I did!'

'Because I was so happy being her.' She frowned. 'Always think before you say "of course". Sometimes you answer too fast.'

… And she was tearing at my face with her nails as those church bells of Vico Conte di Mola rang out into the dark sky, my mobile telephone was broken on the floor, the screen pierced by a stiletto heel, and she was throwing glasses, cutlery, anything she could find – *bastardo, bastardo!* – and I was shouting back at her words empty of meaning, the terrible drivel of a man who is ashamed.

Hello, happy traveller! How are you? Been nearly a year now since my mum's crazy phone call! Sorry but

I just couldn't resist any more and thought I'd have to find out how you're getting on. Got your number from Stephen, hope you don't mind. I've finished at Nottingham – got a First! – and I'm moving to London to do a PGCE…going to be a teacher! Anyway, I've realised I miss you so much. Love, Sophie.

On such things do destinies at first sight appear to depend – the cute coincidences, the seemingly inconsequential decisions such as the choice to stay for another drink to celebrate the end of the course at the language school, and then to continue the night with some Americans at the *baretti*, which meant that I only saw Sophie's message at around midnight when full of potent cocktails. And so I was sitting alone in ridiculous tears on Via Toledo, typing the glib response:

I miss you too, Sophie. More than anyone in the world.

With the tears soon left behind in the past that arrives so quickly in drunkenness, the need to see Mariella, the careless decision to surprise her in the early hours, staggering up Vico Conte di Mola, barking at the street dogs. Mariella shouting at me that I was irresponsible and that I could have been robbed, apologising to the neighbours, putting me to bed; and, as I snored, my mobile phone buzzing and Mariella, sitting alone in the moonlight, all of a sudden surely intensely alert, living one of those rare moments that arrive from nowhere and materialise before our eyes. She was taken by lucid curiosity, perhaps – that need for reassurance that cuts through dreams. Waking at midday in her flat, I found the mobile phone on the table, saw Sophie's message and knew. Upon Mariella's return, her face was dark, her voice calm.

'Tell me that you love me,' she said. 'Say it to me, in your language. Say that Sophie is nobody.'

'Now, Mariella, listen. First of all, you shouldn't be going through my messages.'

She collapsed at this, before I was ever really sure what I would have said; which way I would have gone. But perhaps inside I knew. Now the nails tore and the insults screamed around me as, scratched and shaking, I escaped from her debacle and ran down the stairs... and, as she was collecting those photographs from the street and I hurried away down Vico Conte di Mola, Mariella Esposito gave me a lifetime of chances, she gave me all the time that could have ever existed between us to put things right, to turn back to her, to tell her that I loved her. And human relationships once begun do not then depend on fate – on good or bad timing, coincidence, fortune or misfortune, misunderstandings or moments or words – for human relationships give you the lifetime of chances that Mariella gave to me as I rushed on, out of her life, out of the Quartieri forever.

9

THE VOICE OF A MAN whose need to sing did not derive from vocation but from loyalty to a cause, from passion for a Republic, the incorruptible voice of that most essential desire to belong, had been gradually strengthening, becoming an imminent threat to my peace, a threat that my subconscious had been busy resisting. But then some fleeting image that spoke to Kim the artist's core, hurling him into disarray, led him to cling to that song as if it were the only security. And the voice rose, bold.

'Kim, please!'

The Cuban sunshine was dancing in excitable patterns high up on the kitchen walls, and for a second I stood dazed and bare-chested below its flickering, before an impeccably dressed man whose hands were held tightly behind his back, his morning's work – a pleasantly presented bowl of eggs and noodles, unconventional for a morning but hearty – completed and on display.

'Sorry, but it's just too loud.'

'Breakfast. You. Me. Kim.'

'Not for me, thanks. Very kind, but I'm going back to bed.'

'Breakfast.'

'I said that's very kind, but…'

And, following a daring raid on the bathroom and another large glass of water from the bottle I had taken from the fridge, the coolness of which provided an almost unseemly pleasure, I was back in my room, on my bed, desperate now to return to my story, fearful lest I could not. Tomorrow Rupert would call, and there was so much still to remember. The singing had stopped, but, in my keenness to escape from the present, suddenly I could make out every background noise, and my back was itching a little and I needed to move the pillow a little to the left. No, I needed to move it a little to the right. There we go, that's it… the noises were fading… I was falling back into my story…

… And Naples without Mariella had nothing more to offer – there was no new chapter to be made of the remaining two months. But there was no reason to go anywhere else either, as all I needed was the desk and the books and the *focus* – because the dissertation was becoming very urgent now. Focusing though was hard, as so often I would think of her as I sat there at my desk, high up on the Corso looking out to sea. Seeing clearly the wrong that I had committed, the upset I had caused her, the bastard I had been, perhaps as a form of self-punishment I decided not to reply to Sophie's latest message.

Oh, Simon – I can't believe we both still feel the same! Should I come out and see you?

Or maybe the truth was that I didn't reply to this, or to her further messages, because I had not forgiven her, or maybe because I was scared of being hurt again by her, scared of the strength of my feelings that in previous years had been channelled into the obsessive drive which, ironically, I now desperately needed back. And as I continued to reflect and these emotions continued to mingle, finally I became angry, through a perverse, circuitous route: angry at myself for not being brave enough to love Mariella; for my fundamental dishonesty; for secretly blaming Sophie for the mess I'd caused.

And with the fury I had it back, the energy. I devoured that chapter of Calvino with an intensity that blocked out the summer. I was back in love with the material, but was a wiser lover now, ruthless and manipulative in knowing what the professors were looking for, evading the traps that swallowed up those who played the dangerous game of pure, unfettered curiosity. My translation work, just like my analysis of the pages, was instead obsessively correct, dressed up at times in a disingenuous show of enthusiasm, and, as I emphasised the childish keenness that would make the professors smile indulgently, that acutely embarrassing self-importance (*'we would submit that…'*) – as I refined the lie, one morning, as I looked out through my bedroom window across the iridescent bay, I realised with a jolt that I was telling multiple lies. That I was lying to myself in being cynical, because this work was all I had ever wanted – the infinite ideas, the deep private pleasure of limitless words. But why, then, why was I shouting to myself that it was the cleanliness of the result that mattered now, that I needed a *real* goal? Why was I shouting to myself that they could all go to hell? Who were 'they'?

And the dissertation flourished and Sophie sent message after message – and nothing. It was time to go home, to promise Naples I'd be back again one day, and the day the Twin Towers went down she called and called while I was in Naples airport – but even then I couldn't bring myself to speak to her.

I assume you're OK, I texted instead, breaking finally – a small but insistent thought needing to be calmed.

Of course I'm fine, she wrote. *I was thinking more about you – I guess you're still in Naples. I would stay there for a while if I were you – don't get a flight for a few days. I do love you, Simon.*

I didn't reply, and after that the messages stopped. There was no contact with Sophie during that final year of mine at university – indeed, there were no romantic stories that year. Nobody I really knew was still there, and so there was nothing to interrupt me – only overworking, only a fixation gone too far, would have prevented the First. And with the gaping abyss of the future resolved that night of the Kants, with the London flatshare found, the place at law school to start in September secured and paid for by Fiennes & Plunkett, one sweltering day my parents came to Cambridge for my graduation, my dad bringing a parcel they had received, from Naples. The sun swam across the lawn of Senate House, down King's Parade and towards the water, through the carved gateposts and into Old Court; and in scenes made sure and clear by their tradition, by their deliberate eccentricities, the Fellows pottered, offering slowly pronounced, wise observations.

'You've been one of our stars,' Professor Bonini noted, as he removed a cup of undrinkable red wine from a monstrous, college-emblazoned plastic tray that allowed one to potter holding cup and plate – he'd taken me aside for a word. 'You're made for academia. But,' he sighed, 'no doubt you have a fine future ahead.'

'Well, thank you – that means so much.' I bathed for a while in the safety of the words, the tradition, the fine gardens, before Professor Bonini, with that sad distracted gaze, sipped his wine, nodded, ambled away...and soon, to the fading sounds of the end of an afternoon, I was following him towards the arch, out of Old Court. But then, while Bonini was veering left, climbing some stairs, gaining the refuge of his rooms, I was carrying on past the Porter's Lodge, through Warren's iron gates...

'Here,' said my dad, as the three of us walked down King's Parade – passing the same Tesco where my mum had bought me the strawberries years earlier. He stopped and reached into his bag, passed me the small parcel. 'This arrived from Italy. It'll be that young woman, no doubt.'

Later, back at home in my old bedroom in Lincoln that night, I was finally opening that parcel, laughing at my own nerves. Out spilled three photographs – Mariella and Simon soaking wet under the rain at the Bay; Mariella kissing my cheek as we embraced on the ferry, Capri to our backs; a picture with that extended family in Nola, the father smiling hard and proud, Mariella serene and beautiful. Then I saw the note, wrapped around a disk.

You left this – I am moving apartment, and I found it under my bed. I hope one day you can use it. Ti voglio bene, *Mariella.*

I hurried over to my laptop, stuck the disk in and, as it loaded, I remembered what this must be – my Notes from Naples! I'd forgotten all about that little endeavour – the memoir Mariella had encouraged me to write during those lazy afternoons on Vico Conte di Mola. I hadn't put much effort into it, just written freely, only semi-thinking. Pages and pages of fragments, in no particular order. A jumble of memories that I soon gave up reading.

She's leaving that little studio apartment, I thought. *I wonder where she's going? Funny that we're both moving, at the same time.*

I was moving down to that flatshare on the New King's Road, to that City Law School shining bright with cold reality, financed and dictated to by some of the leading law firms in the world. I was moving down to attend the first year, the transitional 'conversion' course for the non-law graduates, a conversion that exists nowhere else in Europe, the English law firms having the foresight to understand that all a good future lawyer needs is a willingness to be converted. There were among us that year, mixed with the Dan Serfonteins, talented English graduates who might have become literary critics, graduates in music who had yearned only to play, all become suddenly hard, their new dream shaped by the certainty of four years – two at the school, followed by the further two years of the training contract at their firm. These were graduates who would go on to be the leading legal minds in the City but who, arriving fresh on their first day, knew nothing of how to analyse a statute, how to draft a contract, how to look at the world through wary eyes. And like them I soon became irritated by the flickers of humanity, inconstant amid the grey throngs of the sponsored future, provided by the rare students – the semi-aristocrats, the offspring of foreign magnates – who were unsponsored and who had signed up to the course as you might sign up to learn French at night school. Those infuriating questions, their lazy interest, their time.

'But I am not sure that it would always work. What if the company just refused to pay?'

'Dimitris, I'm so sorry, but we really need to move on!'

Under enormous pressure, these teachers, charged with providing the *information*: the methods of contractual interpretation and legal research, the advocacy techniques and drafting tricks, the EU directives that we could never have imagined might one day become irrelevant. 'We have to finish lesson 4.3 today!'

The true wilderness year, this, through which I charged headlong in pursuit of a dream that needed to be mine. I was on the Tube, squeezed between tense, irascible heads, worried that I would be late for class; I was in the library of the law school, exposed through the large glass windows to the anti-war protestors, studying until late evening in the midst of the collective hysteria; suddenly the week had passed, it was Friday night… and there were the pubs and the bars in Parsons Green, on Upper Street, in Chelsea, it didn't matter where, as long as I drank enough to quieten Mr Naples…

And the exams arrived and were soon over, so we celebrated in the pubs and the bars; and the summer break began to drift by in the pubs and the bars. Soon I was broke, awaiting the next injection of Fiennes & Plunkett funds that would come in September, and one morning I became wildly angry, without knowing why, when my parents suggested language tutoring as a way of making some money over the summer: a solution that would have allowed me to spend some time back in Italy. After their call, in a fit of inexplicable rage, I went to the bank and applied for an overdraft. It was approved, almost immediately. And so I celebrated again, in the pubs and the bars…

…I'm awake on a sofa in my flatshare now, my flatmate snoring face-down on the other and Dan Serfontein, back from the Greek islands, somehow twisted into a sleeping position on the chairs opposite. He is awake too, suddenly, and we look at each other, for a second dumb. As he runs his hand through his blond hair and begins to yawn, the stability that he exudes, which I know now is false, nevertheless calms the anxiety without a name that is building in me… packet of cigarettes and bottle of vodka on the wooden table between us… *What happened to that bird you pulled, Dan? Did she stay over too? No, she went home. Mate, can I use your shower? I stink*…the cigarette smoke hanging in the air as he comes running back up… *Mate, she* is *still downstairs, she's in the bathroom! Oh, Jesus!* Soon afterwards he's kissed her goodbye and we're on the New King's Road, the summer morning retreating fast as Fulham's bright young lights, a generation of City professionals, resurface from their beds, the embarrassment of the previous evening dispersed by their need to start again, to 'get on it', the middle-class charge to the alcohol. And hours and hours later I'm still in the Ram, as I am every afternoon, but today I'm different, strangely disengaged. I'm not really drinking and I can feel something stirring inside. And as the pub becomes more crowded and the noise grows louder and the afternoon slips into evening, suddenly, with frightening intensity, my perception alters: I no longer recognise the scene before me. A fog of twelve months has cleared, and I understand something so simple: I'm lonely in here. I see a room of arrogant stares, biting of the lower lip, people devoid of conversation, sincere only in defending their right to be. And I begin to think about what it is to be sincere: I begin to think about Sophie. I think of her fine sincerity; I think of how she would hate it in here, as I watch some young men wearing the uniform of polo shirts and jeans pass drinks from the bar to rosy-cheeked girls who all speak in the same voices. *Oh, no way? That is sooo harsh. Arno just can't take the lash – it's, like, so random?* Defiant faces pulled at the recipients of this language, born of a terror of having been unmasked, perhaps – but then relief, a gulp of wine as the recipient replies in turn: *Like, whatever? He's loving it there?* A play with no end, dizzyingly circular, everyone a banker or consultant or lawyer, everyone secretly tense and insecure... Dan seems concerned, he's shooting me glances.

'You alright, mate?'

'Yeah, I'm going for a walk – I need some air.'

It was early August, a month before the beginning of the second year – I was halfway through City Law School. I called the the house in Hubbard's Hills, sat in silence as her mother's voice rose, left the flat again and turned back up the New King's Road as the darkness began to fall...and I walked on through the drunken crowds, past the antique shops and the ethnic restaurants, through the quiet, pretty terraced streets, and arrived finally at the black water – the houseboats bobbing on its swell. The air was cooler now, invigorating, as I looked up at the steady stream of lights crossing Albert Bridge. On I hurried, up to its centre, and, stopping there a moment, with my eyes I followed the river that shimmered, a thousand reflections, and beyond to the City.

Fiennes & Plunkett were somewhere there.

I walked down from the centre of the bridge and then on into Battersea Park, peopled still by Londoners of a summer afternoon overtaken by the day. Couples heading home with empty picnic bags, teenagers picking up bibs used as goalposts, women throwing sticks raced after by their dogs. Feeling free, feeling certain, I crossed the park as it emptied, became quiet. Prince of Wales Drive stood elegantly before it, before the returning summer night. Number 120, Flat A, Deborah had told me. I pressed the doorbell.

'Mum said you'd come.' Sophie's tears were flowing. 'Please forgive me for what I did that day. I knew you were just being brave.'

'You didn't do anything. We were just kids.'

'Oh, no; I was such a bitch.' Her arms clung to me, her lovely face drawing closer, until it became all that I could see. 'But we're both safe now, if you'll have me.'

And almost immediately Sophie and I did become safe again, rediscovering as if uninterrupted our rhythm and companionship; safe again within a rapidly drawn new world. The summer air became steeped in magic, and it was beautifully insane, ridiculously impulsive, that we should be living together a mere two weeks after I had walked to find her. Sophie had a month's break clause in her lease, while I had to give three months' notice to end my flatshare arrangement, so there were sound reasons for a law student and teacher to wait before renting a flat on Munster Road that was in any case rather grand given their current means. But, when it came to money, I had the future on my side – and, more importantly, the overdraft. We wanted stability, a flat we could call our home for a good while, and there was something about that particular flat with its skylight and its roof terrace that formed a natural part of the story, something that could not wait. Sophie had fallen under the same spell.

So we had a home and each other and a shared elation – nothing else was required. Not for us the surrogates, the litany of dinner parties or the hundreds of friends. There was only really Dan with his latest girlfriend – the slightly surprising development being that Sophie liked Dan. Or the geography teachers, Jason and Eleanor Cantle – the minor low of those first golden days, Eleanor never able to look me in the eye...

Apart from them, virtually nobody – we were delightfully alone, together within the walls of that newly rented flat on Munster Road, inseparable in a reignited passion that was all the stronger for its history, inseparable in recounting to each other the past years. And that accent of mine that Sophie said with amusement had changed soon returned to my real voice, at least when I was with her, and as I sought to explain the world to Sophie and she explained it to me, I began to tell her my secrets. I told her the truth about Mr Naples, the difficulty I was having at times in convincing myself of the new dream, my disappointment at the cold, hard incontestability of what we were being taught at law school – but as soon as she embraced this, as soon as she agreed with Mr Naples, saying how relieved she was that I was finding myself, I explained to her why he was wrong, why these were just immature, self-indulgent doubts, why it was time now to grow up. *The thing is, Sophie, we're independent adults now, and I'm prepared to do what it takes, to get through this second year of law school and then build something, to go out into the world and toil, use my brain to make us money, make us crazy amounts of money* – and thus I adapted myself without altering the dream. And she would look at me with kind eyes, saying that, fair enough, she agreed that I should at least see how it went once I got to the firm – maybe there, once I was actually working, it would be more enjoyable than studying at the law school. And, yes, she also agreed that it *was* important to try it, so that I would understand, so that I would know. But, she added always with a smile, she was with Mr Naples; and she had no doubt that he would end up winning. Years later she would become all agitated when remembering these conversations, saying she was cross not only with me, but with herself too: cross for not being more honest, firmer.

But those first twelve months back together, before I started work at the firm! It was impossible to be more deeply in love than this, and I think she knew it too. In the very first days, that mad August of 2003 when we moved into our new home, we made up for the years of absence with a desire that was inexhaustible, making love three or four times a night, and there was a quiet emotion as we admired each other's best traits, reacted gently to each other's insecurities, drew each other out, loving each other for everything, all our weaknesses. Sophie's rich smile as I told her that one day she would be proud of me, calling me a silly bugger, reminding me that she already was so proud of me. Sophie's own excitement a short time later, in September, on her first day at Burnaby Street Primary, the new school.

'God, it's late – I have to go. I need to set up the classroom! And I've got playground duty, too!'

'It's not seven yet.' I looked up from the bed as she stood in front of the long mirror, brushing her hair quickly. 'We did the dry run yesterday, Sophie – you'll be there before half past.'

'Yes, I know, I know. You're right.' She dropped the brush, picked it up from the floor quickly and then turned to me with an apologetic smile. 'Sorry. I'm all over the place this morning!'

'You'll be fine, I promise. You were a star at Moreton.'

'Assemblies!' She was brushing again, faster and faster, and talking more to herself than to me. 'I'm going to have to do three assemblies a term at this place! They're so terrifying! I think this is going to be tougher than Moreton.'

'The kids will love you.'

'And there's so many more after-school clubs at Burnaby Street! And wall displays, the school's absolutely full of wall displays – there's not a square inch of the place that's not covered by them, ha! They always take up so much time. But, I must admit, I do love wall displays.' She stopped for a second before the mirror. 'Simon, I reckon I'll be doing near fifty-hour weeks, if you take into account the homework. I don't believe in giving the kids homework at the age of six or seven, do you? I mean, it's completely unfair – they have such long days anyway, and they should be allowed to enjoy learning, without all this pressure.' She took a deep breath. 'Right, I'm off.'

'Go get 'em – you're the best teacher in the world!'

'Silly. You say such silly things.'

'You know you are!'

'Well.' She bent her knees a little as she brushed her hair one more time. 'Anyway, wish me luck.'

After a kiss goodbye I listened as she rushed down the stairs, out of the house, and then I darted across to the window to see her walking down the Munster Road, a young woman full of nerves and purpose and belief.

Later, in the early evening, she was back, a little out of breath and with rosy cheeks and big happy eyes.

'There's this little boy called Peter,' she gasped, as I poured the wine. 'Oh, Simon, he's outrageous! So cheeky! He told me that their old teacher, Miss Pickering, had a big moustache. And then he drew her for me. I mean, *really*.' She giggled at the memory.

'Ha! Here, have a glass of Malbec, my dear – one day down, many to go!'

'Have you been drinking? Anyway, yes, he's so funny. But so bright too. I can tell bright kids a mile off, you know.'

'Sophie?'

'Yes?'

'I...'

'I what?' She laughed; nestled up close. 'I what? Come here, give me a kiss.'

Those halcyon days, when we ambled together towards the future again, euphoric and dreaming and free. Those weekends. Arm in arm in a reverie down the tree-lined Embankment, following the swollen river as it surged on. There was the sun waking us through our skylight, the skinny guitarist in Leicester Square, the old Cypriot who ran the drycleaners and who would never let us leave. There were the antique markets and the strange men with piercings in Camden, the pub with live jazz that we found hidden near to Brixton Tube, our endless conversations and long peaceful silences, the Saturday nights when we would come back, throw our clothes into a pile and make love, switch off all alarms and sleep for eleven hours. There was the London Eye on November 5th when we gazed down at London as if from the moon and the girl poured champagne and Sophie squeezed my hand as the fireworks began in the distance. The quaint long garden at St George's Square that we stumbled into by

254

chance, the snow dropping magically onto Munster Road; cinematic Sloane Square with its lights at Christmas, Notting Hill and all the freezing Italian tourists on Portobello Road; the day we found Chepstow Villas, wandered in enchantment past the homes of kings. The absurd Scandinavian plays at the Arts Theatre on Ashburnham Road, our picnics under the branches of Battersea Park; the way Sophie would put her hand to my face when she said she loved me, how she would make me feel sure and strong when she said that I could do anything I wanted, that she was lucky to have me.

There was that icy morning in February when I took her to south-east London to watch Charlton Athletic play. What a weird choice! A team devoid of any famous players, a tremendously unimportant game, a girlfriend who had never suggested she was remotely interested in football. A decision that many young professionals might call 'random'. And yet look at Sophie Williams standing next to me now in the crowd, look at her glow! Our understanding of each other was profound and private, our reactions surely incomprehensible to anyone watching us; we were two selves embracing in those days. Only Sophie could be so delighted by the nonsense of this idea, the knowledge that this was me being truly me. The day was a beautiful disaster, the crowd thin, and it was almost thrillingly cold. 'This is authentic, Sophie!' I was shouting, defensively, as some guys chanted obscenities around us and the players came out, seemingly reluctantly, onto the pitch. 'This is an authentic match, with real fans! You'll never forget this!'

'Yes, I know!' And how she laughed, filling me with relief as the smile burst across her face. 'Don't worry – I love it here. I feel a million miles from everything, all alone with you.'

And spring arrived, then summer, City Law School was over, then summer was over, and suddenly the firm was banging at the front door on Munster Road. Rupert Plunkett forced it open, wedged his foot in the gap, and out flowed the warmth of our hideaway.

'I bought you this.' Sophie walked across to the living room window where I was standing and handed me a black briefcase.

'Wow – that couldn't have been cheap!'

'Well, now that you're an important City slicker.'

The young lawyers at Fiennes & Plunkett, I discovered, didn't use briefcases – print-outs were not permitted to be taken outside the firm's offices except for meetings, and for these the firm had its own bespoke collection, promptly delivered to us by the office boys who could have been our dads. The trainees and associates arrived instead with their gym bags, so that I was laughed at on my first day. It was past nine o'clock when I was back in Fulham, bubbling with nervous energy.

'What a place! You should see the offices inside! I've got my own secretary, you know. Shared with others, of course – but even so! Dan's office is just down the corridor.'

'I'm so pleased it went well. I've been worried all day.'

'I've been put right onto a major transaction, Sophie. A big restructuring deal, called Project Candy. Candy's a code name, of course – everything is code-named. My supervisor briefed me like an army officer!'

'I see. Goodness! Listen, shall we just order a pizza tonight? It's a bit late and I've got to prepare for this bloody assembly tomorrow.'

'Sophie!' And each of us suddenly horrified. 'I'm telling you about my first day!'

'Yes, I know.'

'But—'

'And *I* was trying to tell *you* that I've been waiting for you, it's nearly half past nine and I'm hungry! And I've got a big day tomorrow too! What's the matter with you?'

'What do you mean, "what's the matter"?'

In this exchange was the first drop of poison, the commencement of the bitterness that began to seep into our affection, to pollute it slowly, to change things. Gradually but persistently it grew, the bitterness, for seven more years – *seven more years* – the tension between us intermittently abating, disappearing for months on end, rising up again then disappearing once more, blown away by our intimacy, our love that fought on. But as the years passed the truces grew shorter, the deteriorations more acute, the laughter and happy times still there but more precious, more fleeting – until towards the end, those last two years from 2010 onwards, they merely punctuated a haze.

'What on *earth* is that?' Sophie's hand was to her mouth in surprise, her eyes smiling despite herself.

'Well, rooftop pools are all the rage among the Knightsbridge set. So I thought Fulham should start too. It'll reach thirty degrees in London today.'

'Are you sure the terrace will take the weight with all that water in it?' But then she surrendered, her tight mouth dissolving into a giggle. 'So you're the guy they were talking about.'

'I'm which guy?'

'The guy who went to the petrol station on Warburton Street, and asked to use their bloody air pump to blow up a paddling pool!'

'Yes, and they didn't let me. I had to go back to Lucy & Davies.'

'But it's pink.'

'So? It was the only one left.'

'I was in the petrol station, and they were talking about you. The man with the pink paddling pool. The attendant looked dazed.'

'Fancy a dip?'

'I told you, this terrace will collapse.'

'Rubbish.'

The lengths to which people will go in an attempt to resurrect the magic, the warmth of the touch. Reaching out to each other, to the spontaneity floating away, even when they know its outline is just a mirage. In reaching for it, Sophie was in her bikini, climbing into a paddling pool and for a second there, together in the water, blinded by the sun, we held each other with that intimacy, that reminder of what it was to feel impulsive and young. And then:

'It's just too cold, Simon. Sorry.'

'You'll warm up.'

'No. No, it's too cold.'

Rancour.

'Fair enough. I might work here this afternoon. On my laptop.'

'What? You'll electrocute yourself!'

'It was a joke.' Silence. 'Actually it's a shame, given the effort I put in.'

'Well, Simon, it was a stupid idea!' She rose from the water. 'There were a million other things we could have done this afternoon.'

'I suppose I should have known you wouldn't be so keen. After all, it might have involved *fun*.'

'Right. Well, given that you allow us about two hours a week to even see each other, perhaps you should let me know your plans in advance next time.'

'Feel free to come up with some ideas yourself. Anyway, I'm sorry that I'm working so hard for us both.'

'You're *not*, though – I've told you. You're not doing anything for me.'

'I am!'

258

'Shut up, will you? The neighbours can hear all this.'

Later in the evening, a self-deprecating voice said, 'Sophie, I've done some sardines on toast. Care to sit outside with me, to dine by my pool?'

'You're not funny.'

Piqued by her rejection, I became defensive of the pool. So I sat down by it alone, took a sip of cool white wine while looking out at the smoky sunset. But my elbow knocked the plate balanced delicately on the pool's edge and the sardines fell into the water.

'Sophie! You won't believe this – there are fish in my pool. Come and see! We've got an aquarium out here.'

Sophie was engrossed in marking homework. 'I'm not interested. Really.'

Slowly, almost imperceptibly, with the passing of the years she'd become her final self, assumed her definitive personality, a woman who each day had grown a scintilla more certain, more impatient, less willing to compromise. The sincerity that had always existed as an independent quality had by 2010 attached itself to the specific – to concrete opinions, established perspectives, developed philosophies. And in all this, in the accumulation of all this, she'd discovered a grating sense of purpose. Her purpose was to teach, she would tell me now; she had a *mission* to take care to *really* teach her pupils well, to ensure the sensitive transmission of knowledge – the truth of the solar system, the plants and the animals and the properties of materials, the alphabet, the irrefutability of the times tables, the basics of grammar. Suggesting, indicating gently a set of morals, but taking care not to disrupt the growth of their malleable character – how often she would talk to me about this as I lay exhausted on the bed. It had become so internal, this project, so isolated and self-contained, that one day I understood that my girlfriend had declared war on an undefined enemy: on the outside world, any perceived threat, anything that challenged the value, the superiority, of her mission. And finally, in that same year, the enemy found embodiment, assumed a distinct, unequivocal form, at Sophie's seventh Fiennes & Plunkett Christmas party.

'PLEASE RAISE YOUR GLASSES.' The whisper of an invisible lunatic was transmitted by the microphone through the vaulted Undercroft of Banqueting House, through its arches, into the tight alcoves, each containing one sole table of guests. The structure of the floor here was antithetical to any sense of a firm, any sense of a party – the events manager's career was over. So splendid, Banqueting House: the last vestige of the Palace of Whitehall, as impressive as any national monument in Europe, with its Main Hall that had been home to the royal court's masques, receptions and balls – ceremonies among the finest in history. The Main Hall that had been the pride and devotion of Charles I, with that grand window from which one morning he stepped out to his scaffold. The Main Hall that was available now for Christmas bookings, where bankers would dine and cavort under a ceiling painted by Rubens, but which had, alas, proved too expensive for this law firm's budget committee. And the events manager had continued on blindly, incapable of collecting herself, changing the plan, choosing any of the thousand other possible venues in London – for Rupert had approved of the idea of Banqueting House, which she had floated far too early on, before checking. And so here we were, all one hundred and fifty of us – the partners, a select number of senior associates and their guests – crammed into James I's dark, underground drinking den.

And while the bankers above us, illuminated by chandeliers, clinked glasses to the history of our nation, below, in each of the discrete, isolated corners of the Undercroft, we clinked glasses to another profitable year for the firm.

'To Fiennes & Plunkett,' came the whisper.

'To Fiennes & Plunkett,' rang out voices from caves.

The fine reds, enlivened by the Bollinger's fizz, resumed their flow. The food was light and sufficient, pleasant and uncomplicated, secondary forever to the wine. Soon a division was forming at each of the tables, the guests left behind as the members of the firm together held hands and stepped forward out of the hell of the week, into the magical world of freedom that arrived with the third glass. A dichotomy that created tomorrow's recriminations. The only guest joining in on our table was Dan's companion for the evening, our former colleague Clemmie Mandeville – a girl who had lived the entirety of her life on one of Kensington's finest streets, who unaccountably was *not* stupid when it came to exams, but who had never in my presence made an original or intelligent observation. She was faintly attractive, and attractively silly, her petite figure impervious to champagne, her blondish hair expensively coiffured, her wardrobe one that spoke of effortless luxury. Clementine had been in love with Dan in a vague, drunken way for years and they still dated from time to time, when they were both bored or lonely or just fancied some lash. After her training contract at Fiennes & Plunkett, Clementine had lasted two weeks as an associate before encountering Rupert on a deal. Shortly thereafter, she had moved on with brilliant CV to a 'kind-of-like, hedge fund', where she now earned around a hundred thousand pounds a year, doing nothing...well, doing securitisations...she wasn't quite sure what they were but, you know. Her current boyfriend, a fund manager, was a really nice guy – but, like, Dan, she couldn't *remember anything* about last night...*listen, listen!* This new guy was quite special – Clemmie's face dead serious now, loaded with sincerity – 'I, like, think he might be *the one*.' She had so much to tell Dan. And he was nodding with that acquiescence that tears at this sort of person's heart, absorbing the weight like all the best cushions; turning occasionally to Sophie…

There were eight of us at the table. Clemmie talking to Dan turning to Sophie – it was a bit annoying how he kept turning to her. Sophie was engaged in the challenge of Emma, the real estate department's rising star, seemingly invulnerable in these, the days before Project Dynamite. Emma's female friend – what was her name? – a serious-looking academic type who seemed to be regretting an error that had cost her an evening, was making dreadfully sincere comments about current affairs. I was listening principally to Ed Griffiths himself, the young partner of the wandering left eye, who had beside him his expensive French trophy wife who was surely no older than twenty-four, and who was all cool stare and indifference, a picture of undeserved authority. But Ed had forgotten it all in the warmth of the wine, in the rebellion of his glowing cheeks. Believing himself to be happy, he sought intimacy.

'Don't be under any illusions – we partners find Rupert as mad as you lot do! And he's positively chilled these days compared to the Rupert of old, trust me. Back in the day, I can tell you! He once locked me and an associate from another firm in a meeting room, telling us we weren't coming out until we had agreed the doc. And then he forgot we were in there! *Fucking* hilarious!'

Slight but unmistakable, the wince of Ed's French wife mirrored by Sophie and by Emma's friend. But he was oblivious, poor Ed, churning out his empty war stories. The jazz band had begun, the double bass's soothing chords following the beautiful voice that came searching for us through the arches. I nodded, distracted by the wonder of the Barolo, the heaviness of the air, this slowest of songs, the song of the end of a night, the hint of danger in the conversation to my left, the edge in Emma's voice.

'I *do* envy you being a teacher, Sophie.'

'Really? Why's that?'

'Oh, it just seems so idyllic to me.'

'Idyllic?'

'Well – that was silly of me – it depends on the school, of course. I imagine those inner-city places like the school I went to are an utter nightmare for the teachers. At my school...'

'So, you two, what's the vibe in the trenches? How's morale among the associates?' Ed's forehead is glistening with sweat. He needs to be careful.

How she waits up late as he hides outside,
Back at dawn, all afraid...

'Not much to report, Ed. But you know how it is at this firm: we all just exist in our own little bubbles.' Impeccable, Dan, impeccable!

'I teach in Islington – at one of those inner-city places you mention.'

Oops! No, it's OK: there's no sting. Sophie's smile is accommodating, self-deprecating. I adore that smile.

'I know *exactly* what you mean, Daniel. I'm the same, I wouldn't be able to tell you how morale is among the partners! Ha! So, what are you guys working on?'

'No, I'm at Burnaby Street, the primary school.'

Then she said that, if he dared
She would sing this lonely song...

'Oh, fab.'

She's doing fine, Sophie. I squeeze her hand under the table. She squeezes back; she knows I'm here. Wow, I feel like I want to sing.

'Ah, Project Mercedes! Great stuff – nothing like a club loan! Do you know Rupert and I devised the first ever club loan?'

Baby, see my hope...

I take a sip from my glass, with the affected manners of the man who is about to become drunk, as my feet tap below the table and I rock gently to the beat, the tune now inside me; only I know what it means. So rich, so full-blooded, the Barolo.

'Well, teaching toddlers must be fascinating. Another drop?'

'Oh, no, thank you. I'm fine.'

'Don't be silly, pass me your glass.'

Sophie has yet to understand how much she dislikes Emma, that little Rottweiler – she's too intimidated to dislike her yet. I don't think she's ever spoken for this long to a girl like Emma. Maybe I'll intervene. No, she'll resent it if I do that. Anyway, it'll all come out when we get home.

Baby, see my hope...

'A little refill, Simon?'

'Oh, thanks, Ed.'

'Hi, sorry.' Clemmie reaches over to Emma's friend. 'I didn't introduce myself properly. So, you're a researcher, right? I could have stayed at Bristol too, but – I decided—' She knocks a wine glass; Dan catches it in time.

Sophie will take it out on me when we get home. She's wonderful now, though: look how composed she seems. Making such an effort, all for me. How I love her.

'It becomes easier when you're a partner. Well, easier in some respects. It's definitely worth it. Just keep slogging away. We wish you all the best, you two, in your ambition.' And Ed looks out, beyond us into the distance, full of buffoonish pride. He wants us to ask him how much a partner earns, so that he can shake his head at our impertinence.

'I always tell people that the most important thing – you know what I tell them?'

Ed is looking only at me now, the left eye broadly back in place. Dan has lost interest, subtly shifted his attention without causing offence. He's looking over at Sophie again. He's about to speak. Emma will resent being interrupted like that.

'You alright, Soph?'

A tad protracted, that meeting of eyes. And such familiarity! Who does he think he is? Annoying – they're a bit flirty, those two, tonight.

'Ah, yes, all good.' She sighs softly. He understands with an indulgent smile and – I'm sure – a wink! A wink!

'I tell them that it's pure hard work. I mean, I made it as a partner and I'm no genius – far from it! Right, darling?'

Wow! *What* a shrug! Oh, and look – the Parisian gaze is dwelling for a second on me! Unimpressed, her condescension assured, off it goes, off it goes – goodbye! The gaze returning to her remote horizon, to somewhere infinitely better.

Baby, just read my mind…

'Well, actually – ' Emma's friend is all earnest again ' – for me it's Philip Roth every time. I've just finished reading—'

'Yeah, sorry, one second.' Clemmie is rummaging in her handbag. And then, far too loud to Dan, 'Quick ciggie lash outside?'

Emma's friend falls silent. Sophie looks a little cross now – jealous, perhaps, of Clemmie? Is it true: does part of Sophie – part of her she tries so hard to repress – dream of what it would be like to be with Dan and not me? Is she more physically attracted to him? It wouldn't be hard to see why. There is something evil germinating here in this alcove, isn't there? An accumulation of tension, and someone's going to say or do something wrong, I just know it. I feel lightheaded. Oops, I nearly spilt my wine.

'How could I forget *him*! A true character!'

What? Oh, how marvellous – Sophie and Emma have a mutual acquaintance! Emma went to school with someone, and Sophie studied maths with him at Nottingham. What a guy! Didn't catch his name, but what a guy!

'OK, quick ciggie.' And Dan and Clemmie get to their feet. I haven't said a word to Clemmie all night – I should try harder. Maybe a joke or something.

'Hey, you two – you should have a dance on the way!'

A little cough from Sophie. Yeah, the joke didn't work – a bit too loud, forced. Dan shakes his head with one of his sure smiles. Everything seems to bounce off him. Bastard – I wish I were like that.

It happens just as Dan and Clemmie vanish through the arch. Ed is too tired to be drinking, you see – he should be in bed. Standing up, his face all sweaty, he sways a little, asks the French wife to dance, she declines, he is humiliated, he shakes his head at me ... and then he seems to remember that that is not why he has stood up. He has stood up because his bladder is full.

Baby, read my mind ...

I watch as Ed straightens his tie; I watch him giggle for a brief moment at some silly thought that must have come to him, only to then become all serious once more. He is a man so profoundly alone. As he squeezes clumsily around the table to get out, his breathing is heavy, the left eye off again, the face redder by the second. Across from him, Sophie and Emma are talking about teaching still. Ed hasn't spoken to either of them yet – so maybe it is at this point, as he looks at them, that he begins to think that this has been rude of him, that he needs to rectify it, be witty, because he's the partner at the table. So, Ed wipes his forehead, smiles down at them and says, very loudly, 'Bloody teachers – can't stand them myself.'

And somewhere in his mind he must appreciate the idiocy of what he has just said. Surely he must see it in the shock around the table, Emma's sudden neutrality, Emma's friend raising her eyebrows; surely he sees it clearly in Sophie's straightened back and my arm stretching across to her. He must hear it in Sophie's voice.

'Well, I must say that I'm not overly fond of all City lawyers.'

She's right, good for her, a damn weird and stupid thing for Ed to have said, but I know Ed and, with all the things I truly dislike about him, I know that this was completely out of character. I know that he doesn't think like that and, moreover, even if he *did* think that, it's the last thing he would normally say. If Ed is anything, it's smarmy, overly careful – certainly not a man who would be offensive at a social event. What happened? Oh, *that's* it – he really is drunk, isn't he? I hadn't realised how drunk – it's unheard of for a partner. He's looking at me now like a confused and awkward adolescent, as I say, 'Ha! Yes, I'm with Sophie, I think. Come on, Ed, you don't really think that?' He's looking at me as if to ask, *why this tone of reconciliation, there was never an issue* ... but then suddenly he changes. He has realised something – and he is horrified.

'Messing about, old boy,' he mumbled. 'Got all mixed up. Not quite sure why I said it. Ha!'

'We know, Ed, no worries.' But he's too drunk, he has lost control; maybe something finally burst inside him tonight and now he's all tied up in his own little story. He's passing behind Sophie, the expression on his burning face suggesting that he's keen to fix this issue, make it right by her and calm everyone down. He gets it so wrong. He places his big hands on Sophie's bare shoulders – and rubs them.

'Come on, I was only joking.'

'Ughhh! Please, take your disgusting hands off me!'

Emma's back turns immediately. Emma's friend looks as though she wants to cry. The French wife is alive, sharp, deciding whom to pierce with her ice. Ed is laughing like a fool, supremely embarrassed. Sophie has risen, I am close after her...

'Excuse us.'

... and I hold a hand that does not want to hold mine, as in her loyalty she walks with me slowly, with elegance, through the white-haired gentlemen and the proffered hands and the long dresses spilling from the alcoves, past the small dance floor...

Golden and bright

My kiss with you...

Daniel and Clementine have forgotten their ciggie and are on the dance floor after all, holding each other close; she has melted into him and they are in a sort of harmony. He glances up at us from her neck with a distant, inebriated face, sees us. We collect our coats and leave in silence, Sophie unreachable in her dignity; not a word is spoken up the steps, on Whitehall, in the taxi, outside on Munster Road, not a word until we are in the living room and she pushes me away as I try to hold her.

'Never again.' The mascara streams down her cheeks. 'Never again will I do that for you.'

And we are lying in bed, apart in the darkness. She is thinking surely of her mission, the pupils that need her, the importance of her task, how it has all been mocked, sneered at by a drunken millionaire. She must be thinking of him as he mocks her, his pointless exhaustion and stress, his wife who hates him, his lack of substance, the emptiness hanging over him. She must be thinking that, finally, she's put a face to her enemy. Meanwhile I'm thinking of poor old Ed, feeling for the first time some sort of empathy, thinking of that same

268

exhaustion and stress that brought him to this. Thinking how the exhaustion and stress are not *pointless* at all, but part of his job. Imagining the shame he will be feeling tomorrow. And I'm thinking about Sophie too, why she's so vulnerable – not tonight, but generally. Why she wants to lock herself away inside her own private mission. And for some reason, quite suddenly, I remember Anna Cowley's words – the words that upset Sophie all those years ago. And I wonder, in a sort of epiphany, if this is all somehow tied up with her parents having split up when she was young; with the abandoned father of whom we never speak.

'Sophie.' My voice is low. 'You know when your mum and dad broke up, when you left Derby?'

'What?'

'Well, I'm only—'

'Why bring that up now? What's it got to do with anything?'

'I just mean that, if you ever want to talk about it, I'm here.'

'But why tonight? Why now? Honestly, Simon, you go off on the oddest tangents.' She sighs. 'I don't think I'll ever understand you.'

We lie awake, uncomprehending, careering away from each other.

10

IT WAS MIDDAY in Havana, the blinds absurd now in their ineffectiveness against the force of the sunshine, like the last wall of a sandcastle before the incoming tide. The quiet in the flat was absolute as I raised my head from the pillow – no singing.

'Time to eat something,' I mumbled.

The living room was at peace, the windows reaching up to the fine sky, giving views of the endless, rolling ocean. My friends were sitting very still on the floor, amid the pots of white *mariposa* flowers, before rays that lit a blue horizon – they were not quite meditating, but their faces seemed at once determined and serene. Or almost serene: Kim the artist roused as he saw me.

'Breakfast.' It was no longer a mere invitation, or request. It was an irrefutable statement of fact made by a man whose mind had been unable to defeat hunger.

'Please don't tell me you've both been waiting for me.'

'Breakfast.'

'Of course – understood.'

The egg and noodles were perfect for a hangover.

'Have either of you heard of the Playas del Este?' I was wrapped up in the guidebook that I no longer quite trusted, but which gave me the respectability of a purpose. 'They're meant to be lovely beaches and not too touristy – pretty close, too.'

'So, so.'

'As in, you've heard of them? Been there?'

'Breakfast.'

'I was thinking of going there for the day.' Was I? 'The best one's Playa Santa María del Mar, they say. Fancy coming with me? Do you want to come with me, to Playa Santa María del Mar?'

'No – we stay in Havana!'

Of course. The tripod stood impatiently by the door. They had much to do today.

'Very good, these noodles, Kim!'

'Yes.'

'Where did you get them?'

'OK.'

'I was asking…'

What I was really asking was whether they were cross with me; it had become somehow very important to me that they weren't.

'Kim?'

'Yes?'

'I'm so sorry I made you wait for breakfast.'

'No – not sorry!' He spoke to Kim the engineer, and they both put their hands to their heads and began to laugh excitably. Kim the engineer stood up and slapped me on the back.

'Not sorry!'

They were fine – just ravenous, the silly buggers! Busy helping themselves to seconds now, with that special, panicked hunger of a man whose strict routine has been disturbed.

Later I was in my room packing a rucksack, my mind on Fiennes & Plunkett. It was so strange, this nagging feeling that I needed more time to reflect, that I wasn't ready for the news that would come tomorrow; and even stranger was this new, vague sense that I needed urgently to do something before Rupert called, something terribly important that I could not define – the anxiety seemed predicated upon the bizarre notion that I was somehow still in control of the news, that I could influence it. But the partnership vote, the news that would follow it, did not depend on me now – and maybe my problem, I thought, was that I was reflecting too much as opposed to too little. While it was true that I did not feel *ready* for the news of the vote, the point was that possibly I would never be ready – for what did *ready* really mean? The perceived need to be *ready* seemed a futile attempt at procrastination.

'You're coming with me.' In an act of rebellion against Rupert Plunkett's crazy rules, I brought out the BlackBerry from my suitcase and popped it into the rucksack. And then, after a careful reading of what the guidebook had to say about Playa Santa María del Mar, I made my way to the Hotel Nacional. On the way, at the intersection of two streets, I bumped into a man from whom this time it was too late to escape. *The thief, the thief.*

'Morning, Nathan.'

'Simon! Long time no see!' The perspiration swept down his cheeks, either side of a nose white with sun cream. Again it would have been charmingly geeky, had it not been for the eyes: Angus's eyes.

He was sort of pleased to see me – this was clear. But it was equally obvious that he was also angry with me; cool and calm, but angry – he must have spotted me fleeing in the past days.

'I guess we've both been busy,' I said.

'Yeah. What you up to, mate? Wanna hang out, have a couple of cold ones later? I'm having an easy day in the city today – too many day trips! We could head into Habana Vieja – there's some awesome places I've found. Full of ladies, too – tourists, of course. Not suggesting we go pulling locals, ha!'

'Ah, what a shame,' I said, watching him watch me. 'How about tomorrow? I'm in a rush at the moment. I'm off to Varadero, it's all pre-paid – you're right about the day trips you can do from here.'

'I've not been to Varadero.' He smiled, in a cold, pensive way. 'Listen, mate – can I ask you a question? A personal question?'

'Sure.'

'I get the sense you think I tried to steal that money from you the first night.' His face was icy now.

'Don't be silly,' I said. For I was English: anything but be honest and confrontational in a situation like this.

'OK, then, mate.' He shrugged. 'If you're sure. But I'd be mortified if someone thought that about me.'

'Oh, come on!'

'Alright – apologies, then. I'll be in touch tomorrow, mate – enjoy the sea at Varadero.'

… But once we'd said goodbye and I'd walked a couple of metres down the street, on an impulse I turned back and caught the thief, motionless, still watching me. He had hatred in his eyes. And as it vanished and he smiled again, waving at me, I thought suddenly of the day Engelhardt had come to the

273

firm of Fiennes & Plunkett; what Engelhardt had said to us, what he had said about Angus Peterson...

Minutes after my encounter with the thief, I was walking up the Hotel Nacional's grand driveway under the sun. Suddenly I stopped and took out my mobile phone, looked again at the draft sitting there. And then, after a long period of rumination, finally I sent the reply to Sophie – the message that I'd written and rewritten a hundred times.

I'm so sorry. Drunken ramblings, and I am deeply, unspeakably ashamed. All I can say is that it won't happen again, I promise. Hope all well. Simon.

Clear and rational and unambiguous – in line with a briefly imagined new maturity, a new focus on the present. And yet as I neared the hotel, passing the line of chinos and moccasins stepping out from Chevrolets, the rapid response:

No harm done. But do look after yourself please! You're a lovely guy, Simon. With a lovely secret, remember! Sophie

A response that led me to wander off, just before the entrance to the hotel's lobby, towards a bench standing before two ancient cannons, under the shade of a palm tree. It faced the lawns tumbling down from the promontory, into the ocean. I sat now, contemplating the water below, the waves blown towards this island since time immemorial. Presently a young member of staff came to sit down next to me on that bench: he was out-of-this-world tall, crazily lean and muscular, resembling those American basketball players I used to watch on TV. Startlingly handsome, with his big round eyes and perfectly symmetrical deep black face, he was dressed impeccably in the Hotel Nacional's dazzling white uniform. I thought for a moment of the ludicrous manner in which human beings organised themselves: how it could be that this radiant, beautiful, vastly superior human being, this apotheosis of manliness, was looking at a hungover, red-eared, white-cheeked and bitter Englishman with something approaching respect. He should have been laughing at me; he should have been asking himself what a Martian popped down to Earth might make of the notion that we were both 'men'. In a funny sort of way, as had happened in the past when I had come across super-alpha males, I thought happily of Dan Serfontein: of how this guy before me, who was now shaking my hand and introducing himself in English spoken in a slow, rhythmic voice, was far taller, and indeed far more handsome, than Dan. Childish, wasn't it?

His name was Evaristo, and for reasons I would soon learn his English was extremely good, albeit unlike the accents I had heard in Cuba – his accent had Spanish inflections, but not at all similar to the inflections of the natives of Havana. He must be from another part of the island, I thought. It soon became apparent that, despite having outgrown me thoroughly, the custodian of this absurd physique was still a kid, surely no more than twenty – youth shone through his eyes, through the innocence of his curiosity.

'Evaristo's a cool name,' I said. 'I'm Simon.'

'You're a guest, in the hotel?'

'No, no – I'm just sitting here for a while.'

He laughed softly now, pleasant laughter; as if my reply had relaxed him, he sat back into the bench, lighting a cigarette. 'Don't worry,' he said. 'I won't be tellin'.'

'You mean I'm not supposed to be here if I'm not a guest?'

'It's not a problem,' he chuckled again. 'Buy a *ron añejo*. Then you stay *all* day. You know why I sit here?'

'No.'

'The internet!' He clapped his hands in amusement. 'There is Wi-Fi. When my boss is not looking, I come and write to my *novia*.'

I wanted to get back to thinking of the person who used to be my *novia*; to Sophie's message about my lovely secret, the place to which my mind had been turning before this guy had interrupted. I could not imagine that a prolonged conversation with Evaristo would be of any value to either of us – my initial friendliness was fast turning into a desperation to be left alone.

'English, no?' he persisted.

'Yes.'

'I know it – you speak like my *novia*!'

'Really?' I turned to him. 'You have an English girlfriend?'

'*Claro* – look, look.' He became all busy on his phone, whizzing through photos – he really was young: all silly enthusiasm and energy. Then he found the photograph he had been searching for and moved up close to me on the bench, passing me the phone; when he showed me his girlfriend, I felt a jabbing in my chest. She was a middle-aged woman easily twice his age, unattractive, with short red hair and a burnt, half-drunken face. She was kissing Evaristo's beautiful clean face, a large, full wine glass in her hand, and he was staring proud into the telephone's camera. The woman had a 'London professional' look about her – perhaps some middle-manager in a blue-chip company; or a recruiter, or in marketing, maybe…

'She came here one year ago,' Evaristo said. 'She stayed in this hotel. And now she came back two times for me.'

'That's good.'

'She will take me there, you know? To England, *amigo*! Me and you, we will live together, *jejeje*!'

'Did she say that to you?'

'Yeah, *claro*, my friend!' He gave me a huge smile. 'We're making plans!'

I looked out to the horizon – a light wind was blowing now from the ocean, rustling through the palm trees' leaves above us, creating a strange dance of shadows. *Do I tell him*, I wondered, *do I break his young heart with the words 'be careful – she's lying to you'*? It would be typical of me to interfere righteously like that; or rather it would have been typical of the man I had been until not so many years ago. Now I was just so tired all the time; wasn't it weird how tiredness had washed beyond my body and mind and seeped into my very being? I had lost any sense of conviction that I was necessarily *right* about things. Maybe this woman loved him – what the hell did I know about human beings? Wasn't love between a man and a woman often just a series of compromises anyway? Compromises I had singularly failed to make? That photo of them was depressing, but only to my mind – it was only an idea of mine. My mind was wandering again, through fields and fields of ideas. Somehow I was back to last year, the summer of 2011, around a month before Campaign had begun – the last time we had all gone out together, Clemmie and Dan and Sophie and Simon. We were in Pimlico, on an early Friday evening. Why had that image come to me now? Of course, yes: that was the night Sophie had asked me to tell her again what she called the 'lovely secret'; the night she'd reminded me of the Sophie of old.

'You want to be alone,' Evaristo said. 'Don't worry, I know. That's why you came here.' He punched my shoulder gently, in an amicable way. 'OK. I use internet.' He showed the phone to me again and *of course*, I thought, *he's proud of it – she bought it for him.*

'*Está volao*,' I said, nodding towards his toy in admiration. He looked surprised by this – but then became very amused. I had no idea why, but his humour came passing through me – so we both ended up laughing.

'*Sí, sí, amigo*,' Another punch, before he moved away, to his end of the bench. '*Está volao*.'

Yes, it was an early Friday evening, it was the summer of 2011 – incredible to think that nearly a year had passed since then. It must have been only a week or so later that Dan had cracked, handing in his resignation. An early Friday evening – the moment of the week that, for every Fiennes & Plunkett lawyer, used to make sense of it all. A moment to savour, because soon it would be gone. The drafts could wait till Saturday, the timesheets until Sunday – for now, the lawyer was free.

A balmy, dreamlike summer's evening, Dan and I now on the cusp of Campaign, each of us increasingly lost, each of us increasingly sure. Did he know yet that he was about to leave, the suffering behind the cool smile having become too much? Anyway, now it was Friday…

'Lash on!'

…and the air was rich with a particular promise tonight; the golden mists of alcohol awaiting as I contemplated a fine and cathartic aimlessness. The July sun fell gently onto the wooden tables outside the Marquis of Westminster as I sat with Sophie, Dan and an excitable Clementine, who was running her hands through that head of smooth fair hair that fell to just below her shoulders. Her summery beige dress matching the beige Mulberry handbag. Very touchy already with Dan…Dan, tie loosened now, radiant and cool, the Lothario under the sun. Sophie – tonight I'll watch her interaction with Dan carefully – Sophie in a lovely white dress that accentuated those brown eyes, and sort of half-relieved, half-concerned, to see me wanting to forget, to let go, to have fun. But relaxing herself now, just a little – it was contagious, tonight, this sense of release. Although, condescending, so superbly condescending, Sophie's squint when Clemmie spoke!

'You know what?' Dan lit a Marlboro Light and looked down the Belgrave Road. 'There's something really *odd* about Pimlico. It's all very grand, but there's something artificial that I can't quite articulate; something not quite crass but a bit flimsy.'

'The buildings are just *too* white, maybe?' I ventured. 'Sense of seediness lingering beneath the paint?'

'Yes – that's it! They're too white. Like shiny shoes. Or a man who waxes his car obsessively – there's something not quite right about it.'

'Daniel!' Sophie nearly spat out her drink, her eyes amused. 'What an odd thing to say! Why should a man waxing his car be troubling?'

'Random!' Clemmie finished texting and looked up. A definite spray tan, I thought, as she continued. 'Like, why are you talking about, like, such a *random* thing?'

Sophie looked away, biting her lip. I adored those brown eyes when she was amused despite herself.

'Isn't it weird that not one of us around this table drives?' Dan continued to puff thoughtfully on his cigarette. 'We're a funny lot, City professionals. In our early thirties, and very few of us have a car. Go out of London and they've all got cars! They've had cars since they were eighteen! They had kids when they were eighteen, too – now they're on to grandchildren!'

'Really, Dan! Grandchildren!'

'They have, I promise! Children and grandchildren! Great-grandchildren! Dogs and cats and beer bellies and an absolute contentment! Whereas, in our case, we've never grown up.'

'I can drive.' I finished my pint and looked quickly around the table, buzzing now. 'I passed my test at nineteen.'

'But you don't own a car.'

'No.'

'Nor a house.'

'No.'

'I've got a house!' objected Clemmie. 'I've had my place for two years.'

Dan took a swig of beer. 'Yes, dear Clementine, but you and I don't quite count. We did not exactly independently buy houses.'

'Oh, fuck off.' Clemmie laughed adoringly, threw back her head, inviting more.

'Mummy's Christmas present doesn't count,' Dan explained. 'Your total effort was, I imagine, having to watch while some foreign musclemen moved your stuff; and having a slightly uncomfortable first night before they brought the new bedsheets.'

'You're such a knob!'

'Anyway – back to cars. It's strange, isn't it? It's almost as if there's something very non-Londoner about driving a car.'

'Not true either! My sister drives a…oh, what does she drive now?'

Loud, aggressive laughter spilled outside the pub, followed closely by a gang of jubilant men who looked far too young for their suits.

'Well,' Sophie said, 'I think owning a car is sensible. It shows that you're able to commit to something. You're right about not growing up – I find it so strange. You're all – at least, I imagine you're all – so mature when you're in the office, advising people twice your age, but in your personal lives…'

Much too sincere, this, for Clemmie. She turned away with a *yikes* face.

'Sofia, Sofia,' murmured Lothario. 'There's so much time for commitment and all the rest. For now, let's have fun! Haines – your round!'

'I thought we were going back to ours.' Sophie glanced at me. 'I bought the clams.'

'A quick one, and we'll go.'

'Simon.'

Dan stood up to take off his jacket – a couple of tipsy female colleagues from the firm, whom we vaguely knew, gazed at him longingly from the wobbly table in front of ours.

'Be gentle on your boyfriend, Sophie – he's done ninety hours since last Sunday. It's not even eight o'clock yet. Look at him, he's panting for a pint.' And the assured smile broke her.

'Mm, that's what I'm worried about. One quick drink – then we're going.'

Soon I was back with a tray of lagers and G&Ts and Sophie was laughing, really laughing now about something Dan had said, and despite a little pang of jealousy I wanted the night to go on forever.

'Can I have a ciggie, mate?'

'Simon, no! I hate it when you smoke.'

'I'm allowed a ciggie!'

'Hey!' exclaimed Clemmie. 'I forgot to say – I've got a printout of the mental email!' The handbag seemed almost to become animate as she searched for something impatiently, wildly.

'No – the Wilkinson email?' Dan's face was eager. 'I haven't read it yet.'

'What's this?' asked Sophie.

'It's an email that's been doing the rounds in the City today.' I took my seat. 'I've received it twice, I think, but I still haven't read it either. It's this kid, Bruce Wilkinson. He trained at Raynott Mirren and just quit his training contract today...'

'Raynott Mirren?' Sophie looked nonplussed. She knew exactly who they were – classic Sophie.

'Raynott Mirren,' I repeated. 'One of the best law firms in the world. Anyway, today, his last day, this trainee decided to send an email to all his fellow trainees. Advising them to go and change the world, or something. But by mistake he sent it to the whole firm – all lawyers in all forty-two offices; about three thousand fee earners.'

'Who knows if it was really a mistake?' pondered Dan. 'It was all about getting attention, after all.'

'Well, I confess I'm interested now too,' murmured Sophie.

'Yes – come on, Clementine, read it out! Come on!' The beer was so cooling. I could drink pints and pints tonight!

'Simon,' Sophie turned to me. 'Calm down!'

The group of young men who looked so absurd in their suits walked recklessly into the middle of the street to stop a taxi, which, to their fury and my great pleasure, drove straight past them and on towards the river, the insults chasing it down the Belgrave Road.

'Wanker!'

'Twat!'

'Apparently, he's off abroad,' Dan was saying. 'And then he's going to become – wait for it – a dentist! He's going to do his bit for the mouths of the human race. I must say, actually, it's so annoying when people mistake weakness for strength. I bet you he was a smart guy – did amazingly at uni and law school, no doubt – but he just couldn't hack the hours. He's too ashamed to admit it, and so now he's trying to portray his defeat as some magnificent rebellion.' He shook his head. 'An egomaniac.'

'Do you actually *know* any of that?' asked Sophie, a low fire in her voice.

'Actually, you're right,' added Clemmie. 'That's what I was going to say – my sister actually *knew* someone who *knew*

Wilkinson at Trinity. He was just like that, apparently – super clever but, like, how do you say ... '

'You say egomaniac.'

'Clemmie!' I said. 'Please read the email!'

'OK,' Clemmie took a gulp of G&T. 'Here goes.'

Dear all,

Given that we have all shared over a year together – a very intense 15 months – I thought I would leave you with some thoughts, which may or may not be of interest/assistance.

'Can't you already tell?'

'An egomaniac!'

'Shh! Let her carry on!'

'Yes, Simon, *please* shut up.'

Don't believe this lie that people peddle about cynicism meaning superiority. Cynicism is the poor man's prop – it is insecurity and fear. You can have a lot more fun being open-minded, interested in life and culture, caring about others, caring about the environment. A pursuit of prestige alone is a form of madness that will lead only to true madness.

Clemmie stopped for a second, then finished off the G&T with a flourish.

We all need to remember that somewhere inside us we all have big hearts. Sniggering now, aren't you? But we do, we have hearts, and we have a responsibility. Society is a contract based on respect. And we

need to start respecting each other again – every-
one, from the senior partner to the people who
drive you home in your midnight taxis – everyone.

You have, all of you, forgotten about your hearts,
but don't worry – you can all find them again, find
yourselves again, with only a bit of concentration; a bit
of bravery.

'He's fucking mental!'

And while you laugh at this and laugh at me with
your mates tonight when you're lashing it up, while
you forward this on to your friends at other firms, do
remember that I understand. You're putting on a front,
like everyone else. I will not hold it against you if one
day you revisit this, calmly, and thank me.

Clemmie paused again. 'This is, like, so embarrassing to read?'
'Carry on, Clementine!' Dan ordered. 'I'm hooked now.'
Clemmie shrugged; murmured, 'Whatever?'

And so – you may ask – what are my plans now? Well,
I am off to remote lands – the Shetland Islands, to be
precise. Where I will walk, camp and climb. Watch
birds. All for long enough to rediscover myself.

And, once done, I will be back, to try to relaunch myself
in a career in: dentistry! It will be a long haul, even if I
do get into dental school – it will require studying with
people many years younger than me, and will doubtless
lead to my being called eccentric. But never again will I
have that emptiness that I had each day when doing the
due diligence on Project Smoke.

Alternatively, I might become a professional preacher and wander the planet spreading wisdom. That last point, for the avoidance of doubt, is a joke.

Anyway, keep well and I hope to see you again some day. In particular, do come and visit me in the Shetland Isles. There may be no conference call capacity out there but hey, you could try shouting!

All the best,
Bruce Wilkinson

Clemmie finished, mouthing, 'No way,' as she dropped the printout onto the table. Thin wisps of cigarette smoke danced through the summer air.

'Now, Sophie,' said Dan. 'Tell me that that email does not make you cringe.'

'No. I'm sorry, but it doesn't.' Oh, how proud she could be! 'It reminds me actually of Simon, years ago when he was a trainee.'

'Sophie!' I was aghast.

'Don't you remember, when you had that awful supervisor who never explained anything, what was his name? And one night you said you'd started getting a bit philosophical, and—'

'Oh, really!' Dan thumped his fist down onto the table in delight. 'Now, I want to hear this! A rebel in our ranks!'

'Don't be ridiculous.' I glared at Sophie – honestly, in front of my colleagues! But there was not much damage. Minds and thoughts were loose and itinerant now.

'What's *so* bad,' Clemmie was noting as she texted away, 'is his attempt to be funny! The "no conference call capacity" thing? It's, like, so NOT funny!'

'Give him two months.' Dan narrowed his eyes. 'Two months maximum and he'll be back in the City, applying for an in-house position at a fund or a corporate, trying to explain that email away to a recruiter. I guarantee it.'

An old tramp staggered towards our table, asking for spare change. He had a large stomach that bulged below a filthy green shirt. His ripped grey jogging bottoms touched the pavement as he came near. Behind him was his companion – an Alsatian on a lead – and there hung in the air a stench of urine. With a flick of his hand, Dan waved him away.

'Got a magic trick,' mumbled the tramp.

'No, thanks!' exclaimed Clemmie, rolling her eyes. And then, in a conspiratorial voice, 'Fuck me, Pimlico's nice but, like, sometimes it's really *grim*?'

'What's particularly awful about the spoilt middle class,' I said, as the tramp stared, wiping his face, and Sophie, with great drama, took out her purse and gave him fifty pence, 'is this assumption that we can do any job we want. That we can switch from being a lawyer to a dentist just like that. It's all arrogance and caprice – there's no substance to it.'

'How do *you* know there's no substance to it? How are you so sure that you're right?'

'What a random place to choose, anyway: the Shetland Islands!'

'I *am* right, actually, Sophie!'

'Well, I don't agree!'

'Alright, alright, you two!' Dan was grinning. 'Easy, tigers! Now, one more lash?'

'One last round,' I declared, jumping up. 'I'll get it again, then you owe me, OK? Very quick, then back to ours!'

'Simon!' Sophie stood up, alarmed. 'You're manic tonight! Simon, listen to me!'

But I was drifting now; drifting away in the boozy, eddying currents of a river with sunlit shores. Later the night was still warm and we were on our roof terrace, around a table of empty bottles of Malbec and Chablis, three cigarettes flickering in the semi-darkness. The conversation had returned to the email of Bruce Wilkinson – as if in a strange sort of way something remained to be resolved.

'So, he was at Trinity with your sister, you said?' Dan's voice was hard, suddenly.

'No, with a friend of hers, I've told you that!' Clemmie was texting her new boyfriend – texting him increasingly as Dan's indifference increased.

'That email was so self-indulgent.' Lothario sighed. 'Of course, many of us feel frustration, I suppose.'

'Really?' Sophie bit. 'So we have another rebel, do we?'

'A rebel? Ha! No, not me. I'm just talking generally, not about myself. I'm saying it must be a bit frustrating for some people, when they start to realise certain things. I mean, years ago we all arrived as cocky trainees without a clue what we'd signed up to, but with this assumption – no, certainty! – this certainty that, whatever it was, we'd excel at it. And we all knew already what excellence meant, and how it would be measured – it was the only thing we knew. Excellence meant partnership.'

'Well!'

'It's true. And so we assumed that, as things took their natural course, we'd become partners. The most basic research would've told us what our real chances were at our very particular family firm – i.e. about one in a hundred. But nobody bothered to think about that, or wanted to think about it. Or maybe we were all just too self-important, I don't know.'

'So when people *do* have to accept, after years in the game, that they might in fact not be ...' Dan paused now, as if angry with himself that it was too late to change his sentence '…might not be *good* enough, or hardworking enough, or that simply they might not want it enough – it must be pretty galling! And that's already been the case for many at our firm – although hopefully it won't be the case for me. I don't think it will be Simon's case. In fact I'd say that, of the four of us left – me, Simon, Emma and Angus – Mr Simon Haines here has the best chance. But the ironic thing…'

He sighed again – and I felt so awkward listening to this.

'The ironic thing is that, deep down, with only a tiny minority of exceptions, I suspect that none of us ever really wanted to become a partner of a law firm in the first place. But we've been in this hermetic world for so long now that it's easy to be convinced. I suppose a mature approach would be to keep an open mind at this point.'

Ah – there we have it. He's rewriting his story, I thought. *He knows he's not going to make it, so he's begun the formulation of a new narrative. Better this way – better for him. Write your story, Dan – write yourself out of the mess.*

'It's lovely to hear you say that, finally,' murmured Sophie. 'You're such a weird pair, you and Simon. Despite how much you go on about it, and these insane hours you put in, I've actually doubted for a long time how much you really do understand your own goal – but it's impossible to make you listen! I mean, have you ever reflected on what being a partner of Fiennes & Plunkett means in practice, what it means in reality? Have you ever asked yourselves whether you really are so desperate for the prestige and the million-pound salary? I reckon the fixation is on something else – some deeper idea. Or rather, some shallower idea – the idea of being able to say you *made* it.'

'It's not, like, actually a *salary* when you're a partner, by the way. It's called *drawings*.'

'Exactly, Sophie!' Dan interrupted Clemmie, stood up and looked out into the night sky. 'None of us really *wants* it. But we're all horrified at the thought that we might not get it.'

'What *do* you guys want?' Sophie wondered aloud.

Silence descended upon the terrace. Sophie infuriated me when she spoke like this, spouting this sort of righteous pseudo-intellectual nonsense, not understanding or even wanting to understand the bare minimum of what I did, what I thought. Ignoring the substance, the intermittent but intense enjoyment that my job brought, the intellectual rigour – reducing it all to a race for the money. Of course I'd questioned what I'd wanted – on any objective basis I had a fantastic career, and how easy it was to criticise, to sow doubt. But I would leave it now, for Dan's sake: I was relieved, happy even, that he was telling himself this story now, justifying in advance what he would do…

…And it was easy to leave it, for I was not in the mood for an argument – I was relaxed, it was Friday evening and it was lovely out here on the terrace, although there was a slight chill now in the air. Sophie brought out some blankets; Dan poured himself a drink. Presently, a sharp intake of breath. It was the noise Clemmie made when a thought came to her.

'It's even harder for women!' she blurted out suddenly. 'There's *major* discrimination in the City still! Just look at how few female partners there are in the top firms! It's really tough for us!'

'I must say, I read the other day about the number of women who enter the law versus the number of female partners, and it's pretty damn shocking.'

Sophie turned as I spoke, as if surprised I was still awake. She moved her chair nearer to mine. 'You OK?' she whispered. 'You were a bit tipsy earlier. This is all quite interesting – Dan's opening up a bit.'

'I know, Sophie, I know. Dan this, Dan that. I've been listening.'

But she leant over now and surprised me: covering us for a second with the blanket, she kissed me warmly, in a way in which she hadn't kissed me for years.

'Yes, I agree.' Dan had re-engaged. 'It's still a real issue – something that needs putting right. For a female lawyer in the City generally, the odds are indeed still shocking. When I think of Emma Morris – if she were a man…'

'It's not just about Emma Morris – it's the same for me too, at my fund! And not to mention the natural disadvantage of childbirth!'

'Did you hear about Angela Gill?' I said, emerging from the blanket. 'I heard she worked right up to the day before the day she gave birth, and that she was back a week later.'

'Insanity,' murmured Sophie.

'It's the system that's insane,' I said. 'It leaves women with hardly any reasonable options; it makes it almost impossible for them.'

A pause again now – some footsteps and then a pleasant gurgling noise, as Clemmie emptied the final bottle of Chablis. Presently, the outraged voice of a golden girl.

'Archie says it sounds like I'm being totally bullied, by the way.'

Sophie pinched my leg.

'Oh, babes!' said Dan. 'You mean your boyf, the journalist? He should write about it!'

'He's, like, an editor actually? Anyway, yeah – it's about this, like, total *bitch* at work.'

'Clemmie – you've told me three times!'

'OK, OK. Um, Soph, what do you think, can we put some music on?'

'Not really – not unless we go inside.'

From somewhere afar, somewhere lost among the rooftops of Parson's Green, came the sound of a baby crying…

'Now, all of you.' Dan had adopted the voice of a leader – some grand military commander of old. 'Listen up! Pass me a whisky or a glass of wine – one last drink for the road – and I'll tell you my theory about all of this.'

'Simon's got the whisky behind his chair!'

'Simon?'

'Hmm? Yeah, alright. Here you go.'

'He's a million miles away.'

'Sorry.'

As was often the case when a little tipsy, I'd been thinking for a second about Naples. The porter at my old *palazzo* who would wake the residents each morning with his yelling as he opened the grand old doors to the courtyard and the sun flooded in…the city exploding into wild joy late at night, fireworks ripping through the black sky, for reasons unknown…the fine quiet of crazy blue Sundays, the broken glass in the Greek ruins at Piazza Bellini, Mariella on the dance floor of L'Arancia. Ha! Mariella indeed! What was I doing, thinking of her? I loved Sophie – it would be alright with Sophie. There had been moments, tonight, which told me it would all be alright. Her kiss had been so loving.

I moved my chair nearer and reached out to hold Sophie's hand, my scotch balanced expertly on my lap. She put her blanket over both of our shoulders and we cuddled up. Yes, we were close tonight – safe again together.

A voice boomed out.

'Now, my theory, which I've just come up with tonight, is about what a young lawyer like this man Bruce Wilkinson, coming up to qualification, about to enter real City law – what this young lawyer should now do. He is the same man Simon and I were many years ago. Let us say he is not actually totally mad like this man Bruce, and he at least sees the training out – so he qualifies. And the theory, my children, is that his options now boil down to four, which we shall call Options A, B, C and D.'

'Let me guess.'

'I know!'

'Quiet, and I'll tell you. His options are as follows. Option A is that he realises he's got it all wrong – if that is indeed what he believes – and he draws back, with much drama and just in time. It's a seductive image, but – bullshit. Never – or *extremely* rarely – followed in practice.'

'But that's what that guy Bruce Wilkinson has done!' protested Sophie.

'No,' I interrupted, 'no, I don't think that *is* what Bruce Wilkinson has done.'

'Excellent, young Simon,' declared the Wise Man. 'And please explain why what he's done – by moving to the North Pole or wherever it is – please explain why it doesn't qualify.'

'Because what Bruce has done isn't real,' I said.

'Bravo!'

'It might be.'

'Highly unlikely, I'm afraid, Sophie. Because this Bruce Wilkinson here is just making a scene! He's *telling* other lawyers what he's going to do. In other words, dear Sophie, he's still attached, not free. Now, if he'd just gone and done it – if he'd really organised his place at dentist school or whatever you call it, if he'd come up with a plan, well, that'd be another matter. The dentist nonsense is just that – a fantasy. If there'd been any substance to it, he'd have given the details.'

'He might need a period of time to clear his head,' Sophie replied. 'I imagine he would need to, after all that work.'

'He won't do it, and that's that.'

'Oh, for fuck's sake.' Clemmie yawned. 'Tell us Option B.'

Sophie squeezed my hand. 'God, she really is appalling,' she whispered.

'Hmm? Oh, yeah, I know.'

'You're daydreaming as usual. Are you even listening?'

'Yes, I *am* listening. I was just thinking of Naples too. Shall we go to Naples this summer? I could finally show you the Corso, where I lived. You'd adore Piazza Bellini.'

'Naples? You told me once you'd never take me there. You said you'd never go back, remember?'

'Yeah, but tonight—'

'Shh!' She giggled. 'You're not that drunk, actually – you're funny tonight. Listen, Dan's moved on to Option B. Or rather, he's *trying* to move on to Option B. He needs to go home.'

'Yes, Option B. We turn... Now, what *is* Option B? What the fuck is Option B?'

'Presumably, Option B is to go all the way,' I said. 'To dedicate eighteen, nineteen, twenty-two hours a day for six years – focus on becoming a partner, regardless of the consequences.'

'That's right.' Dan hiccupped. 'Fucking lashed. I...I've forgotten Option C.' And then, with the voice reverting, thankfully, to his real voice, with that trace of an Essex accent, 'Need to go soon.'

'I know Option C,' I said. 'Option C is to continue for a few years and then go in-house. Irritate the shit out of people like me by talking about your better hours, your work-life balance. You'll ask anyone who listens why a lawyer would need to earn a million pounds a year. Now and again you'll tell war stories about the mad old days, talk about what awful lives the partners must have...'

I stopped, cursing myself silently for the insensitivity in relation to Dan – this was not what he needed to hear tonight. And it was stupid to be blasé about it anyway – on any rational basis, Option C probably was the best, or at least the most sensible option for most.

But it was alright – Dan hadn't heard. He was far away now, completely hammered.

'Simon'll do Option B.' He was slouched in his chair, talking to his feet. 'He'll make partner. He loves the work too much. Too good at it. Fucker. Hey, Clemmie!' He looked up. 'Can you call a cab?'

'I said I'd already called it!'

'Alright, calm down. Now, Sophie – it would be a pleasure if you would accompany me to the door.'

Getting to his feet, he reached over to take Sophie's hand. She let him take it, laughing – it had seemed an inappropriate request to me, and they stayed holding hands a little too long as we waited outside, before the taxi pulled up and our guests clambered in, faced by a young driver's disapproving stare.

'Please.' Sophie smiled cheekily at me before I could speak. 'Not the Dan flirting thing again. You're so ridiculous. Let's go upstairs.'

It was extraordinary to kiss Sophie again that night; it was like knocking down an ugly wall we'd been building for years; like unblocking a dam, and dipping our feet into a fresh bubbly stream. Were we back again? Had we somehow, unwittingly, started afresh? Or was this just a snatched fleeting happiness, a snatched fleeting dream?

'Dan doesn't know your funny secret, does he?' she whispered, as we lay naked together. 'When he mentioned you loved the work at Fiennes & Plunkett so much, I almost said it.'

'What secret?'

'You know: that you love your job sometimes, but only when you do it your way – that you're scared you might be a bit of a fraud, and that you're not actually sure you're very good at the law. Tell me again.'

'Ah, that.' I laughed – I felt warm now as she came close. 'It's really true, you know,' I whispered, as we gazed up through the skylight at a pale moon. 'Often I'm convinced that I have no idea what they're on about during the meetings. But without my realising it some part of my mind is taking it all in. I go back to my office, look at the notes and they still don't mean much, if anything – and I have a massive panic! But then I concentrate on the agreement and all of a sudden I start tweaking things, playing with the clauses, moving words around until it all fits … you know, creating a new exception here, or a new proviso there, a few new definitions … and it always ends up alright. Then sometimes I get all this praise for having shown such a focused approach, but in truth I never know quite what happened!'

'For you it really is just all words.'

'Lots of us are like that, I reckon.'

'Really? I don't know why, but for me it's such a lovely image, somehow – probably because I know you so well, that's why. I can just see it: a meeting room full of serious business-men and women arguing about all these important things, and you understanding even less than I would – but at the same time understanding it all. I do still love you, you know.'

'Sometimes I'm not sure.'

'Soon, very soon now, you're going to change your mind. Don't start that stupid Campaign thing, Simon. You've still got a month to find something else before it starts. Think what you could do instead. Maybe you could do something grand. Something with value and meaning. Can you imagine?'

'Yes, who knows?'

I didn't want to argue with her now – I didn't want to try to explain everything again, make her see how heedless she was being of the real world, how romantic and immature her arguments were. Because, for that second, I really didn't know.

'Yes,' I repeated. 'Maybe you're right.'

'Oh, Simon.' She put her arms around me. 'It's such a sweet thing, that lovely secret.'

The morning found us embraced in a soft white light under soft summer sheets – a picture of the couple we'd once been.

11

I COULD HAVE grown old, I could have sat for a hundred lonely years on that bench, looking down at the Atlantic spinning out, the waves rising high before the rocks. The improbably handsome athlete Evaristo had abandoned the bench but was back now, loosening his tie – his shift was over.

'You're still here, *mi amigo*!'

'Actually, I must go,' I said. 'I've got a trip half-planned – I wanted to go to the Playas del Este – get a bit of *playa y sol*, you know.'

'*Playa y sol.*' He had a strange habit of repeating what I said, as if we were singing together. But now, once the repeated words had been assimilated:

'You're crazy!' he cried, suddenly.

'Why am I crazy?'

'*Tormenta, amigo.* A big storm is coming today – see?' He was on his treasured internet again – showing me a forecast that took me by surprise, despite the slightly cooler air, the clouds grouping slowly out there on the horizon. For the moment it was still fine weather – perhaps it would be for a while. But there was change ahead, Evaristo warned me...

'I'm writing to my *novia*. I write real good now.' That friendly punch to emphasise the point – met by that most English of reactions. I was thinking how I was quite happy to give up on my idea of the Playas del Este – I was tired, pleased to find a justification to do nothing. A trip to the Hotel Nacional and back, then, today. I took out my BlackBerry, enjoying a quick silly thrill at the thought that I was going to breach Rupert's rules. *Tomorrow, he'll call with the big news. He's going to tell you either that you're a partner, or that you're out – one of these two outcomes is certain.* It was all very curious, this repetition of the point to myself – it was as if I were trying to elicit a reaction, trying to make the fact real. And I couldn't quite manage it, the words bringing about only that troubling idea that there wasn't much time left for something, that there was a sort of extreme urgency to do something or get somewhere, and that I'd left everything too late. The incomprehensible sense of urgency elicited a memory of an episode of my childhood. I must have been around twelve or thirteen when I had read an article about self-recognition in which the author had stated that very few animals are able to recognise themselves in a mirror. The article had captivated me, stuck with me throughout the day at school, and that evening before bed I had stood too long before my own mirror, looking deeply into my own face, only to turn away suddenly, run from the room in anguish and terror, which became then muted by a sort of detached realisation – a thought that, even if I were to know everything there was to know about myself, *I could never know for sure whether I was real.* And this in turn had brought about the imperativeness, the need to do something...

I remembered now that the sun was shining on Green Park, and that Sophie and I were having a picnic below the swaying branches, when I'd told her about it – back in those early days, when I'd only just started at the firm as a trainee.

'I love you to bits, *precisely* because you are so utterly and fabulously round the bend,' Sophie said.

'Well, you say that, but have you tried the test?' I insisted. 'I did it again recently, and had exactly the same reaction I'd had as a kid. You try – try staring into the mirror tonight, the full-length mirror, and repeating to yourself, more than ten times, "This is Sophie looking back. I am Sophie. And I am real". Then tell me you don't feel a little freaked out.'

'But Simon, that's the point.' Her tone was kind, reassuring. 'You *think* about things too much.'

'Maybe.'

'I'm not saying your reaction is wrong; it's your putting yourself through it which is nuts. Sort of wonderfully nuts, in a way. It really isn't healthy, though – what will it achieve?'

'Well, maybe I'll write a book – *Expeditions to the Borders of Sanity.*'

'I'm sure your boss Mr Plunkett could help with that.'

Sophie had always had this wonderful ability to bring me down to earth, to make me experience things with her – a capacity to pop the balloon of thoughts, of wondering, in an instant. I loved how she would click those fingers, half-jokingly, if she saw that I was 'off'. With Sophie, I thought, there had never been urgency – because she had always been grounded. But then, slowly, she'd changed, consumed by her own words, the words of her mission, her philosophy…

'So,' Evaristo said, 'you got a woman?'

'My girlfriend and I split up,' I said. '*Se acabó.*'

'And you have friends?'

'Sorry?' I turned to him, an unexpected indignation in my throat. 'What a weird question. Of course I have friends – I have lots of friends.'

'*Ya*. I have many friends too,' he laughed again – he was always laughing, wasn't he? 'I have hundreds of friends, you know?'

A silence fell between us – only the wind through the palm trees was audible. I was looking down at the BlackBerry again, but for some reason still hadn't brought myself to switch it on. Presently:

'Evaristo,' I said, 'shall we have a drink?'

'For me too?' He jumped up, his gigantic smile revealing those perfect white teeth.

'Why not – yes, I'll buy you a drink.'

'OK!' He nearly knocked me off the bench as he gave me a high five. '*Dos presidentes?*'

'*Dos presidentes.*'

'You like to drink?'

'I do,' I said. He was already off with my *pesos*, bounding across the fine gardens into the bar of the Hotel Nacional, when I added, quietly, 'Rather hard not to, with my job.'

The temperature was lovely out here in the garden now; I would have the most fantastic view of the storm's approach by sea and air, if ever it did come. But there was not much sign – the grey clouds out there above the water, far away, seemed still uncertain as to their plan. I switched on the BlackBerry – time for mutiny.

You must not *access your work emails, Simon.*

I knew that none of the emails would contain any real clue as to my future – the partners were obsessive in their confidentiality – but nevertheless it was natural to want to check; it was absurd of Rupert to imagine that we would accept being cut off from the firm, unable to receive gossip, banter, maybe some messages wishing us good luck for tomorrow. The prohibition, I suspected, was set out somewhere in the ravings of The Manual, the logic behind it disturbing in its simplicity: any lawyer who had made it through a Fiennes & Plunkett Campaign would be skipping on the edge of sanity, liable to trip at the slightest push. The little shove of an email from an irascible client, or a regulator; the glancing blow from a partner who had forgotten that the lawyer had just completed Campaign.

After Campaign, a lawyer needs to rest, Rupert had said, when explaining the rules for the first time. Perhaps there was, in some part of England, a recovery clinic full of gaunt young men and women, babbling:

I got through Campaign but then they wouldn't leave me alone!

All I needed was a week or two!

There's a typo in that prescription! Please, nurse, please let me correct the typo!

Men and women who would pull faces of horror upon the sight of an incoming email, the sound of a ringing phone, the mention of the name 'Plunkett'.

After Campaign, a lawyer needs to rest.

I had heard a few stories of alleged mental breakdowns at Fiennes & Plunkett, but had only been a direct witness to one case, which happened to be the firm's most notorious (this, of course, was on the somewhat dubious assumption that Rupert Plunkett himself had not broken down badly decades earlier and that we were not still experiencing the fallout). The case was that of Tim Douglas, a slight, red-haired, wonderfully gentle guy from Newcastle, a man with the at once accommodating and awkward smile of the truly bright. The only lawyer of his intake to make it to Campaign, he was about midway through the eight months when it happened. The story was passed down from one intake of Fiennes &

Plunkett to another, but Angus and I were two of the very few lawyers who had seen it first-hand, having been trainees on the final deal of Tim's career. Poor Tim Douglas. The mere recollection of the man's name made me wince.

To the emails, then. I'd been sent or copied on an impressive two hundred or so. But I was good at the 'relevant email spotting' game – comprehensively trained. It took a very short amount of time to understand that only three new emails were worth reading. The exercise had been facilitated by the point that over three-quarters of the emails were from Rupert Plunkett to others, copying me in – judging from the subject headers, to get to UK time, I had seen that the lead madman continued to shun sleep, and that the happy days continued to roll.

Client is HUNGRY. Expedite coffee/pastries to meeting room. Time of sending 03.26, UK time – this had been sent to Giles, Rupert complying with The Manual in copying me, Giles's direct supervisor, on all correspondence to the trainee. Two days later, one Tuesday morning, an email with that red exclamation mark indicating high importance, sent to the entire firm: *General notice: new LMA wording now DEFECTIVE,* time of sending 01.59; followed, at 02.03, by a computer-generated: *URGENT: RUPERT PLUNKETT HAS ATTEMPTED TO RECALL MESSAGE;* followed, at 02.12, by: *General notice: new LMA wording now EFFECTIVE (for the avoidance of doubt, NOT defective).* At 02.30, an email to Giles: *Major issue re preparation of draft emails.*

There were no good-luck messages from other associates or partners – it was uplifting, the camaraderie at Fiennes & Plunkett. But there were two emails from the little shit himself, Angus; and one from Giles. Evaristo was walking across the garden with our cocktails, so I jumped in, concentrating on Angus's. His first was addressed to both me and Emma. It was false and strange and disquieting.

My dear competitors,

On the assumption that you too have been unable to respect the rule as to no email checking, I was just writing to say that I do hope you are both holding up! Simon, I trust Cuba is treating you well and that you've made some friends on your tour, and got yourself a nice tan. Knowing you well, I'm sure you've been savouring the mojitos. Not too many, I hope!

Emma, I'm sure you're enjoying Dubai – I can see you this evening (it's already evening there, right?) on some luxurious balcony with a glass of vino (and maybe even one of your sneaky ciggies ☺)

I just thought I would write to say that, regardless of what happens tomorrow, I believe you should be proud of yourselves. Not many have come through Campaign unscathed – and I don't think any of us ever really flipped during the eight months – do you?

If either of you wishes to let off steam over the course of the next 24 hours, feel free to give me a call.

Finally, this being our last day as associates of the Firm, I say that we should raise a glass or two – but, as I say, NOT the moment for megalash, Simon ☺

Best wishes,
Angus

If Emma was on her Dubai balcony, she would be stubbing out the secret fag in fury. It had been a small but unpleasant dig – Angus just wanting to emphasise her inability to quit; her weakness. The man delighted in weakness – I remembered a time when, at around 6 a.m. on one particularly unpleasant deal, the company we'd been negotiating against had suddenly caved in, conceding every point on the document – it was clear that their alternative option had just fallen away, and so they had no cards left. In the meeting room, sitting next to me, Angus had been hyperventilating with a predatory excitement.

'If we were playing hardball,' he'd whispered, a spot of saliva on his lips, 'we'd reopen all the agreed points now, and absolutely *fuck them over*. Literally, every single point – we could *fuck* them.'

A charmer, young Angus. He'd latched on to what he'd perceived to be a weakness in me too and hyperbolised it – for a while now he had been developing his weird little narrative about my drinking. Laughable, of course – I drank a little too much, but there were hundreds of City solicitors like me. Or rather, it would have been laughable, had it not been so potentially damaging. The thought reminded me of when Angus had first raised the point a few months earlier, the fear I'd had then of Angus Peterson. The memory led me back to that rainy day at Fiennes & Plunkett, a picture of the cold eyes that I'd remembered earlier too, when speaking to Nathan. What Engelhardt had said, the concern in Engelhardt's voice …

'*Eh, amigo.*' Evaristo had arrived at the bench, beaming. '*Un presidente.*'

He passed me the large cocktail, and I took a sip, then another, before giving my approval – to more not-quite-understandable amusement. I knew the drink well, having become something of a connoisseur – it was white rum, white vermouth, grenadine – and something else that I'd forgotten.

'I'm not sure you're right about that storm, you know,' I said cheerfully. The clouds were still just hanging there, before giving way to the blue that came swimming back over the water, the land.

'OK.' He insisted on another high five now, for reasons unknown – he hadn't been listening. 'Now,' he said, 'you tell me of your English friends!'

'I was saying I'm not sure about the storm—' But I stopped. His question had passed through me in that same sharp way that made no sense, had no reason; again I'd felt that indignant, unaccountable rage. 'Evaristo, what is it you want to know about my friends?'

'*Todo*, man,' he laughed. 'You love your friends?'

'No, I *like* my friends. We say *like*.'

'No, not like – *love*. Me, I *love* my friends. You here in Cuba, with your friends?'

'No.'

'Your *novia*?'

'No – I told you. We split up.'

'So what are you doing here in Cuba, man? You all alone?'

'I am all alone.'

'Ah.' Suddenly Evaristo looked wary, as if urging me to tell him his new conclusion was not true. 'You here for *jineteras*.'

'No,' I said bitterly. 'No, Evaristo, I did not come out here alone to find prostitutes.'

'Hey, *tranquilo*.' He took my wrist, pulling me down to the bench. 'I'm joking – we're friends, no?'

'I'm just a young guy, travelling abroad for a bit of an adventure,' I said. 'I really don't see what's so unusual about it.'

'A young guy?' And he began to rock with laughter.

'Yes. Why is that so funny?' My hand was clenched around the cocktail glass – part of me wanted to throw it all over him.

'You're not young, man. *Jejejejeje!*'

'How old do you think I am?'

'*Jejeje*.' He regarded me, with amused but friendly eyes – it must have been very hard for him to judge my age. 'You're thirty-eight, man. Thirty-eight.'

'Thirty-eight?' I cried. 'For God's sake, I'm only thirty-two.'

'You look older!'

'Evaristo,' I said, 'you may be with an English woman, but I don't think you've quite picked up the famous British reserve.'

But he was sipping his *presidente*, a picture of humour, oblivious to my words – with no idea that he was somehow hurting me. 'Anyway, man,' he was saying, wiping his eyes, 'thirty-two is still *old*. Me, I'm twenty, man.'

'Good for you.'

Part of me was screaming that I had to get rid of Evaristo now, and quickly – it was just a question of gulping down this *presidente*. But the cocktail came loaded with pure liquor – it would burn my insides if I necked it. And there was something else too in my not making my escape – there was something addictive about this conversation with Evaristo, which made me think that perhaps I *didn't* have to get rid of him. *Maybe we should go deep, Evaristo, you and I – maybe you should ask me more, ask me anything.* And despite his words he had a suffusive warmth that went beyond them, exuding goodwill no matter what he said, his big arms so close that they touched mine, making me feel at once embarrassed and oddly happy.

He was back on the internet now, so that it was time for me to return to the BlackBerry – to read the final two messages.

'*Jejeje*,' he was mumbling from time to time. 'Thirty-two.'

I moved to Angus's second email. But then on an impulse I stopped and looked again at his first – it had occurred to me that there was something in one of its paragraphs that had the tone of a victory speech. On reflection, though, there wasn't much to read into that – there was no way, surely, that he could have known something I didn't. Never since the founding of the firm had a secret left that Partners' Meeting Room. His second email was shorter.

Simon,

Just as a little extra, see Emma's response to my email below. As you will note, our esteemed colleague is as amiable as ever!

All good here in Cornwall with the wife. Cold, but you can't beat Blighty.

Have a cerveza *on me,*

Angus

P.S. I did mean that point about how strong we've all been. With the exception of Emma's 'doctor's appointment' on Dynamite (I never believed that, did you?), there was not even a threat of what you would call a 'T-bomb' – so far as I'm aware. We're tough and stable alright.

Throughout his career Angus had forwarded others' emails without their knowledge – just as he had constantly sought to divide and conquer fellow associates. There was a lack of self-awareness, an absence of emotional intelligence in him that in its way was more perturbing still than the sadistic streak – he did not have the ability to understand that I would not approve of what he had done. The email that he had forwarded was itself entirely uninteresting – Emma had just replied to his first one, abruptly and rudely, a little meanly – *Ta*, she had written, neglecting to reciprocate – but the giddy naughtiness that sang out from his email made me feel a little sick. The reference to 'T-bomb' was worse, and it was funny that it was just now that I'd been

307

thinking of Tim Douglas's breakdown. Tim, that short, lovely Geordie with the twinkle in his eye, the overriding gentleness of character that was his finest trait and his downfall. Angus had invented the code name hours after it had all happened, sniggering hysterically with joy in the early hours of a winter morning many years ago when he and I, still trainees, had been smoking the last cigarette of the deal on which Tim had broken…

'The T-bomb! Did you see Tim's *face* before he did it?'

I had seen it, and I would never forget it – Tim's face had turned as white as snow. It had been long after midnight, he hadn't slept for days, we had had ten minutes to wait before the final conference closing call and Rupert had said, with that perfect mix of the rational and irrational that was his defining characteristic, that we might as well use the time to check on progress on Project Green, Tim's other deal. *As white as snow*, the face. The junior partner had understood something, removed himself quickly from his squatting position on Tim's desk and then, 'Do you know,' a lost and haunting voice had said, 'I can't really *see* any of the words on my screen – they're all moving about.' Rupert had become all rattled, and had ordered us minions out so that he and Tim could 'have a quick chat'. Angus and I had been the last ones in the queue to leave: we'd shut the door behind us and for a second looked back in through the glass walls to see Tim Douglas rocking madly in his chair as Rupert took a seat. And then, as if in a nightmare, we'd seen Tim leap to his feet, pick up his hole punch and, with a manic, animal's glare, smash it and smash it into his screen.

'T-bomb! This place is fucking *awesome*! I want to see another!'

Nobody knew for sure what happened to Tim Douglas later that night, or afterwards – except the partners, presumably.

But it was generally believed that he had never worked in the City again. Emma once told me she'd seen Tim in a bar near to the firm. She said he was still *Tim*, the short Geordie: he had the same vulnerable face, the same embarrassed cough, the same hearty laughter. But she said he'd looked so much older, and that he was drinking heavily, which was unlike the Tim we'd known. She'd said that he'd had sweat patches all over his shirt.

'A fucking T-bomb!'

And Angus was still saying it even today, still mocking him, apparently entirely incapable of feeling Tim's pain – or maybe he did, and he enjoyed it. It was odd to admit that in some way I was frightened of this side of Angus, the side that was hinted at by his vacant eyes. The fear had always been mixed with, and hidden by, a social superiority on account of his geekiness, so that at times I forgot how real that fear was. I remembered that Sunday when I'd caught him going through my papers in my office – what the hell had he been doing? But it wasn't the question of what he'd been doing that had wedged itself in my memory – it was the fact that he hadn't blushed when I'd caught him. Instead he'd looked up slowly, with a thin smile, and said, 'Morning!' Just like the thief, actually...

'Simon.'

Evaristo was pointing to the screen of his phone – it was the first time he'd addressed me by name, and it felt nice – perhaps he was testing new boundaries.

'Look at this, *mira*.' A photograph of Evaristo and his friends, some of all those hundreds of friends he had. They were all tall and handsome like him, lean and strong, and they were on the Malecón, posing for the camera. 'My best friends!'

I was turning to the final email of interest – from one Giles Glynne-Ponsonby.

Simon,

I do hope that you are enjoying your break. I know people have said that I am not to email you directly on any matter, but merely to keep you copied in on client correspondence. However, I just thought I would wish you the best for tomorrow – I am keeping my fingers crossed.

Back here it is absolute madness on Project Wall – Rupert has near enough the whole of the ninth floor on it, and it looks like we're going into our second all-nighter!

Giles

I began to type a response.

'What are you doing, Simon?'

'I'm writing to *my* friend,' I said, surprising myself with the momentary emotion in my voice. 'I'm writing to my friend Giles.'

'Your friend Giles.'

'That's right, Evaristo – my friend Giles.'

I was writing in my serious, slightly distant supervisor's voice.

Giles,

Thank you for the message – much appreciated.

As you will gather, I've been unable to resist checking emails – but not to be mentioned to Rupert, please. Incidentally, if you hear any rumours feel free to pass on – it has been an interminable wait. No need to go looking, of course.

*And please take care of yourself on Project Wall – don't
do the usual trainee thing of getting caught up in the
madness and just staying for the sake of it. Unless
someone specifically asks you, I strongly advise you to
go home to get some sleep.*

Best,
Simon

'Hey, Simon.'

'Evaristo.' I looked up. 'I'm just writing here.'

' "I'm just writing", *jejeje*. Look at this.' Again that phone,
showing me photos on that phone. 'Look, my *mamá y papá.*'

*Hmm. Mamá is a tad large, isn't she, Evaristo? And papá
quite short – an unlikely set of parents for you. But it's sweet,
you all huddled up close like that in your homely, busy kitchen.*

'I love my *mamá y papá,*' he said. And as he let the words
hang in the air between us, I was tensing up, feeling an arrow
of adrenalin shooting up through my stomach. The question
was coming.

'You love your *mamá y papá*?'

'Yes, I do. Very much,' I said.

'You speak them much?'

'Oh, yes – we're very close.' And he must have thought
I was mad, because I had to stand up quickly from the bench
– I had a big ball of anxiety in my chest that was nothing but
the strength of my love for them…

It was months ago now, that night back in Lincoln, when
I'd overheard them talking on the stairs – they'd thought I
was asleep in bed, but I was on my way to the old shared
bathroom. Tiredness – that age-old plea for mitigation. That
was what I'd heard my mum talking about.

'He was just shattered, Paul – that's all. Couldn't you see?'

'God, he's up himself these days.' But my father spoke fondly, his voice flowing with deep, tender love. 'I confess I got quite cross for a second there, when he was telling me all about that bloody marvellous Engelhardt. Christ, Abbie! I might not be in Engelhardt's league, but if he'd ever suggested he was interested in psychology I could have taught him all he'd ever want to know! And now that bloody firm bring in the big shot for some speech, and Simon tells *me* about it all.'

'He was only wanting to show off a bit. You know Simon.'

'But he kept interrupting me! In fact, he bloody corrected me at some point. Honestly – ' and he chuckled now ' – that posh voice of his!'

'Stop it.'

'That voice, when he's talking about the firm. It's like making Rick down the street try to imitate Prince Charles. I thought it was just Cambridge, but it gets worse every year. He still hasn't quite got it, either.'

'Paul!'

'And he'd certainly had a few, tonight – I could tell as soon as he got off the train.'

'It's that *ridiculous* job he's got.' Her voice had become almost a whisper, but there was a trace of real anger in it. 'We do need to make a plan, love, decide what to do about it. He says it's all fine, but it's just not right – he had huge bags under his eyes, and he's manic now, isn't he? And it seems he's completely messed it up with Sophie. I can't say I blame her, by the sound of it.'

'There's nothing more we can do, Abbie – it's been years that we've been telling him. He's a man, a top lawyer – it's his decision.'

'Oh, how can you be so cold?'

'I'm not cold.' And it was true – he was all worried, but he didn't want to tell her. 'Come here.'

I heard them step towards each other, coming up and down the stairs.

'He'll be fine, I promise,' I heard him say. 'He's hardly daft, is he? He's told me, he's sworn to me that when he becomes one of the bosses, or partners, whatever they're bloody called, it'll all get easier. And if he doesn't make it as a partner they'll kick him out, so one way or another it'll be over soon.'

'He'll be so upset if they kick him out. But is it really true he'll work less as a partner? Has he checked, do you think? I hope he's not just kidding himself?'

'No, he'll have that one right.' My dad's voice changed. 'Hey, can you imagine his voice if he becomes a partner?'

'You're terrible.'

'Prince Simon of Lincoln.'

My mother had been right in her suspicions, of course – I'd been lying to them, to everyone else, lying to myself that it would ever get easier. It wouldn't be Campaign, obviously, but the partners worked the same hours as the rest of the associates. Better not to think of that too long though, that I'd been lying to myself – and anyway, the money would help ease things. And, given the money, I wouldn't have to do it forever.

My mind was turning to Emma Morris – the hamster was single as I now was too; did she have the same support of family love? I hoped so – I did worry about her, but at the same time could never quite trust her. I knew that she was alone, just like me, on this enforced holiday. I wondered how she would have been passing her days there in Dubai. A daily sushi lunch, for sure – she was obsessed with sushi. A few magazines would be there below the sunlounger, from the morning till sunset, and she would have raced through some novels too – some thrillers, probably, or maybe a love story set in an exotic part of the globe, infused with a dose of mysticism. Late in the afternoon a member of staff would bring her a large glass of imported white wine and some nibbles on a tray as she sat on a luxurious terrace, alone at her table; afterwards over dinner there would follow another glass, perhaps. At night before going to bed she would have that last cigarette on her balcony, and be cross with herself immediately for it…

I'd never thought how she was the only person I knew who was as lonely as me. Probably she'd feel the loneliness acutely at times over there, while she lay on her sunlounger surrounded by the sorts of English couples and families who went to Dubai, all of them affluent and lazily reading… what would they be reading? What did the type of English person who went to Dubai read? Maybe nobody read anything…

I reflected that, if I had been given the choice between the Cuba I had experienced and five-star Dubai, even with the Monument to Hemingway, I would have chosen Cuba.

What would she be doing now? Staring at her BlackBerry, probably. Waiting for any sign, knowing that nothing would come until tomorrow. Angus was right, it would be evening there already in Dubai – it was three or four hours ahead of London, wasn't it? Whereas here I was five hours behind – I had not considered previously the implications of this time difference. *Five hours* behind! I'd perhaps still be sleeping tomorrow if Rupert called me in the UK's morning – imagine if I missed Rupert's call! I would have to set the alarm for half past four at the latest, or else stay up all night…

Emma would be finishing that large glass of white, while here I sat on a bench with Evaristo in the early Cuban afternoon and Angus, I imagined, was in a warm coastal pub with his Lithuanian wife. I'd never met her – they said she was very attractive, and that she had very poor English. I could see his pale face concentrating on the BlackBerry, thinking, thinking. I could see the gorgeous wife taking care not to disturb him; remembering to speak only when she was spoken to, Angus perhaps grinning suddenly as he thought again of the T-bomb.

'*Mi amor, mi amor!* Simon, my friend – look! She wrote me!'

'Bravo – good work, Evaristo!' A quick handshake, then another – he had the almost sheepish face of the man who had won the big prize; and now the face of the cocky winner. How hilariously expressive he was.

'Bravo,' I repeated, 'but, no, sorry – I can't look at your messages.' I was imagining my nausea at what the old crow would have written to her Cuban hunk. That *presidente* really had been strong – it had sort of cured the hangover, but simultaneously made me feel sleepy. My eyes were nearly closing as I put my BlackBerry away, batted Evaristo away, thought again of Angus Peterson. Of how rare it was to know a human being who was *bad*. Someone who was playing an entirely different game, with a mask of humanity. Presently I began to relive moments of that day at Fiennes & Plunkett – the day Angus had truly scared me, the day Engelhardt had come. The memories were returning, but it was as if they needed first to make it through this kaleidoscope of images that felt so close to dreams...

'*Mi amor!*'

Finally, the kid fell silent. I was in London again now, Evaristo would likely never see this land so exotic and cold. It's cleaner there, Evaristo, where your *novia* lives; the streets aren't potholed and ever-odder glass buildings soar into the sky. People in my London move in subtlety – they send messages in nods and winces, a syllable stressed, modulations of tone. It's good for drinking there, Evaristo. I'm tasting my favourite whisky, Glenmorangie Signet, on the terrace of Boisdale of Belgravia; soon I'll be tipsy enough to be fleetingly cocky. I was at Clare, mate, I work at Fiennes & Plunkett – I'll keep the tie on, delight a little longer in irony and prestige. Yes, we're in Belgravia here, Evaristo – where Dan lives. Have you met him, my friend Dan? Funny that I never mentioned him in Cuba – maybe it's because inside I'm not sure I do love him, the way you love your friends. I knew really what you meant, when you asked me. Anyway, no, I don't live here – I live in Fulham. It's more or less over there – come over and I'll point it out to you from the terrace. The journey into the City isn't great but it's a cool place, full of young professionals like me. And, well, it's as close to Chelsea as I can afford, currently.

12

THE DAY THAT DR ENGELHARDT visited Fiennes & Plunkett began for me at around half past nine in the morning – the usual time I arrived in the office. I was tired, dog-tired that morning, because I'd only finished the previous day's work a few hours earlier: Rupert had caught me at midnight as I'd tried to escape and so I'd found myself back in my chair, reading the comments he had scribbled all over the loan agreement. The monstrous handwriting was the special code, the key to the only true understanding of the document, the transcript of a stream of consciousness crawling around the margins of the pages, crammed between each of the typed lines, searching passionately for space, colliding violently with other wording. There were arrows next to certain clauses that pointed ostensibly nowhere; there were arrows pointing at each other, as if he were deliberately taking the piss. There were obscure references to legislation, question marks that might mean *no* or might mean *yes*, or might mean nothing at all. The game was all about exercising sound judgement in interpreting and communicating these thoughts, *getting it right*. It was rather important to get it right, for the loan was for six billion pounds.

It had been a grim night's work, the agreement running to over two hundred pages. And yet, as I arrived back bleary-eyed in my office that morning, to my dismay I encountered Rupert Plunkett – who had a worn, comprehensively reviewed document in his hand. I sat down behind my desk after a brief, tense exchange of pleasantries, and then waited to hear the issues he had with my draft; waited for him to berate me. But he seemed momentarily distracted. He was peering down from his great height at the sheets of paper in Giles's bin, in the corner.

'Are those my comments?' he asked suddenly – very darkly.

'Yes!' Giles turned from his computer. 'Yes, that's right – I've typed them all up into the electronic version.'

'But those pages are a record of my thoughts.'

'Sorry.' Giles's face was horribly confused. 'As I say, I've made the changes to the electronic version, so I didn't think the pages would be needed now.'

'They are a record of my thoughts, Giles. Get them out of the bin. Get them into the file.'

'Erm, Rupert,' I said, as Giles dove down into the bin and the pinstripe suit turned slowly, magnificently – I'd decided that I might as well try this on now, before the drafting interrogation began. 'Given that you're here, I wanted to ask you about the training scheduled for this evening – the Enterprise training for the associates on a Campaign.'

'What of it?' Scratching the neck now – so much to do this morning.

'Well, we all wondered whether we might cancel it.'

'What?'

'All three of us are going to be terribly busy this evening – in my case I may well be stuck in the meeting with you and the client.'

'Of course you'll all be busy this evening. You're all on a Campaign. As for you – you can step out of the meeting, if necessary. I'll be able to fill you in afterwards.'

'OK,' I said, mechanically. 'Understood.'

… Outside it had begun to rain, the drops tapping against the glass wall behind me as he whispered…

'The firm has paid very good money for these people. My younger partners are rather fixated on the idea. *They* will tell you it's a privilege that you won't find in the larger firms.'

He had winced, though.

'Is there Enterprise training for the partners too?' I asked, suspecting something.

'Yes.' He sniffed. 'We were all divided into small sub-groups. As a matter of fact, it was a disgraceful waste of time.'

There you are.

'Which is why we've changed the structure of the course for you three. In any case, future partners of this firm need to be able to manage their time effectively. You all need to get a grip. Now,' he whispered, looking at me with narrowed but somehow excited eyes as he sat down on the chair before my desk, 'let's talk about your *peculiar* draft. We don't have long to fix it. The client will be here soon.'

TEN HOURS LATER, Rupert and I were in the lift alone, heading back up to the ninth floor – the disastrous meeting had finished abruptly and Giles was still in the breakout room, gathering papers.

'You'll make the Enterprise training, then,' Rupert whispered. 'That's about the only good thing to come out of this after-noon's nonsense. Incidentally, I intend to pop down myself, to see what they've put together. We've paid a fortune, and I confess I have my doubts as to the *point* of it. Anyway – ' he shook his head ' – the man, our client Henderson, is far too aggressive. You can't treat banks like that – that's why they walked out.'

'Yes, you're right.' I looked at my watch in a manner I hoped was pointed. 'Actually, I'll have missed the first half-hour of the training by now. Sorry, Rupert – I should've seen the time when we were in the meeting. Maybe I should get on with the drafting instead.'

'Don't worry about being late – not a problem. In fact – ' Rupert drew back suddenly as the lift stopped and the doors began to open ' – in fact, why are you in the lift?'

'Because—'

'I'll see you down there.' With a rare expression of pleasure, he pressed the button to send me back to the floor whence we had come. But then, realising the foolishness of what he had done, my leader was compelled to evacuate at great speed, charging forward in the manner of an action hero before the doors closed on him too.

'We've paid a fortune for that course,' was his parting reminder as he charged.

So minutes later I was walking towards Meeting Room Three, which, for reasons ascribable to the quirks of Rupert's mind, was the room in which all training sessions of the firm *must* take place. Opening the door, I saw my two competitors for partnership. They were facing each other across a white desk and a ghastly stillness enveloped the room. Emma, I saw, was flustered, close to tears. Opposite her was the blond hair, the pale face. Angus was smiling a detached, unnerving smile.

'Hello there,' came a voice. 'You must be Simon. Welcome – better late than never, we say!'

My competitors had just finished a negotiation session: a form of role-play in which they were given separate cards, which they were told to keep confidential, and on which were written instructions specifying what they needed to obtain from the negotiation, and what they could concede. The spectacle had been filmed. This was explained to me by the young man who shook my hand with gravitas. His name was Owen. He was clean-shaven and suntanned and wore a well-cut grey suit with no tie. His eyes flashed intelligently, he had the business-speak of a City trader, and yet his secret leaked from every acronym, every buzzword – he was appallingly nervous. I sort of liked him for this – or rather, I feared for him in the presence of Angus and, imminently, Rupert.

'Good stuff,' he said to himself, and then again to the projector screen, where Emma was frozen, small mouth open and more a hamster than she had ever previously been. In front of this unflattering picture stood a very serious young businesswoman, also dressed in an elegant suit, who rushed over to introduce herself.

'I'm Philippa and I work with Owen.'

'Hi, Philippa,' I said. This was going to be unbearable, especially given that hours of work were waiting upstairs.

'Now, Emma, what was your *mistake*?' Owen was asking, with solemn authority.

'I didn't make a mistake,' she hit back, placing her BlackBerry down on the desk.

But the guru shook his head.

'I'm afraid you did. Watch this back now. And remember what your instructions were. In fact, Emma: tell Angus what your instructions were.'

'I'm happy for you to tell him, Owen.'

I gave her a silent cheer for this – I was immediately going off the teacher. He seemed to be one of those people who, when nervous, would pick up on any ostensible weakness around them and attack it in the hope that from this they might draw strength.

'OK – I'll say it. Emma, as seller of the car, *cannot* sell for less than twenty thousand pounds. This is because Emma needs twenty thousand pounds to pay off debts that Angus doesn't know about. The debts are Emma's big secret. However, Emma, what was your *aim*? What did the instructions suggest your *aim* should be?'

'To get twenty-five thousand for the car.'

'Not really, Emma. The instructions said you could settle for twenty-five. But they also said you could make a reasonable argument for thirty. And that, if the buyer was desperate to have the car, you'd push to forty. So what should your aim have been?'

'Well, I understand that,' hissed Emma. 'But it was a negotiation, Owen. I ended up getting a thousand pounds more than the instructions said I could settle for – twenty-six. So I don't think it was a bad result.'

'Yes, but ... ' Owen paused as Emma glared at Angus, who had let out a little laugh. 'What was Angus's big secret?'

'Well, he gave it away!'

'It's not what you think. Let's watch the video. Then I'll tell you what Angus's instructions were.'

Philippa, nodding slowly with a thoughtful, professional expression, now pressed Play. The video was disturbing but uncomfortably gripping, like a wildlife documentary filming a predator catching its prey. A small part of you is frozen in fascination by the sheer horror of it; the rest of you wants desperately to turn it off.

'Good evening,' says the young woman, sneaking a look at something on her lap – no doubt her BlackBerry. Her voice is anxious in front of the camera and she is blushing and she cannot hold the gaze of the fair-haired man. 'Now, we both know you have come all the way here to purchase this lovely little classic, so you must be keen.'

'I'm not here for the car.' The voice is cold, poisonous.

'Well, OK.' She smiles a profoundly human, embarrassed smile, reaching out to him in an unconscious, natural request for reasonableness. 'Well, that's strange, because we're meant to be here to discuss the car.'

'I came because I'd heard you needed some money. I wanted to make you a loan.'

'What?' Emma turns to someone out of view, as if to seek reassurance. Yet, from her expression, it is not forthcoming. She turns back – a forced attempt at joviality remains because this is, or should be, a game. But, in the complexity of psychological interaction between two human beings, there is soon no such thing as a game. She's uncomfortable and – though she must know it's absurd – she seems even a little frightened.

'Right,' she says, looking at Angus. 'If you're going to be silly, we'll start again. Can we play this properly?'

No response.

She turns again to the invisible person. 'Owen, I'm stopping this now if Angus is going to be daft,' she says. 'He's got to play by the rules.'

'He *is*, Emma. You're both playing by the rules. Carry on.'

'Ridiculous.' Her voice falters for a second. Then: 'Whatever. Anyway, right: I don't want a loan and I don't need money. But I *would* be happy to sell you my car.'

'Ha!' The violence of the laughter makes her pull back in her chair. The blond man leans over and asks contemptuously, 'You want to sell your car but you don't need money?'

Emma says nothing.

'Look, both of us have a secret written on a card.' Angus is charming suddenly, changing mood in a second, and she is reacting physically to this abnormality, holding herself tight. He says, 'My secret is that I've got three minutes to close the deal because my wife'll be back and she'll talk me out of it.' He looks at his watch. 'Over a minute has gone. Shall we do a deal?'

Her natural disinclination to be confrontational, which makes Emma a social human being, means that she cannot resist a laugh of her own – it bursts from her, as spontaneous and unwanted as a hiccup. 'OK, I'll sell you the car for forty thousand.'

'No. Two thousand,' he orders, excitable now. 'Deal?'

'Two thousand?' she cries in horror. There appears to be an understanding forming in her that she must fight. The unreason-ableness has triggered a defence instinct, maybe. Something more essential even than pride. 'No, I'm not doing it.'

'Come on.' He raps his knuckles on the desk. 'Come on!'

'No – stop being a prat, Angus!' The game has sucked her in, and there is something appalling about what is happening, something that brings back so many things to me: the voice of Mr Naples, the face of Freddie, the young waitress in Cambridge, crying. It is as if every value Emma has been taught, every value they did not have to teach her, she is now being told by this game is negative, something to be shed so that she might be stronger in a negotiation that is no different from brawling naked for a scrap of meat. She is defending herself now, true, but the boundary is so subtle – how many more lessons are needed for her to become the unreasonable aggressor?

'You *know* it's worth way more than that, Angus.'

'You're right. Five.'

'No! Thirty!'

'Ah. Yes, it's obviously worth thirty thousand.'

He spits out some more laughter. She swallows hard.

'Look,' he says, 'I need it. I'll give you fifteen thousand pounds. That's it – me exposed. My wife's here. End of game!'

'Twenty-six!'

'Done!' he reaches out to shake her hand, jubilant.

'Get off me, weirdo!'

'OK, pause!' comes Owen's voice.

And now we were all silent, Angus's mouth twisted firmly into that unpleasant smile. Emma was indignant.

'I don't think I made any mistake. I needed twenty. I got twenty-six. And he was being mental, as usual.'

'Your mistake was that you never tested what Angus wanted,' explained Owen. 'Or what his secret was.' He looked past us, towards the back of the room as if someone behind us were listening – or, perhaps, further back still, to the remote glow of Truth. 'You never tested him,' he repeated.

'He told me his secret – the wife coming, his rush to get the deal done.'

'That was a lie.'

'Well,' she gasps, 'I mean, if he's going to lie, what's the point of this stupid game?'

'People lie in negotiations, Emma. That's why this is such a great *learning*.'

'Learning? Don't you mean lesson?'

'Out of interest, do you know how much I would have paid?' asked Angus happily.

'Go on, then.'

'One hundred and twenty!' cried Philippa. 'Angus's secret was that he knew the car was worth a fortune to collectors and that you hadn't realised it.'

Emma pulled the unhappy face that we pull when we want to reject something as absurd. Angus whistled to himself. 'Want to play?' he asked, turning to me.

'No, thanks.'

'I'd destroy you too.' He was fidgeting suddenly in his chair and the fixed smile had been replaced by a naughty little grin and a slight dilation of those grey eyes. The image of Angus Peterson orgasming was one I knew would stay with me always.

'Anyway, guys,' Owen was continuing, 'there are two key *learnings* that come from this. First, in order to win at negotiation, you have to understand, or imagine, what the other side's weaknesses are. *Not* fixate on your own. Angus guessed yours immediately, Emma! He knew you needed the money.'

'Well, I thought that I knew his.'

'And that's the other issue!'

'Yes,' affirmed Philippa, her hands behind her back. 'Yes, that's the other issue.'

'You kept *thinking*, Emma.' Owen took a step towards her. 'You must remember that negotiation is not about overthinking.' He paused, melodramatically. 'Negotiation is about emotions; about human beings.'

'Or rather, a *lack* of humanity,' I said. I found the trace of contempt in his voice unacceptable. 'It seems to me the bully always wins. Empathy is the enemy.'

'Well, true.' He seemed ready for this. 'But young lawyers need to have a bit more of the bully about them, Simon. I'm not saying you have to go all the way to full-blown tyrant, but you need to be more robust. If you do this training with traders, you see the difference immediately. They're *strong*, as Angus was.'

'Yes,' enthused Philippa. 'Yes, Emma, you just need to have a bit more of the bully about you.'

'Alright – we all got the point.' Emma and I looked around in unison. Our leader, standing at the back of the room, had stolen in without a sound. Rupert had a talent for roaming stealthily through the rooms of corporate institutions, especially those of his own firm – and especially when night

326

began to fall and lawyers began to dream, to plan their escape from the work.

'In my view – and I only caught the end – I think that went too far, Angus. Bad form. But you, on the other hand, *were* weak, Emma. Weak.'

'Well, Rupert,' objected Angus, 'I mean, I *won*.'

'Yes, I know you won.' Rupert was fixing Angus with a mix of apprehension and troubled love. My leader's interaction with this particular associate was characterised always by a struggle between admiration of his efficiency and a lingering revulsion at the personality, leading me to imagine the likely interaction between a dictator who was once a good man, and the head of his internal security service. Unknowingly, Angus Peterson subjected Rupert Plunkett to a form of test.

'Let's move this along now.'

Owen obliged. But Angus soon became dominant and, to judge by the scratching of the neck, Rupert Plunkett's internal struggle was intensifying. The Executive Chairman had moved to sit among us and was eyeing Angus with concern as my competitor interrupted me, held out his hand to silence Emma, jumped in with answers, chuckled at Emma's answers, was endorsed with a dash of wariness by Owen and Philippa. Presently we arrived at a *learning* about how to manage our time. Or, as the slides would have it, 'The Fundamentals of Efficiency'. Rupert, as was his way when presented with any document, had his fountain pen out and was marking up his copy of the slides, striking through the word *learning* at the top, scribbling comments in the margin, drawing his arrows. It is spontaneous, instinctive, the reaction of a Fiennes & Plunkett partner to the written word.

'Now, what gets in the way of performance?' asked Owen, as Philippa sought to elicit answers with irritating expressions.

'Distraction, obviously.' Angus was quick.

'Excellent, Angus!' Owen turned to the rest of us. 'There are many unimportant, everyday distractions that, if dispensed with, would save every professional a lot of time. The question, actually, is one of awareness. Most people have never thought about this, but I want to ask you to think about it now. Each of you, try to think about two things you do, each day, which you could easily omit.'

A pause. And then, predictably:

'Emma – do you want to go first?'

'Well, I don't know yet.' She looked agitated. 'You've not given me time!'

'I'll go first, if you want,' I said.

'No, it's fine. Just let me think.'

'Cigarettes,' murmured Angus. 'You and Simon both have that as a distraction.'

'Sorry?' Emma was furious.

'You heard me.'

'It's none of your business what I do. Anyway – ' she looked at Rupert ' – I've stopped smoking.'

'Not true,' said Angus, 'you were smoking last night. I could smell it on you. *I* stopped smoking shortly after the training contract – because I realised it wasted time. You never did.'

'Yes.' One aspect of Rupert Plunkett's mental make-up was an inability to comprehend that sometimes truth lay deeper than the literal, with the consequence that, for him, pedantry would prevail always. Angus was *correct* here, you see, and Emma was *incorrect*. 'Yes, we all know you still smoke, Emma. I shouldn't worry about it. Now,' and then, for the second time, as if the phrase had become a short-term obsession, 'let's move this along.'

We all looked at Emma.

'You want me to name another distraction? Oh, I don't know, my crack habit.'

Angus was greatly amused by this; there was from Rupert Plunkett no sound.

'Right – your turn, Angus.' The general tone of things, the mere presence of our leader, seemed to be worrying Owen. 'What are your two main distractions?'

'Well, I think the main one is the way I interact with colleagues,' he replied smoothly. 'It's sort of twofold, I think. First, I definitely spend too much time listening to colleagues when they go on about non-work matters. Listening to their excuses. Like the fact that they have a football match that evening, or a date, and so can't do the work.'

'Hmm.'

'And second, perhaps more seriously, I spend far too long explaining tasks to juniors. When I was at their level, I was given a task and left to run with it. These days the juniors get too much spoon-feeding. I mean – ' a quick glance at Rupert ' – it's probably down to my desperation to get things right. Because that's all that really matters – that the firm gets it right. But I should be harder with them.'

'Good,' said Owen. 'That's very thoughtful, Angus.'

'Well, hang on,' whispered Rupert. 'Part of being a good lawyer is giving instructions that are not opaque. And I certainly don't agree that you, of all people, need to be harder on anyone!'

'Oh, yes.' Angus offered up a vilely sweet smile. 'I wasn't clear. All I meant was that I've not quite found the correct balance yet. I've not yet managed to do it the way you do it, Rupert. That is to say, hard in a good way.'

'OK.' Rupert was vulnerable to flattery. 'Very good. It will come with time. Very good, Angus.'

Owen, in line with his mandate to drive things forward, interrupted this terrible spectacle with:

'And Simon – your two, please?'

'Smoking. He smokes.'

'I do smoke. Thank you, Angus,' I said, as Emma put her hands to her face in mock amusement.

'And he drinks *massive* amounts – even on weeknights.'

A few seconds passed before I grasped what he had said. I came to understand it from the depth of the silence that followed – from those infinitesimal human reactions, rapid movements too brief to record, that together paint a story. First, I felt nothing. Presently, a sort of buzzing sensation and then together they came – the sweat on the palms, the quickening of the heartbeat, the adrenalin that would be a tremendous release if only it could be released.

'Would you care to repeat that?' I heard Rupert ask.

'I'm not saying that he's *definitely* got a problem – yet. I'm just saying that he goes out drinking loads during the working week.' Angus was smirking, unaffected by the atmosphere he had created. 'Any night that he's not working, you'll find him standing outside a quiet little pub in the City – usually the Windmill, or one of the other ones at a decent distance from the firm – necking pints until closing time with his mate, Dan Serfontein. You remember Serfontein, Rupert?'

'Where is this going, Angus?' Rupert had stood up.

'Well, I mean, it must be a distraction. Being so tired in the morning. Take away the hangover and there'd be more efficiency!' He laughed. 'And far less pain!'

'Guys,' intervened Owen, 'I think we need to calm down a bit here. This isn't meant to be an opportunity to make accusations. I think Simon has a right to reply.'

Ah, yes, my reply. I'd considered briefly the idea of mentioning that Angus was often out too. True, he was never drunk, but there was something worse to bring up in front of Plunkett – Infinitum, that strip club that was Angus's little

330

distraction. He would have considered that possibility though, so there'd be more fighting, probably a few lies.

'Simon?'

'Well, I confess, I've got a couple of bottles of whisky under my desk,' I replied weakly. The joke elicited no reaction in the room. But then:

'I've never heard such utter nonsense.' Emma had got to her feet. 'I've had enough now, Rupert, if that's OK with you. This is all so messed up! Totally exaggerated and totally irrelevant!'

'Think so?' Angus was alive, ready.

'Moreover, we all know that Mr Peterson enjoys the odd tipple – and all the rest.'

'You *shut* up.' And, from his tone, suddenly I had the vague impression that Angus might be capable of harming her. I stood up too now, instinctively.

'I suggest you calm down, young man,' Rupert was whispering, placing himself between Angus and Emma, as if to protect her. 'You and I will have a word later.' But it was not without a distrustful glance at me that he began to place his printouts into a file. 'Thank you for your time,' he whispered to the Enterprise training team. 'We shall provide feedback in due course. Apologies for this tension – people are rather tired.'

'Thank you, Mr Plunkett. But please don't head up yet. There's still the final session – we won't be taking it, of course! But I shall be introducing it.'

'What's that?'

'The corporate psychologist is next. To talk about "The Law and the Mind".'

'Psychologist?' Rupert looked distraught. 'I thought we'd communicated our point about all that stuff.'

Owen and Philippa exchanged puzzled, embarrassed looks. 'Well, Mr Plunkett, we understood that you wanted the individual who came last time to be replaced, not that you didn't want the session at all. In any case, it'll be a very different type of session from—'

'Where is he? Who is he?'

'He's not due for another ten minutes.' Owen gulped. 'We've finished a little early.'

'I'm not sure about this.'

And then I made the mistake that ensured we would remain.

'Actually, Rupert, I could really do with getting on.'

'What?'

'I need to start on the document.'

'It can wait.' He grimaced. 'We shall all wait for the psychologist.'

It was a while before he arrived but the time passed quickly, all four of us engrossed in the narratives playing out on our BlackBerries. Despite my exhaustion I was thinking how my dad would be so excited when I told him about this – how funny, a man from his profession coming to talk to City lawyers. Often he had told me I should show more interest in psychology – and more recently he'd been keen to see if he could help. But always I would be embarrassed, decline quickly his proposal of a 'session', even an informal, half-serious one. 'I'm off for a pint,' I would add, 'best therapy for me!' He would sigh, say he wished that I would look after myself better…

So I looked forward to telling him about the experience I was about to have – who could say how it would go? Rupert's reaction was already so weird! Meanwhile, while we waited, it was interesting to watch the others interacting with their BlackBerrys. Angus typed methodically, relentlessly, from time to time sneering down into his; Emma picked hers up and put it down again every fifteen or twenty seconds. Rupert

Plunkett held his as he paced the room, no doubt debating whether he shouldn't just escape now, still in time, on the reasonable grounds that these sessions were for us, not him, and that he had things to attend to upstairs. But he appeared shackled by a strange sense of duty – perhaps, according to his own system of rules, the very thought that he was terrified compelled him to stay. I had moved closer to Emma and, when she looked up from her BlackBerry for the thousandth time, I mouthed, 'Thanks for before.' But she didn't like it – she waved me away.

Finally, an erudite-looking man of around Rupert's age – and, like him, silver-haired but without the quiff – was shown in by a member of Fiennes & Plunkett staff. He was introduced by Owen, whose own desire to leave had manifested itself in his proximity to the door.

'Excellent! Now, guys, please can I have your attention.' Moving back towards us, away from the door, with great affectation Owen consulted his notes, which I rather hoped did not include a long script. 'I'd like to introduce Dr Max Engelhardt, who'll be leading the next session, "The Law and the Mind". Guys, is everyone ready?'

I watched Rupert, who was now sitting, as he raised his head from the BlackBerry. He sat courageously, back straight, a picture of fatalistic acceptance.

'As you may know, Dr Engelhardt is one of the leading psychiatrists in London.'

'Psychiatrist?' Now Rupert turned and whispered to me. 'Psychiatrist?' he insisted, as Owen continued. 'I thought he'd just said it would be a psychologist. No attention to detail.'

'He's a fellow of the Royal College of Psychiatry, and a *thought leader* in the areas of anxiety, phobias, obsessions and addictions.'

The rash was sweeping hot across Rupert's neck.

'A key part of Dr Engelhardt's *core belief system* is that no approach should be exclusive. For this reason, he believes deeply in psychotherapy – indeed, he's a renowned expert in cognitive behavioural therapy.'

Yes, it would be great telling my dad about this. I wondered if he had heard of him – surely he had! It sounded as though Dr Max was pretty famous; it also sounded as if he had seen the whole range of cases. But this room was not bad.

Owen was continuing to read from his notes.

'Recently, Dr Engelhardt has begun to take an interest in psychological issues relating to our relationship with work. He has focused particularly on how best to equip professionals with the tools to deal with the enormous stresses that come with the top roles.'

Owen paused, looking up for a second from his notes.

'And how to minimise the risk that these stresses result in mental or physical problems.'

The psychiatrist had sold himself to the corporate devil, then – perhaps. Regardless, I was mildly interested now – even if he wanted to convince me that I, not the job, was the problem. And, I thought now, perhaps I *was* the problem. I remembered the session with the GP, the weird thing that happened to me in the early hours, touching the desk with my right hand, then my left. Or Rupert becoming a witch for a second at around 4 a.m. on the second all-nighter. But no, the GP had asked me a thousand questions and had ended up fully convinced I was fine, that it was all about exhaustion. Perhaps the better argument in support of my own madness was the theory that I *needed* this sort of job. It had not been forced upon me, after all. Did he know all this, Engelhardt? Would he touch on deep stuff? How much would Fiennes & Plunkett pay him for this, though? Lost in a muddle of thoughts, I placed my BlackBerry in my suit pocket.

'Good evening, all.' There was no trace of the German accent that I had anticipated. Dr Engelhardt approached us to shake hands, and I thought immediately how he was kind in his seriousness – professional with a sort of avuncular reassurance.

Rupert stood and shook his hand vigorously. 'Welcome to my firm,' he whispered. But then, quickly, '*Our* firm, I should say. *Our* firm.'

'Thank you.' The words were spoken gently. I imagined Rupert needn't have worried – his condition must have been clear to a psychiatrist, and it wasn't megalomania.

'Yours is a curious profession.' Engelhardt had returned to the front of the room, and had begun. 'In most areas of life, to worry constantly is a very negative thing – in some cases, it can have a profound impact on people's lives. But of course, for a lawyer it's different. For a lawyer, a tendency to worry is a *plus* – something you need.'

'Yes, it is,' came the whisper, 'yes, it is.'

'And so, what to do?' Dr Engelhardt paused. 'I've given this question much thought.'

But the first of his theories – the weakest – did not work for Rupert. Nor did it work for me – Engelhardt had not grasped the true nature of the job, the only consolation being that he was clearly not a hired gun. His argument that the lawyer, even if working late into the night, must always 'switch off' for at least one hour – for example, by popping to the gym, or eating in the canteen and not at the desk – wasn't practical.

'Unrealistic, Doctor,' Rupert noted.

'Please – call me Max.'

'Fine. OK.' Rupert was being watched with some interest now by Engelhardt. 'My point is that, when there's a deal on, we're paid to be on call all the time. A City lawyer cannot switch off for too long, Max.'

'Not even for an hour?'

'Not always, Max. Sadly, sometimes that is impossible. It's the same in any other firm.'

'Wow – I've worked with people from many different professions, and I've never heard of anything like that. Sounds as if I have a bit of learning to do myself! So, is there always a "deal on" for these young ones?'

'For these three, yes. They're on a Campaign,' Rupert explained.

'They're on a *what*?'

'Campaign. Final step before the vote. It's an eight-month thing, Max – only lasts eight months. Only eight months.'

'Goodness me – that's surreally tough.' Engelhardt spoke with easy humour, but his shock seemed real. 'And what about you, Rupert? I mean, today's session is about these three, not you, but the question just interests me. Surely you don't stare at that thing – ' Rupert was staring at that thing now ' – all day with no break? Rupert?'

The Executive Chairman looked up, but did not understand.

'Do you take breaks?' insisted Engelhardt.

'Not often. But when I sleep – ' he squinted ' – I sleep deeply.'

'Sounds very unnatural.'

'The strategy has seen me through over forty years of hard work.' Rupert pushed down his quiff. 'And I feel just fine, thank you.'

There was a short pause in proceedings now – during which Engelhardt had his first experience of being *fixed* by Rupert Plunkett. Then he nodded.

'OK,' he said, addressing those of us still young enough to permit hope. 'Now, while your boss might not agree with them, let me talk to you about a few other simple tricks that I promise will help all of you, if you embrace them.'

And these theories, or at least the one he was about to explain now, made the course worth something – at least in my view, which Emma later said she shared. Max Engelhardt conveyed a new, beautifully simple idea – an idea my despairing father told me weeks later he'd been trying to explain to me for years. I'd never listened – I'd preferred to roll my eyes! Why is it always like that between loved ones? I was fascinated now as Engelhardt encouraged us to imagine worries, thoughts, as independent objects, with their own physicality. He invited us to conceive of worries as little bubbles that appear and upset the still water, but which – if you watch them – disappear in seconds. Often they come, but they are nothing more than their brief appearance. To stand before, to objectify the worry, Engelhardt said, was the key.

'Does that make sense?' This was, indeed, a kind man – I saw that now.

'Absolutely,' Angus replied enthusiastically, as Rupert sat still, aghast, profoundly confused. Following which, Engelhardt's gaze lingered on Angus Peterson.

'I mean, it's not the easiest thing to understand,' I began. 'But—'

'Are you alright, son?' Engelhardt asked Angus, suddenly.

We all turned.

'I'm good, yes,' said Angus.

'Are you sure?'

'Max, what's wrong?' Angus asked pleasantly. 'Please, carry on – this is fascinating.'

'You looked very hostile towards your colleague Emma for a split second there. That look you gave her.'

'Hostile? Me?' Angus laughed. 'No, just the opposite. I wasn't looking at anyone in particular – just reflecting on what you were saying. It's such a clever way of putting it.'

'Now, now, don't try to flatter me.' Engelhardt's tone too was playful, but the air was heavy. 'You're the one out of the four who doesn't seem to me to be a worrier. You don't suffer from nerves, do you?'

'Oh, you've got me wrong, Max. Ask my wife – often I can't sleep through worrying.'

... Then Engelhardt was talking to us about reality ...

'The only things that exist right now are you, me and the sound of the rain against the glass.' He searched our faces as he spoke. 'In this moment, the rest, everything else, is *imagined* – by our amazing, but overly busy minds.'

'But the emails coming in on the BlackBerrys, Max,' whispered Rupert, who now bore the face of a man whose mission was to save the world. 'They are real, Max. I can assure you.'

'Let's talk about the emails,' said Engelhardt. 'And, Rupert, I'd like you to do me a favour. I was wondering if you wouldn't mind looking at your last email, and telling us what it says. If you wouldn't mind reading it aloud.'

'I cannot do that, for reasons of confidentiality,' he replied, with fine pride.

'OK.' Engelhardt did not appear at all ruffled. 'I was wondering then if you could read out the first one you *can* share with us. Omitting anything confidential, of course.'

'I don't see the point of this, Max.'

'Please, Rupert. This will be of help to the associates.'

'Very well.' Rupert stared into the BlackBerry, shaking his head. 'A message from my evening secretary.'

'What does it say, Rupert?'

A little gasp. Then: 'I haven't time for this, Max.'

'The whole exercise will take just a couple of minutes.'

'Very well. OK.' There followed another of those awful pauses that only Rupert Plunkett could create. But then, quite suddenly:

'*Brian T. has phoned. He says you have his number and that it is urgent.*'

Engelhardt considered this.

'How does that message make you feel, Rupert?' he asked presently.

'What?'

'The message. What is your emotional reaction? How does it make you feel?'

'Well, anxious, of course. Anxious.'

'OK. Now, read it again.'

'This has to stop, Max.' The tone was his gravest.

'Rupert, stay with me, please. Read it again.' Engelhardt looked at us apologetically. 'I know I'm being a pain, but it's just to show how you can objectify words, if you want to.'

'*Brian T. has phoned. He says you have his number and that it is urgent.*'

'Good, Rupert. Again, please.'

'*Brian T. has phoned.*' And now something had clicked – but I was not entirely sure that it was what the psychiatrist had intended. Asking Rupert to repeat a phrase was playing to all the wrong things. '*He says you have his number and that it is urgent.* Yes.'

'Do you see what is happening? One more time. Just the words in the message, though.'

'*Brian T. has phoned. He says you have his number and that it is urgent.*'

'What do you notice, Rupert?'

'*Brian T. has phoned—*'

'Rupert! Stop for a second, and tell me what you notice. Can you see that they are just words?'

'Possibly,' he whispered. 'Possibly, you are right, Doctor.'

'Again. Once more.'

'*Brian T. has phoned.*' But Rupert's tone had changed, dramatically. '*He says you have his number and that it is URGENT.*'

'One last time.'

'No, I'm sorry. On reflection, this doesn't work.' Rupert fixed him again. 'It's making me *more* anxious, for Christ's sake.'

My leader would never understand the theory for the simple reason that his mind did not allow for the existence of two contradictory truths. Rupert Plunkett's genius was limited to the law – the man was no philosopher. Neither was I, but the lesson had sort of worked for me – it was fascinating, although I didn't like it quite as much as the previous idea about thoughts as bubbles. It did occur to me that you could play the objectification trick with everything, not just words – indeed I'd played it with my very identity, by looking too long at the mirror. Maybe in other circumstances I would have brought that up to see what he thought – his opinion would have been so interesting to get – but I was becoming distracted. Increasingly I was watching Angus – his body language – because, immediately following the odd exchange between him and Engelhardt, I had had the sudden creepy thought that my colleague might be *acting*; that he might always have been acting. As he nodded, frowned, became pensive, he evoked the image of a man standing before a large mirror – like that mirror from which I had fled as a boy – mimicking voices he had heard, performing idiosyncratic gestures he had seen, slight changes in expression. In his embarrassing quest to charm Engelhardt – and I didn't understand why he was so desperate to charm him – he was displaying that usual failure to appreciate how he was *actually* coming across.

'Amazing stuff, isn't it?' he said quietly. 'So much we can take from this.'

The final theory related to problem-solving techniques and how they could be adopted to help us at work. Engelhardt emphasised one message: accept the daily little problems and irritations, the minor issues, for what they were. Accept that you would have to be two minutes late for that next conference call. Accept that you might have made a mistake when drafting a clause of a loan agreement. The key was to be able to *lean into* the problem.

'Our job is to get things right, Max,' noted Rupert, with bitter indignation. 'Your last example was not a good one. A drafting mistake is *not* a minor issue.'

'I wasn't judging its quality as a problem, Rupert.' Engelhardt grinned. 'I was discussing how we should deal with it.' Surprisingly, he seemed to have really taken to my leader. Maybe it was because they were contemporaries. Or because nobody had challenged him like this for a long time.

'The best way to deal with a drafting problem,' Rupert was saying, 'is to correct the damned mistake.'

'But, Rupert, you can only correct it by accepting it. It's exactly my point – if one of your associates decided not to point out the error, wouldn't things be infinitely worse?'

'There, possibly, you may have a point.' And then, to my relief, Brian T.'s message became too much. 'Now, excuse me – all of you.'

With Rupert gone, Dr Engelhardt spoke to us for a little longer about some practical matters, such as the importance of eating properly, limiting alcohol – Angus raised his eyebrows at me – and grabbing as much sleep as we could. He seemed still incredulous at the firm's rhythms. He wondered if there were any questions. Not one – it was past nine o'clock, and we were all thinking of the night's work ahead.

'These two will be out chain-smoking in the rain shortly!' Angus informed Engelhardt, with thrilled amusement.

'Yes, that won't really help,' said Engelhardt. 'But I can understand why you do it – it's a sort of release, I imagine. And it allows you to escape physically from the office for a brief period. Don't you smoke, then, Angus?'

'No,' he replied scornfully. 'I did as a trainee but stopped. It's a disgusting habit.'

And so the Enterprise training ended. Angus offered to take Engelhardt down in the lift but then became torn as he had now received an email from Rupert on his deal. Finally, Angus decided that he could not wait. Emma and I led the placid man back to the lift and then went down with him to the main reception of the glass dome.

'My father's a psychologist back in Lincoln, you know,' I said. 'Although I've never been interested. It's strange.'

'I'd say it was entirely normal,' he said. 'Now that you're a grown man yourself, though – ' his glance was gentle ' – you might want to start listening to him a bit more.'

We looked out into the busy traffic, the lights flying through the darkness.

'Can we get you a taxi?' asked Emma.

'No, don't worry. I'll be fine with my raincoat and umbrella. I hope some of that was useful.'

'Incredibly useful!' she exclaimed. 'Sorry if it was a bit of a case study!'

'Well, your boss is certainly highly strung.' Engelhardt chuckled. 'I suspect he's got a good heart, though. Don't you think?'

The question was sudden and confusing.

'Not sure,' I said slowly. 'Rupert can be terribly selfish.'

'We can all be selfish when we're caught up in things.' Engelhardt's voice was hushed. 'Rupert seems to have had an unusual life, and to have been caught up in things for decades. Stress, tiredness, they can all lead to bad decisions.'

342

And then, with a pointed laugh, 'He's full of worries though, isn't he?'

Afterwards, Emma told me that it had been at this moment that she too had understood that Engelhardt did not yet want to leave; that the man had something to say.

'Full of worries. I suppose you could take the view that that's what makes Rupert human.' We were watching Engelhardt's face, which was very serious now. He delayed before speaking again – as if to resolve first an internal struggle.

'The people to watch are the people who have no fear at all,' he then said, hurriedly. 'Or rather, the people who have only one fear – the fear of being unmasked. I'm sure you'll have heard the term "sociopath" being used by the media. The truth is, it's all much more complicated.'

We stood entranced.

'But it *is* true that there's a type… Anyway, this type of person can be quite dangerous – especially if you stand between that person and his or her goal.' Engelhardt spoke a thousand words now as he stared at us. 'They really do lack empathy, you see. That's why they sometimes do so well in politics, business or other competitive fields. But it's also why some of them have it in them to hurt others, if necessary. They live to win.'

The kindness in his voice was chilling.

'They live only to win.'

Then he was gone, an old man in the rain, and Emma and I were walking back towards the lifts, each of us silent, pensive.

'Feels obvious, doesn't it, once someone has said it?' I blurted out suddenly.

It took her a while before she agreed.

'Angus certainly freaked me out this evening,' she admitted, a little sullenly, when we were inside the lift.

'That's an understatement. But thanks for sticking up for me when he started on about the heavy drinking. It was decent of you.'

She looked away. 'Well, I mean, I don't see the big deal,' she murmured. 'Who cares if you have a few beers with your mate now and again? It was more that it was just such a stupid accusation.'

'Very stupid – but the intent was malicious.'

'Yeah, well…' Quiet seconds passed as we climbed. And then, to my horror, she grinned. 'Well, I can always use it against you now, if necessary.'

'I hope you're joking?'

'Hmm? Oh, I see – it *is* true.' Now she was looking into my face. 'You *do* get hammered a lot, don't you?'

'Of course not!' I was startled.

'Don't worry, I'll never mention it. We've all got our problems.'

'I said that I don't! And what's wrong with you? What problems do you have?'

'I didn't mean that *I* had any problems. I was speaking loosely.'

'Sure?'

'What are you fishing for, Simon?'

'Nothing.'

The lift stopped at the eighth floor – the floor of the real estate department. My competitor hurried out, turning right towards her office. I followed her with my eyes until the lift doors closed behind her.

13

'Now, I TELL you a story,' Evaristo said. 'A story about my *novia.*'

Back on that bench atop the promontory of the Hotel Nacional, my friend was being proven correct in his earlier forecast: the temperature had dropped considerably now, the wind had obtained a fresh strength, and we were watching as the ink-black clouds ventured towards us slowly, menacingly from the sea. I had been quite right about the dramatic view we would have of nature's change – a whole new sky gobbling up the old, the water poisoned dark as if through the casting of a spell. A panorama of impending doom – I was enjoying it immensely.

'I'm listening, *amigo!*' I said. 'Look at this storm coming!'

The excitement at the imminence of the *tormenta* had been given an extra kick by the two further *presidentes* we had each had – I had given Evaristo some *pesos* for a fresh round, partly to continue my recollections, avoid having them interrupted by some incipient new mumbling of '*Mi amor*'. I suspected he had become lost halfway through his love's email, but had then understood things again towards the end. So off he'd gone – and then we'd both enjoyed the fresh round so much that he'd got us another. Now I was feeling *extremely* well – that brief, lovely lightness that only alcohol brings.

'*Mi novia,*' he said, '*es abogada.*'

'Fancy that. I'm a lawyer too.'

'*Ah, sí?* You too?'

'Yes – you see, the thing is, Evaristo,' I said, drawing close, 'everyone in London is a lawyer. Every adult.'

'*No! Jeje.*'

'It's true – I promise.'

A first raindrop, fat and heavy, hit my knee, flattened and then became a trickle down my leg – moments later there was a roll of drums from afar in the Atlantic. Over the savage choppiness there hung a luminous ring piercing the clouds, as a flash of lightning cracked down like a whip. Evaristo and I were up and running now as the rain came down in earnest, the last moving figures in gardens ready to slide into the sea…

We rushed up the stairs of the Hotel Nacional, splendid white and Arabian against the storm, came inside into the 1930s all wet and breathless and excited – it was fun and conspiratorial to rush through the busy lobby under the grandeur of the chandeliers. The Churchill Bar though was busier still, ever busier, and the atmosphere felt unfriendly. We were on our second daiquiri when in the confusion a member of staff must have said something to Evaristo that offended him, or perhaps just reminded him of where he was, for soon afterwards he decided to leave. Accompanying him out of the bar, I trod hard on the ankle of a refined, beautifully dressed lady whose white-bearded husband then barked something at me; I was apologising but had seen my BlackBerry flash with a new email from Angus, entitled '*Big news*', and I really needed to read it.

'*Watch* where you're going.'

It transpired that the email was a hoax.

Got ya both! Angus wrote. *Speak tomorrow.* Less than a minute later, I received an email from Dubai, too. Reading it, I realised I was very tipsy now – I had to make an effort to concentrate.

Don't know about you, but I'm feeling a bit weird tonight. God, isn't Angus just SO horrid? Hope you're OK and, on the basis you might be a little anxious like me, let me know if you fancy a chat. In any case, we should have a catch-up together when we get back, regardless of how it goes – if you're up for it.

Emma

'Evaristo,' I said. 'Remind me later to phone a woman called Emma Morris.'

'OK, my friend.'

I was quite lightheaded. We were back in the lobby, resurrecting some vague but important conversation we'd been having while in the Churchill Bar. That was right – I'd been explaining to him that I was waiting for news, that tomorrow I would know if I had become a partner. And he'd found it *hilarious* – while laughing away with him, I'd sought to guide him towards an understanding that actually there was nothing funny about this, that it was all complicated and I was feeling a little stressed about it, just as Emma now said she was. And for the first time Evaristo's face had borne a flicker of hostility.

'It's not a problem, *amigo*. It does not seem to me a problem.'

'I'm not saying it's a *problem*. I'm saying tomorrow's going to be a massive day – things will change for me tomorrow, professionally – change dramatically, one way or another.'

'But it's not a problem.'

'We're not following each other.'

'You are free – in your country you are free, you have many possibilities.'

I'd felt a surge of blood up through my body, turning my cheeks hot, bringing about those palpitations that had accompanied me throughout Campaign. In some obscure part of my mind I'd concluded that Evaristo was trying to kill me – he was trying to smash me up into little pieces psychologically, asking about my friends when he knew I didn't have many, asking if I loved my friends, implying that I was spoilt and self-indulgent, making me recall that night when I'd heard my parents worrying for me, loving me despite my clownish self-importance. Now, in the lobby, he was returning to the theme.

'You are free.'

Outside the doors, Cuba was all wild and dark – the rain slamming into the glass, wanting desperately to break it. Inside, the lobby was warm and calm and suddenly oppressive – we were receiving stares.

'Yes, there's nothing to moan about,' I said. 'Don't think that I ever feel sorry for myself – I remember Dan accusing me of that once.'

'Dan? Who is Dan?'

'Yes, I don't feel sorry for myself. It's all bullshit, you see – and it would be offensive to say to you that I feel sorry for myself. Often I'm furious with myself, but you must understand that that's something quite different.'

'In your country, you can do many jobs.'

'Well, some of us in my country can,' I said wisely. 'There are poor people in England too, though, and they can't. But in my case, I agree – I had a pocketful of tickets, and one morning I ripped them up and threw them into a bin on Oxford Street. You've made me quite sad, Evaristo.'

'Come on, man! You're my friend. I love you!'

'That's nice. It's nice that you love me. I think the Kims might love me too – did I tell you about my friends, the Kims? And Giles, I reckon he definitely loves me. He's just emailed me again, see?'

Simon,

That's very kind to suggest heading home when possible – thank you. However, tonight is shaping up to be rather grim – Rupert's just had us all in his room, handing out tasks.

As for tomorrow's news, there are now LOADS of rumours flying around. Including that the real estate department are saying they have needed a new partner for years and so, if Emma is not made up, some of the current partners may leave. I cannot verify any of this but am just keeping you updated. It might be nonsense…

'This email is too fucking long,' I said, looking up at Evaristo. 'Giles's email – it's way too long! It often happens – he just rambles. And I'm – I'm too drunk to read it.'

'*Jeje.*'

'Very important for a lawyer to be *concise*, you see, Evaristo. I'm going to just skim it.'

Also, while two partners will be retiring, people are saying that the firm is going to reduce the total number of partners from 30 to 29 out of 'economic caution' – so only one of you will be made up! This rumour

349

might have some truth in it, I reckon – the partners
have suddenly all begun to talk about the importance of
being far-sighted in business. I've heard this three times
in the last forty-eight hours!

I may be speaking out of turn, for which apologies, but
I do think it will be very unfair if they only allow one
of you in. Perhaps I'm confused, but, if they reduce the
partnership from 30 to 29, surely all it actually means
is that each of the 29 will get a larger share of profits!?

Giles

In his loyalty to me, my trainee was being a little harsh
– the partners' job was to ensure that the firm continued as
a successful enterprise – and he was, of course, out of line.
But, for once, Giles was not entirely confused. If the rumour
was true, maintaining or increasing profits per partner would
indeed be the rationale. This was all bad news for me, I
supposed. But I was having difficulty thinking about it: I
was sort of remembering and forgetting it at the same time. I
typed my response very slowly, read it twice for typos before
sending.

Thanks, Giles – good luck for tonight. But do go home
if you feel too exhausted at any point.

Meanwhile a sombre, affected, very elegant man of around
my age, his face the picture of that special Latin formality, had
arrived before me.

'Everything OK, sir?'

'All fine here,' I said.

'Yes.' He cleared his throat. 'We wanted to check whether
he was bothering you.'

'Who? Ah, *him*? Evaristo?'

'Yes – you see, he's a member of staff and he shouldn't be drinking in this hotel – at *any* of the bars in this hotel. He shouldn't be drinking with guests or customers.'

'That man,' I said, 'has been utterly outstanding! It was my fault – I asked him to come into the bar with me.'

'Very good. But you understand that we have rules about members of staff.'

'Yes, I understand. But look – ' I reached into my pocket ' – he's been so helpful that I want to tip the hotel. I'll tip him too, of course.'

'There's no need for that.'

'No, no – please take it. Now,' I said, pointing out through the doors, feeling mischievous, 'do you think it's safe to walk home from here? My flat is pretty close.'

'We wouldn't recommend it. The storm is very strong. Perhaps stay here for a coffee, wait for it to calm.'

'Nah,' I said, 'I want a strong drink and then bed – and I'm an adventurer at heart. Did I tell you—'

'Simon,' Evaristo was mumbling with his head down, the man in the suit looking at him severely as he spoke, 'stay here inside.'

'As I say, I'm an adventurer at heart.' The truth was I was just drunk. 'Goodbye, Evaristo,' I said, passing him a bunch of *pesos* as I shook his reluctant hand. 'I'll always think of you here, on this hill.'

… So there I was outside in the premature Cuban darkness, descending the stairs of the Hotel Nacional as the trees swayed and the wind howled, bringing fear and melodrama from the sea. Five hours ahead of me I could see Angus brooding over dinner, refusing angrily his wife's suggestion of a bottle of wine. Over in Dubai Emma's alarm clock, placed inches from her, was ticking loudly while she lay awake, working out how many calories she had consumed today and thinking how unfair it was that she had the sort of skin that never tanned. Maybe now she was putting down her book, closing her eyes tight only to stand up again, too agitated. Later, I would write to her; or call her, that was it. Wow – look at that wind! Listen to that thunder!

And the beautiful scene, a little mawkish yet at the time deep for me, occurred as I was walking down the hotel's driveway and Evaristo, the friend who loved me, came running under the madness of the rain, laughing wildly, and we embraced, tears running down my cheeks. Then, as the sky exploded again, we walked in hysterics, giddy at the thrilling danger, playfully punching each other's arms, pointing at tiles flying in the wind, cars skidding, swerving left and right, worried Cuban faces pressed against windscreens. Before we parted Evaristo had the very bad idea of buying a bottle of *ron de la calle* from some guys sheltering under a bar's awning – bootleg rum that was like drinking petrol. After that, until I somehow got back to the flat, there were just a series of suggested images that I couldn't swear to: becoming incensed at a recollection of Sophie's words of the day earlier, but then experiencing such unbearable affection as I remembered her message about my being *lovely*; wondering in a vague way why I hadn't replied; a big sheet of rain drenching me just outside my building, the lift going up so slowly, climbing like a resentful old man as I stood alone inside it...

I did understand, though – and I had it confirmed the next day – that the Kims had prepared dinner for the three of us. It was *lobster*, and this disconcerted me at the time – lobster, in Havana? I hadn't known you could get it so easily. I remember their looking so disappointed as I staggered past with the small plastic bottle full of Evaristo's noxious rum, apologising, telling them I was not hungry. They said something about a special dinner, something about a text message they'd sent earlier that day and that I'd not replied to – because it had made no sense, I explained, it having been simply a random grouping of letters. They were shouting after me about my day tomorrow, 'Big day, tomorrow big day,' and we all jumped as the pots of flowers were snatched from the balcony by a bellowing of air. And I laughed a bit more about the lobster, about how on earth they had managed to find lobster in Havana, and I remember they didn't understand, that they didn't seem to like me laughing like that...

...The next day my parents said I had sounded het up, confused; that I'd kept telling them about how crap the food in Cuba was, and something about a lobster. I remember only that I'd felt so happy to hear their voices, when they'd said they'd be bloody proud of me whatever happened tomorrow...

And the next day I also found emails sent and received, none of which I remembered.

Simon,

I can't imagine how nervous you must be – but I confess I'm getting rather excited now myself about tomorrow! Drama! But Project Wall has got so long to go.

I'll let you know if I hear ANYTHING new – as I imagine you won't be sleeping much tonight!

Giles

And my response – how could it sound so sober?

Thanks, Giles. Appreciated. Make sure you get a day off for your efforts.

There was an email from Emma:

Simon,

I am a bit sad that you decided not to reply to my last message – I can't really believe you're not checking your BlackBerry. Anyway, I repeat that I hope you are well, and the invitation for a drink remains open upon our return.

Your insomniac colleague, Emma

A failed attempt to call her had followed this, then the email response – reasonably lucid at the beginning, but then rambling and mad at the end.

Emma, hi –

Sorry for the delay in replying – missed email. When we are back in London, and we have the drink, I will tell you about the time I have am having in Cuba. Not relaxing! But SOOOOOO glad you wrote (I am eight or nine hours behindt you here, unbelievable right?) I too am feeling odd tonight too but safe back home now in flat. Yes, Angus humour NOT THE BEST.

I hope you are OK I was a bit worried by your last email. Are you OK? You in touch with family. I know it's impossible, but important. I'm still remembering Dynamite and not sure you were OK. Please CALL whenever.

TIRED more than anything! You – ? So much shit and all that! xdo try hard, to try not to get worked up about stuff.

SimonXx

A short one back from Emma:

Thanks. Sorry I missed your call, bit late here now to speak. You sound like you need to get to bed! Speak tomorrow.

And another from Giles, a little later – he would have been passing through that stage of a deal when even trainees become pompous.

Simon,

Just to say, I may have trouble replying to any further emails tonight as I have been sent down to the signing room and it is essential that I check all the documents very carefully without interruption.

Speak tomorrow – can't believe Rupert's going to be here all night again and then go straight to the partners' meeting.

Giles

And his supervisor from Cuba, eminently sensible:

Understood. Thanks, Giles.

Those were the emails. But there was other stuff too, bits of which I recalled the next day. Like calling Dan Serfontein, being vile to him – how vile I can't quite remember – and asking him repeatedly why he hadn't bothered wishing me good luck. Was he maybe too polite, deliberately too polite, in return? Something like that made me even angrier, and I think he mentioned with a cough that it was very late there, so if I didn't mind; then something about *Lawyers' Latest* having talked about the vote for days. There was something unpleasant in his voice. Next a gap in memory, and something grim and I was standing up in my room, screaming down the phone at him. He'd said something like: *You upset Sophie with that message. She called me in tears.* And I was yelling deeply embarrassing things, such as that he might be better-looking than me, he might be more stable, more of a man, but he wasn't going to touch Sophie. And he was laughing – but very on edge too now – saying I was being an idiot and that I sounded bladdered. That Sophie and he had been friends for years and he wasn't going to delete her number just because I had fucked things up with her.

'Think it's best to speak once you've slept, Simon.'

'You stay away from her!'

'Goodbye.'

Those words I remember. And I remember too that later I kept telling myself that I needed to sleep as I'd have to be up so early, in case Rupert called first thing UK time – how long would the partnership meeting take? What time would it be held? If I put the alarm on for half past four, surely that would be OK? And then that part of my mind that was never affected by drunkenness focused in, and I thought of dates and times and practicalities and anything I *needed to do*, for this, strangely, was my greatest preoccupation, that I might do something wrong – miss Rupert's call, not sound awake, not sound gracious in victory or in defeat. The dates were fine, tomorrow was Thursday, the 26th, Rupert would call, and I would fly back on Friday and, yes, the alarm was set...

And then from somewhere obscure, an echo from a bottomless well, there came Sophie's golden, sleepy voice.

'Simon? What are you – it's two o'clock in the morning here. Simon – *what*? Me and Dan? Don't be mad! Of course I'm not living with him – I'm still living at Eleanor's. Simon, you're crying! Calm down, please calm down. Listen, I'll call you back in a second.'

And I don't know if or for how long I slept before we spoke again but when I heard her next I was in a diabolical state, half-hungover and half-drunk, my face and chest and belly plastered with a lash rash more severe than anything I had previously achieved, those palpitations ringing in my ears. I told her to wait – I went off to be sick, which cleared the mind a little, and then I lay on the bed, trembling and gazing down at my blotchy body. Sophie was still there on the phone.

Yes, she was still living with Eleanor...our conversation moved in strange, arbitrary directions...yes, she *knew* I hated Eleanor Cantle – I'd told her a hundred times about how rude Eleanor had been to me during *Dick Whittington*, the first play Sophie had organised at Burnaby Street Primary. Yes, yes. Enormous sacrifices to make it, just for Sophie, right in the middle of Campaign. Yes, what a cruel shock to find myself having to sit next to that obnoxious woman with that comically short dark hair. Yes, she'd been outrageous, tutting when I'd silently checked emails, refusing to acknowledge me when I needed to leave in the middle of the play.

Why were we talking about Eleanor? Anyway, Eleanor had said I'd been a prat throughout it, that I'd made some stupid joke about the stage, remarking that it was nice how they'd mixed old and new London by painting the Gherkin in the background. When it was clearly not the Gherkin. That sounded like me – so humorous.

No, she wasn't with Dan. But she was glad I'd called. She wanted to speak to me tomorrow, when I was sober.

'Simon, are you listening to me?'

I was looking out of the bedroom window – the night was calm now, the storm over. And I remember telling Sophie how the view reminded me of the universe seen

357

through our skylight in Fulham. A universe lit only by our favourite stars.

'What are you *on* about? Oh, God, what a mess!' She'd become all emotional now too. 'I wish you'd listened to me all those years. What a stupid position you've got yourself in! Campaign's finished, hasn't it? Dan told me everything. Tomorrow they'll tell you if you've "made it", that horrible expression.'

'Dan?' I murmured. 'And "stupid position"? Not what most people would say.'

'Well, I *know* you.'

'Ah. Why did you leave me, then, Sophie? Hmm?'

'Yes, that's right. Selfish old Sophie. But—'

'But?'

'But the work was *every* night, wasn't it?'

She waited for me to answer but I was too tired now, so I just continued to gaze out at the vast black sky.

'It was *every* night. All you cared about. Every weeknight, every weekend. And the drinking after it. Working and drinking, working and drinking.'

'Didn't you ever think about the pressure I was under?' I said suddenly. 'Didn't you know that I felt nauseous, every single morning? Couldn't you see that I was struggling?'

'But *why*, then, Simon?' she pleaded. 'Just tell me this: tell me why! Come on – why do you still want it?'

She knew the reason, of course, deep in her heart. Not all the details, but she knew enough. I wasn't going to tell her now, if she didn't have the courage to say it herself. I'd just lie back instead and look at the universe, thinking quiet, meaningless thoughts. Wondering whether there might be an alien as lonely as me, looking back down from one of those distant stars…

'Loneliness,' I mumbled.

'I don't think I've ever heard you this drunk.'

Well, I'd had quite a few, hadn't I, today? Indeed most recently I'd consumed a rather large amount of Cuban petrol, which was why my stomach had become a red and white chessboard. But the vomiting had helped stabilise things, and I wasn't going to let Sophie goad me now into shouting out the reason I had toiled night and day, risked my mind; if I had any pride left, any trace of self-respect, I wasn't going to let her make me say it.

She was crying now.

'All I'm asking is *why*? Why force yourself to endure this? Tell me. Do you really want it so much?'

But I'd never tell her. She'd never hear from my mouth that behind the drink and cynicism and arrogance there was just a frightened man, yearning for approval. She knew this, so I wouldn't tell her. She knew that I was desperate for her to admire me, and that once she'd hurt me very badly, so I'd never tell her that in a strange way her sincerity had always been an inspiration, a cherished value that gave meaning to the dream. I wouldn't tell her that these days I was so tired that at times I feared I had lost my identity; feared I might be just a receptacle of unconnected emotions, thoughts and fears, a ghost ship adrift on the high seas...

I wouldn't tell her how much importance I'd ascribed to her and us, that I was secretly so insecure. That the day she had left me in Nottingham, that day so many years ago when she'd looked at me as if I was not welcome in her student room, in an instant the lights had gone out and the whole house of cards had come crashing down. Never would she see me the way I'd been upon my return from Nottingham that evening. She would not see me alone in the corner of the Cellars, downing shots like a madman; she would never know that later I'd sat for hours in the icy cold of Cambridge's

Market Square, drinking from that bottle of Jack Daniel's, not tearful, but afraid. That I'd thought of running, starting a fight with the guy queuing for food, smashing the bottle of whisky, anything to forget for a moment the terror at her having obliterated the outline of a personality.

I wouldn't tell her that the relationship between the firm of Fiennes & Plunkett and its loyal associates was addictive, intense, based on a potent combination of needs. That, with the rare exception of a lawyer like Angus, the firm attracted people just like me – honest, hardworking but dependent souls, people-pleasers whose fulfilment was found in the occasional smile from a partner; from an email saying:

Well done.

She'd never hear me blame her, for none of this was her fault. But what she should know was that if I'd worked this hard, if I'd staked so much, then I'd be *damned* if I was going to turn away now.

'Please, Simon,' she begged. 'Please tell me why you do it.'

I let out a deep, drunken sigh, and closed my eyes.

'If I make it as partner,' I murmured, 'it'll all be just fine.'

PART THREE

14

MY BIG NEWS was delivered with a quintessentially Fiennes & Plunkett form of abruptness that made all the pondering I had been doing in Cuba, all the self-flagellation for not having pondered enough, seem rather silly in hindsight – rather a waste of time and mental resources. I thought afterwards of how peculiar it had been, the return of that indescribable sense of urgency to do something, and how peculiar and ironic too that insistent reminder of a moral duty to wonder – my news would have been the same if I had not thought at all, if I'd stayed out all night with the street rum.

But these thoughts came later – for now I was standing on our balcony in Havana, dry-mouthed, agitated and befuddled, as I listened to a whisper coming through my mobile phone. It was 5 a.m. here in Cuba, still a couple of hours before dawn, the dull glow of a streetlight hanging in the wet air below the balcony, revealing glimpses of the aftermath of the storm. I could see an upended bicycle, tree branches, a fallen signpost ...

'Right, here I am. Simon? Are you still there, Simon?'

'Yes, Rupert. I'm here.'

'Good. Very good.'

I had slept through the alarm, but the ringing of the mobile phone had woken me, the noise ricocheting out from a dream of a dark ocean and a raft and Evaristo and the Kims. It was ten o'clock in London – the time in Cuba was not a matter of concern to the caller. As I had tried to rub the madness of the hour, the pain of the drink, from my eyes, Rupert Plunkett had announced himself, and then gone to shut the door to his office. After which – embarking on one of his mental expeditions to the border – he had gone back again just to check that the door really was closed. Finally, the Executive Chairman was ready.

'Well, the meeting has just ended,' he whispered.

I realised that the balcony was wet; and that I had no shoes on. I wondered for a second why I was on this balcony, before remembering that it was because I had wanted a cigarette while I received the news. Moving back to the step that had remained dry, I went to light one but then changed my mind: I still had Cuban petrol inside me and it was too early – it would be sub-optimal to puke down the phone.

'And – oh, Christ, what is he *doing*?' Rupert was evidently looking at his computer screen. 'Apologies, Simon – please bear with me. I have not been to my bed for two consecutive nights. I'm having an appalling time on Wall. It seems I can't delegate any matter without it going wrong.'

Silence followed this, punctuated only by an intermittent tapping, an occasional soft cursing. Before my leader even returned to the call, the only thing left unclear to me was the way in which he would convey the news. For I knew what the news was – I had looked at the BlackBerry and seen Giles's email, which had been sent an hour or so earlier.

Simon,

I suspect Rupert will call you shortly, so this email is probably out of place. But, just in case he delays – at the moment he's back upstairs at the reconvened partners' meeting – I thought I should let you know that it's not good. Angus is already in the office – and he's about to be crowned partner.

Apparently he was summoned early this morning as they'd assumed the vote would be pretty quick, but there was then a big argument upstairs. People are saying that Eliza Hayfield went nuts about the decision, threatening to leave if Angus was made a partner. As you know, she's not a great fan of his – I understand that once, a while back, she saw his true colours!

However, people are saying it may be a bit Machiavellian, i.e. Eliza may be just trying to get something for herself in return – possibly the role of sub-head of a department. Anyway, they adjourned the meeting, Eliza has been down in Rupert's office, and now they are all back upstairs to finalise matters, presumably to agree a new deal for her.

There's lots of whooping going on in Angus's office, lots of people shaking his hand, so I do think this is pretty definite.

I am very sorry, Simon.

Giles

He's quite right, I was thinking, as I waited for Rupert to return to the call to confirm the news, *Eliza Hayfield is not a fan of Angus Peterson's*. It felt good to dwell on this irrelevance – *yes, Eliza hates Angus* – good to cling to the thought; maybe it would protect me from the intolerable vacuity growing inside. *Yes, Eliza Hayfield – now there's a lawyer.* She was one of the firm's most brilliant young partners, her gentle, librarian's air – with those terribly sensible clothes, the embarrassingly large red glasses, the colourless hair pulled back in a bun – hiding a ferocious energy and an acutely strategic mind. Years earlier, when we'd all been junior associates, Angus Peterson had seen her sudden onset of appendicitis as an opportunity...

'Sorry about that, Simon.' Rupert was back on the line. 'Now, there is to be only *one* new partner. As you know, these are uncertain times for all law firms – and so we've decided to adopt a cautious approach.' He coughed, a little uncertainly...

...Angus had been young in those days, when he'd shafted Eliza on the deal – not yet the fully developed sociopath, so prone to error. The mistake had been exuberance – later he would learn to rein it in. It had been a bad mistake, though – earning him an enemy who from then on had done everything in her power to trip him up, spoil his holidays, push him that little further towards the edge.

'That silly bitch Hayfield,' he'd said to me recently, just before Campaign had begun, 'she came to my room just now, ordered my trainee to leave, and then with a smile said she would work "night and day" to stop me from becoming a partner. I mean, I could bring a claim against her for that, couldn't I? I'll record her secretly on my phone next time.'

But Eliza hadn't managed to stop him. For Angus had won. He'd beaten her. He'd beaten Emma, beaten me.

'And I'm sorry to tell you,' Rupert whispered, 'that the new partner is Angus Peterson.'

He'd won. And it really was a mess down there on the street – the fallen signpost was blocking the road. There was probably still some rum left in the plastic bottle. Perhaps later I would take a chair out here, smoke some ciggies and finish Evaristo's petrol, watching the Cuban sunrise.

'Simon?'

'Yes, I heard you. Thanks for letting me know.'

'I don't know if you would like me to elaborate.'

'Not really – seems no point.'

'Fair enough. Look, to be frank…' Rupert paused. 'I'm personally very sorry about this. We were a very good team, Simon, you and I. And as your mentor I did make your case very forcefully to my partners – influencing a significant number of them, I might add. But Angus has an extraordinary number of admirers within the banks, and it wouldn't be in the interests of the firm to ignore this point. Clients know him already, you see – they ask to work specifically with him. Nobody asks to work with you.'

'Thank you. But just one thing.' I took a breath. 'Did Eliza tell you what Angus did to her when we were junior associates?'

'Eliza?' A hint of panic in the whisper – but then it disappeared. What did it matter now? 'Ah, you've heard the rumours, then; you've consulted your BlackBerry, haven't you? Well, to answer your question: yes, she did tell us. Not a pleasant story at all. But it was rejected by my partners – derided, in fact. The consensus is that there must have been some mix-up: it wouldn't have been deliberate on Angus's part.'

'A mix-up? But you know that the story, how he exploited her appendicitis, is fully believable, surely? You know there are many stories like that about Angus?'

'Alright, Simon – that's enough. I did my best. I won't stand for anything defamatory.'

'Well, speaking of defamatory,' I said, 'may I ask, was my alleged heavy drinking – you remember, that false accusation that Angus made – was that brought up? Was it a factor?'

'Oh, no,' Rupert seemed embarrassed – offended, even. 'What a very strange question. Of course not. There was nothing personal like that – we know full well that you're not a heavy drinker. How could a lawyer be a heavy drinker at this firm, with the hours we all put in? Indeed I made a related point most vociferously upstairs – that it's all very well Angus having this excellent competitive streak, and it is true that the chap is very tenacious, but at times he goes too far – and that evening his behaviour was utterly unacceptable. The general point about his, erm, zeal, will be underlined to him during his admission process.'

'I see.'

'Yes. So, I repeat, there was nothing personal. I mean, you had a few detractors.' Rupert paused for a second and gasped – some new horror must have appeared on his screen. 'Ed Griffiths was a little negative – apparently there was a scene of some sort at that Christmas party, the ghastly one we had in the dungeon? And my former partner, Duncan Green, wrote to inform us of some funny episode, a conversation during which you displayed a particularly argumentative attitude. About Italy, of all things! But, as I say, nothing substantive; nothing that affected the outcome.'

'Rupert,' I said, 'I'm sorry, but I've got to go.'

'Understood – but listen, don't get too down about this.' The voice was very unfamiliar and gentle. Paternal, even. Maybe Engelhardt had been right: possibly deep inside there was real goodness in Rupert Plunkett. It was just a shame that it was overshadowed so often by certain other characteristics. The constant severity of the stress, the overwhelming—

'We'll talk about your career options when I see you all *tomorrow* at the *meeting* at *5 p.m.* to discuss next steps, including for you two *non*-partners. There are some excellent positions available at a couple of our clients – a straight route to the board of directors at one of them, too. The firm can be of genuine help here. We owe it to you.'

'Thanks, Rupert – that's very kind. Just to be clear, though – ' for what he had said was a little weird ' – I'm not flying back till late tomorrow night, UK time. So when you talk about a meeting tomorrow—'

'I'm sorry?'

'I'm sure you said we wouldn't be meeting until next Monday. I thought you knew I was flying back on the Friday. We talked about it.'

But I stopped as my leader emitted a noise that made me shiver: the whimpering of an animal that had not been born to whimper. There was a rustling of papers, the sound of typing. Then silence, punctuated suddenly by a voice elevated above a whisper for possibly the first time.

'That boy!' Rupert wailed. 'That damned, rotten boy!'

Later, as the Cuban night was beginning to fade and the Kims were still sleeping, Giles was telling me about Rupert's key meetings in Warsaw that had been rescheduled to begin on Monday, and which would likely mean that he would be a week out there – following which he was taking a holiday. So it was very important that we meet this week instead, because Rupert wanted things 'arranged' immediately – i.e. he wanted me and Emma out, safely in the hands of a good employer. The relevant trainees had been tasked with the job of making this happen: the task of liaising with us, the secretaries, the travel agents… Poor Giles was spluttering awfully now as he saw the other emails that had also remained in his Drafts folder.

'So sorry for having such a lousy memory – it's been a horrendous couple of nights on Project Wall!'

And finally, with touching dedication, he was performing his last job before bed, which was to organise a new flight home for his former supervisor.

Right then, I thought, as the call ended and a great quiet returned to my Cuban balcony. *Where's that plastic bottle of rum?*

15

IF THE TRUTH OF every city lies somewhere within it, then in Havana it will always be on the Malecón. The present-day personality of the Key to the New World, a front line of intermittent hope, its forays into the blue resisted by the godlike force of the swell, by the power of the ceaseless waves. Behind me sat the profound complication of the capital, restoration accentuated by neglect, wealthy tourists and ration books, the promises of change, of an emergent middle class and aspiration, all lost from time to time in the terrible pull of the past. Before me was the sky, and walking past were musicians, lovers, pimps and their broken prostitutes, lone Canadian men with predatory eyes, sad-faced local guides rhapsodising to the ingenuousness of awestruck, selfish travellers...

It was approaching early evening now, not yet time for the goodbye of a sun that had long burnt out the puddles of yesterday's storm. The voodoo music, notably absent all day, as if its musicians had been washed away to sea, was drifting once more as we stood looking out at our own horizons, all of us so far away. Young Evaristo was in England, wandering through Hyde Park hand-in-hand with his love; Kim the engineer back to the fresh spring morning he had met beautiful Ji-min, who with her smile had convinced him that the world was made up of no more than her and Kim. I was in Italy with Mariella, as the water before me sighed, became the Tyrrhenian. She was out there, in that blue that laps Posillipo, bobbing musically, her breasts bursting from her white bikini, her dark hair wet, calling for me to join her – '*Viene ja*', *viene!*' – we'd been so happy that day on Capri, we'd laughed all afternoon – but now it was evening, the restaurant was too exclusive and I felt guilty, I felt sad.

'I don't like it here,' Mariella whispered. 'Let's go home, to Napoli.'

And I was in Lincoln, wandering the summer fields behind Sophie's house; I was at the Charlton Athletic game with her on that day she glowed; I was with her, looking out of our skylight, into the dark universe. But I preferred to be in Naples, because it was painful and terrifying to think about Sophie, her new message saying she was going to ring, the fact that she would ring very soon, while I walked the Malecón with my friends – *I mustn't let her know my news; it's so important that she doesn't find out.* I was in Cambridge too, in Belgravia even, under the maple tree; I was anywhere but here, in this great hole of the present. My defeat had broken in two inside me. One part of me had taken the news as Emma Morris apparently had – to my relief she had not flipped out at all, but had sent me a very reasonable email, writing to me that, in a way, it was like a huge weight off our shoulders now. She'd added that she was feeling surprisingly calm, and reminded me of our catch-up drink. Very reasonable; very mature. One part of me was just like this, like Emma, taking the news so admirably well, a fine example of a rational adult – after all, there would be no more eighteen-hour days now, there'd be a new, sensible job somewhere at one of our clients, a salary that was more than sufficient. But this part of me was secret, and I resented it – loathed its existence. Because it was *crucial* never to confess to being fine with the news – to confess it would mean that I was a loser. Indeed it seemed necessary not to admit the news at all – not to tell anyone, except Evaristo and the Kims because they would not understand its full import. It would be somehow grotesque, vastly inappropriate, to articulate the news to someone back in England.

'It's bloody cruel of them making you hang on like this, Si,' my dad had seethed down the telephone, 'Abbie – they've *still* not told him! You poor lad, I don't know how you can bear this suspense!'

'I told you, it's a complicated thing, the partnership vote – there's a lot of politics involved. It's just a question of being patient.' I'd spoken very clearly and calmly; the voice of a lucid, professional man fully in control. 'It may well be that we won't know until tomorrow.'

'Tomorrow? Oh, this is bloody ridiculous.'

Yes, but I'm fighting for time, you see – please give me some time to come up with something. Because at the moment it really is crucial that I don't tell people the truth. It would shatter something most precious to me. So please give me some time – just enough to plan an escape route, a way around this.

'Afraid so – it could well be tomorrow. Just relax – do something to keep your mind off it. There's no point fretting.'

That last conversation with my parents had taken place a good number of hours ago – the whole day had slipped by, surreally fast. Now it was nearly time to head to the airport, to take the overnight flight back to London. I was all packed and it had been worth it, and very pleasant, this farewell walk on the Malecón. I doubted I would ever come back here to Cuba and so I was very glad I'd spent a couple of hours with my friends, the sole custodians of my secret. One of them, Kim the artist, was calling to me now as we looked out to sea.

'Simon?' The voice was gentle.

'Yes, Kim?' I turned to him.

'One more photo.'

'OK. Just one more, though.'

My flatmates had been kind to me all day, in spite of my shameful behaviour when I'd come home the night before – refusing to sit down with them, laughing manically at the lobster, waving the plastic bottle in my hand. The Kims had forgiven me, and as they had emerged in the morning in their sleepy stupor they had looked at me with hopeful eyes, and then looked away, their eagerness to know my news restrained by a most human sensitivity. There was no expectation in their stares today – it was perhaps precisely this lack of expectation, the absence of any invasiveness, that had led me to tell them the news, immediately. I had spat it out to them, much too quickly, then rambled on, giving far too much ancillary detail, the sort of detail that they would never understand – but they had understood the core, cutting through the bullshit with the same precision Kim the engineer displayed with his lobster-meat extractor.

'You did not win,' he had said.

'That, Kim, is correct – well put, sir.'

Not only had they done me this wonderful favour of allowing me to tell them, to unburden myself just a little, but my flatmates had also saved me from my recurring Cuban nightmare – the dream about not having enough money to pay the departure tax. Throughout my days in Cuba I had been haunted by the guidebook's reminder that, in order to be permitted to leave the country, I would need to pay the departure tax and present my tourist visa when at the airport – this had found a pathway into my subconscious, so that in my dreams I would arrive there, realise that I had lost my wallet and, with a weird sense of resignation, nod to the fierce military man, before returning bowed to the Rococo building, where the barman from Cojímar would be waiting for me. The fear that arose during the day could be traced back in turn to the terrible promise of inevitability the dream contained…

So it had been a little grim earlier, watching that Cuban cash machine swallow my Visa card, as the queue grew restless behind me. Grimmer still when I'd stupidly tried with my alternative debit card – which had also been promptly eaten. I had gone for it because that cash machine, opposite that multi-chambered, gigantic ice cream parlour that seemed more likely to be an alien ship crashed down into Havana, was the only one I had found that would permit international withdrawals. A disaster – but the Kims had stepped in, lending me *pesos*, giving me their bank account details for repayment. After an emotional hug, I had packed my bag, gone to wait for a fantastically hungover Evaristo to appear at his special bench – he'd received a further bollocking that morning but, to my relief, had retained his job – and then I'd organised my little walk with all my friends. They'd been most interested to meet each other.

'I'm Kim!'

'*Mucho gusto. Evaristo.*'

'I'm Kim!'

We'd set off, the Kims soon nattering away to each other, Evaristo telling me that my defeat was not a problem, not a problem, while I kept thinking that time was passing, and that I needed a plan to resolve this point about the news – for nobody back in England must know that I was a loser. We'd walked a long way, up and down the Malecón. Now it was time for the final photo before the goodbye, the airport.

'One more photo,' Kim repeated.

'I said OK!' I laughed. We were just passing the spot where I'd first perched on the sea wall to gaze at the sea, all those days ago.

'Here's good.'

And yet, just as Kim's tripod was being assembled for the thousandth time, my phone began to ring. It rang for a long, long time. Finally it stopped – then it began to ring again. I motioned to my friends that I needed a minute.

'Hi, Sophie.'

'Hi.' She paused. 'Right, I've got something to say.'

The words were irrelevant – it was the tone that made me gasp with emotion. For it was the tone of a kind person – a person who loved me. *Sophie loves you*, that nervous teacher's tone was telling me, with its hint of threatened authority, *she loves you very much, just as your parents and the Kims and Evaristo love you.* I understood this, but Sophie must not know my news – not under any circumstances. If she already knew, then I needed to find my solution right now, to trick her or confuse her. Without knowing why, I hoisted myself up and sat on the sea wall.

'I'm glad you called,' I said. 'I was going to phone to apologise for last night. It was disgraceful to ring you like that, especially so late. Not to mention my text message of the other day.'

'Please, Simon. Just listen to me.'

'Yes, I should have rung much earlier – ' I heard myself cackling ' – but it's been a mad day today – absolutely insane, with all the drama at the firm! We still don't know, can you believe it?' I clenched my fist. 'It's remarkable how it's dragging on.'

376

'Simon.'

'Please, Sophie,' I whispered.

'Dan told me.'

'It's not certain.'

'I checked – it's pretty easy to find the news on the internet. The firm itself has it on its website.'

She paused again, as I jumped down from the wall, began to pace. *Shit, of course – the news is public.*

'It's very sad,' Sophie said, 'that you didn't want to admit it to me. You're so proud. But this is silly, because I think it's bloody great, actually – you always were far too interesting for that lot. Now,' she said, very matter-of-factly, 'I want to talk about something much more important than that. I want to talk about *us*. I do still love you, Simon Haines – I've always known it, but I knew it especially last night, when I heard your voice. I want to say sorry too, because I let you down, walking out on you. But I do want you to hear my side: I want to talk about what we've done to each other, how we can sort this out.'

I heard myself gasp again – but with a different emotion now: outrage. Sophie had dismissed my news. She had dismissed it without consideration – for her, it didn't matter. An ambition that had lasted so long: nearly eight years of backbreaking work for us, for her, years of extreme stress that very few humans could tolerate and which I was not even permitted to complain about, for complaining would just be self-indulgence. She couldn't care less. It was just the business world – we all knew that the business world was a load of nonsense. So it wasn't important.

The Kims and Evaristo were gazing towards me – I felt very deep into madness now. My friends were uncomprehending, but the anger I felt and which they must have seen on my face was all the languages of the world. I wasn't turning back, either – what I felt now was something new; something real.

'So you've caught me out.' I chuckled. 'Well done – hands up, you win!'

'Simon, don't be weird. I'm very sorry you didn't want to tell me – that itself is *extremely* weird.'

'Yes – especially when it's so unimportant. But can I just say: when you tell me that you want to talk about "what we've done to each other", I don't think you need the reciprocal bit. And the answer's quite simple – you left me, Sophie. You've left me twice in my life.'

I stared back at my friends; stared at them for staring at me.

'I didn't phone to argue.' The voice was so absurdly injured, when it was she who had hurt me! 'With you, it's always about conflicts. Me versus you. You just can't see it both ways.'

'See *what* both ways, exactly?' I hissed. 'I worked my arse off for us – and you coldly analysed it all and decided that, on balance, you'd be better off out of it. Just like you did at university. It makes me *fucking sick*!'

The Kims were still gazing, a little upset; Evaristo was listening intently. In the ensuing silence I walked further away, waving my hand at them to indicate privacy.

'How sweet,' Sophie said. 'I don't think you've ever spoken to me like that before.' There followed another pause, as if we were both adjusting, taking our first steps in this alien new world – a world not English, a world where people *said* things. Then, her voice close to breaking:

'I've got something I need to tell you, something I've never told you.'

'Really.'

'Yes. Now, you know I used to nag you about your drinking with Dan— '

'Oh, you're *joking*.' Instinctively I let out a laugh. 'You want to talk, today of all days, about my beers with my mate after work? You're really set on destroying me, aren't you?' I

378

added this last bit because somehow I'd felt the earth move moments before she'd said this – beyond the words, in the communication of emotions and values, there was a profound intimacy. 'Any imperfection, Sophie, anything you don't approve of, you go on and on about. You never understood my challenges, how strong I was.'

'I *did* understand.'

'I like a beer from time to time, my one little vice, and you *obsess* about it.'

'Simon, I've never tried to make out that it's a big problem. You're so defensive. If you'd just listen to me for a second without interrupting—'

'You know *why* you obsess about it? Because you get your self-esteem from putting me down. All you've ever done is throw your crap at me.'

'Ah, right, it's like that, is it? So you don't want to hear what I have to say. Right, well – that's fine!' She was terribly agitated now. 'Yes, let's talk instead about how I put you down all the time – Simon, I'm going to have to break it to you!'

'Break what?'

'I'll carry on, if you want. I'll tell you how you're a self-obsessed little *shit* who convinces himself he's so good, so dedicated. Yes, you were so strong getting through that idiotic Campaign. So, so strong. Whereas the truth is you're weak.' She laughed evilly. 'You're almost *comically* weak.'

And with these words she took away my final prop, removed my last finger that had been holding on to the cliff's edge. I felt myself swirling, free and afraid – and then evil too.

'Damn you,' I murmured.

'That's clever.'

'Damn you. I'm not the one who's hiding from the world, hiding away in my pathetic little mission.'

She fell quiet. I was walking back to the Kims, who were

379

busy photographing Evaristo, while I waited for her response, feeling nervous now about what I'd just said. Then:

'You malicious bastard!'

'Hold on.'

'And there I was, just about to open up about something, finally – there I was, about to open up! You sick bastard!'

And the screaming went on, this sound and this language that were such a new part of her. I listened to her, the girl I loved, yelling hatred down the phone, and wondered how it could be that two people who loved each other so much, two people who had loved each other so long, could find themselves embedded in a narrative that was written for anyone but them. How despite our words, our hurting each other, we could yet be crying out our affection…

'Sophie!' I couldn't bear any more. 'I'm sorry – I do want to listen.'

'Had enough now, have you?'

'Please. I'm all over the place today.'

'I was *going* to explain why I always have to escape, when things get unpleasant.' The voice was now soft again – but troubled. 'Which was why I wanted to talk to you about my dad.'

'Then, tell me – I do want to know. Obviously I do.'

'Fine, I'll tell you, then. Right.' She took a breath. 'The thing is, my dad wasn't an alcoholic either. But when the relationship with my mum broke down, towards the end, he'd drink – he'd drink a lot. And he was horrible with it – he could be the best dad in the world for weeks, months on end, big Dad who knew so much – and then when he drank he became a sad excuse for a father, spiteful, arguing nastily, really viciously, laughing at my mum.'

'That's horrible.' Surely, though, she wasn't implying that I was in any way similar?

'He'd walk around the house trembling with anger, smirking like a madman. You know what he did one night, when he argued with my mum?'

'You don't have to tell me.'

'He spat in her face.' Her words were cool suddenly – as I remembered little Benedict from the Kants spitting into my face. 'I watched my parents' marriage, a relationship between two reasonable, intelligent human beings, deteriorate to the point where a full-grown man bent down, looked at his wife, and then – in front of his daughter – spat into his wife's face.'

'Sophie.'

'He always told me, after the divorce, that he wasn't sure he'd ever be able to look me in the face again because of what I'd witnessed – he's a very intelligent man, as I say, and so I think he's always understood the stupidity of any defence like "it wasn't the real me". He's never defended himself in that way. The day I went to see him in Derby, it really did upset me, because his prediction was right: he wasn't able to look at me. We saw each other as I stepped off the train but then he just turned and hurried away into the crowd, even started running – running away!'

And it was mortifying to acknowledge but, as Sophie was telling her story, suddenly I surprised myself by yawning. Uncontrollably. A big, deep, heartfelt yawn. Then another. I had to cover my mouth.

'He started running away from me at the station,' Sophie was repeating. 'Can you believe it? Running from his daughter in shame? And what upset me most was thinking how sad he must have felt. He'd been looking forward to seeing me for a whole year!'

'That really is awful,' I managed – I was in the grip of a yawning attack!

Later Sophie had calmed and I was apologising again, the words between us becoming gentler, conciliatory and almost forgiving. But inside I was remembering what *she* had said – that I was *weak*. And she'd called Campaign 'idiotic'. It was a horrible story she'd told me, and it was true that I had no experience of that sort of thing, that I was lucky. I understood that it must have marked her – marked her profoundly, maybe. But taking sixteen years to tell me? We could have spoken about it so long ago, talked it through!

'You've got no idea what it was like in that house between the two of them at the end. They despised each other.'

'I *don't* know, you're right.'

'You see, that's why I always have to escape,' Sophie said. 'I called you weak earlier – but I'm the coward. Whenever things get nasty, I have this intense anxiety thing – I've seen how low human relationships can get, you see. It's a real phobia, and it's why I left you when we were arguing on the phone every night at university. It doesn't cast me in a great light, I know, but I could sense where it was all leading, with those vicious rows we used to have. And it's why I just had to walk out again recently. I knew the stress you were under and I didn't want to abandon you – I hate myself for that. But I just couldn't cope with the nastiness.'

'But Sophie,' I said, 'there wasn't really so much nastiness, was there? We would never have sunk as low as what you've just described. I've never shouted at a girl in my life.'

'Until today.'

'I wasn't shouting.'

'And nastiness can take many forms, Simon – ours was quite subtle. Silent, even – but it was pretty intense. There was such animosity at times, in that flat.'

'I think you're exaggerating. Or perhaps you're right, I don't know. I hardly had time to think – maybe I just didn't notice.'

'Anyway, phobias like mine aren't rational. And you *did* used to look at me so unpleasantly some days. And then there was the drinking with Dan, too. You see, for me it was another anxiety trigger. It brought it all back.'

'Sophie.' My voice was as calm as I could make it, but I could feel the strain now. 'I'm not like your dad. I'm not a bad drunk. We've never argued when I've been drunk. In fact you used to *complain* that I didn't engage if I came back drunk. I used to just fall asleep.'

'Yes, but you used to huff and puff, getting into bed.'

'Because you'd be having a go at me! And anyway, I'm not sure my drinking suddenly increased, or anything.'

'Maybe not, I don't know – but it was a more general sense I had. The whole thing between us – it was reaching a climax.'

'I'm still not sure I agree.'

'Oh, stop it!' she cried. 'Can we talk about this properly? When are you back?'

'Tomorrow, around midday. I have to go into the office at five.'

'OK, so can we meet tomorrow night? I'm supposed to be getting a train up to Glasgow for a friend's wedding but I'll stay to see you – I can go up the next morning instead. Really, I will – I'll stay to see you.'

'Sophie, I don't know. What's triggered all this? Is it just because of my news?'

'Of course it's not your news – I've told you I don't care about that. It was your phone call last night, hearing your voice.'

I felt a sudden fire in my chest. It was quite simple, it seemed: I could not cope with the very sound of Sophie talking about my news. Talking about it with that profound indifference.

'Don't be upset about the news, Simon. Even if partnership *was* what you wanted.'

'Of course it was what I wanted. I worked like a madman for it, for years and years.'

'But there are so many other jobs you can do now! And the important thing to remember – I know that you think this sort of thing is all glib and everything, but the important thing to remember is … ' She was losing control. 'Oh, you know. Oh, Simon, please!'

Sophie was a kind person, and she loved me. I loved her too. But I'd nearly ruined myself through exhaustion, and yet for her it was irrelevant. What mattered was that, because sometimes I had a few beers after work, even though I'd behaved fine, I'd somehow triggered a memory of a nasty scene in her past. That *really* mattered. I felt something switch inside me now.

'Please let's meet tomorrow,' she was saying. 'After all, you're the one who got back in touch.'

'No,' I said suddenly. 'I'm sorry. But this conversation – it's helped me understand that it really is over now, for me.'

'What? But you called me, yesterday!'

'It won't happen again, I promise. I'll delete your number, all the messages. That way, it *can't* happen again.'

Now I was back with my friends on the Malecón – I felt safe with them. They seemed to have forgotten about the phone call, the rage. Instead the Kims were very busy ordering Evaristo about – and he was happily obliging, enjoying his role of model, as he had throughout the walk.

'Right, guys, I'm ready,' I said. 'One of me – then I really need to get going!'

I had not realised, until this final walk that Sophie's call had now ruined, that the Kims were known on the Malecón. Tourists pointed at them; locals hurried past, heads bowed. The reason for their notoriety had become clear: Evaristo and I had watched as they entrapped an attractive young French couple and insisted on a lengthy, romantic photo shoot. It had been the same formula with other unlucky tourists too – as Kim the engineer assembled the tripod, Kim the artist would procure email addresses, promising to send the pictures on.

In an attempt to limit embarrassment and the risk of arrest, I'd told the Kims early on to concentrate on me and Evaristo instead – that we would be their models. A heavy price had been paid – and now, right at the end, it was never going to be just one more photo. Instead, as the sun began to fade slowly in Cuba on the day I had learned that my professional dream was over, that I had missed out on becoming a partner, a millionaire, I was standing on a sea wall again, my face cocked to the left; then I was looking straight into the camera, searchingly, with Evaristo's arm around me; I was half-turned, fully turned, shouted at, encouraged, praised. Evaristo and I had our arms outstretched, as if about to perform a joint dive into the water; I was sitting on the wall, wise and reflective … and, finally, I was with all three of them, as we huddled together for a group photograph. The shutter clicked. And then, after I had shaken Evaristo's hand and told the Kims that it was time to head back to our apartment, my phone rang. To my surprise the call was from Fiennes & Plunkett.

'Hello?' I said.

'Simon,' came a whisper. It was Rupert! Sounding more tired than I'd ever heard him.

'Simon,' he repeated, 'can you speak?'

'Yes.' I gripped the phone tight. 'Yes, I'm listening.'

'Good.' He cleared his throat. 'Now, I don't know if you've heard about the drama, but nothing has been decided yet – there are still two of you in the running.'

'What do you mean?' I was still, before the waves. 'You told me more than twelve hours ago that Angus had got it – everyone knows, it's on the internet.'

'Yes, but there's been a change of plan,' he whispered. 'Angus Peterson is no longer a lawyer at this firm. It's you or Emma.'

NEVER UNDERESTIMATE a lawyer whose appearance brings to mind a librarian. Angus Peterson had been outsmarted for the first and only time in his professional life – Eliza Hayfield, she of the very large red glasses, had finally got him. Giles told me all the details – he had been snoozing all afternoon in his flat on Sloane Square but was fully up-to-date on everything now because he'd been ordered back to the office a short time ago. Wall had unexpectedly failed to close, it *still* had not closed, so that Rupert Plunkett, who had certainly not been home, was now approaching consecutive all-nighter number three. Giles told me twice all the details of what had happened that evening, in fact – in an increasingly passionate voice. The third time of telling I had to ask him to stop, confirming that I'd got it. And, just after that call, Eliza Hayfield herself telephoned me – she thought it right to let both me and Emma know of the day's developments.

Now, as noted, Eliza's unassuming look was most deceptive, for lurking below were a frightening work ethic, raw ambition and, most notably, a very rare intellect. Eliza had an extraordinary capacity for cold logic – she was a born strategist, a planner. This was a woman who at City Law School had achieved what remained the highest overall mark ever achieved by any student. Perhaps no less impressive, she was also the official chess champion at Fiennes & Plunkett, having beaten the Executive Chairman in a drawn-out, unspeakably tense final in the Partners' Meeting Room several years earlier. I still remembered her quiet, patient demeanour, while dozens of lawyers looked on, enthralled, and a purple face fixed the board with a look of pure terror. Christmas fun, Fiennes & Plunkett style...

Eliza was still very junior as a partner, being only a few years older than me, Angus and Emma – she'd joined as a trainee in the intake three years ahead of ours. So for the majority of our time at the firm we'd known her as a fellow associate, rather than a partner. Specifically, Angus, Emma and I had been newly qualified associates, Eliza a middling associate, at the time of the appendicitis story – when Angus had shafted Eliza with that savagery that had left many of us disbelieving, a savagery that had begun their long, cold war.

The appendicitis story: as Rupert had said, it was not a pleasant one. It was the summer of 2006, nearly six years before I'd be wandering around in Cuba, and Eliza and Angus were working on the restructuring of a large private company. It was all extremely urgent, of course, and as always stress levels were as high as stress levels can be. These two young lawyers were shining; they were shooting stars who had soon left behind the rest of the large team. They were also getting on each other's nerves – interrupting each other in the weekly update meetings, drawing attention subtly to each other's mistakes in front of the partner on the deal, dropping hints to the partner about unequal workloads, accusing each other directly of creating work, avoiding work. So far, all well. But there were and always had been lines that were not crossed at Fiennes & Plunkett. Eliza had been in a meeting room with Angus, preparing the piles of documents to be signed the next day, and that pain she had been feeling in the right-hand side of her abdomen suddenly became a lot worse. She called a taxi from that meeting room, which drove her at high speed and wailing straight to the hospital where, after much fuss and not a little confusion, her appendix was finally removed. On the way, in the taxi, she had nearly passed out, and had not managed to email the rest of the team. No matter, though – Angus Peterson had promised that he would let people know, and that he had everything in hand. She'd told him about the points on the warranties, that they were all covered.

So she was rather surprised and disappointed twenty-four hours later when she caught up on the email traffic. Particularly by Angus's email to the partner, copying the whole team, which had been sent while she was in the taxi.

Alastair / All,

This is to confirm that we are effectively all done on Project Robin. There are just two outstanding points – and I would be grateful if the relevant lawyers would confirm once these are dealt with, by replying to everyone on this distribution list.

***Graham C.** – we need all the notices to the US custodian to be prepared **this evening** and added to the docs. Please confirm when this is done.*

***Eliza H.** – please could you confirm **as a matter of urgency** whether all your documents are now ready, and in particular whether you've covered off all the warranty points. I think we should be confirming to the client expressly that the warranties are OK, before signing.*

Angus

Nor had Eliza appreciated Angus's shorter email to the various people at the client, copying the partner, which had been sent when she was coming round.

Dear all,

We're nearly good to go, and will see you at our offices shortly. Once my colleague Eliza H. (copied) has confirmed on the warranties, we can proceed to signing.

Angus

No, not a great story. Eliza had dealt with it rather impressively, though – emailing the partner and requesting a meeting upon her return. She had not made a big fuss, and had never discussed the matter directly with Angus. Instead, she had applied that patient, logical, brilliant mind to his destruction, no matter how long it took. The psychological pressure she managed to put on him was very great – Angus often complained that she must have obtained secret access to his calendar, for the poor little sociopath would very often receive a monstrous avalanche of emails from a client just as he was setting off for holiday, relating to something that she too was working on. For nearly six years she had followed carefully his contributions to meetings, too. In an attempt to disconcert him she would always take notes when he spoke, her face one of profound concentration; and then she would ask him evilly difficult, very relevant questions in front of the partners. Anything Angus missed, she was on it. And the day she had become a partner he had finally looked rattled – he had known what was coming and he'd been right: Eliza was always terribly keen to work with him, particularly on the big horror deals. Always she was professional, always calm – secretly she would force shocking workloads onto him. And then as her final step she'd even told him her aim – confessed to her objective of ruining his chances.

It must have been very disturbing to hear those words when he was so tired, so stressed. But the sociopath was strong. He'd survived the years of Eliza's games. And now he would also survive her final tricks, her lobbying of the other partners during his Campaign. He would get through it, and now she had lost, dramatically – so it must have been delicious for Angus to hear Eliza's voice down his office phone at around seven in the evening London time, on this, his great day.

'Eliza! Time for an apology, is it, my fellow partner?' he purred.

'Yes, indeed,' she said. 'In fact, given all our history, it's fallen to me to give you the original version of the formal letter – to "admit" you, as it were. It's a tradition here – rather a quaint one. Rupert says I must do it because he won't stand for tension between partners – a kind of punishment for me, I guess.'

'Brilliant!'

'Anyway, please do pop by. I'll be in my office.'

Angus Peterson did not know that the moments that followed would be the most important of his career. He should have noticed; he should have seen so many things. Why was she waiting for him *outside* her office when he arrived, and not at her desk? Where was her trainee? Where were all the lawyers on the ninth floor? Wasn't it risky to talk in the open corridor, especially when she was standing just before the point at which the corridor turned sharply to the left, so that he couldn't see what was behind the corner? But things were often quiet at this time of the evening – the lawyers were usually refuelling in the canteen around now – and presumably he was still giddy, not thinking straight, the assimilation of this news so beautiful that, after his congratulatory lunch, he had sat for many hours in his office, gazing at the pile of admin he was required to complete, apparently unable to focus on it. This news had changed *everything*. All those years of crazy work made sense. He could see the money; he could smell it. Angus Peterson was drunk on euphoria – his guard was down.

'Well, well, my fellow partner!' Eliza cried as he walked towards her, eyes on her. 'I've got the letter here. Prepare to be knighted!'

'I've already *been* knighted, thanks – enough of this ceremonial bullshit.'

He reached her now, snatching the letter from her. She remained very courteous, as if she hadn't heard him.

'I know this is a massive day, Angus – I remember when it happened to me. You feel so proud, don't you? And you should be proud.'

'I *am* proud.'

'We're all delighted to welcome you into the partnership. You'll have had a lot of congratulations today already, I'm sure, but you'll have to prepare yourself for more over the coming days, I'm afraid – clients, partners of other firms, City journalists!' She laughed warmly. 'Trust me, the congratulations soon get exhausting. And they will just keep coming. *Ad infinitum.*'

She'd emphasised heavily those last words. Angus laughed too now. Then:

'You silly cow. Why say *ad infinitum*? It's a dig, isn't it? A threat!'

Her face surely utterly confused. Or did she quickly wink?

'Angus! I don't know what you mean.'

'Yeah, yeah. The strip club. You've found out that I like to go to a strip club. Who gives a shit?'

'Honestly, you've lost me,' she said, the voice so convincingly innocent...

Until this point, probably, Angus was still, and would have remained, a partner of Fiennes & Plunkett. It was embarrassing, of course, with all the lawyers who were left in the office listening just around the corner – Rupert Plunkett flanked by two secretaries at the front of the crowd, holding a magnum of champagne. It was embarrassing for the firm that the young lawyers and secretaries should hear a partner describe the receipt of his formal letter as 'ceremonial bullshit'; more embarrassing still that they should hear about a partner frequenting a strip club, especially habitually – but these were unlikely to be things that would end his career. The 'cow' insult, and the aggression in it, was not fantastic either, but probably could just about have been explained away, or else denied – not everyone would have heard it. But what happened next could not be explained away. For Angus drew up close and went to slap Eliza Hayfield in the face, stopping just as she flinched.

'You give me *any* more shit at *any* point in my career,' he spat, 'and I'll fucking crush you. Although I must say – ' and now he stroked her face for the briefest of moments, his tone transforming as she stood motionless in shock ' – you're quite fit, aren't you, behind the glasses? A secret hottie. We could have fun one night, if you like.'

'What?' she gasped, far from feigning now – her game had become both better than she could ever have imagined, and indescribably worse. But she still had enough strength, enough cunning and cold logic to add, 'Did you really just say that? Did you *actually* just tell me that—'

'You heard. We could get together – have a bit of fun. How do you like it best?'

And she stepped backwards now, and backwards again, and he followed her menacingly, turning left with her. Apparently, it took him a while to understand the sight before him: the magnum of bubbly, the Executive Chairman and, behind him, stretching down the long corridor, all the lawyers and evening secretaries.

'Come with me,' came the whisper.

Upon reflection, I changed my mind and called Giles back, let him tell me the story a third time – Rupert Plunkett taking Angus by the collar, dragging him to the lift; Angus's vacant expression; Eliza in tears as she confirmed she would call the police. Rupert giving a speech to those who had witnessed what had happened, imploring them to keep it within the firm, reminding them of their duty of confidentiality. No chance of that.

Why hadn't Rupert told me? Presumably because he didn't have time; or because, in my case, he had not deemed the details of the story to be relevant – the only relevant fact for me was its consequence. It was such a disturbing story, absorbing in its horror, that on its initial telling by Giles it had distracted me for a moment from this point – from the enormous relevance of the event for me personally. Angus was gone, hopefully soon to find himself in a police station, while back at the firm it was game on again! I might never have to tell people that I hadn't been voted in! It was nearly 8 p.m. in Havana – I'd said goodbye to the Kims and now I was in my taxi to José Martí International Airport. In London it was long past midnight and the partners were back in the Partners' Meeting Room and Giles was going *insane*.

'By the way, as soon as you finish your work, you must go home, Giles.'

'Actually, I've finished my work already. It was much quicker than I'd feared – we're all done now on Wall! But I'm very sorry, Simon, I hereby disobey!'

'You what?'

'I said that I disobey – I'm staying right here in the office till I know. You're going to do it, I can feel it! I just wish they'd hurry up!'

'Please, Giles – calm down!'

But I too was silently begging them not to take much longer. Imagine if they hadn't told me by the time I was in the air! I still hadn't heard anything two hours later, when I was waiting at the gate, having made it through security with my departure tax duly paid. As a high-pitched voice declared that they were about to start boarding, my BlackBerry flashed – an email from Emma.

I presume you've heard what happened re Angus. Pretty sickening – I always thought he might be capable of something like that. Anyway, I hope your nerves are holding up – not sure mine are!

I replied immediately.

Yes, I've heard the story – horrifying! My nerves are the same as yours. And, even worse, I'm about to board my plane – so I might not know for hours!

But then, moments later, as I was walking across the tarmac towards the waiting plane, Rupert called.

16

IN LONDON WINTER HAD remained, brazen and ugly like the drunken guest at a dinner party who stubbornly ignores the signs that it is time to leave. Grey sheets of rain swayed above the tale of a city that served as a backdrop to a grand desk, a red neck and a silver quiff. Inside the glass walls, all was as it always was – courteous and precise and unbearably tense.

'You'll all need to mill around,' Rupert was whispering. 'Look intelligent and energetic. Keep away from the senior people.'

Above me and Emma as we sat opposite his desk there stood four young associates, who had the privilege of having been invited to attend a client event taking place later – a private evening viewing of the Caravaggio exhibition at the National Gallery. It was being made clear to the young lawyers that they were to engage in conversation only with people of their level. The risk of their saying something inappropriate, or letting slip something confidential, was too great.

'And Rupert...' one of the future stars of the City began. 'Erm, if a senior guy decides to speak to us, what should we do?'

I watched, only vaguely interested, as the Executive Chairman frowned at this, looked down at his desk. They waited uneasily, hoping for clarity on the matter, before his head rose.

'Just mill around,' he whispered, biting his fingernails.

Twenty minutes had passed and he had yet to speak to the two lawyers sitting before him – the two lawyers who had taken up his previous night. For there was always an order of things – and the Caravaggio viewing was due to begin in less than an hour.

'OK,' he whispered, raising his hand to the line of four. 'Close the door on your way out.'

The door clicked – and silence came to the cage.

'Well,' Rupert began. 'Here we are.'

Then he stared at me for a while.

'You look utterly exhausted,' he whispered. 'Pale. Not at all refreshed.'

'My plane only touched down a few hours ago. From Cuba.' If he wanted to talk to me about exhaustion, he should look in the mirror.

'Yes, I know that.'

'Can I just say – ' Emma reached over and took my hand ' – I want to say congratulations, Simon. You really deserve it!'

Her eyes were kind and clean – brave, too. Emma's profound intelligence was apparent in the speed with which she had adjusted to the news – rationalised it and realigned the walls of the game. But those eyes also spoke of an integrity – a decency she had hidden from me for years.

'Thank you. I'm not at all sure I deserve it over you.' Her hand was warm and I squeezed it hard as our gazes locked.

'Neither am I,' whispered the picture of delirium before us. 'Not at all sure – it was a damned close thing, Emma. And so, exceptionally, if you did want to try again, I should let you know that next year there'll be another senior partner retirement. The partnership has resolved that—'

'Oh.' She giggled. 'Thanks, but there's no way I'm going through a Campaign again.'

Thanks to Emma's dignity the atmosphere in the room was pleasant – except that Rupert could not contain a moment's fury at being interrupted. He bit those fingernails again in a doomed attempt to conceal the rage, as we remained holding hands before him. The moment passing, he stood up and began to pace, as if some terribly complex matter were playing out in his magnificent mind. We waited, wondering what it was that troubled him so deeply – yet we were destined to never know. After a solemn nod, he sat down, forced a smile at Emma and told her that he would like to discuss a position that had been offered at Ove, one of our top banking clients.

'Remember to apologise to Ed Griffiths,' he whispered, looking up at me suddenly as I was at the door. 'As I said, it sounded like quite a little scene, that night at the Christmas party.'

I caught Emma watching me, seemingly a little moved.

'Right,' I said. 'Will do, Rupert.'

AND AS IF BY MAGIC the evening sun made a brief appearance from behind the wintry sheets of rain to bathe me in the glory I deserved: close to eight years of intermittent all-nighters now all made sense, and I could see a rainbow and I was on a million pounds a year! And a sort of wild happiness that was not quite happiness boomed inside me, the air around me charged with a fire of excitement.

'Like, fucking hell!' Clemmie punched her fist into the air, gave me a huge sloppy kiss on the cheek. The Amber Light was buzzing, City lawyers charging through its doors towards the submerged bar. But this Friday night there was a corner of the bar, a corner somebody had reserved for *Mr Simon Haines – the legend*, that had a special energy. I had just arrived, dazed by how quickly the news had spread. My BlackBerry was flashing permanently, my mobile phone on silent because the calls were incessant.

'I'm so proud of you? You're, like, my first partner friend!' Clemmie displayed her delicate hand, adorned by a rock of an engagement ring that seemed too heavy for it. 'If it weren't for, like, Archie, I'd marry you now!'

'I'd marry you too!' Big, handsome Dan Serfontein slapped me on the back and grinned. I'd phoned him earlier, as soon as I'd touched down, and we'd sorted things out. He'd been his reasonable self – he would never mention my moment of madness, the horrific, drunken abuse yelled down the phone. 'You were wrecked, mate, don't worry. You were under a lot of pressure too. Anyway, you can make it up to me now, can't you? Maybe a little country house for me for Christmas, what do you think? Ha!' Now in the bar Dan's shirt sleeves were rolled up and his tie was off. Like Clemmie, he looked as if he'd had quite a bit to drink already.

'To Mr Simon Haines!' someone shouted.

'To Haines!' said a strange, rat-faced man with enormous glasses, whose name I could not recall immediately. Oh, that was it: Handley! I hadn't seen him for years. Always a networker, he'd resurfaced in an instant – quickly, cautiously, just like a rat. He was in real estate, that was right. A very talented lawyer, who now worked at the US firm across the street. He hadn't made it at Fiennes & Plunkett.

I felt a surge of arrogance. None of these guys had made it

at Fiennes & Plunkett.

'Yes, really! An incredible achievement.'

I turned. 'Toby! How did you know? How did you get here so soon?'

'Oh, Clemmie's been phoning round!' He patted me on the shoulder and from behind him I acknowledged the warm smile of his darling Arabella. My old flame from Clare, the charming, red-haired girl who had once said that I had all the excitement she'd ever known. I counted her still among my friends.

'There are a lot more coming too!' yelled Clemmie. 'For fuck's sake, it's early!'

I liked Toby – he was a lawyer too, and had gone in-house early, to an asset manager. He didn't need the money of any City job, of course. Arabella's father's funds ensured that the couple could wander up and down the King's Road for fifty years...

It was lovely that they had come, Clemmie, Dan, Toby and Arabella – so kind of Clemmie to organise. And more on their way: how touching! But the rest of the people circling me – an arbitrary assortment of junior associates and trainees from the firm, who had turned up uninvited – were already becoming annoying. The enthusiasm was all feigned, each of them sneaking glances at a BlackBerry while exchanging observations and pleasantries that were at a level of banality that exists only between colleagues:

'How's stuff, anyway?'

'Not ideal. Got a few small things going on as well as my two big things.'

'Sounds tough!'

'Yeah, it's ridiculous how stuff always seems to kick off at the same time. I was quiet on Monday and then, all of a sudden, everyone wants a draft of something from me!'

'I'm the same – everything blew up this week. And I just got bollocked for not turning up to training this morning. But if I'd gone, Plunkett would've killed me!'

'I don't think he would have, mate. Better just to flag that sort of thing earlier on in the week. We're qualified now, in charge of our own time. We need to step up a bit.'

'Hey! How are you? Have you said congrats to Simon yet?'

I thought how I was a star, in the eyes of these lawyers now – all hanging on any inflection, any hint of a reaction, any pulse of a point of view. One of them, a slim, very pretty girl with fair hair, made it into the inner circle.

'Congratulations, Simon.'

'Thank you.' I caught an approving gaze from Dan. But I wished she'd just piss off.

'I know this isn't the time, but Rupert says you'll be supervising me on Project Rana. I just wanted to check – should I open the matter tonight? I can if you want me to.'

'Not tonight, thanks. Let's catch up on Monday.'

'OK.' She took a little breath and then, her dreamy eyes swimming into mine, she put everything she had into her second attempt. 'I really look forward to working with you. Or rather, *for* you.'

Go now, all of you, please go. Leave me alone with my friends. But no – not you, not you! One man I wanted to stay all night – to see me through into the early hours. That man was Mr Giles Glynne-Ponsonby. There he was, making his way through the crowd of suits, knocking people's pints as he went. He stopped before our table, holding up two bottles of champagne like a prize, his eyes gleaming with victory.

'Stick 'em in the bucket, mate,' said Toby. 'Keep 'em cool.'

'Will do!' Giles paused. 'Can I, um, sit here with you chaps?'

'Of course!' I laughed. 'We did it, didn't we?'

'*You* did! Despite me, some would say!' He shook that mop of hair.

'Rubbish. Now, one more instruction – drink up!' I passed him a shot glass from the tray. White rum, served neat: a tribute to Havana.

'Oh, so *you're* the famous Giles!' Clemmie was texting again. 'I've heard so much.'

'All good, I hope,' said Giles, necking the shot. He was with the big boys now – away from his jealous trainee friends in the corner. And how he loved it! 'Shit,' he gasped. 'That rum burns. I feel that – is it alright if I open the champagne?'

'Simon, you open it! We're all waiting.'

'So, Arabella, how's the gallery going?'

'Oh, absolutely fab. You know who we had in yesterday? Surrounded by bodyguards?'

'Si, how was Cuba, anyway?'

'It was very odd, Clemmie. But I ended up living with two South Koreans, who were very nice.'

'Huh?'

'I'll tell you another time.'

'You're, like, quite pale? Like your neck's a bit tanned but your face *isn't*?'

'So,' the rat began, from behind his looming glasses, 'you're a colleague of Simon's, are you?'

'I'm his trainee,' Giles clarified.

'Ah.' The rat lost interest immediately.

'I don't think Archie can come,' Clemmie was mumbling to Dan. 'But that's kinda fine, actually – tonight's about Si, and he wouldn't know anyone here? It'll be like the old days, tonight.'

The music in the pub was becoming louder. Suits were swarming in like wild bees.

'Oh, *absolutely*, mate.' Toby and Giles had bonded. 'Yes, we're practically neighbours.'

'Dan?' I leant across. 'Have you got a ciggie?'

'Indeed – telepathy. Let's go and have some partnerial ciggie lash outside.'

'Ha!'

The chat outside with Dan ended up deflating me, though – as we reminisced about law school days, the trainee dramas, the stories of associate life and the rare, colourful personalities we had encountered along the way – Mark Conlan, who had left law school to set up a rock band; that other guy, the former trainee who had painted and distributed photographic copies of 'A Portrait of Plunkett', the neck deep purple – as we laughed and reminisced, I understood with a start that he was not at all happy for me; that he was sick with envy.

'Can't you insist on a couple of weeks' more break now you've made it? Cuba seems to have been less than ideal!'

'I'll ask.'

I wondered if we would remain friends for much longer. I wasn't sure. When we were on our second cigarette, he brought up Sophie.

'To be clear, I'm sorry if you think I interfered unduly. She called me. And we *have* been friends for a long time now, Simon. It's easy to forget, but we've all known each other for years.' The drink had loosened him, allowed him to say it.

'Look, no worries.' I blew out smoke, barely controlling my anger at this *crap* about their friendship. *Say it, Dan. You quite like her, don't you? And don't worry, I'm sure she secretly wants you too!* It was stunning, how Sophie could implore me to see the folly of my world while being such *great friends* with a man like this. A small-timer, too...

'Look, I hardly think you're sleeping with my girlfriend – my ex, I mean. As you say, I was pretty wrecked.'

'I know, I know – I don't want to go over it again.' He raised his eyebrows, uneasily. And then, in a remarkable testament to goodwill, 'She *was* very emotional, though, mate. I do think she still cares about you. Are you sure it's not worth one more go?'

'I'm sure.' I dropped the cigarette on the floor, crushed it out under the sole of my shoe. 'She doesn't know the news, by the way – at least not from me.' I paused. 'Have you—?'

'No!' He tutted. 'I haven't told her. I'm not in touch with her every day, Simon.'

'I wonder what she'd think. Wonder what she'd say.'

Dan shrugged his shoulders, perfectly polite. And, for a dismal second, I wanted to roar with laughter as he said, 'She's be as proud of you as the rest of us.'

He'd deflated the whole evening. Everything seemed to take a downward turn after that. Soon the further friends Clemmie had promised had already come and gone: they'd all seemed a little uncomfortable at the noise in the bar, all offered a quick hug or handshake and promised a proper celebration in due course. The throng of sycophants had largely dispersed and the remainder were forming their own little groups. Giles, who had overcooked things, had caught a taxi to Sloane Square with Tony and Arabella, declaring loudly as he got in that Haines was the finest lawyer in the City of London. Emma had shown her face briefly, courageously, but the atmosphere hadn't really befitted her honour, and she wasn't one for bars. We'd agreed to have our catch-up another day, sometime soon.

So it was just the old core that remained now – Simon, Dan and Clemmie. Along with the rat – who was still sitting close to us, still laughing too loudly at the jokes.

'I wish he'd fuck off,' I whispered.

'Does he really think you'd be interested in talking business tonight?'

'Possibly he does.'

Dan stood up. 'Sorry, mate, we're off now – taking Simon for something to eat. Nice to meet you anyway.'

'Yes, indeed.' Handley shot to his feet, entirely sober. 'Well, I'm sure you're getting tired of this sort of thing, but my congratulations again, Simon. Here, take my card.'

We watched him scurry out – head down, typing away on his phone – and raised a glass of rosé to Dan's excellent work.

'The mental thing about lashing early,' said Clemmie thoughtfully, 'is that you end up totally lashed when there's still, like, the whole night ahead. I'm such a lightweight really – always have been, not like some girls. I can't take more than—'

'What time *is* it?'

'Right,' I said. 'My round.'

'Ooooooh,' giggled Clemmie. 'A partner's buying. Back to the champagne, then, methinks!'

'We can't have champagne, then rosé, then champagne again!'

'Oh, yes, we fucking can!'

'Get some more shots, too!'

Then I was drinking a bit faster, to try to forget that Dan had deflated things. I was still way behind my two friends on the drunken scale. He was very keen to leave now. We were both keen to leave. In our desperation to leave we were staying, being nicer to each other.

'All those happy days,' sang Clemmie, arm around Dan's lean shoulders. 'We always said you'd make it, Si!'

'No, you didn't!' I was amused.

'We did, we did. Don't you remember that night on the terrace with you and Sophie, about a year ago? Options A, B, C and D! Ha! When you cooked us your Neapolitan dish and you fucked up the clams?'

Dan and I both had to think.

'You've got a good memory.'

'Well, that night Dan definitely said you were going to make it.'

'I've said it many times,' Dan noted. And then, quickly, 'What a night, though, that one!'

'We've had loads of good nights, us three!'

'Yeah, totally! It's a shame Soph's not come tonight – she should have.'

Hmm, thanks, Clemmie.

'I wonder whatever became of that guy,' I said. 'What was his name?'

'Who?'

'That trainee who never finishing his training, and wrote the email to all his colleagues, to the whole of Raynott Mirren, last summer.'

'Ah, yes! The wannabe dentist who went to the Shetland Islands? Brian something?'

'No – Bruce! Bruce, that's it!'

'Yes! Bruce Wilkinson.'

'Google him,' I said. 'First person to find out what he's up to can skip a round.'

'Where are you off to?'

'Quick ciggie lash.'

'I'll come.'

'Nah, nah – it's OK. Just got to make a call.'

'Who are you going to call? Plunkett?'

No, no. I didn't call Rupert Plunkett. I called Eleanor Cantle, Sophie's dear friend. Scrunching my eyes shut in my effort to sound calm; to sound sober.

'Simon?' The discomfort hung there.

'Hello. How are you?'

'Are you after Sophie?'

'Yes.'

'You have her number, don't you? Oh, no, of course – she told me, you were going to delete it.'

'She told you? Listen, Eleanor – I just wondered if she was in, or if you can tell her to call me. I've got some big news – some *very* big news – and I said a lot of stupid things yesterday.'

'She's not here. She left a short time ago for Euston, for her train.'

'Euston?'

'Yes, she's going to Glasgow. Some wedding tomorrow or something.'

'Oh, that's right! I remember, she told me! So, Euston station? She's just left?' I was only ten, fifteen minutes from Euston.

'Yes, she's just left. But please, don't keep interrupting,' Eleanor hissed. 'I don't know how to say this, but she talked to me about your last conversation. She said you're both clear now that it's over.'

'Thanks – but there's no need to get involved. Can you just call her instead, tell her to call me? Or just give me her number, please?'

'Would you allow me to offer some advice, for what it's worth?'

'Just please give me her number.'

'I won't do that,' she said. 'I'm sorry, Simon – it's probably best if we end this call now.'

'Fine, then. As you wish, Eleanor.'

Eleanor Cantle and the new partner of Fiennes & Plunkett ended their call...

A hundred thousand pounds a month. Put your seatbelts on, ladies and gentlemen. This rocket is about to take off!

I found Dan and Clemmie snogging absentmindedly, slouched on their chairs behind a row of empty bottles of champagne. Clemmie pulled away when I approached – I pretended that I hadn't seen.

'So listen, some developments.' I put the new bottle in the ice. 'I'm off to tell Sophie the news shortly. She's headed to Euston. I'm going to catch her before she gets her train.'

'Aww, no way!' Clemmie purred. 'That's, like, so romantic?'

'Why not just call or text her?' Dan looked unconvinced. 'That's a mental, drunken idea.'

'I'm not so pissed.' It was odd, and very unhelpful, but if I had ever known anything it was that there was no way on earth that I was going to ask this man, Dan Serfontein, to help me now, by giving me Sophie's number. There was no way I was ever again going to allow him to have any part in our story.

'I'm just a bit tipsy – not like you two. You both had a good hour's start. And it needs to be face-to-face. Girls love a bit of drama, don't they, Clemmie?'

'I wouldn't do it tonight,' Dan shook his head. 'It'll all go wrong.'

'Oh, fuck off!' shouted Clemmie. 'You're so boring!'

And then:

'Simon, have another drink first, though? You just got the bottle.'

'OK.' Yes, another glass of champagne would do first – to give me a little courage. I had Googled the train times. She'd be getting the eight forty-five – there wasn't another train for a good while after that. So there was plenty of time – she wouldn't be anywhere near the station yet, if she'd just set off. This *was* romantic, actually.

'So?' I covered my eyes as Clemmie pointed the champagne bottle in my direction. 'Did you find out about Bruce Wilkinson? Let me guess: a year on, he's already a lawyer again?'

'No, funnily enough,' Dan said. 'It turns out he really is going to go and study dentistry, up in Liverpool. He claims he's starting this coming September. In his year out, he's also become a certifiable maniac, by the looks of it. Look – he's got his own website.' Dan passed me his phone. 'I was wrong about him not seeing the dentistry thing through. But I was completely right about one thing – he's an egomaniac!'

'A total dick!' yelled Clemmie.

Following which, my friends began to chat again between themselves in a forced, polite way that in their drunkenness was embarrassingly transparent – they were burning now to go back to Dan's, to rip each other's clothes off – as I sipped my champagne and gazed at Mr Bruce Wilkinson, the man who was staring back at me from Dan's phone. To my annoyance, I found that there was something immediately enigmatic – something charismatic, even – about him: he did not resemble in the slightest the man I had imagined. There was a hilarious but likeable intensity in his eyes under that dark hair, an inner turmoil that he exuded in a sort of hunted look. He was dressed in running gear, urging people to join up to the Great North Run. Below the photo, I now saw, scrolling down, there was a link to Discover Shetland – and then another picture of Bruce crouching down on the grass to photograph a bird perching on a solitary rock in a dark blue sea. Then another link, to the Woodland Trust. And then there were more links still, links to things which, to my surprise, made my heart begin to beat fast. A link to CongoVoice...

'Here,' I said, passing Dan his phone – I wanted suddenly to try to forget about the website.

Dan grabbed the phone without looking at me, immersed in a hollow anecdote, in Clemmie's gushing laughter. I glanced at my watch – yes, it would be very early to leave for the station, but I'd go anyway, in a minute. Feeling alone now, for the first time since my news, I looked around the bar, unable to stop thinking of Bruce Wilkinson, the insolence in his demand that I join up to the Great North Run. In the far corner of the pub there was a table of kids, younger even than Giles, who were bubbling away, high on tequila and the thrill of cash.

'One, two, three!' the leader of the pack shouted. They licked the salt from their hands, downed the shots, stuffed lemon wedges into their mouths.

'Again!'

They were the first-seat trainees, fresh off the boat of law school. Fine young minds, yet to become accustomed to a monthly payslip, yet to know what they were doing or who they were, still borrowing against their stellar academic success, the promise of intellectual stimulation, the heady golden dream. A new generation dancing the same old dance, appropriating the same fantasies, a generation that had not sought to learn from those that had come before. They did not know, but should have known, that the challenge that lay ahead would become an addictive game; that it would never get better than it was for them tonight.

Unless they made partner, of course – as I just had.

'Right!' I yelled suddenly, slamming my hand down onto the table and jumping to my feet. 'You two – I'm off! I'm going to catch Sophie before she gets her train!'

17

LONDON EUSTON AT a quarter past eight that Friday evening was undergoing its weekly transition from ebullient chaos to dark melancholia, like a pub in the City at around the same time. The nascent idea that the party might have moved on; the sense that, while the station remained busy with people, those people were somehow not the right sort; not the people who carried the vitality of the evening. The great crowds had surged northwards on the six forty-five to Glasgow, and those for whom there had been no space had followed an hour later, having enjoyed a couple more pints of London Pride. At a quarter past eight that Friday evening in Euston station, the beauty of the weekend that lay in its giddy contemplation was becoming sullied by its actuality. Those who still drank upstairs at the Eagle, the station's bar from which one could view the departure screen and the scurrying masses below, were either drinking too late or drinking too much.

If one of those lonely drinkers had been looking down from the Eagle that night, he might have seen a figure in a smart suit emerge from the escalator. He might have watched, a little intrigued, as the figure looked left and right and then, with a sudden, wild shriek of excitement, as if his craziest fantasy had become true, charged across the station towards the huge departure board. Presently, following the figure's course, the drinker would have seen a young woman too, standing under that departure board, waiting for her platform to be announced. She was very tall, with lovely auburn hair, and she had a wheeled suitcase beside her. She'd turned as the figure in the suit had shouted towards her. The drinker up at the Eagle wouldn't have been able to hear what was said; but he might have ascertained a great intensity as the man seemed to proffer a letter.

'I've done it, Sophie.' I was unable to hold her astounded gaze. 'I'm the new partner of Fiennes & Plunkett – look.'

She took the piece of paper from my hand and read it carefully.

'My goodness! I thought—'

'It was all complicated in the end – but it doesn't matter now. We're *insanely* rich, Sophie: we're millionaires.'

'What on earth do you mean by *we*?' Tears crowded into her eyes as she passed the letter back to me. 'You were rather definitive yesterday – I think you promised that I would never hear from you again. And anyway – ' she shook her head ' – you *know* I never cared about the money.'

'I'm so sorry, really.' In the emotion I held on to her shoulders and pulled her towards me gently, thrilled now by the promised climax of a song that had been playing since I had jumped on the Tube. A climax that was so delicate, and maybe I was holding her just a touch too eagerly.

'You stink of booze,' she said, suddenly. The tears began

to fall now in streams, as she gazed at me. 'You're so lost,' she whispered. 'You're so lost, my lovely Simon Haines.'

'What?' I stepped back from her, horrified. 'Now, this stuff again, in my finest hour? Why can't you be proud of me instead, like everyone else? I had a glass of champagne in the Partners' Meeting Room, and a couple more with Dan and Clemmie – that's all!'

'You've had far more than a couple of glasses of champagne.' She dabbed her eyes. 'I'm not saying it's strange – I'm not judging. It's normal that you would want to celebrate this evening. It's just that, when I look at you, I know you don't really know what you want.'

'What?'

'Well, you don't.'

'Stop it, Sophie! Stop it!'

'You don't!'

'Oh, fuck off! You always ruin everything!'

'Simon!'

And the drinker in the Eagle would have seen these two people stand before each other, the tall girl with her hand to her mouth, apparently in shock. Presently she shakes her head again and turns away. The figure in the suit – transformed or unmasked, it's not quite clear – seems suddenly to go mad. Devoid of the conviction that earlier had driven him, his sprinting away back across the station is now bizarre, and moments before the escalator he bangs into an elderly man, whose coffee spills onto that elegant suit. Apologising profusely, the young man – surely a City lawyer or banker – wipes himself down with a handkerchief and then, after a moment's pause, disappears back down the escalator to the Tube.

'WHAT'S THE NAME again, mate? The name of that place Angus used to take them all to?'

'Simon,' Dan's voice was vague. 'Clemmie's just vommed in my bathroom. I'm battered, mate.'

'The name. The name of Angus's place! Where they used to go after the lash.'

'What?'

'Come on!'

'Infinitum,' he said. 'Why do you want to know? How was Sophie?'

Infinitum – yes! How could I have forgotten the name, after the story they'd told me of the previous night when Eliza had brought it up? Infinitum – Angus's little secret. Someone, maybe Dan, had once said that every person who worked as hard as we did must have his or her little secret. Even Emma, with her sneaky cigarettes. A secret is an outlet and without an outlet such a person will break, that was what someone – was it Dan? – had said...

Yet I'd never really had one – no little refuge when the black clouds were lowering from the sky. Sophie, of course, would say that the beers after work were my and Dan's outlet. Maybe she was right, but they weren't a secret... and anyway, I didn't want to think about Sophie. She'd ruined things. She'd destroyed the moment.

So, after returning home briefly to change my suit, and then spending a few hours by myself in a Soho pub, drinking just the one pint, or maybe two, I finally went to Infinitum, all by myself. It turned out that it's an inconspicuous place, at the intersection of two relatively quiet streets of all-night cafés and restaurants. The passer-by could easily be unaware of its existence, the only sign of *something* being the smartest of security guards, who shakes your hand and after a look at your suit and a flash of your cash leads you down...

...leads you down into a new world of warmth and security, romantic like an old Parisian hotel. The chair you sink into is of an exquisite comfort, the lights are low and sensuous, the champagne like a long-lost love, returning with the glow you remember. The music is loud enough to ensure intimacy without being invasive – you can speak as freely as you like with the three, four supermodel types who sit with you at your table, safe behind the velvet curtain.

'I love this song!' I yell. 'It's "The King of Hollywood"!'

'No, is not! Is different song! You are so funny!' A Russian girl who might indeed have been a supermodel places her hand on my thigh and begins to draw circles with her fingers. 'You are cute – you make me laugh!'

'I make everyone laugh!'

There are four of them, yes: the Russian, then one who says she's from Argentina, but I'm not sure, then a Polish girl and then, I don't know, is that another Russian? Why am I paying for four? How expensive will this place be? Oh, who cares?

'I'm a millionaire,' I slur.

'We know, honey.' The hand is moving up to my groin. 'You told us. More champagne? You want us to dance?'

'Yes, yes. Champagne! More champagne!'

As if by magic, through the velvet curtain steps a middle-aged gentleman in a dinner jacket, who observes the debauchery of our table – all four of them topless, the Russian playing with my leg entirely naked, my face and neck feeling warm, my shirt half-unbuttoned – as if it were a formal dinner.

'Another bottle, sir?' he asks, looking only into my eyes.

'Yes, please. Now, I wonder if you could help me – what's the name of this song?'

…And then through the gap I see a Latin young woman walking across the floor, wearing a thong and black boots that stretch up her legs. She flicks her head in my direction…

'I'm afraid I don't know the name of the song, sir. I can check.'

'Hey,' purrs the Russian, 'handsome – drink some champagne.'

...and that girl on the red-carpeted floor, as she flicks her head, looks so like someone I once knew. Oh, my God, Mariella! Mariella Esposito! I extricate myself gently from the Russian's arm, button my shirt and indicate to the man in the dinner jacket that I need a word.

'I would like to sit with her.' I point at her, as we walk through the curtain.

'Of course. You would like her to join your table?'

'I don't want the rest. Just her.'

'As you wish, sir.'

The nameless song ends and I wait back behind the curtain, putting on my tie. The room is emptied of the four girls in seconds, as if they had been mere figures glimpsed in a dream. And then Mariella comes in and smiles.

'Hello.'

'You're gorgeous.'

She grins. 'What is your name?'

'Brian. Well, not really. It's kind of the name I'm using, you know.'

She sits down and is especially attractive in her contradictions – her olive skin soothing and warm, the thong harsh and thrilling; her naked breasts irresistible yet her eyes mocking and cold; her lips beckoning yet her voice distant.

'Are you Italian? I used to know someone who looked like you.'

'Really?' Her mouth opens. 'Yes, I am from Naples.'

'Naples! What?' To her bemusement, I stand up, exuberant. 'That's where she was from! Naples, it's the most beautiful place in the world!'

She shrugs her shoulders. 'It has its problems. But yes, it is beautiful. May I?'

'Of course, sorry.' I pour her a glass of champagne, and as I slip and it spills all over the fine tablecloth she helps me out with the first trace of bitterness – as if, with the mess that I have caused, she has lost her last shred of dignity.

'I love Naples,' I stammer. 'I fell in love there.'

'Tell me about her.'

'Her name was Mariella. She was beautiful, like you. I loved her.'

The bitterness fades; she seems almost a little touched.

'You know, Brian – may I tell you something?'

'Of course.'

'You have very soft hands. Men who come here – they do not have hands soft like this.'

She is holding them tight, caressing them and nearly upsetting me.

'Yes, well, Brian's not the sort for strip clubs. First time here.'

'Does he think it will be the last time?' She is on her feet, her breasts looming over me, her legs opening wider, and I see a figure commensurate with my most colourful fantasies. She is naked now, bending before me.

'Hmm? I speak a bit of Neapolitan, you know. Not very well – but I lived in Naples for a year.'

'You speak *napoletano*? I don't believe you!'

'A tiny bit. Listen – *stongo chin' 'e sorde*.'

She stops, laughs and then seems unable to decide whether she is charmed, bored, or about to be offended by my apparent lack of interest in her performance. But then, as I reach across to pour myself another glass, she understands something and sits back down, takes a sip of her champagne, holds my hand.

'You really speak *napoletano*.'

'Just some words – never really got the hang of it. Shall we try and talk in Neapolitan? Or maybe just plain old Italian, instead? I *do* speak good Italian!'

'Sure, soft hands.'

And we talk for hours about so many things and it is only later that I realise she never says a word but just listens, naked, and smiles patiently. I talk about Mariella and the day that I let her go, of Sophie, of my job and of how I'm the most eligible bachelor. Actually, does she want my number? Of course she does. I'll give her my card and – does she like London? But she doesn't want to talk about herself.

'You love Napoli – so sweet.'

'Yes. Listen, I'll tell you one more story.'

'You told me so many.'

'Just one more.'

'Not tonight.' She leans across and brushes her lips against my cheek. 'I must go.'

'But your number. You said you'd leave me your number.'

'I have your card. I will call you.'

For a second I'm so happy – she likes me. But, as she disappears through the curtain and the lights of the end of the night come on, I remember that my card is still in my jacket pocket. It's the biggest humiliation imaginable and I'm seething with anger and heartbroken. But then I forget it.

'That was such a lovely chat,' I say to the dinner jacket.

'Yes, sir.' He passes me the bill. 'That's, um, three thousand tonight.'

'Three thousand pounds?'

'Yes, quite a big one. Should I put it all on the same card?'

18

As I EMERGED from Infinitum, after another handshake from that smart security guard, I glanced furtively up and down the street for the minicab that they had promised me was waiting, only to then freeze as I saw Sophie Williams. She was regarding me through the glass windows of an old all-night café, with a small white cup in her hand and a smile as sad and uncertain as all the loveliest smiles. Our eyes strained across the shadows...

She was running out of the café now. As she arrived up close, her expression changed – it seemed that she was stifling a giggle. 'Oh, Simon, your face! Oh, stop it.' Yes, she was giggling – how bizarre. 'That guilty expression! It's only a strip club.'

I was standing still before her under the drizzle, my hands behind my back in an attempt at dignity, my cheeks now alarmingly hot.

'I know you so well – tomorrow you'll wake up in one of your fits of paranoia! Without admitting the truth, of course.'

'What's the truth?' I heard my voice trying to be clear and firm.

'The truth is that this is so sad, Simon – so hapless. I mean, a strip club! You, the handsome, academic young man, the superstar lawyer set to earn millions of pounds! The man who tomorrow will be the talk of the City, or whatever.'

'Yes, the City.'

'What are you *doing* here? I called Dan.'

'Dan, *again*?' But I stopped. Her words were coming fast and there was something more potent than the alcohol now – a fever! Yes, I was burning up.

'Oh, shut up – you're so odd. I called *you* hundreds of times and you didn't ever answer. I was worried about you. He only told me where you were when I insisted. He offered to go in and get you – I told him you weren't in a great state.'

'Dan! Not exactly in a great state himself!' I turned away for a second and punched the air.

Her voice trembled. 'He's atrociously jealous of you, you know. Even more than you are of him. I only realised tonight.'

'I know, I know,' I mumbled.

'Oh, you do? I thought you'd never have picked up on it. Because you need a minimum of self-esteem, to understand that someone's jealous of you.'

My head was nodding meaninglessly. I had realised that my back was wet with sweat, not rain, and I was shivering violently. My soaring temperature had overtaken the drunkenness, making it negligible, and, just as when I'd had a fever as a child, I felt a trace of delirium as I listened to the voice that continued …

'Ingenuous, you are, and you're so lacking in confidence – you're such a bag of contradictions! But do you know,' Sophie murmured, 'I must be pretty complex myself. I confess my heart went wild when you came towards me in the station.

You had that affection that is *all you* – the same affection you showed me when we first met all those years ago, after those girls had hurt me in the sixth-form common room. Yes – ' she let out a gentle, nostalgic laugh ' – that kiss in the woods – neither of us knew how to kiss properly, do you remember? But I didn't say anything, as I'd realised you were the kindest person I'd ever met.'

'Jesus! I thought you'd liked that kiss!'

'Oh, now what are you doing?'

'Right. So even my kisses make you feel sick?' I was glaring at her with defiance. 'I've worked out where it all went wrong for me.'

'Really?'

'Yeah! I'm going to get a flight to Naples – to find Mariella again! Maybe I still love her!'

'Mariella? You don't mean that girl from your year abroad? From eleven years ago? Simon, you silly thing.' Sophie put her hand to my face, the way she used to when she would tell me she loved me. 'Mariella will be married now – she'll be someone's wife, maybe a mother. We're not young any more. Oh, don't be so melodramatic.'

But I shrank away suddenly, sat down on the kerb and then collapsed into a sea of tears. And I just sat there, bawling out the depths of my heart, my new Church shoes motionless in the stream of dirty water flowing down the gutter.

'Come on, stand up. You need to get out of the rain. You don't look well.'

'Who cares?' I looked up. 'So, what, then? What shall we do, if we're not young any more?'

'That's a question I've asked myself so often, recently.' Her voice came and went, as my head rocked above the running water. 'I think it's all tied up with an acceptance of who we are. Listen, just listen to me for a second.'

But I didn't want to listen. I wanted to go *home*. I wanted to go home to 2001, to Napoli. I could see her on Vico Conte di Mola, beautiful, achingly beautiful, winking at me with those mischievous eyes…

'I think it's really up to each of us to decide, to know, who we really are,' said Sophie. 'And that's something that seems rather hard for this generation of ours. Maybe it's just London, but it does seem to me that there's a whole generation of people who want everything and nothing at the same time – a generation that believes in nothing. And it's important to believe in something, and to know what you want for yourself – nobody's going to know it for us. Do you understand what I'm saying?'

'Mariella.'

'What I mean is that it might irritate you, but I'll tell you again that I do believe in teaching. And the only reason it annoys you so much is, well, it's because you're such a special man. Because somewhere deep inside, you know yourself too.'

My hands were pressing on my temples.

'You do, don't you? It isn't true what I said before. You *do* know what you want, and it isn't this, but you don't do anything about it and then you feel so lost. I've always known it, but it came to me more vividly than ever, after our conversation the other night. You charged off down the wrong path at twenty-two, and, when you realised it, you told yourself it was too late. But no matter how hard you try to convince yourself otherwise, you know what you want.'

'All I want is Mariella.'

'Yes, yes, Mariella. Oh, you idiot!' she cried. 'Don't you realise, she wouldn't understand the first thing about you? Haven't you got it yet? Haven't you realised there's only one way to stay young in your heart?'

'What's that?'

'Accept who you are! Throw that letter, the partnership letter – throw it away!'

'You've gone mad.' I chuckled softly.

'Oh, come on, let's go home now! Your teeth are chattering.'

'You'll come back home with me?' I got to my feet. 'Sophie.'

But she shook her head as I held her. 'I meant that I'll take you home – you look all feverish.'

'You meant that it was your home too.'

'I didn't.'

She walked with me to the minicab that was still waiting at the street corner. The car made its way slowly through the grid of narrow streets and then crawled along in the ceaseless traffic of Piccadilly and Knightsbridge, eventually coming out onto a quieter stretch of road. Having gained finally its freedom, it began to race towards the lovely flat with the skylight, the flat that we had shared for all those years.

'Accept who you are.'

My cheeks were ablaze now, my feet so wet, so cold, and I was beginning to hallucinate, a myriad images flashing into my mind. There was the snow of King's Parade, Ilha Preciosa, that white villa above Portofino, Rupert nodding in approval as I showed him my lush sunken gardens, my marble swimming pool. Later we'd take him out on the boat, glide majestically through the blue towards Santa Margherita. But then Rupert was confused, horrified: I'd transformed into an academic in a faded green jacket, a protégé of Professor Bonini, looking well, looking fine. Except that now I was a politician, with steely eyes. I was a man who would leave his mark on the history of the world…

And then, quite unexpectedly, I was Simon Haines.

A man with the loveliest, if also the most earnest, of wives. I was the best friend of Bruce Wilkinson, the dentist. Bruce surpassed even Sophie in sincerity, and I would argue with him about coppicing until I'd be insane with laughter – in the summer we would all go on bike rides – *ting-tang* – the two of them chattering away, debating as we cycled. I was Simon Haines, curious intellectually, but certainly not what you'd call a careerist. What *does* Simon do? Some job or other, he's always home by six. But then, in the evenings, Mr Naples comes alive. He's learning the grammar of the dialect, you know – how obscure is that? He's taking his wife to Pompeii, boring everyone with his knowledge of Campania. He's not a strong man, not a leader of men, not a *great* man in any sense of the word – but he has a colourful imagination and a muddled, sensitive heart. Each year there's a week out there, he and Sophie in the Congo. He's a bit of a stickler for planning these days, Simon – apparently there were so many years when he could never plan anything because of work that now he plans everything. He has the next six months all organised in advance – there's Christmas with his wife and parents and then there's loads to do, they're moving house, buying somewhere outside London, because Sophie – look at her – Sophie's three months now. They can't afford to bring up kids in central London and anyway Simon says he can't stand the place, he says London is full of jumped-up buffoons...

'Simon!' Sophie was tapping me. 'Wake up, we're nearly there.'

'I've been awake all the way.' I opened my eyes, feeling my mouth breaking out into an excitable smile.

'You're bright red, you know.'

'Yes, I know. I'll be alright.' She watched as I reached into my jacket pocket and took out the letter appointing me as a partner of the firm of Fiennes & Plunkett, before winding down the window.

'Do you dare me?' I cried wildly. 'I'll throw it away, I promise you I will! Would you come back to me, if I did that?'

'Simon, wait!' She grabbed hold of my arm and wound the window back up. 'Not tonight,' she whispered. 'Sleep on it. See how you feel tomorrow.'

'And if tomorrow—'

'Well, if tomorrow you throw that letter away…'

Sophie's voice was straining now, as if she was daring to believe, but as she spoke I saw in those brown eyes how some part of her knew that I might not be able to throw that letter away. And she was right, I never did throw it away. I wanted to, I wanted to so much the next morning, but I couldn't bring myself to do it, you see: it was too late, I was in too deep, and when I looked at the letter I became afflicted by some horrible, intrusive fear, before curling up into a ball in my bed…

So I've never spoken to Sophie again after the brief phone call we had that same morning. By chance I've seen her a couple of times – once in a restaurant, an Italian place on the Fulham Road; we sort of smiled awkwardly and rushed past each other to our respective tables. She was with a guy who had the face of a man for whom this sort of restaurant was a *very* big deal; I was with Clara, the sexy but irritating interior designer… The last time I saw Sophie Williams was three or four years later, at Sloane Square station. We were in a new world by then, and that morning on the train I was engrossed in my newspaper, absorbing the daily dose of the unpredictable, the volatility extending across continents. Fidel Castro might have gone but Cuba's future, I was reading, held only uncertainty. In the United States, Obama was imploring the young people not to despair, telling them that it was OK, America's path had always zigzagged… as my train arrived at the station and began to slow I looked up from the newspaper and out through the carriage window at the line of waiting passengers, my hangover accentuating the sense of loneliness. Suddenly, as I gazed, I saw Sophie's face, one among so many, glide by on the platform. She had her mouth open, as if she were calling to me. In that fleeting second, I heard again the last words she had said to me the night in the taxi...

'...if tomorrow you throw that letter away, I'll be so proud of you, Mr Simon Haines! You'll be my hero!' She took a breath. 'Please do it, Simon. Call me tomorrow, first thing, and tell me you've thrown the letter away.'

Acknowledgements

Thank you to Anna Burtt, Clare Christian and Heather Boisseau for the fantastic support, encouragement and guidance throughout the editorial and publishing process. Thanks to M. Jones and Virginia, both of whom have followed the novel's development all the way from its first draft, for their respective invaluable feedback and observations.

With thanks also to Gabriele for the considered and constructive advice and comments provided from Italy. Thank you to Corrado Grasso for the excellent contribution and support with respect to all things Neapolitan, and to all those who assisted with the Cuban-specific aspects of the novel.

A huge thank you to Linda McQueen for the editorial professionalism, incredibly hard work, constant patience and good humour throughout.

About the Author

Tom Vaughan MacAulay currently lives in North London and is in the process of completing his second novel.